PR

FORCE OF GRAVITY

"Absolutely addictive! I was captivated until the very end."
— Penelope Douglas, *New York Times* bestselling author

"The writing in this story is rather consuming. It's not often enough that a book grabs you from the very first page and doesn't let up. This story reads like it flowed effortlessly from this author. That doesn't happen often in this writing climate and when I find it, I feel like I discovered a gem."
— *Angie & Jessica's Dreamy Reads*

"I find myself sitting here mesmerized by this book. It blew me away. Absolutely, 110% wowed me. There were a few moments in the story where my heart was racing, or I felt like I couldn't breathe....This story packs a powerful punch and leaves no emotion untouched. You'll laugh, cry, feel anger, and longing. It's all there. I adored everything about this story. The journey these two travel, together and apart, will definitely end up as one of my new favorites."
— *Southern Belle Book Blog*

"This is no cliché student/teacher romance. It's not light and fluffy. It's real. It's genuine. It truly depicts the life of a teenager who deals with real life issues with friends, her family, and of course love. *Force of Gravity* grabs you from the very first page. You will not want to put this one down."
— *Biblio Belles Book Blog*

"[Stevenson] has done a wonderful job of taking a taboo subject...and turning it into something extraordinary and beautiful. [Stevenson] was able to grip my heart and my soul with her words, make me feel for these characters, paint a picture for me, make me laugh and cry in the same chapter, and fill my heart with joy."

—*Who Picked This? Book Blog*

"I am a sucker for student/teacher books and while some of them fall flat, *Force of Gravity* did not. The writing is so fantastic that you feel each and every emotion first hand....I wanted to call in sick and just hide under the covers and read....The feelings and emotions jumped off the page from the very beginning and kept hold of me until the very last word of the epilogue."

—*One Chick Bliss*

"This may be my favorite student/teacher romance....This book totally took me by surprise....It had a realness that I think is missing in many [New Adult] romance novels. This is a fantastic debut from Kelly Stevenson and I cannot wait for the sequel."

—*Love Between the Sheets*

FORCE
OF
GRAVITY

FORCE
OF
GRAVITY

KELLY STEVENSON

Slate Publishing

FORCE OF GRAVITY

Slate Publishing

Copyright © 2014 by Slate Publishing, LLC and Kelly Stevenson

All rights reserved

Cover design by: Regina Wamba of MaelDesign.com

ISBN 978-0692241578

*To Darin,
for never doubting me.*

PREFACE

I GASP FOR AIR.

The white tiled floor is icy against my knees. My heart pounds erratically, my chest tightening around it like a boa constrictor. I clutch my stomach.

Just breathe.

The tiles sway, then rush toward me, and I slap my hands against the floor before it smacks my face. I hover over the floor as my lungs burn, wondering if this is what it feels like to drown.

Why can't I get any air?

I collapse on my side, pressing my face against the cold stone, and close my eyes.

Maybe I *am* drowning.

I've been treading water for far too long, and I can't do it anymore. I'm tired. Tired of hurting everyone around me. Tired of living a lie. Tired of staying afloat.

My body sinks into the unwelcoming tile, and I imagine being submersed in the frigid water as it swallows me whole. The harsh fluorescent light penetrates my eyelids, but soon fades as I sink even deeper into the darkened water.

My body goes limp as I let go.

CHAPTER ONE

I HIT THE SNOOZE BUTTON for the countless time and squint at the numbers on the clock.

6:55 a.m.

Panic shoots through me. I rip off the covers and race to the bathroom, striking the corner of the wall with my hip.

"Ow!"

"Kaley?" my dad calls as he walks out of his bedroom. "You okay?"

"Yes," I croak, hobbling into the bathroom.

"Are you just now getting up?"

"Yes! I have to hurry!"

I shove the door closed and frantically brush my teeth, catching a glance of my hideous reflection in the mirror. The whites of my eyes are bloodshot and invading on the blue. *Oh, hell. I look like a walking ad for substance abuse.* After washing my face, I force a comb through my tangled hair, but it's near hopeless. Giving up, I decide on a ponytail. I sweep blush across my cheeks and throw on mascara in an attempt to look less like a zombie, but the dark circles under my eyes will only fade with sleep. Agitated, I hustle back into my bedroom to change.

7:10 a.m.

First period starts in ten minutes. Not good. Mr. Hanson not only detests tardiness, but uses humiliation tactics to ensure it's never repeated. I snag a crumpled pair of jeans off the floor and throw them on before ripping a plain white T-shirt off a hanger and pulling it over my head. I slip on my sandals as I double-up on my deodorant, then snatch my bag and sprint down the stairs. The smell of coffee lingers throughout the house, and I hesitate for a split second.

No time.

I will have to endure first period precalculus—the worst subject in the entire universe—and grumpy old Hanson without my morning coffee.

On a Monday.

God help us all.

I dash out the front door and toss my bag into the backseat of my 1970 Chevelle and start the engine. Even in the mild March weather of Phoenix, Arizona, my car prefers to be warmed up before driven. But today won't allow such a luxury, and my car groans as I slam on the gas.

The Chevelle and I have a love-hate relationship. I love finally having my own car, but I kind of loathe the beast. It runs okay—as long as it starts—and the chipped black paint is a dull shade of embarrassment. My boyfriend, Tommy, was able to hook my parents up with a great deal through his dad's auto shop. And I really am grateful . . . for the most part.

Tommy is the reason I'm late this morning. We stayed up until two in the morning talking on the phone. There's no excuse, really, since we just spent our entire spring break practically inseparable. Part of me was worried how he'd take the news about me moving to Los Angeles for college, but he's been nothing but supportive. Even though he has no college aspirations, he's surprisingly relaxed about us being in a long-distance relationship. I wish I could say I felt the same.

We've hung out in the same circle of friends since junior high, but it wasn't until last summer that we finally started dating. We became exclusive on the last day of summer vacation and things have never been better. Well, except that he's become a little restless about going all the way. I know he gets a lot of flak from his friends about the fact that he hasn't scored with me yet—sometimes I overhear them asking him about it. Boys are so vile.

Tommy isn't a virgin, but he's only had sex once in his life. It was at the first party of the summer with some random girl about two weeks before we started dating. Classy, I know. But he isn't a bad guy; he's pretty great, actually. He's just . . . well, a *guy*. I know any other girl in school would have slept with the dark-haired, blue-eyed hunk by now, but I'm not ready to lose my virginity just yet. I'm still waiting for the perfect moment.

I pull into the crowded parking lot and circle around twice before parking on the side of the road. I glance at my phone and groan.

7:35 a.m.

I made pretty good time, but I'm still terribly late as far as Horrible Hanson is concerned. To be blunt, Mr. Hanson is a grouchy old man who's probably been on tenure longer than I've been alive. I got stuck with him because I procrastinated on my registration and missed out on the good teachers. Now it's mid-semester and I am somehow holding onto an A. But to be honest, I always feel like I am hanging on by a thread.

I snatch my bag and dash across the student lot. It's a pretty large campus—home to a huge two-story building and several sports fields, including the baseball diamond where Tommy is currently in mid-season.

When I arrive at the entrance, I yank open the heavy blue door. It slams against the brick wall, and I flinch as the sound ricochets through the silence. My footsteps echo as I sprint down the hallway, and I try to mentally prepare myself for Mr. Hanson's wrath. I've never been late to his class for this very reason. It's cringeworthy just watching him lay into a student. This time, that student will be me.

I round the corner and rush through the classroom doorway, avoiding all potential eye contact, and plop down in my seat—which unfortunately is front row center. I literally brace my body as I stare at my desk, waiting to be humiliated.

But it never comes.

Instead, I hear an unfamiliar voice.

"Are you Kaley Kennedy?"

I look up and see a much younger man than I'm expecting. He's holding the class roster in his hands and is wearing what looks to be a very expensive three-piece suit. His warm caramel eyes pierce into mine, and I try to find my voice.

"Um . . . yes?" I say, unsure why my answer comes out as a question.

He erases what is probably an absentee mark, and I take advantage of his brief distraction to quickly look him over. I have no idea where this guy came from, but there's no way he's a math teacher. First of all, he looks like some Ivy League professor, or a prestigious lawyer. And yet, he's so good-looking and youthful, he gives the impression of a European fashion model—so much so that I'm surprised a British accent didn't come pouring out. Either way, he looks completely out of place in a public high school in the middle of the East Valley suburbs.

He catches me staring at his perfectly disheveled locks—that remind me of milk chocolate drizzled with honey—and I drop my gaze to my desk, remembering how unsightly I look. *Wait . . . why do I even care?* I should just be grateful I'm late on the one day Mr. Hanson isn't here.

His dark-brown designer slacks interrupt my thoughts as they come into view. Standing directly in front of my desk, he peers down at me as I slowly raise my head, meeting his focused eyes. Suddenly, I can't feel my lips.

He speaks softly, and I force myself to hold his tranquilizing gaze. "I just got through informing the class that Mr. Hanson passed away last week."

"Oh shit." My face grows hot at my explicit reaction, and I quickly mumble "Sorry." I sense the faint hint of a smile in his eyes for a moment before he continues.

"He died of a massive heart attack Thursday night," he says. "The school counselor was here at the beginning of class to offer counseling for all of his students. I wrote her office hours on the board, if you need them."

I peer up at the board and admire his perfect handwriting in all caps.

"I'm Mr. Slate," he continues, "and I'll be your new math teacher for the rest of the semester." He pulls his gaze away from mine as he turns to his desk, and my mouth goes dry.

Okay, so he's *not* a substitute. He'll be here every single day . . . no big deal.

Mr. Slate instructs us to open up our textbooks and asks us where we left off as I shuffle in my bag for a pencil. The class begins to buzz with chatter, and I desperately try to smooth out my ponytail. *What is my deal?* My reaction to him is so silly. It's probably just my lack of sleep. And let's face it—it's shocking to have such a hot math teacher. I mean, has there ever been one before in the history of time? He's like some kind of mathematical unicorn. I scan the classroom and notice Avery—who sits three seats to the right of me, directly in front of his desk. She's sitting up straight, gazing at him like a pit bull salivating over tenderloin. I roll my eyes and bring my attention back to my textbook.

In what normally drags on, class flies by in a blur. I try my best to pay attention to the equations we're working on, but he's so mesmerizing that I end up observing *him* more than the assignment. And it turns out he's funny on top of everything else. He has the class laughing as he frets over the dirty whiteboard.

"Sorry, I'm a little OCD. I'll be fine though," he jokes as he vainly tries to clean up the smears of old dry-erase marks. "Hmm ... I'll have to bring my own cleaner, apparently." He hesitates before setting down the eraser.

He brightens the mood of the class with his light-hearted quips and genuine smile. The guys all seem to appreciate his comicality, while most of the girls just swoon. He finishes his lecture with ten minutes to spare and instructs us to start on our homework. As he settles into his desk, the class quiets down. I search in my bag for my favorite lip balm, thankful when I find it. My lips are dry and my entire body feels dehydrated. I pull off the cap and slide the bubble gum flavor along my lips, closing my eyes in sweet relief. Instinctively, I glance over at his desk and find him studying me, his eyes resting on my mouth. I pause before slowly rubbing my lips together, my heart palpitating. Our eyes meet briefly before he rises from his chair and makes his way to the back of the classroom where Seth's hand is raised.

Heat sweeps through my face, and I shield it with my hand as I dig my elbow into the desk, trying to slow my pulse. *Clearly, he was just watching the class to see if anyone needed help. Get over yourself.*

The bell rings, releasing me from this disorienting first hour, and Avery is out of her seat before I even stand up. Mr. Slate walks past me and sits back down as Avery twirls her blonde hair around her finger and leans against his desk. She asks some lame question about the homework assignment, and I cringe at her sad attempt at portraying innocence. Avery and I have mutual friends, but she's half sweet and half nails-on-a-chalkboard.

Mr. Slate leans back in his chair, and I watch their interaction through my peripheral vision while I pack up my stuff.

Now that I'm standing, I'm able to take in more of his attire. His shoes can only pass as some high-class Italian loafers, and I still can't get over his designer suit. *Who is this guy?* I check out his dark-brown leather messenger bag sitting next to his desk before my gaze lifts to his spectacular face. His eyes flash to mine as Avery babbles on, and my stomach flip-flops in disobedience to my brain. I drop my gaze and throw my bag over my shoulder and walk out the door . . . no longer in need of caffeine.

I rush to my locker and swap out my books before heading to second period. My hands are shaking a bit, and I feel light-headed. No coffee, no food, not enough sleep, and my math teacher just passed away—*of course I'm out of sorts*, I assure myself. When I walk into my English lit class, Tommy is already seated. His first class is next door, so he usually beats me here. I slide into my seat next to him and smile.

He regards me with curiosity. "Everything okay?" He probably wonders why I look so hideous.

"I slept in!" I say, running my hands over my ponytail. "I couldn't even shower, or have my morning coffee."

"You look fine, Kay." He laughs. "But you really didn't have any coffee? Because you look like you just downed about six cups."

"Really?" My voice cracks.

Great. So whatever I'm feeling shows.

His giant water jug distracts me.

"Hey, can I have some of that?"

He hands it over and I take a greedy swig. All the athletes carry a gallon of water with them throughout the day, and today I am grateful.

Tommy's eyes still question me as I hand him back the jug.

"I don't know," I say. "I had a weird morning . . . Mr. Hanson died of a heart attack over spring break."

9

"Oh shit!"

"Mr. Bradford," warns Mrs. Taylor.

"Sorry, Mrs. Taylor," says Tommy, flashing his boy-next-door grin.

DURING LUNCH, TOMMY sits next to me as he discusses the upcoming baseball game with his best friend, Derek, and the rest of his teammates. My mind begins to wander just as Emily slams her tray down in front of me, startling the entire table.

"Did you see?" is all she says.

"Huh?"

Her eyes are wide with excitement. "Did you see our new math teacher?"

"Well, I have his class right before you, so yeah," I say.

"Holy hell! How are we supposed to get any work done?"

Tommy and Derek's conversation halts as they gape at us in confusion.

"What do you mean?" I ask in a lame attempt to seem oblivious.

"Mr. McHottie!" Emily squeals.

"Oh, I know," Avery chimes in as she takes her seat nearby. She and her fellow cheerleaders always sit at the end of our table. "He is *so* gorgeous!"

I try to act nonchalant as the girls gush about him. "They're totally overreacting," I say to Tommy, hoping I sound convincing.

Derek turns to Emily. "Do I need to escort you to second period now, babe? Who the hell is this guy?"

"Oh, please," says Emily. "Like you guys didn't talk about Ms. Guess in front of us constantly when she was new."

A lazy grin pulls up the corners of Derek's mouth as his

eyes glaze over. "Yeah, she's hot."

Emily playfully punches him on the arm. I've been best friends with Emily since third grade when I fell off the monkey bars during recess and she ran over to help me. She even walked me to the nurse's office and stayed with me until I stopped crying. After the nurse cleaned me up, she gave both of us purple lollipops, and we've been inseparable ever since. She is annoyingly beautiful, however, and popular, with gorgeous blonde hair and legs up to her neck.

I've known her boyfriend, Derek, since junior high, and he is one of my favorite people on the planet. He's great-looking, a high academic achiever, and excels at every sport—so much so that he's all set to go to USC on a football scholarship. On paper, you'd think he was a jerk. But he's the sweetest guy I know. He's beloved by everyone in school, and his light-brown hair, emerald-green eyes, and positive spirit, complement my best friend in a way that makes me believe they are made for each other.

Emily turns to Avery for support in the how-hot-is-Mr.-Slate meter, and I scoot closer to Tommy and squeeze his hand while I pick at my salad. He may not be concerned about me leaving in a few months, but I can't help but feel guilty. Maybe I'm overcompensating, but I know if he was moving away for college, I'd be extra sensitive about him drooling over some hot new chick.

As I plant a kiss on his lips, Emily interrupts.

"Hey, what's up with you? It's finally payback for Ms. Guess. Do you seriously not find him attractive?"

I shrug. "I don't know. I guess so. For an older guy."

"You are *crazy*," Avery says. "He's gotta be in his twenties."

"I wouldn't care if he was in his thirties," Emily deadpans.

Avery giggles. "He doesn't wear a ring."

Derek smirks. "Girls. They look for a ring, while guys never even make it to a girl's finger." The guys all laugh, and I quickly change the subject.

"So, have you heard anything from USC yet?" I ask Emily.

She sighs. "Not yet."

After Derek got his scholarship, Emily and I rushed our applications in, so we could all go together. I just got my acceptance letter last week, so I'm anxious to see if our dream will become reality.

"You're bound to hear something soon," I assure her.

"I know. I just hope it's good news."

THE LACK OF sleep and caffeine hits me hard by the end of the day. I make my way down the hallway and slump down on the wooden bench next to the gym, where the four of us always meet after school. Tommy's late. I rest my head against the wall and close my eyes. Emily and Derek have already left and the halls are beginning to thin. Just as I'm drifting off, Tommy rushes me from the side and lifts me up over his shoulder. I scream as he twirls me around, laughing.

I squeal. "Let me go!"

He sets me back down, and I hold onto his arms for balance as I wait for the room to stop spinning. I brush my ponytail out of my face and catch Mr. Slate's eyes as he strides past us. My stomach drops, and I watch him walk outside to the parking lot, then quickly turn my attention back to Tommy and try to smile.

"You okay?" Tommy laughs. "You look like you're about to puke."

"I'm good . . . y-you just caught me off guard," I stammer.

Something has definitely caught me off guard. No lie there.

He pokes me in the ribs and gives me a quick peck on the

lips. "I'm late for practice, I'll call you later."

I TRY TO calm my mind as I slide into my car. I don't feel like myself today and can't wait to get home. As I pull out of the student lot and onto the street, Mr. Slate appears in my mind. I blast the stereo in a vain attempt to drown out my thoughts. I don't want to be thinking about him and analyzing every detail of first period. It makes me feel like a young, foolish girl, and I'm embarrassed that I can't control the way my body reacts every time his eyes meet mine.

Once I'm home, I trudge upstairs to my bedroom and work through all of my homework—even some extra credit. I could really use a nap, but there's a sudden need inside me to stay busy. I don't come downstairs when either of my parents come home. Instead, I work straight through until my dad calls me down for dinner.

My mom is a hairdresser and works all kinds of hours, so it's rare when we eat dinner as a family. We have similar features with our dark-brown hair and blue eyes, but I have my dad's nose. While a lot of my friends complain about their parents, I couldn't be happier with mine. We've always had an easy, loving relationship. And up until recently, I'd say the same for their marriage. I would think their relationship is perfect if it weren't for the late night fights. But even though things have been strained between them lately, they never bring me into it. They haven't spoken to me about it, nor have I mentioned how they've been keeping me up most nights.

My dad sits across from me at the dinner table and looks at me with his loving hazel eyes. "What's up, Kay?"

I'm playing with my spaghetti when he addresses me. "Nothing," I say. "Just really tired. I think I'm gonna go to bed early."

"How's school? Everything okay?"

My mind flashes to Mr. Slate before I answer. "Actually, no. Mr. Hanson died of a heart attack over spring break."

My mother gasps. "No!"

"Yeah. We already have a new math teacher, too. It was kind of a strange day." A tingle runs down my spine as I recall Mr. Slate's eyes on my lips.

"Unbelievable," my mom whispers. "Are you okay?"

I shift in my chair. "Yeah, I'm fine."

My parents stare at me with concern, and I know they think I'm upset over his death. I admit, Mr. Hanson's death was a shock, and obviously I didn't want the guy to drop dead, but that isn't what's pestering me.

My chair screeches against the tile as I stand up. "I'm gonna go crash." I reach for my plate, but my mom stops me.

"We'll get that, sweetie," she says.

I stop an eye roll. They're both looking at me with pity, and nothing irritates me more. I bid them goodnight and go upstairs to wash my face and brush my teeth. I slip into my pajamas and try to push today out of my mind. My phone chimes just as I'm climbing into bed. It's a text from Tommy. Suddenly, I'm not in the mood to talk. I text him back, letting him know I'm going to bed early and turn my phone on silent. My body is desperate for sleep, and I sink into the mattress.

But I toss and turn.

My mind is restless.

It's not long before I hear my parents arguing downstairs, and I groan. I wanted to fall asleep before the fighting began. It's become almost routine in my house, but as long as I can fall asleep before I hear them, I'm able to get my much needed eight hours.

Frustrated, I lift the pillow over my head and press it tightly against my ears, begging my body to sleep. As much as I resist, the idyllic image of Mr. Slate continues to permeate my mind. Normally, I don't remember the specific features of a person I've just met. But somehow, the details of his face are already etched into my memory. *Ugh! Why on earth am I thinking about my math teacher right now?* And what was with my body's reaction to him today? I'm just as pathetic as the rest of the girls. *A lack of sleep is the culprit*, I convince myself. All I need is a good night's rest, and I'll feel like my old self again.

After a while, I pull the pillow off my head, and I'm relieved to hear silence throughout the house. My mind finally gives in to my body's exhaustion, but Mr. Slate's face is still the last thing I see as I drift off to sleep.

CHAPTER TWO

I WAKE UP TWENTY MINUTES before my alarm goes off. After nine solid hours of sleep, I feel well rested and decide to get a head start on the day. Feeling grimy from skipping a shower yesterday, I take my time underneath the warm stream of water. My mind shuffles through the events of the last twenty-four hours, and I laugh at myself. *Who was that girl?* I'm definitely not forgoing the coffee today. When I'm finished with my shower, I wrap a towel around myself and plug in my curling iron. I hesitate before heading back to my bedroom.

Maybe I shouldn't curl my hair today.

I glance at my reflection as my buried thoughts begin to surface. I don't want it to seem like I'm trying too hard in front of Mr. Slate. I especially don't want him to think I'm going out of my way to look nice for him. But why would he even think that? What makes me think he'd even notice? *You curl your hair all the time, what's the difference?* If anyone knew I was standing in my bathroom unsure of whether or not to curl my hair because of what my math teacher might think, I would die from embarrassment.

I unplug the curling iron and walk back into my bedroom.

After choosing a pair of formfitting jeans, with an aqua shirt that hugs my curves and complements my eyes, I make my way back to the bathroom to dry my hair and apply my makeup. I have to at least admit to myself that I'm trying—without trying to *look* like I'm trying.

Oh, man. What am I doing?

My mom enters the doorway and sets down a fresh steaming cup of coffee.

"Thank you," I say, grateful, bringing it to my lips.

"I still think you're too young to be drinking this."

"I'm eighteen," I say. "And you're just an enabler."

She laughs and then examines me. "You look really beautiful this morning."

My heart skips a beat. "I do?"

"Yes. I mean you're always beautiful, Kay, but I don't know." She smiles, her eyes glistening. "My baby's growing up."

"Mom," I grumble.

She laughs at her own weepiness. "Sorry, I'm just having a moment here." She admires me as I put the finishing touches on my makeup. "Will you be home tonight?"

"Yeah, why?"

"Your dad and I want to have a family meeting."

I turn to her. "What's going on?"

She glances at her watch. "You better get going, or you'll be late. We'll talk tonight." She gives me a kiss on the cheek before turning away.

Apparently, I took an extra twenty minutes getting ready this morning. Underneath my denial, I know the reason, but I plead ignorance to my conscience.

THE NORMAL BUZZ and chaos swarms the hallways as I enter the building. I slowly make my way to first period and take a deep breath before entering. Mr. Slate is vigorously cleaning the whiteboard as I stride up the center aisle. Butterflies tickle my stomach while I quietly slip into my seat.

Stupid butterflies.

He wears expensive-looking gray slacks with a white button-down shirt, neatly tucked in. The thin material suggests a muscular back as his arms move back and forth across the whiteboard. I cross my legs as I take in his full body and realize this guy is packing quite the physique underneath his designer clothes. When he turns around, I snap back to reality and flip open my math book. With my gaze fixed on a random page, I hold my breath as he walks over to his desk. I can't handle any possible eye contact right now. After the last of the students trickle in, he takes attendance.

When he calls my name, our eyes lock, and electric shock rushes through me. My throat tightens, stifling my reply, so the best I can manage is a slight nod. His penetrating eyes release mine, and I exhale, sinking into my chair. *So much for things being back to normal today.* I've had nine hours of sleep and a cup of coffee—I'm out of excuses.

After he's through taking roll, he writes on the upper right-hand corner of the whiteboard:

STUDY SESSIONS

FRIDAYS 6PM

"Okay, you guys," he says, unbuttoning the cuffs of his shirt. "I'm offering study sessions to anyone who wants extra help. I know they're on Fridays, but after going through the grade book, many of you could really benefit." He sets his cufflinks down on his desk and slowly rolls up his sleeves, revealing nicely sculpted forearms. "I will stay as late as needed, so I don't want to hear any excuses. It's right here," he says, tapping the board with his knuckle, "so don't make me say it over and over. It's your responsibility to get some help if you need it. Okay?"

Sorry, can you repeat that? I couldn't hear over your forearms.

My palm sweats around my pencil as I scribble down notes throughout his lecture. He's pretty good at explaining things, but if I don't start focusing on precalculus instead of his broad shoulders, my grade is going to plummet fast. *This*

18

is absurd. So his body is cut like an equilateral triangle, big deal. I've never been distracted by muscles like this. I'm a sensible girl—an honor student for goodness' sake!

At the end of the hour, Mr. Slate hands back our tests we took the Friday before spring break.

"I'm sorry I couldn't get these to you sooner, but I just got them yesterday and graded them last night."

The thought of someone retrieving our ungraded tests from our deceased math teacher is not only morbid, but disturbing. The class falls silent, and I'm sure everyone is picturing the same scene. Since Mr. Slate is still learning everyone's names, he has to call each student up to get their tests. But when he calls my name, he looks directly at me. My legs are weak as I stand up to approach his desk.

"Nice work," he says, his warm brown eyes burning through me.

I peer down at my test and frown—a low B. As I walk back to my desk, I examine each page, analyzing every mistake. After a few minutes, I collect my things and wander toward the door, still scanning the last page of my test. By the time I look up, I realize everyone else is already gone.

With my books cradled against my chest, I stand at the back of the classroom and observe as he diligently erases the whiteboard, his tantalizing back muscles rooting me to the floor. Feeling my gaze, he turns his head and does a double-take. He stops erasing the board and slowly turns around.

I blush.

"Kaley? Are you all right?"

I nod, unable to speak. *Leave, just leave!* But my feet won't move.

"Is there something you need?"

I burst out a nervous laugh and my face burns.

He furrows his brows. "Is something wrong with your test?"

"No. Well, yeah, just the grade," I stammer. "But that's not your fault. Um ... I just want to know what time the study group is."

Idiot. He just went over that and specifically said he didn't want to repeat himself. I stare at the ground and brush my hand through my hair. Nervous habit.

Still waiting for his reply, I peer up at him and see that his expression has turned into something else. Confusion mixed with something ... unreadable. Without breaking his gaze, he slowly points to the top right-hand corner of the whiteboard. He had to know I was paying attention when he gave the announcement. My façade is so unbelievable; I want the floor to open up and swallow me whole.

"Oh, right," I say, letting out another nervous laugh.

"It'd be great having you there. You have one of the highest grades in class. You'd be a big help."

"Thanks."

Why am I not walking out the door?!

"Are you sure you're okay?" His eyes hold mine with an intensity that makes me breathless. I nod just as students begin to trickle in, and the classroom quickly fills with chatter.

Emily enters. "Kaley, what's the matter?"

I shake my head and try to manufacture a smile. As I head out the door, I glance over my shoulder—he's still staring at me, his expression indecipherable.

Holy hell.

I rush to the bathroom and splash cold water on my face. *What is wrong with me?* I've never lost control over my body like that. I'm always in control—I don't even drink! Sure, I've had plenty of crushes before—*wait, this isn't a crush; he's your teacher*—but I've never had this kind of physical reaction before. And just because I haven't had sex yet, doesn't mean my boyfriend doesn't turn me on.

Does he turn me on?

Maybe I thought I knew what it felt like to be turned on ... until now. *What the hell are you saying?! You are not turned on by your tea*—I can't even say it to myself. If I do, it will make it true, and I am perfectly happy living in the land of denial.

Happy? Okay, more like desperate to live there.

I face my reflection and find mascara running down my face. *Way to go, Kay.* At least the bathroom is empty. I wipe it away and try to freshen up my makeup, but it's no use. I have a wildness in my eyes, like I'm hopped up on amphetamines. *Get a grip!*

I take a deep breath and gather my thoughts.

This man is my teacher. Even if he wasn't, he'd still be too old for me. He's a grown man, with a grown-up life and would probably laugh his ass off if he knew what I was feeling. I'm sure he thinks I'm a freak after gaping at him like a moron just now.

But what was that look in his eye?

No! He doesn't want some stupid, doe-eyed teenaged girl. He wants a woman. He probably *has* a woman—a grown-up, beautiful woman who doesn't fumble when she speaks to him and calls him by his first name. She's probably some supermodel and sleeps in his bed every night. *Why are you thinking about his bed?!* The late bell rings, and I swear out loud. I take one more glance in the mirror before rushing to second period with my face still flushed and my body trembling.

I BURST THROUGH the door while Mrs. Taylor is mid-sentence. She gives me a disapproving frown, and I collapse into my seat. I've never been late to her class before, so I hope she'll let it slide.

Tommy leans over and whispers, "You okay?"

I nod and give him the same forced smile I gave Emily: *fake*. He isn't buying it. He's known me for too long.

"Um, Kay? You have the wrong textbook."

I notice my math book gripped tightly in my hands.

"Damn," I whisper. "I forgot to stop by my locker."

"Are you sure you're okay?"

I nod. Why does everyone keep asking me that? *Because I'm not okay*, I decide. Hoping he'll let it go, I turn my attention back to class, my body still tingling.

EMILY PLOPS DOWN next to me. "So, what were you and Mr. McHottie talking about?"

Tommy's eyes meet mine across the table.

"Who?" I ask, picking at my lunch.

"Oh please, Kaley. Mr. Slate! What the hell was going on?"

"Nothing." I shrug. "We were just talking about the study group."

Emily purses her lips. "That's it? It looked a little more intense than that. I thought you were in trouble."

Oh, I'm in trouble all right. She seems to have bought it, though. I mean, technically, that *is* what we were talking about, so it's not a complete lie.

"You're not going, are you?" she says as she cracks open her soda. "It's on a Friday night!"

"I'm thinking about it," I admit.

Tommy breaks his silence. "Don't you have an A in that class?"

I feel the heat on my face betray me. "Um, yeah, but it's still a hard class. In fact, I just got an eighty-one on my last test. And besides, he said I would be a big help."

"So, wait," says Emily. "Are you going because you want help? Or are you going because you want to help out?" She winks at me, and I silently curse my face as I feel it blush.

"I dunno—I mean . . . both, I guess."

"Well, you can tell him that I'd *love* to be his big help," gushes Emily dramatically.

Derek turns to her. "What the hell, babe?"

Emily laughs and throws her tater tot at him. "What? You jealous?"

"Please. What do you want an old man for when you've got this?" He flexes his arm and grabs her around the waist. She giggles and they fall into a kiss.

Someone behind me shouts, "Get a room!"

Tommy leans forward. "I thought we were going to the movies on Friday night."

"Oh, right," I say, hoping he doesn't sense my disappointment.

Emily breaks away from Derek. "Thank God, Kay! If you were going to ditch us *and* Ryan Gosling for a study session on a *Friday* night, I'd have to disown you."

I try to smile, then turn to my lunch. I don't know what I was thinking. Whenever the boys have a game-free Friday night, the four of us have automatic plans. A study session with Mr. Slate—*and his forearms*—will probably never happen. *Why does that bother me so much?* I shove my uneaten food back into my lunch sack.

"I have to go to the library," I say to Tommy. "See you after school?"

"Yeah, I'll see you then," he says, his eyes guarded.

I give him a light peck on the cheek and stand up. As I leave the table, I throw out my untouched food and catch Tommy's concerned eyes lingering on the trash can as I walk away.

BY THE TIME my parents get home, I'm deep into my homework and have forgotten all about the family meeting. When they call me downstairs, dread washes over me. Are they finally going to address their fighting? Or worse—what if they're getting a divorce? No, not *my* parents. I push the unbidden thought out of my head.

They're sitting in the formal living room when I make my way down the stairs. My mom looks worried, my dad tense. No words pass between us as I take my seat on the leather couch.

"Just spit it out," I say quietly. Whatever terrible news they're about to give me, I'd rather they rip it off like a Band-Aid than drag it out. I slide my hands in between my knees as suspense suffocates the room.

My dad leans forward in the chair across from me and takes a deep breath. "We need to talk to you about college."

"College?" I say, dumbfounded.

"We're so proud of you for getting into USC, Kay. You should be really proud of yourself." Something in his tone sets off my inner alarms.

"I am," I say.

He hesitates like he's struggling to find the right words. After a period of thick, awkward silence, my mom shifts in her seat on the other end of the couch and speaks for him.

"Kaley," she says softly. "We can't afford it, sweetie."

A sudden coldness hits me at my core. "What?"

I don't understand. With my mom working as a hairdresser and my dad managing a small hardware store, I know we aren't exactly rich. But we definitely aren't poor.

"Kaley," my dad finally speaks up, "the University of Southern California is over sixty grand a year."

The University of Southern California? What, is he avoiding the abbreviation for dramatic affect?

"Yeah, I know that." I try to choose my words carefully. "But tuition hasn't exactly changed in the last few months. You knew the cost when I applied." I look back and forth between them. "I don't understand. You've always wanted me to go to college."

"And we still do," my dad replies. "ASU is a good school, Kay."

"ASU? Why do I have to go to ASU?" I try to stay composed, but my voice rises. "You've *never* put limits on what college I could go to!"

"We never really talked about it," my mom says gently.

"I can't believe this," I say, gaping at them. They've been pushing college on me my entire life—silly me for assuming they were prepared for it. A thread of ire weaves through me. "So tell me something. Why have I been busting my butt in school? Why have I been wasting my time with student council and community service? What was it all for? Why did you even let me apply?" I exclaim.

"Well," says my mom, "it's a really hard school to get into, Kay."

Her sympathetic voice masks the truth behind her words, and it takes me a moment to process.

"You guys didn't think I'd get in," I say, my voice faint. Confirmation flashes across their features, and I don't wait for them to reply. "Well, I *did* get in," I cry, rising to my feet. "So what now? That's it?"

"Sit down," warns my dad. "Since when are you too good for Arizona State?"

"What is your obsession with ASU? Quit turning it around!" My nails dig into my palms as I tighten my fists. "Newsflash! Your daughter isn't a moron! You lied to me—you *both* lied to me!"

"We didn't lie to you," says my dad, his voice stern. "Now sit *down*."

I cross my arms and remain standing. "Is this what you guys fight about every night? Money for my tuition?"

My dad lets out a loud sigh. "No," he says, sounding defeated. "That has nothing to do with you."

Nothing about that statement makes me feel any better.

"I'm going to USC," I demand. "I'll take out student loans; I'll get a job." I'll be damned if I let their lack of responsibility and preparation ruin *my* life.

My dad leans back in his chair, his face pained. "Kaley. We'd have to co-sign. We just can't do it. I'm sorry."

The truth is, he looks sorry. Painfully sorry. They both do.

"Can I go to my room, please?" I ask, my legs starting to weaken.

"We're not done talking about this," says my dad.

"I just need a moment, okay?"

"Let her go, Don," says my mom, her voice soft.

As soon as he nods for me to go, I sprint up the stairs and into my bedroom. My acceptance package stares back at me from my desk, and I collapse onto my bed. My phone chimes with a text from Emily:

I'm on the waiting list! Not what I was hoping for, but I have a good feeling. Our dream will happen, Kay!

That's awesome, Ems, I reply. Keep me posted!

I toss my phone aside and burst into tears.

CHAPTER THREE

"Damn, I'm sorry, babe," says Tommy after I get done telling the group how my parents blindsided me last night. I left out the part about how they never expected me to get accepted. Tommy sets down his sandwich and wraps his arms around me.

"Yeah, Kay," Derek agrees. "That sucks."

Emily looks like her whole world has crumbled. "There has to be some way," she says.

"Nope, I'm destined to go to ASU," I say with a heavy sigh. "All by myself."

"You're going to ASU, Kaley?" Avery says as she slides into her chair. "That's where I'm going!" She beams.

"Great," I mutter, exerting a smile. I know she means well, but can't she see I'm devastated?

"Don't give up," says Emily. "We'll figure something out."

"Like what?" I say, hopeless.

"I don't know yet, but it's going to happen."

"Ems, you don't even know if *you're* getting in or not."

"I know *two* people who were on the waiting list, and they already got their acceptance letters. I'm going to get in. And you're going too, I promise."

I shake my head. Sometimes my best friend can be positive to a fault.

THE WEEK GOES by without any more embarrassing incidences in front of Mr. Slate. On Thursday after school, I'm the first one to arrive at our usual meet-up and take a seat on the old wooden bench. Emily walks over with a bounce in her step and practically hurls herself on top of me.

"So, I found out some stuff about Professor McHottie," she says, grinning.

"Don't you mean Mr. McHottie? He's just a high school teacher," I say, trying to hide my thirst for details about his life.

"Nope. Professor. He's going to be teaching a math class this summer at the community college. So technically, he's Professor McHottie." Emily beams. "Doesn't that make him even hotter?"

"I guess."

"Come on! Don't you think he's sexy? I can barely concentrate in his class, and it's already a boring subject."

"You have a boyfriend."

"So? He probably has a girlfriend, or a freakin' fiancé," she blurts out.

My insides cringe.

"He's also your teacher," I remind her.

She giggles. "Duh! It's not like I can actually boink the guy, but I can dream about it."

Jealousy sinks into me, viciously spreading its venom. I don't want her fantasizing about him. I don't even want her thinking about him. Emily is so confident and beautiful, I bet she *could* boink him if she really tried. I shove my insecurity down and try to appear indifferent.

"So, what else did you find out?"

"Well, I don't know if he has a girlfriend, but I'm going to find out. He's definitely not married, unless he's one of those jerks who doesn't wear a ring. I hate that. Anyway, he has his master's degree, obviously, since he teaches college classes, and I know he got his undergrad at NAU."

A master's degree. That's so . . . adult. I'm not even old

enough to buy a wine cooler.

"I also found out where he lives," she says, her eyes glittering with excitement.

My head whips around. "What? How?"

"Well, you know how I'm an assistant in the office fifth period—"

"You didn't."

"I did. I peeked at his file while Mrs. Miller was in Mr. Bentley's office. I was only able to see it for a second, but I couldn't resist."

"Ems, that is so . . . freaky."

"I know, I'm a total stalker. Do you wanna come with me?"

"What, to his house?" I blink at her in disbelief. "What are you gonna do? Go knock on his door and say 'Hey Professor McHottie, take me now?'" We burst into laughter.

"No!" says Emily. "We're just going to drive by to check it out."

Before I can object to the "we" part of that sentence, a sultry voice interrupts.

"Hi, girls."

Emily and I look up, and there he is, striding toward us. My face grows hot while Emily laughs harder.

Please God, say he didn't hear us.

"Hi Prof—uh, Mr. Slate," I say.

Kill me. Kill me now.

My slip-up has Emily silently shaking with laughter, and my face is probably the same shade as an overripe tomato. Very attractive.

After a quick hesitation, he smiles his gorgeous, picture-perfect smile as he continues toward the gymnasium. "See you tomorrow, ladies. Don't forget to study for the quiz."

"Oh we'll be seeing you *tonight*, Professor," Emily says under her breath.

"We?"

"Yes! Aren't you the least bit curious?"

"Not really," I lie.

"Come on, Kay! You have to come with me. We'll go after the boys' game tonight—what else are you going to do? And don't say study! It'll be fun."

I sigh as my curiosity gets the better of me. Suddenly, I wonder what kind of house he lives in . . . I wonder how his kitchen is organized . . . I wonder what his bedroom looks like . . . if he lives alone. Guilt washes over me as Tommy and Derek approach.

Emily turns to me and whispers, "Come on, let's do it!"

"Fine," I say through gritted teeth, then stand up to greet Tommy.

"Hey, babe," says Tommy, slipping his arms around me. "You're coming to the game, right?"

I smile. "Of course."

With his arms wrapped tightly around me, he turns to Emily. "Hey, your boyfriend will be at the game today."

Emily and I exchange glances.

"Um, he's on the team, so I would hope so," she says.

Derek covers Emily's ears. "Oh, don't tell her that!"

Tommy laughs.

"What?" squeaks Emily, struggling to escape.

"Your boy toy has been appointed new assistant coach."

My smile fades as a pit in my stomach grows. The universe has a sick sense of humor. Emily releases a wide grin and Derek is quick to wipe it off with a kiss that should only be performed in private.

Tommy turns to me. "Are you okay? You've been a little off this week. Are you still upset over USC?"

"Yeah, I guess."

He tucks my hair behind my ear. "Would it be so bad to stay here with me?" His sparkling blue eyes linger on mine as a twinge of guilt pricks my heart.

"No, of course not," I say, glancing down.

He cups my chin and pulls me into a deep kiss. "I'll see you after the game."

Emily squeals as soon as the boys disappear around the corner. "He's coaching!" She jumps up and down.

Her enthusiasm is infectious, and I playfully lift a brow at her. "Did baseball finally get interesting?"

She tugs on my arm. "Let's go right now."

"Where?"

"Mr. Slate's house. We know he won't be home," she says, pulling me outside. "Just really quick before the game."

I attempt to stall. "What if the boys notice?"

"So what? We'll just say we grabbed a bite to eat or something."

"Fine," I say as an unwelcomed excitement springs up inside me. I couldn't argue with her even if I tried—when Emily wants something, she stops at nothing to get it.

She's a ball of energy as we drive off campus toward his neighborhood, and I try to downplay my interest. But when she starts talking about his forearms, I can't hold back my laughter. As much as I want to add to Emily's amusing observations, an undulating possessiveness over him has me guarded.

Before long, Emily is slowing down the car, pulling me from my thoughts. On my right, a rock waterfall greets us, gushing next to a large stone sign that reads Sunset Meadows.

"I think this is it," she says, turning in.

Emily's car vibrates over the cobblestone as we pass through the entrance of his subdivision. The main street is lined with Queen Palms, giving the community a resort-like feel. I zoom into the map on her phone as we mischievously weave through the streets.

"This is it," I direct. "Ironwood Drive. Take a right."

Emily slows down as she reads the house numbers. "Four-five-two-oh—yep! There it is! On the right."

I sink into my seat as the car crawls down the road. Even though I know he's not home, it still feels intrusive. The house is a light sand-colored one-story with a typical desert stucco finish and Spanish-tile roof. A mahogany front door sits between the two-car garage and several large windows adorned with white shutters. His lawn is the greenest on the block and manicured to perfection, like he edged it with a razor blade.

"His yard is cleaner than his whiteboard," I quip.

Emily giggles and makes a U-turn. "I just need one more peek."

She slows the car and gawks out her window as we pass his house again. I glance around to see if any neighbors are watching us. When she turns off his street, she speeds back up, flashing a satisfied grin my way.

"You'd be terrible at a drive-by," I tease.

She bursts into laughter and turns up the radio as we head back to the school. We arrive at the game twenty minutes early, and I slip into the restroom to check my appearance before Emily and I take our seats near the top of the bleachers. I have to admit, this is definitely the first baseball game I'm not completely dreading.

I'm scrolling through Facebook on my phone when Emily squeezes my arm.

"Kay, he's in uniform," she says. "Good God."

My head jerks up, and I search the field until I spot him. Mr. Slate is carrying a clipboard while he and Coach Miller observe the players warming up.

And yes, he is in the team uniform.

Coach Miller is fit, too, but he's never looked like *that* in uniform. The team gathers in front of the bleachers while Emily and I ogle from the stands. After they break, and the team takes the field, Mr. Slate lifts his foot onto the bench and bends over to tie his cleat.

Emily gasps. "Kaley, I love my boyfriend, but baseball pants have never hugged an ass like that before."

Laughter explodes from me, and Mr. Slate looks up to where we're sitting. His mysterious brown eyes penetrate mine as they peer from underneath the brim of his cap. My heart stops as he holds my gaze for a moment before turning away.

"Holy. Shit," Emily breathes. "That was hot."

I can't speak, so I just nod slowly.

After the first pitch, Emily's focus is back on Derek. She is a good and faithful girlfriend, whereas I am a shameful, distracted whore. Yes, I cheer for my boyfriend, but I'm guilty of watching Mr. Slate more than anyone else. It's near-impossible not to. I mean, how is a girl supposed to pay attention to anything else but those damned pants? Seriously, they should be officially banned in baseball, right along with steroids.

THE LAST OF the evening light fades into dusk, transforming the pale sky into a spectacular display of fiery gold. Emily and I cheer as the team gathers in front of the bleachers, celebrating their victory. A slight breeze sends a chill through the air as Emily and I descend the stands. Just as I'm about to step down onto the grass, she yanks my arm back.

"Look, look!" she whispers.

I follow Emily's line of vision and see a gorgeous blonde walking up to Mr. Slate. She's wearing a designer dress with pumps that show off her trim calves, carrying a handbag that I know costs more than what my parents paid for my car. Holding her oversized sunglasses, she embraces Mr.

Slate in a hug, her arm wrapped tightly around his neck.

Emily clutches my elbow as I stand frozen. "Do you think that's his girlfriend?" she whispers. "She's drop-dead gorgeous."

"Definitely his girlfriend," I say.

"She looks like a supermodel."

I frown. "I'd expect nothing less."

Emily smirks at me.

"What?"

"I knew you thought he was hot." She jumps down to greet Derek as I watch Mr. Slate introduce the blonde beauty to Coach Miller.

Tommy hops onto the bleachers, creating a booming echo, snapping me out of my trance. He lifts me up on his back and jumps down to the ground, almost dropping me. I scream as I clutch onto his neck.

"You're choking me, babe!" he says, fighting for breath.

I giggle at his strained voice. "You almost dropped me!"

He lowers himself down, and as I slide off his back, my shirt rides up, revealing my entire midriff. I quickly yank it down as Tommy slips his arm around my waist, grazing my bare skin, just as I catch Mr. Slate's stare. I glance at the blonde next to him, who is also looking my way.

"Hit the showers, Bradford," hollers Coach Miller.

Tommy squeezes my backside before running off to the locker room, and I cringe as I scrape my hand through my hair, forcing myself not to look back at Mr. Slate. I rush to catch up with Emily, and we huddle underneath Derek's letterman jacket while we head to the parking lot.

AFTER SAYING GOODNIGHT to Emily, I wrap my arms around myself as I make my way to my car. A faint clicking sound behind me grabs my attention. When I reach the Chevelle, the quick-paced steps grow louder, and I glance at The

Blonde as she strides past me. I slide into my car with overwhelming curiosity. *Is she waiting for him?* Feeling like a creepy stalker, I duck down in my seat as she walks up to her car . . . a gleaming, white Mercedes convertible.

My stomach hardens as reality sets in. I'm so pathetic. There's no way Mr. Slate would ever think twice about me. And not just because I'm a student. The way he dresses alone is a dead giveaway he dates only the hottest, most elite women. Even if we met later on, when I'm older, graduated—maybe in a bar or through mutual friends—he still wouldn't be interested. I'm such an idiot for even crushing on him. I can't believe I let myself get so wrapped up today. And then the realization dawns on me . . .

I wanted him to want me.

The headlights of the Mercedes flick on—apparently, she isn't waiting for him. I watch her car leave campus and glide down the road. Feeling completely deflated, I turn the key in the ignition and my car roars to life. Laughing at the gruff motor that isn't exactly a Mercedes Benz, I shake my head and turn on the radio. What the hell am I doing pining over some teacher anyway, when I have a great boyfriend? *Back to reality.* I send Tommy a quick text saying I love you, before shifting into drive and heading home.

CHAPTER FOUR

Mr. SLATE ANNOUNCES TO THE class that he's the new assistant coach for the baseball team, and that he'll still be holding his study sessions—the times just may vary according to game days. But since there's no game tonight, the session is still being held at its normal time.

After he finishes today's lesson, the class goes quiet as we all try to get a head start on tonight's homework. He's excellent at breaking down math—just so long as you pay attention. I did pretty well today—seeing his painstakingly beautiful girlfriend last night helped me refocus on reality. And the reality is, I need to pass this class—and do well. I may not be going to USC, but I'm not trying to lose my spot at ASU either. Besides, I think I have a handle on this. All I have to do is put the equation of the parabola in standard form, then calculate the vertex, focus, and directrix. Then graph it. No big deal, just tedious.

But when I hit the graph button, the screen doesn't display the right output. *Hmm . . . my numbers must be off.* I do the entire problem over three times before finally summoning the courage to raise my hand. What I wouldn't give to be enrolled in an all-girls Catholic school right now, so I could actually focus on learning math instead of being intimidated to raise my hand because of my teacher's insane good looks. He's working with another student when he notices my hand in the air and gives me a quick nod to let me know he'll be there in a minute. My palms moisten, and I wipe them down on my jeans, scolding myself for being such an idiotic school girl with uncontrollable urges.

So pathetic.

"My calculator's messed up," I say as he approaches my desk.

"Let me take a look at it."

I hand it to him with swift obedience. "I swear I entered everything correctly."

"I can figure it out," he says. "I can work these things forward and backward."

My stomach swirls as he squats down next to me, pressing a combination of buttons and pulling up screens I've never seen before. I peer over his shoulder in amazement. This man can work a TI-84 graphing calculator like nobody's business. *Am I seriously finding this sexy?* I've just reached a new low.

"Okay, your settings were off, but I also think you entered a number in wrong somewhere."

"I checked three times," I say, annoyed.

He smirks. "It's a machine; it can't make a mistake. It can only do what you tell it to." He places it in front of me and stands. "Is it updated?" he asks, picking it up again. I have no idea what he means, and I think he can tell with the way he smiles at me. "I'll check it for you."

He walks over to his desk and plugs it into his computer. I didn't even know you could do that. I observe him as another student comes up to his desk and asks a question. His self-assurance is so alluring. High school boys seem to overcompensate for their lack of confidence, coming off as arrogant. But Mr. Slate is older, more mature. He never crosses the fine line that divides confidence and arrogance. And even though I try to fight it, I'm finding myself drawn to him like a hummingbird thirsty for nectar. He makes me want to be more mature, sexy, and assertive.

He makes me want to be a woman.

"Here you go, Kaley," he says, dissolving my thoughts.

He sets my calculator on my desk, his chestnut eyes gleaming into mine. "Let me know if you need anything else."

Oh, help me.

"DID YOU SEE Slate's girlfriend last night? Holy shit, dude," exclaims Jeff.

"I'd let her play with *my* bat anytime," says Donovan with a devilish grin. All the guys at the table take turns exchanging crude sexual innuendoes about The Blonde, each of them eager to weigh in on every detail of her "precious assets." My disgust gives way to the prickly vine of jealousy that grows larger with each mention of her.

"You can't go," says Emily, pulling me back to our conversation. She snatches one of my fries.

"Why?"

"Because we have plans for dinner and a movie, remember? You can't waste a game-free Friday night on a study session, Kay."

"You're being so unreasonable," I whine.

Tommy faces me. "Why are we having this conversation again?"

"Because I feel like I should be able to go to a study session if I want. We hang out all the time. It's like *one* hour, *one* Friday night."

"Do what you want, Kaley," he mutters.

"Fine, I won't go," I say.

Tommy scoffs, turning his body toward the guys.

Emily leans across the table. "What's going on with you? Is everything okay between you guys?"

"Everything's fine."

"Then why don't you want to hang out? You can't really be that stressed about your grade."

I struggle to keep eye contact as she attempts to read my face. "My grade is slipping; I need some help. Why is that so weird?"

"It's not, but we're almost out of here. You're not failing the class, Kay. Come on, you love game-free Fridays!"

I nod my head and muster a small smile, appeasing her, as heaviness tugs at my chest.

DEREK DRIVES US to Velocity, his brother's sports bar and grill. It's walking distance from ASU on a street lined with bars, restaurants, and little shops that college kids flock to. My favorite part about this place is that it isn't just sports—it has an artsy side, too. I wouldn't think those two things could go together, but somehow it works. Every Thursday, they hold an open mic night for musicians, singers, and even poets. I still haven't gone to one because Derek's brother always teases Emily and me that if we come, we'll have to perform something. I can never tell if he's serious or not, and I'm too scared to find out. But I've always enjoyed hanging out here. With Derek being the owner's brother, we get first class treatment: free food and drinks, and every server treats us with a respect that's hard to come by as teenagers.

But tonight, I'm just not feeling it.

Tommy's heavy arm is draped around my shoulders as we sit across from Emily and Derek in a dimly lit booth, waiting for our food. There's no space between my body and his, and I struggle for air. As much as I try to enjoy the evening with my friends, I just can't seem to fake it tonight.

I am screaming inside.

A pair of soft-green eyes meet mine as Derek's brother strolls up to our booth. "Sup, guys."

"Hey, Jace," says Emily.

Jace is five years older than me, and I don't see him much outside of his restaurant, but I've known him just as long as I've known Derek, and he's always been nice to me. Although he was out of high school before I even started, everyone in town knows he was quite the football star in his day. He even turned down a football scholarship to Stanford—much to his father's disappointment—and decided to attend culinary school instead. Most people thought he was crazy at the time. Nonetheless, his parents supported his dream by giving him the money to open up his own place. Jace is far from a spoiled brat, though. He takes his responsibilities seriously, and it's evident through the success of his bustling restaurant. And now his parents couldn't be more proud. Although, I'm pretty sure the fact that they have another golden boy in the wings has helped soften the blow.

Jace elbows me. "Hey, Kennedy. What's up with you?"

"Nothing," I say.

"What'd you do to her, Bradford?"

Tommy squeezes me. "Nothing, dude!"

"Fix her a drink," teases Emily.

Everyone laughs, and I grit my teeth. "I'm fine, just tired." Jace cocks his head to the side, and I shrug out of Tommy's hold and slide off the booth. "I need to use the restroom."

Jace takes my seat as I rush to the ladies room. It's crowded when I enter, so I go back out and lean against the wall in the shadowy hallway. *I'm being so ridiculous.* Am I so stubborn that I can't just go with the flow? I'm usually the queen of going with the flow. I always go wherever they want to go and do whatever they want to do. I'm the designated driver. The responsible one. The reliable one. The one everyone can count on. But suddenly, I don't feel like any of those things—I feel like I'm their puppet. I'm *everyone's* damn puppet. Something inside of me has snapped, and I'm desperate to cut the strings. But I know it isn't just my redundant social schedule that's bothering me . . .

It's him.

And that's even more ridiculous.

BY THE TIME we take our seats in the movie theater, the mood of our group has changed. The tension has spread like cancer, and I sink into my seat, praying for the two hours to speed by. Tommy reaches for me midway through the film, and I let him hold my listless hand. His grip is clammy. He inches closer to me throughout the night, but I just stare through the screen. Not even a shirtless Ryan Gosling can perk me up. If I don't shake out of this soon, I'll have to do something about it—but I have no idea what that something is.

TOMMY'S MOUTH IS on mine in the darkened den in the Larson house. He tastes like alcohol. Emily is with Derek in his bedroom, and my life feels like it's stuck on repeat. How was this ever fun for me before? It's the same routine every damn weekend. An endless carousel of drunken weekends and meaningless conversation. Tommy slips his hand up my shirt, and I try to relax. I let out a few light sighs, but that's the best performance I can give.

Every girl in school would smack me across the head if they knew I didn't have fire in my belly for Tommy. And why don't I? I thought by now I'd want to take it further. I swear there's something wrong with me. My body doesn't seem to work right—I'm definitely attracted to him, but I never desire to take it to the next level. Every girl I know would jump at the chance to take him from me. Maybe in some twisted way, I like that. He could have slept with the whole school by now, but he hasn't. He only wants me.

He pops open my jeans, distracting me from my thoughts.

"Whoa," I say, sliding back on the couch.

Without hesitation, his lips are on mine again, and I push him away. "Hey!"

He pauses. "What?"

"You know what."

"Kaley," he groans. "Babe, I love you. We've been together forever." His lips rush over mine as he pulls down
my zipper.

I struggle to push him off me. "Seven months is hardly
forever," I say, hopping off the couch. "Take me home." I
pull on my shoes and secure my jeans—yet another action
stuck on repeat.

He's quiet for a few moments, then says, "Just take my
truck. Leave the keys on top of the tire."

"Are you serious?"

He gives a slight nod, barely acknowledging my presence.

"So, you're going to be angry with me now? Because I
won't let you in my pants?"

His eyes cut to mine. They appear dark in the dim room.
"I'm not an asshole, Kaley."

I say nothing.

"You need to figure out what you want," he says, turning
away from me.

"Oh, so it's all or nothing, is that it?"

His face tightens. "Don't give me that. You know me better than that, Kay. I love you. I just want to be with you. I
want to move forward."

I take a deep breath. "I'm just tired, okay? I'll see you later."

"Whatever." He slumps down on the couch.

I grab his keys off the side table. "Are you sure you don't
want me to take you home?" I offer softly. He always has a
way of making me feel guilty.

He ignores me and turns on the PlayStation.

"Nice," I say as I storm out, slamming the door behind
me.

CHAPTER FIVE

I AM EXHAUSTED ALL WEEK. If it isn't my parents' fighting keeping me up at night, it's my own thoughts. No matter how hard I try to be logical about the whole situation, I find myself more and more unsatisfied in all areas of my life. And to my dismay, it's showing. Perhaps my feelings—or whatever they are—are just an escape from what's really bothering me.

When I think about no longer attending USC in the fall, it upsets me, sure, but I know it's something deeper. I just can't put my finger on it. Was it only a couple weeks ago that moving to Los Angeles sounded exciting? It just seemed so full of possibilities and adventure at the time—and I was thrilled to finally have a piece of my future planned out. But when I step back and think about it all, USC wouldn't have been that different from my life now. Emily and Derek would still drag me to all the parties, only this time I'd be the tagalong friend and fighting off frat boys instead of Tommy. Same life, different city.

The truth is, I've been discontent with my life ever since Mr. Slate walked into it . . . but maybe it isn't just him. Maybe he just struck a chord in me that's been waiting to be plucked for a long time. Maybe I've been waiting to erupt like a volcano for years, and Mr. Slate is just the earthquake that set me off.

All I know is I want something more from my life. Something more than movies, dinners, and pointless parties with our foursome that always ends at the Larson house with

Emily and Derek frolicking in his bedroom, while I'm left fending off Tommy's invading hands in the den.

Tommy says I need to figure out what I want, but how can I? I have no idea what I want. *I want to go to a study session. . . .* The uninvited thought springs into my mind like a reflex. Why do I want to go? Why would I want to waste my time? I know I'm not the first student to find a teacher attractive—national news headlines have made that uncomfortably clear—but how many people would waste a Friday night studying precalculus just to be in the same vicinity as their teacher?

Maybe my attraction to Mr. Slate is just an escape for me—an escape from the reality that no longer quenches my thirst. And whether it's out of pure boredom, or clandestine curiosity, I realize I need to go to a study session. Just once. Get it out of my system. For whatever reason, he's shaken up my small, predictable world. It's gotten to the point where my friends can feel it, too—and it's creating tiny cracks in our solid friendship. When the next game-free Friday arrives, I decide to crack it a little more.

"OKAY," I BEGIN my statement in front of the jury once again. "I didn't do that great on the quiz last Friday, or my last test, and I still hung out with you guys. Let me go to the study session tonight."

"Well, thank you for gracing us with your presence, Kay. We're so happy you chose us over a study session for a class you have an A in," says Emily, her words covered in frost.

"I won't have an A for long," I mumble, knowing my excuse is lame.

"Did you forget that Derek's parents are in Sedona all weekend? We're having a party," she says as if it's an obvious choice.

And maybe it should be.

"Yes, I know. I'll swing by after. That's no big deal, right?"

Tommy's eyes are hard. "Whatever, Kay."

"Seriously? You guys are going to be pissed if I come by later? I'll probably be there by like eight or nine o'clock!"

"What's the big deal?" mumbles Derek with a mouthful of sandwich. "She won't be missing anything before nine o'clock, guys."

Emily's shoulders drop. "But we always hang out before the party. We always get ready together. You were supposed to come over right after school today, remember?" Great. She's resorted to whining.

"Okay, well, it's just one night," I say.

Tommy snorts.

"What?" I snap at him.

He shakes his head and gets up from the table. "Nothing," he mutters before stalking off.

I sigh. "What's his deal?"

Emily raises an eyebrow and gives me a glassy stare. "You haven't been that nice to him lately."

"What are you talking about?" There's no way she knows about me leaving him mid-make-out on the couch last Friday. He's way too prideful to ever let that out.

"All week, Kay," she starts. "You were a drag last Friday night, and you've been kind of distant all week. What's going on?"

I have? I guess I haven't really paid attention . . . maybe that's the problem.

She's still glaring at me with contempt, and I shrug.

"Nothing, Ems. I've just been tired."

Her expression gives away that she isn't buying it, and I don't blame her. Despite it being true, it's still a poor excuse. I'm thankful when the lunch bell rings, cutting our conversation short.

I WAIT ON the wooden bench after school, but Tommy never shows—I can't believe he's this upset. After Derek leaves, Emily sits down next to me.

"He's never not shown," I mumble in disbelief.

"I don't think he's upset because you're coming to the party late. Something's up and you're using math as an excuse."

"It's not an excuse," I say, my tone more defensive than I intend.

"You have an A, Kaley. Yet, you constantly obsess over your grade. You're always saying you're tired. And frankly, you've been pretty bitchy lately."

I give up. "Ems, please. I really don't feel like going to Derek's party tonight. Like, at all."

She shifts her body to face me. "Okay, tell me what the hell is going on."

"Nothing, I'm just over it."

"Over what?"

"I don't know. The same old stuff. I'm just bored, I guess."

"Bored with what? Tommy?"

"I don't know. Just bored with life. Don't you ever want more?"

She scrutinizes my face. "More what? We have our entire lives ahead of us."

"Yeah, but are you happy with your life right now? Are you satisfied?"

"I mean, yeah." She hesitates. "What's wrong? Are you just freaking out over USC? Your parents will come around, I know they will."

"No," I say with a hard laugh. "I don't think so."

"They will," she insists. "They probably just need some time to get used to the idea. And if they don't, just take out student loans. No one can stop you, Kay."

"Yes, they can. They'd have to cosign. And before you say it—no, I don't qualify for any grants. I'm screwed. I don't care anymore, anyway. I don't want to talk about it."

She sighs. "Okay. I get why you're upset, but don't take it out on all of us."

I slump back on the bench. "I'm sorry. I don't mean to."

It's probably for the best that she thinks I'm a mess because of college and the uncertainty of my future. And sure, I'm stressed about all those things . . . but I know there's something deeper stirring inside me.

"Look, Kay. It's fine—just go to your stupid study session, but make sure you make it up to Tommy tonight. Come to the party and show him how much you love him. I think he's worried about you." She nudges me on the arm and smirks. "Maybe wear his favorite dress and make him feel like a man."

I roll my eyes. "I'm not losing my virginity at a party."

She laughs and gives me a quick hug. "I'll see you tonight, math nerd. Say hi to Professor McHottie for me."

My heart flutters against my will.

"If the blonde chick is there, rip her eyes out for me, will you?" she teases before trekking off to the parking lot.

The Blonde. I'm sure she'll be meeting him tonight after the study session. Just like I should be meeting *my* boyfriend. I know it's pathetic, but I'm looking forward to the study session more than the party. I know Emily and Tommy will be mad if I don't show up tonight, but I just want some time with Mr. Slate before going home and crawling into bed.

And that's what I plan to do.

WHEN I GET home, I almost drive over to Emily's and forget the whole thing. I'm furious with myself for overthinking this. I try to distract myself with some homework, but my nerves are in overdrive. Why can't I just be content to party with my friends like a normal teenager? Why do I have to make my life so complicated?

I pick up a novel I'm currently in the middle of, but after ten minutes of reading the same paragraph over and over, I give up. I pace around the house, searching for random things to clean, even dusting and wiping down my mom's cat figurines. I should just pack a bag and drive over to Emily's. Why would I allow a study session to cause a rift in my relationships? Especially with my boyfriend. . . . Maybe I should drive over to Tommy's. That's a gesture that would grant me forgiveness, right?

When I glance at the clock, my stomach twists. I'm out of time and need to make a decision: Tommy's house or Mr. Slate's classroom? Forgiveness or adventure? A flutter stirs in my chest, and I bolt upstairs to my room to grab my stuff.

I PULL MY car onto campus and park in my usual spot. The engine falls silent as I remove the key from the ignition and stare at my math book sitting next to me. Emily's right—I'm not acting like myself. She and Tommy have every right to be mad at me for ditching them on a Friday night. And it's not like I have a good excuse to go—it's a hard class, sure—but I'm not exactly failing. No one realizes how much effort it takes for me to do this well, though—one distraction can cause my grade to plummet. Even still, I have an A in the class, and no one will let me forget it. I have no reason to be here tonight . . . except for the real reason, of course.

I want to be near him.

I check the time on my phone and realize I'm almost ten minutes late. I snatch my things and rush into the school. It's almost eerie being here in the evening. The hallways are quiet and void of the usual student chaos. An overhead fluorescent light buzzes as I walk through the empty corridor. When I reach Mr. Slate's room, the door is already open. I step inside and find him sitting at his desk.

Alone.

I tap on the door frame, and he glances up from his computer.

"Oh, hey." He looks surprised to see me.

"Where is everybody?" I ask.

He leans back in his chair and rubs his jaw. "Yeah, it's a bit of a challenge to get people to show up for a math session on a Friday night." He smiles, flashing his perfect teeth. "Last week I had three students, so I was hopeful for tonight, but as you can see . . ." He gestures to the empty room.

They're probably all at Derek's.

"Why do you schedule them on Fridays then?" I ask, stepping back and leaning on the door frame.

"I know. It's a bad idea. I'm just so busy during the week. I have classes, and it's just tough on my schedule."

"Classes?"

"At ASU. I'm finishing up my master's. Half of my classes are online, but with deadlines and such, it takes up a lot of my time."

"I thought you already had your master's," I blurt out, instantly regretting my words.

Real slick. How am I supposed to know that?

He falters before answering. "Uh, no. Not quite yet."

"Oh." I silently curse out Emily in my head. "I heard you were teaching a class at the community college this summer, so I just assumed."

He tilts his head and regards me thoughtfully. "Yeah I am, actually. I already have the job, so long as I complete the degree." He shuts down his computer as I stand immobilized like a statue.

His eyes are back on mine. "I'd offer for you to stay and study, but the school board says I need at least two students present to hold a study session."

"Oh. No, that's okay. Don't worry about it," I say, swallowing my disappointment.

"I'm sure you have better plans for a Friday night, anyway." His eyes twinkle as he smiles at me, and my inner soul faints.

I slide my hand through my hair. "Not really, actually." I think about my friends partying at Derek's house. Tommy's probably taking his frustration out on a beer bong by now.

"Oh," he says, seeming bemused.

Silence stretches between us and I fidget with the tear on the corner of my textbook. "Well, have a good night, Mr. Slate." I turn toward the door, my legs feeling like lead as I try to focus on one foot in front of the other.

He rises from his chair. "I'll walk you out, Kaley."

My heart sputters. "Okay," I squeak. I clear my throat, and he scoops up his leather bag.

He follows me out of the classroom, and we stroll down the hall side-by-side, the tension nearly strangling me—I know it's solely on my end, and I hope he can't sense it. When we reach the front of the building, he stops and presses the door open for me. I hesitate for a beat, then slip through the narrow space and brush past him—*Good God, he smells amazing*—and step out into the warm twilight evening. The parking lot is almost deserted, our quiet footsteps the only sound interrupting the silence.

"Any plans this weekend?" I ask, too uncomfortable to keep quiet.

He glances my way. "Nah, just studying ... golfing on Sunday."

That's such a manly thing to do—study for a master's degree and then go golfing. I wonder if he drinks brandies and smokes cigars afterward.

"Pretty boring, huh?" He gives me a half-grin, and I almost trip over my own feet.

"No, not at all," I say, trying to keep my voice steady. I have no doubt he's leaving out the part about him having hot, passionate sex with The Blonde all night.

When we arrive at the edge of the two parking lots—one side is for faculty, the other for students—I feel a twinge of sadness.

"It's Friday night, Kaley, go have some fun." He chuckles. "There's no reason we should both have a boring night."

My gaze falls to the pavement, and I tighten my grip around my book. I don't want to go to the party . . . I don't want to go home. I don't want to do anything tonight except stand in this parking lot and talk to him.

"Hey, is everything okay?" he asks, his voice gentle.

I peer up at him. "Huh? Oh, no I'm fine. Just stupid life . . . stuff, or whatever."

He turns away from the employee parking lot and faces me. "Do you want to talk about it?" He's being so nice, but I'm sure he just wants to get home to The Blonde instead of babysitting me.

"I don't know," I begin.

He's silent as he waits for me to speak, and I look away. I should just tell him goodnight and get in my car before I make a fool of myself.

"I'm worried my parents are going to get a divorce," I blurt out. I'm surprised this is what comes out of my mouth. "I mean, maybe it would be a relief if they did, since all they do is fight, but still. It's my parents, you know?"

"Oh, I'm sorry, Kaley. That's rough."

I love hearing my name through his voice.

"Actually, that was the first time I've said that out loud," I admit, glancing around the parking lot. I can't keep eye contact with him for more than three seconds without blushing.

His brows lift. "Ever?"

I shake my head. "I haven't told anyone. Emily knows my parents have been fighting, but she doesn't know how bad it is. She has *no* idea they're on the verge of a divorce."

"What about your boyfriend ... Bradford, right?" His voice is careful, and there's something unreadable in his eyes when he says his name.

I nod. "Yeah, he's my boyfriend. I haven't told him either."

He seems taken aback. "I'm the only one you've told?"

I let out a short, nervous laugh and run my hand through my hair. *Stop fidgeting around him!* "Yeah, I guess. Sorry. That's weird, isn't it?"

"No," he says. "Just surprising, that's all." He scans the empty lot. "Hey, it's getting dark. Let me walk you to your car."

My body goes numb, and I lead the way, hoping my legs won't give out on me. I now know where the phrase "weak in the knees" comes from and pray to God I don't trip and fall flat on my face.

When we reach my car, I'm surprised when he leans against it. He slips his hands in his pockets and watches me as the sun sets across his face, making him even sexier than usual—if that's even humanly possible.

He interrupts my internal swooning. "Hey, I'm really sorry about your parents. Have you thought about talking to the school counselor?"

"No way," I say, lifting a hand in protest. "I don't want to do that."

"Well, okay. I can understand that, but you have to talk about it." He pauses. "You can talk to me if you need to. Don't keep it all bottled up. Take my word for it."

"Thanks," I say, feeling my cheeks flush.

His gaze intensifies as it locks onto mine, and he tilts his head to the side. "How old are you, Kaley?" His voice is low.

I stop breathing completely as I try to remember how old I turned on my last birthday. Suddenly, this is the most difficult math question he's ever asked me.

"Uh . . . eighteen," I reply, my voice barely above a whisper. A brief moment passes before I return the question. "How old are you?"

He gives me a heart-pounding half-grin. "Twenty-five." He chuckles. "That's probably so old to you isn't it?"

I hold his gaze. "Not at all."

His smile fades, and his expression spurs an unfamiliar response in my body. The front door of the school screeches open, and he springs from my car. A custodian steps outside carrying a large garbage bag and plods down the sidewalk, disappearing around the corner.

Hmm . . . Mr. Smooth actually seems a little jumpy for once. I've never seen him less than confident, and it catches me off guard.

"Drive safely, okay?" he says, cutting our conversation short. "And keep your chin up. Go have fun tonight!"

"I think I will."

I give him a soft smile, and his eyes linger on my lips before he breaks his gaze and heads back to the faculty lot. I watch him walk away, savoring the moment before getting into my car.

That was . . . interesting.

As I drive off campus, I flick on the radio. A remake of Joan Jett's "Bad Reputation" plays through the speakers, and I laugh to myself as I crank up the volume. I roll down my window, letting the warm breeze whip around my hair as I belt out the lyrics.

I'm suddenly in the mood for a party.

CHAPTER SIX

I'm in rare form as I get ready for Derek's party. The short time I spent with Mr. Slate has me completely elated. Adrenaline rushes through me, and I try to keep my hands steady enough to curl my hair. Okay, so maybe I'm guilty of a little crush. And maybe my excitement has something to do with the way he looked at me as he leaned against my car tonight. But it was innocent enough, right? It's not like anything will ever happen—he's my teacher, after all. It's just a fun little distraction for me—a harmless indulgence in my mediocre life. It's no reason to ruin my relationship with Tommy—if anything, it makes me want to make out with him all night and let loose. But honestly, Mr. Slate isn't the only reason I want to go out tonight—I really dropped the ball with Emily and Tommy this week, and I want to make it up to them.

I take my time perfecting my makeup—creating a smoky eye and nude, kissable lip. When I'm satisfied with my dramatic look, I slip on my black strapless dress that clings to my body in all the right places. It's Tommy's favorite, and I hope when he sees me tonight, he won't have enough blood left in his brain to question my recent behavior. We've never really fought before, and I hate that he didn't meet me after school today. It's obvious he's pretty upset with me, but he can never resist me in this dress, and I hope it helps him forget the whole thing.

I step into my five-inch black strappy heels and spray my favorite perfume on my wrists and neck. As I turn around in front of my full-length mirror, I admire every angle of my body and smile—I feel good tonight. Sexy. And ready for some fun.

Knowing this is my father's *least* favorite dress, I creep down the hallway—but there's no hiding the click of my heels on the hardwood stairs. He scans my attire from the family room couch and gruffly reminds me of my curfew—even though it hasn't changed in the last two years. I smile and reassure him I'll be home on time, then slip out the door.

THE CIRCULAR STONE driveway in front of Derek's house is jam-packed, so I park down the street behind a line of cars. To say his parents are well off would be an understatement. Their house resembles a mini castle—although there's nothing mini about it. I think I remember Derek saying it was over six thousand square feet one time. The exterior is a deep, rich brown, with a stone faced turret towering over the double front doors. Despite being enormous, it has a storybook charm to it, complete with a courtyard circling a small fountain filled with exotic fish. And if that's not enough, his parents are the type to stay out late on the weekends and sometimes travel for weeks at a time, making their house party central more often than not for our classmates.

Trying not to topple over in my heels, I step over the gravel. As soon as I make it to the pavement, I confidently stride up the walkway that's perfectly lined with solar lights, resembling tiny lanterns. When I push open the massive wooden door, blaring music penetrates the quiet neighborhood, and I slip through the buzzing crowd in search of my friends.

"Damn, Kennedy," says a familiar voice.

I turn around. "Jace? What are you doing here?"

"Just making sure you knuckleheads don't get the cops

called." He surveys my dress. "You turned it out tonight."

My cheeks flush. You wouldn't necessarily know Derek and Jace were brothers if it weren't for the eyes. Jace is taller, with darker hair and a bigger build, but their eyes are identical. That, and the fact they're both gorgeous.

"So what's the occasion?" he says.

"No occasion." *Just kissing my boyfriend's ass because I'm feeling guilty, that's all.*

"Tommy's in the kitchen," he says before turning away.

I head to the kitchen and there he is . . . in the middle of a keg stand. As I stand behind the crowd, waiting for him to finish, my mind wanders to Mr. Slate.

Mr. Slate, who goes golfing on Sundays and is completing his master's degree. Mr. Slate, who grades papers and disciplines students my age. Mr. Slate, who dresses professionally, coaches the baseball team, and has adult responsibilities. I could be wrong, but I doubt he's participating in a keg stand right now. In fact, he's probably sipping wine with The Blonde while sitting fireside as they speak passionately about politics.

The cheering crowd drags me from my thoughts as Tommy finishes his record-breaking keg stand. My classmates seem impressed with his "accomplishment" as they all high-five each other.

Jeff's eyes cut to me, and he takes in my appearance. He smirks, giving Tommy a nod. "Your girl's here."

Tommy faces me and I smile, holding my breath. I expect a joyous grin at my arrival, but instead, I'm greeted with an unwelcomed stare.

My body stiffens.

"What are *you* doing here?" he says, his nostrils flaring.

The girls standing adjacent to me snicker, and my temper flickers—I hate being humiliated, so I fire back.

"You *begged* me to come, remember?"

He sways a bit as his eyes darken. "I thought you chose a study session over me. Why the change of heart?"

Here's my opportunity to soften him—to tell him how sorry I am. This is my chance to fix the whole mess—to bring his attention to my dress and flirt with him. To kiss and hug him in front of everyone. I know how to defuse him—he loves flattery and public displays of affection. He's so easy. But as the girls sneer, and his friends begin to form an alliance behind him, I decide against all of these, and instead, fold my arms across my chest.

"It was cancelled."

The boys say "Oooh" in unison, and Tommy's attitude transcends into anger.

He hates humiliation as much as I do.

His jaw clenches, and his voice deepens. "It was cancelled, huh?"

"Yep."

"Otherwise you wouldn't have come?" He slurs his words a little, and I know I should back down.

But I don't. "Probably not."

He steps closer to me as the crowd watches intently.

"You're such a bitch," he spits out.

A few gasps echo through the crowd, and I swallow over the growing tightness in my throat. He would never call me a bitch if he were sober—I know I'm not talking to the real Tommy and should give him a pass, but we have an audience and my pride takes over.

I turn to Jeff. "How much has he had to drink?"

Tommy narrows his eyes at me. "Don't do that shit." He leans his body against the counter for support.

"You just called me a bitch!"

"Because you're *acting* like a bitch! You've been a bitch all week, Kaley, and you won't tell me what's going on with you. It's bullshit!"

My hands ball into fists at my sides. "Shut up!" I shout. The crowd has at least doubled in size and I hesitate, then lower my voice. "You know it's been a tough week."

"Oh, boo-fucking-hoo," he taunts. "You can't go to USC. Big fucking deal. You didn't even know you wanted to go until Emily talked you into it."

His words cut through me, but instead of cowering, I square my shoulders. "Well, it's a good thing I can't go then, isn't it? I mean, if you're this jealous over a study session, how would you act once I moved to LA?"

"Please," he says, his rancorous eyes burning through me. "You know you'd never leave me."

My throat burns as his words strike me, but I'll be damned if I'm going to let myself cry in front of this crowd.

I glare back at him. "You know what, asshole? Watch me."

Spinning on my heel, I storm back through the crowd as Tommy yells something that's drowned out by the music. I hesitate at the front door and glance behind me, scanning the crowd for Emily. I see Jace through the sliding glass door talking to a crowd of people near the outdoor fireplace, but Derek is nowhere to be found. Tommy is still in the kitchen, but no longer looking my way. Avery hops up on the counter between Jeff and Tommy and tosses her hair back, flashing her fake grin in my direction. She hangs on Jeff and giggles at whatever Tommy is saying.

Rage invades my body, and I push past the group of smokers lingering on the front steps. A girl yells "Excuse you," but I ignore her as I focus on reaching the Chevelle before the tears break free. Tommy has never spoken to me like that before—I hate it when he drinks. And calling me a bitch in front of everyone? Unacceptable.

I slam the heavy door shut and start the engine, catching my reflection in the mirror hanging on my visor—it's obvious I'm on the verge of tears. *Damn, I wish I had a better poker face.* I flip the visor back in place and press on the gas pedal.

Hard.

My car skids out on the gravel before hitting the pavement and taking off. I don't know where I'm headed, but I sure as hell don't want to go home. I check the time on my phone: 9:37 p.m. Where am I going to go at this hour? Normally, I'd go get lost in a bookstore to calm down—they're like my sanctuary. But a quiet, peaceful bookstore is the last thing I need right now.

I brush a tear off my cheek as the fight loops around in my mind: *You know you'd never leave me.* Who the hell does he think he is? I know he was drunk, but he said it with such conviction. Like he really, truly believes that I'd never break up with him. Is that the only reason he was so indifferent about me moving almost four hundred miles away? Because no girl in her right mind would ever break up with him?

Maybe no girl would. Maybe *I'm* not in my right mind. I'm furious with him, sure, but even more so with myself. If I hadn't been acting so crazy lately, none of this would've happened. And after our very public fight, I have no doubt every girl at the party is swarming around him like a hornets nest right now. Not that I blame them—it's not like he isn't extremely attractive, with his crystal-blue eyes, dark hair, and beautifully sculpted body—complete with a six pack. But it's more like my brain knows he's gorgeous, instead of my heart . . . or my body. I've barely had any contact with Mr. Slate and can't even see straight when we're in the same proximity. I've never felt that way around Tommy.

Or anyone for that matter.

The Cineplex comes into view, and I decide to pull into the crowded parking lot. Emily always makes fun of me when I go to the movies by myself, but it's a great getaway. You don't have to take any calls or texts, and you can just be invisible for two whole hours. I usually go in the morning when the theaters are empty, but tonight I don't care. I'm desperate for a distraction. I need to be off the grid, and a movie sounds like the perfect escape.

After touching up any evidence of tears, I climb out of my car and head to the box office. The warm Arizona evening grazes my bare legs, and I take a deep breath, attempting to shake my mood. I feel a little self-conscious going to a movie by myself during peak hours—especially dressed this way. I know it's shallow, but I really thought this outfit would help smooth things over with Tommy—drunk or not.

Boy, was I wrong.

As I approach the box office, a short stocky blond boy with black-rimmed glasses stands up, his eyes widening. "H-hi. How can I help you?"

He reminds me of a hobbit.

I scan the list of showings. "Yeah, can I get a ticket to Flesh Eaters Six?"

He stares at me slack-jawed for a few seconds before turning his attention to the computer. "That's sold out, sorry."

"Damn," I whisper. I want bloody, mind-numbing gore right now.

"There's some seats left for Love Spell: The Moon Rises."

No way. The latest crazed teen series is so not what I need right now.

He pushes his glasses up the bridge of his nose. "It started ten minutes ago, but you've probably read the books, so you'd be fine."

I'm annoyed at his assumption that I've read the corny, teen-love fantasy books. I mean, yeah, I've read them—and maybe even loved them—but it's still rude to assume. Frustrated with my bad mood and nowhere else to go, I mumble "Fine."

He beams. "Great!"

I open my neon-pink clutch that matches my toenail polish perfectly and pay the boy $10.50.

"Just one ticket?"

"Yeah, why?" I say unable to stifle a bitter tone.

"You look like you're on a date, that's all," he says.

"I'm meeting someone here," I lie.

"But weren't you trying to see Flesh Eaters Six? Is your date in there? I can go get him if you want."

This night is a total disaster.

"Um, no, it's cool. He hasn't arrived yet, so I'll just text him."

"Okay. Just be sure you text him before you get into the theater. No texting allowed."

"Got it, buddy," I call over my shoulder as I walk into the Cineplex.

An old man in a wheelchair greets me as he takes my ticket and directs me toward my theater. My stomach twinges as I pass the concession stand, completely ignoring my must-have Watermelon Wedges candy.

When I arrive inside the darkened theater, I drag my fingers across the wall for guidance, hoping my eyes will adjust soon. I hate being the person blindly searching for a seat, knowing that everyone else's eyes have already adjusted and can see you stumbling around like some kind of drunken fool.

I make the trek up the dimly lit aisle and scan the audience for an empty spot, but the theater is packed. So much for nonchalantly slipping into an aisle seat and feeling invisible tonight. The hobbit acted like there was plenty of room, but even the front row is filled. I finally spot one near the back row about ten seats in. *Ugh.* I'll have to climb over people in this tight dress—all I can think about is my ass in their faces.

"Excuse me," I whisper to the guy on the end. He looks annoyed until he glances up at me. His expression shifts from irritation to interest as he stands up to make way. The girl next to him shoots me a dirty look. I apologize to everyone I pass until I reach the empty seat, tugging at the hem of my dress as I sit. My phone vibrates through my clutch, and I let out a soft sigh, disregarding it.

After about ten seconds, the person on my left nudges me. *Oh, please say I haven't taken a saved seat.* I dread the thought of climbing over everyone again. My eyes struggle to adjust as I squint in the darkness. It takes me a moment, but then he flashes that familiar, perfect grin.

A bolt of adrenaline sends shockwaves through me.

"Hey," says Mr. Slate.

"Hey," is all I can manage.

Holy hell!

Isn't he supposed to be home studying? I knew he left out the part about his date. I look past him expecting to see The Blonde, but instead see a preteen girl engulfed in a bucket of popcorn.

"If you tell anyone that you saw me here, I'll have to fail you," he says, smiling.

"You're here alone?" I ask.

He chuckles. "Yeah . . . seriously, please don't tell anyone I came to see this movie. Say you saw me at Flesh Eaters Six or something."

He's still smiling with that damn twinkle in his eye that makes my body hum.

"You got it," I say.

"I take it you're here alone?"

"Yeah, I am."

His eyes sweep over my dress, and tingles erupt through every part of my body—it's as if his eyes can physically touch me.

"You look like you should be on some hot date," he says.

I shrug. "That was the plan, but things changed."

Our eyes hold for a moment longer, and he swallows.

"Teenage boys are so stupid," he says in a low voice. "His loss."

A flush of heat spreads over me, and I hope he can't see my heart pounding through this snug dress.

He holds out a bag of candy. "Watermelon Wedge?"

A beaming smile escapes me. "Seriously? These are my favorite."

He grins. "Really? Mine too. And let's just keep that between us as well, okay?" He winks, and I think I am going to die of a heart attack.

"Your secret's safe with me," I say, grabbing two Wedges.

We both turn our attention to the movie, but I can't see anything on the screen. All I see is his profile through my peripheral view. And is it my imagination, or is he watching me, too?

Dream on, Kaley.

Minutes tick by, and I try to pay attention to the movie, but it's impossible. This is way worse than math class—we are literally inches apart in a dark room. How am I expected to focus? My phone vibrates again, but I ignore it. I shift in my seat, crossing my legs toward him and try to steady my breathing. But when I carefully glance his way, I notice him gazing at my legs.

That sure as hell isn't going to help my breathing.

Fiery heat seeps through places in my body that no one has ever touched. How is it possible he can touch me in a way I've never felt before—and with only his eyes? I imagine what his fingers are capable of . . . his tongue.

Our eyes lock and he offers me more Wedges. I shake my head, but neither of us break our stare. There's no longer a twinkle in his eye—no hint of a smile. His eyes travel down my neck, leaving a trail of goose bumps in their path. They slide down my shoulder. Then arm.

I shiver.

"Are you cold?" he whispers, lifting his eyes back to mine.

"Hm?"

He grabs his jacket from behind him and hands it to me. "I always bring a jacket just in case. These theaters can be freezing. Especially in a dress like that, I imagine." He looks embarrassed after mentioning my dress and turns his attention back to the screen.

My pulse races through my veins as I drape the jacket over my lap and pull it up to my chest like a blanket. The intoxicating scent invades my senses, and I close my eyes, taking a deep breath. I shoot my eyes back open to see if he noticed my reaction. He's still focused on the movie screen—I can only hope he didn't see. I steal a glance at the label on his jacket: Armani. I've never been the type of girl who valued designer labels, so why does seeing this turn me on even more? I still can't figure out how he can afford it, but it doesn't matter. My mind wanders to what label is on his underwear, and I'm thankful the room is dark enough to hide my blushing cheeks. I sink into the seat and snuggle into his jacket as we watch the rest of the movie in silence.

The film ends in what feels like two minutes instead of two hours, and neither of us move while the movie credits roll up the screen. I dread giving him back his jacket—I want it around my body all night since it is the closest I will ever get to the real thing. Stealing one more whiff before I stand up, I regretfully hand it back to him. He's still seated as he takes it from me, and his eyes wander down my body causing me to tremble once more.

"Are you sure you still don't need it? You're shivering."

I let out a nervous laugh. "No, I'm fine." If only he knew

how hot I felt.

He slings his jacket over his arm and rises. We exit the theater together, talking briefly about the movie, even though I barely watched a single frame.

We step outside into the darkness, and the desert warmth envelops me once again. I'll have no excuses if I shiver now, so I try to keep my body relaxed. The lines of palm trees are decorated in white twinkle lights, and I imagine what it would be like to be on a date with him. I imagine my hand wrapped safely inside of his as we stroll through the crowd ... I imagine his lips on mine as he kisses me good-night. Running my tongue over my lips, I taste the faint watermelon flavor of the candy we shared and wonder if his lips taste the same right now.

The blond hobbit yanks me out of my daydream when I feel his stare as we pass by the box office. His quick observation of my dress again is not lost on me—I definitely feel nothing whatsoever as he gawks at my body. His eyes widen when he notices Mr. Slate walking next to me, and I remember how I lied about meeting my date here. Oops! Oh well, it's not like I know the hobbit, right? But panic ripples through me as I hear him call out, "Mr. Slate!"

What. The. Hell.

Mr. Slate whips around and sees the boy. *Why do I think of him as a boy?* He's clearly around my age.

"Duncan!" greets Mr. Slate with a dignified smile. He's so smooth, so sure of himself all the time. I, however, can't even remember how to breathe.

Duncan flicks his stare back and forth between us. "What are you doing here?"

Mr. Slate glances at me and then back to Duncan. "Watching a movie, of course," he answers with poise. "I just ran into Kaley, do you two know each other?"

As I shake my head, I notice Duncan nodding. *He knows*

me? I swear I have never seen him before in my life.

Duncan gives me a toothy grin. "We have gym together. Fourth period."

"Right," I say, trying not to hurt his feelings. His expression turns quizzical, rattling my nerves, and I slide my hand through my hair. "Uh, my date wasn't able to make it."

He nods, but seems to be teetering on the edge of suspicion.

"See you on Monday, Duncan," says Mr. Slate, giving a quick wave.

He leads me to the parking lot as Duncan continues to gawk at us. *Get a life, nosey little hobbit.*

It's a short walk before I am forced to part ways with Mr. Slate. After we say goodnight, I tear myself away and trudge down the aisle toward my car. Almost immediately, an uninvited longing stirs within me. I immediately scold myself.

He's a grown man—your teacher! You are pathetic.

But my boyfriend was a complete asshole tonight . . . don't I deserve to be appreciated by a gorgeous man? It's not like anything happened.

Nor will anything ever happen.

He's harmless. He's . . . an innocent crush.

Innocent? He checked you out tonight.

A smile pulls at the corner of my mouth.

Stop! He's your teacher! He's forbidden.

I tune out the condemning voice as I slip into the driver's seat, my pulse still racing. Releasing a deep sigh, I turn the key in the ignition, but it just clicks. *No, not now!* I try again and again. *Click-click-click.* I hit the steering wheel with my fists.

"Damn!" *What else can go wrong tonight?*

As if on cue, a shiny black Tahoe pulls up beside me. Mr. Slate gracefully hops out as I step out of my car.

"Need help, Kay?"

My heart skips a beat. *Did he just call me Kay?* Only my closest friends and family call me that.

"It won't start," I grumble, hoping to hide my embarrassment.

"Let me see what I can do."

I hold out my hand, and he takes my keys, his fingers leaving a trail of heat across my palm. He ducks into the driver's seat, and I try to cope with the fact that Mr. Slate is now sitting in my car.

My dirty, unwashed—and now broken—piece-of-junk car.

Please kill me.

Why didn't I at least take the trash out? The backseat alone looks like a water bottle graveyard. It's mortifying enough to be driving a beater, but does it have to resemble a recycling center, too? I glance at his gleaming Tahoe and cringe. Even the huge rims shine as if they've never encountered a speck of dirt.

Okay, chill. Maybe there's an upside to this. Maybe his scent will linger in my car so I can enjoy it on my way home.

He steps out of the driver's seat. "Pop the hood for me. I'll try to jump start it for you."

Unable to respond, I slide into my car and watch him attach the jumper cables between his beautiful SUV and my junkyard-bound Chevelle. When he gives me the command, I try to start it, turning the key in the ignition and pressing on the gas.

Still nothing.

"I'm beginning to hate this car," I groan, stepping back out.

"I think it's the alternator," he says, slamming my hood down. "Sounds like you need a new one."

"Great." I glare at the Chevelle. *Unreliable piece of crap.* As frustrated as I am, I don't want to leave my car here, and I definitely don't want a ride home from him. I'm afraid my body can't handle it.

"I'll run up and tell them you're going to leave your car here overnight. It's under a light, so it should be okay. Do you have an alarm?"

I shake my head. "No one's going to steal that thing, trust me."

"It's a classic," he says as he pats the roof. "Just needs a little TLC."

"More like CPR," I gripe.

He chuckles as he locks my door. He returns my keys, and I'm careful to not make contact with his hand this time.

"I'll take you home and maybe your parents or someone can help you with this in the morning."

I hesitate. "A-are you sure? I can try to call someone." My friends are all drunk, and I doubt my parents are awake. . . . "I don't want to be any trouble."

"No trouble, Kaley." Something inscrutable flickers briefly across his eyes. "I'm not leaving you here. Hop in."

He opens his passenger door for me, and I hoist myself in—well aware that my dress is not meant for climbing into a Tahoe. As I sit down, I notice a fire in his eyes and my mouth goes dry. His gaze burns through me as he tells me he'll be right back and shuts the door. Okay, I can't be imagining the way he just looked at me. It was too real—too intense. I shiver again.

The inside of his SUV is spotless. Of course. Not a speck of dust, or a single empty water bottle. The interior smells like it was just hand-washed by angels, mixed with a hint of the same scent I enjoyed earlier on his jacket. A vibration on my lap jolts me out of my thoughts. Annoyed, I yank my phone from my clutch. It's Tommy. A picture of the two of us locked in a tight embrace glows on the screen. Emotions tug at me as my thumb hovers over the display. I hit "decline" just as the driver's side door clicks open. Mr. Slate hops in, and I drop my phone back into my clutch.

His eyes slide over my body. "Buckle up," he says, his voice strained.

I do as I'm told and give him the directions, my throat becoming increasingly dry. We ride in silence for a few minutes before my anxiety can't stand it.

"So, how'd you get this job so quickly?" I ask. "I mean, it just seemed really fast. I figured you were just a substitute."

He rubs the back of his neck. "Well, last summer they offered me a job teaching English of all things, but I turned it down. That would've been disastrous." He chuckles. "I was teaching math part-time at two different junior high schools, which was exhausting. And I substituted a lot before that as well. I've known Stan—I mean your principal, for a few years. He called me up on a Sunday afternoon after we played golf earlier that day and offered me the job. I accepted and started the next day. Normally, I wouldn't leave a job in the middle of a school year, but since there were only a couple months left, I wasn't going to turn it down."

It's interesting to hear him talk about himself—even if it *is* just a snippet of his professional life. He seems so grown up and responsible. I'm surprised to find his life so attractive. I love that he's mature and smart . . . and *not* doing keg stands in the middle of a party.

"What about you? What are your plans after school?" he asks. I let out a groan and he laughs. "Sorry, touchy subject?"

"Kind of. Long story short, I was stoked to be accepted to USC, only to have my parents tell me they couldn't afford it."

"Ouch," he says. "Sorry to hear that; that's an excellent school. I have some family members who went there."

"Yeah. My friends and I were all trying to go together,

but that's quickly falling apart. Derek got a football scholarship, as you probably already know, and Emily's on the waiting list . . . and then there's me."

He clears his throat. "And Bradford?"

My chest tightens at the mention of Tommy's name. "Uh, no. He didn't apply to any colleges. He gets good grades and everything, but he could care less. He's next in line to take over the family business, so he's pretty much all set," I say, hoping I sound nonchalant. I glance at him, trying to read his face, but it's too dark. "Anyway, ASU is my only backup, but I haven't accepted their offer yet. It's like I can't bring myself to do it. It makes it all too real, you know?"

"Don't worry about that. It's wise to accept their offer to lock in your spot. You can always pull out if something changes," he says, stopping at a light. He looks over at me, and my body goes numb.

How does he do that?

When the vehicle is back in motion, I collect myself. "Honestly, I'm more upset over the fact that my parents let me go through the stress of applying, all the while knowing they couldn't afford it." I gaze out the passenger window. "Apparently, they weren't too worried about it because they didn't think I'd get in." *Why am I always opening up to him so much?* I've opened up to him more than Emily lately. What must he think of me?

His glance reclaims my attention. "Seriously? That surprises me. You're more than capable."

I feel a smile pull at my lips. "Thanks," I say. "That means a lot."

Something about this little talk fills me with comfort. *No one ever talks to me in this way*, I realize. Something about it feels . . . right.

When we pull up to my house, I notice that my parents forgot to keep the front porch light on, leaving an unfriendly darkness to greet me.

He peers through the windshield. "Are your parents home? Do you want me to walk you to your door?"

If I let you walk me to my door, I may just lose my mind and invite you into my bedroom.

"No, that's okay." I open the door and climb out of the Tahoe.

"Kaley?" He clicks off the dome light, causing moonlit shadows to spread across his face. He hesitates for a moment. With only the glow of the dashboard, it's difficult to see his expression, but he seems on edge. "This is going to sound silly, but please don't tell anybody about tonight."

I'm silent. I don't know what my response should be. What *did* happen tonight? Does he think something happened between us?

"You know, taking you home and all that," he continues. "As a teacher, I'm not supposed to be alone with a student."

"Even if you're helping out a stranded girl?" I tease.

His face is sober. "Never."

"O-okay," I falter. "No problem, Mr. Slate."

Did he just wince? It's too dark to know for sure.

"Thanks, Kay. See you Monday morning. Be safe."

"Goodnight." Reluctance grips me as I try to bring myself to shut the door. I don't want this moment to end.

"And Kaley?" He leans forward on the console. "He's an idiot for letting you walk away in that dress tonight."

A thrill erupts from every nerve ending in my body, and I struggle to find my voice.

"Thanks," I whisper.

Forcing myself to break his gaze, I close the door to the Tahoe and walk up my driveway. I don't look back, but can feel his eyes on me as I slide my key into the deadbolt. My phone vibrates through my clutch yet again, and I hesitate before entering the house, finally allowing myself to peer over my shoulder. He's staring at me, so I wave a quick goodnight. He doesn't move a muscle and seems to be deep in thought—almost as if he is looking through me. I step inside the foyer and close the door behind me and lean against it, my heart pounding in the darkness. My breaths are uneven, and I try to calm down. I shift over to the window and peer through the shutters and watch him slowly drive away as my phone continues to buzz.

CHAPTER SEVEN

ON SUNDAY NIGHT, I'M FINISHING up the last of my precalculus homework when the doorbell rings. I can hear my mom downstairs, talking animatedly to whoever it is, and the jovial conversation continues for at least fifteen minutes before I peer out my bedroom window. Tommy's silver truck is parked in the moonlit driveway. *Great.*

My phone has pretty much been silent over the weekend, except for a few brief texts with Emily discussing what happened at the party. She and Derek were hidden away in Derek's bedroom during the incident—*what a shock*—and only heard the story from a few witnesses later that night. After I filled her in with the details, I was disappointed when she didn't take my side. She didn't exactly take Tommy's side either, but her lack of immediate support left me feeling like she may as well have.

I haven't spoken to Tommy since our fight. I didn't even attend his baseball game on Saturday. It was an away game, anyway, and I didn't feel like taking the time or effort, although it would've been somewhat satisfying to watch him play with a hangover.

The chatter below my room comes to a halt, and I soon hear footsteps ascending the stairs. After a quick pause, there's a quiet knock on my door.

I stay seated at my desk. "Come in."

Tommy enters with a gentle smile on his face, closing the door behind him.

"Hey," he says as he sits on my bed.

I turn in my chair to face him. "Hey, yourself."

"Why haven't you returned any of my calls?"

"Did you call me?"

"I called you a lot."

"Um . . . you called me a lot Friday night."

"Yeah, that's what I mean."

I roll my eyes. "I wasn't about to pick up a drunk dial. Especially after the way you treated me," I scoff. "Why didn't you call me when you were sober? You've had all weekend."

"Okay, look," he says, ignoring my question. "I'm sorry for how I acted. I was drinking and just letting off steam. I barely even remember it."

I shrug a shoulder. "Okay."

He looks at me expectantly. "Is that all you have to say?"

"What else would you like me to say? You humiliated me in front of everyone—I don't even want to show my face at school tomorrow."

"It'll be fine, Kay. I promise. Everyone knows I was just drunk."

"So that makes you unaccountable for your actions?"

"No . . . but I would never act like that sober—you know that. And honestly, I got plastered because of you."

I laugh in disbelief. "So, it's *my* fault you called me a bitch?"

"No, but I can only take so much. You made me feel like shit last weekend and all week at school. I mean, how *should* I react when my girlfriend acts like she doesn't want to be around me? Everyone could see it, Kay. It's embarrassing."

I blow an exasperated sigh from my lungs. "You're right, I'm sorry." *How am I the one in the dog house all of a sudden?*

"Will you at least tell me what's up with you? I feel like we used to have fun together; now it's like I don't even know who you are anymore."

Yeah, you and me both.

"I've had a rough couple of weeks. I've been fighting with my parents about college, and . . . I'm stressed about the future, I guess." *That, and the fact that I've been lusting over your baseball coach and my math teacher to the point of obsession.* "But apparently, I have no reason to be upset about that because 'it's no big deal,'" I say, thick with sarcasm.

Tommy leans forward and rests his hand on my thigh. "I *said* I was sorry." I can tell he's losing his patience.

"You meant what you said to me. I could tell."

"I don't think you're a bitch, okay?" he says in a rush. "You've just been acting like one. How do you expect me to take that? You want me to just roll over and let you walk all over me? I'm not that guy."

"Oh, I know you're not. That's why I would 'never leave you,' right?" I say, spitting more of his words back at him.

He lets out an agitated sigh. "So, what—are you breaking up with me now?" he says with blatant mockery.

I'm silent. He should be begging for my forgiveness right now. But instead, *I'm* apologizing. Maybe it *would* be easier to just end it now. . . . I lean back in my chair and close my eyes. I really do love him . . . and what am I supposed to do? Dump him for someone I can't have?

"Kaley?" he says quietly. When I open my eyes, his expression has softened. "*Are* you breaking up with me?" There's no hint of mockery this time.

In all the years I've known him, I don't think I've ever seen Tommy vulnerable. His wary eyes drill into me, puncturing tiny holes into my heart. What has he ever done to me, really? Besides the drunken fight, he's been nothing but good to me. I can't exactly hate him for wanting to go all the way—he's no different than any other guy in that area. There's no excuse for how he treated me, but I guess I did push him over the edge.

"No," I whisper.

His lips collide into mine, and it takes me a moment before I can participate. He pulls me to the bed beside him and slowly lays me down. He slips his hand underneath the back of my camisole and fumbles with my bra clasp, but I'm quick to stop him.

He always moves so damn fast.

I break my lips away from his. "My parents are downstairs."

Giving me a wolfish grin, he unhooks my bra. "So? They love me. And you look hot tonight."

My hair is pulled into a sloppy bun, I'm wearing no makeup, and I'm sporting sweatpants—I swear he'd still be aroused if I were wearing a trash bag. I roll my eyes. "Okay, but just for a minute."

I reach for my desk lamp and flip the switch. Darkness floods my bedroom, and I slip out of my bra. He shifts his body so he's between my legs and slides my top off over my head. His fervent hands travel down my body and as soon as his mouth makes contact with my bare chest, my mind drifts to Mr. Slate.

No!

A tremor runs down my body as his striking face flickers behind my eyelids, and I quickly shove him out of my mind—*I'm with Tommy.* It becomes a mantra in my head: *I'm with Tommy, I'm with Tommy, I'm with Tommy.* A spark ignites in my chest, my skin suddenly sensitive to his touch. *Focus!* But I soon feel myself weakening . . . slipping . . .

Oh, no.

The last of my willpower enervates as I surrender to my instincts and imagine Mr. Slate on top of me. My breathing promptly increases, and with my eyes squeezed shut, I pull his face to mine. A light moan escapes my throat as I use Tommy's body to kiss Mr. Slate with a passion that has been building for weeks. I lock my thighs around him, feeling him against me.

"Kaley," Tommy whispers in surprise, but all I hear is Mr. Slate's silky voice.

I quiver underneath a pair of eager hands as they slither below my waist, tugging on my sweatpants. The drawstring tightens as he pulls, and he stops when I grab his hand. Instead of pushing him away, I fumble with the knot until I loosen the strings. He hesitates before returning his hand to my waist, and to his surprise, I welcome the action and quickly unfasten his jeans. I hear him gasp as I slide my hand inside Mr. Slate's boxer shorts. Grunting, he leans into me, his lips moving faster against mine. He cautiously pulls on my sweats, slowly inching them down. I squirm beneath him, hungry for contact, his slow pace torturing me. A pulsating ache grows like a weed below my waist, and I silently rejoice. *My body is finally reacting the way it's supposed to!* I don't want to lose this feeling.

"Touch me," I whisper.

His breathing becomes ragged as I guide his hand farther down. With my eyes still tightly sealed, I focus on Mr. Slate's fingers as he slips them underneath my white cotton panties, and I inhale sharply at the brief contact. His fingers struggle to inch closer, and I yank down my sweats to give him better access. My anticipation is interrupted by the sound of footsteps climbing the stairs, and Tommy leaps off the bed.

Annoyed at the timing, but grateful for hardwood floors, I pull up my sweatpants and search for my camisole in a panic. Tommy flicks on my desk lamp and fastens his jeans. I spot my top on the floor and frantically pull it over my head. Just as I'm kicking my bra underneath the bed, I hear a knock on my door.

"Come in," I say, my voice two pitches too high.

When the door swings open, I'm sitting on my bed with

my knees to my chest, while Tommy plays it cool in the chair. My mom enters, carrying a basket of laundry, and I pray we don't look suspicious. She sets a stack of clothes on my dresser and turns to Tommy. "I forgot to ask about your game. Did you win yesterday?"

"We lost, actually," he replies. I can tell he's still trying to catch his breath, but my mom doesn't seem to notice.

"Oh, that's too bad. See, Kay? You should've gone. You would've been his good luck charm," she teases. She turns to Tommy. "I told her she could've taken my car." She smiles at us both and closes the door behind her—*man, my parents really do trust him.*

Tommy turns in the chair and faces me. "Now that I think about it, your car wasn't in the driveway. Where is it?"

"In the shop. I need a new alternator."

"Oh." Desire returns to his eyes like he wants to get back to where we were, but with the lights now on, I am no longer inspired. I feel guilty as hell for what I've just done, but equally relieved to find out that my body isn't broken. As it turns out, I can feel sexual desires just like everybody else—I just need the right person.

Too bad my body picked the very worst person to react to.

"What are you thinking about?" he asks, his eyes burning with lust.

"Uh . . ." *Quick, change the subject.* "Would you mind taking me to school tomorrow?"

He smiles. "Sure."

I am the worst person on the planet right now. Of course he'll take me to school tomorrow. After what just went down, he'd fly me to the moon if I asked him.

"You know, I think it's better this way," he says.

"What?"

"You going to ASU. We can hang out more, just the two of us. Move forward in our relationship."

Yeah, I know what that means.

"This is a good thing," he says, upbeat.

I purse my lips into a hard line. "Yeah, maybe."

He moves back over to the bed.

Uh-oh.

Taking advantage of the easy access, he slides his hands up my top and presses his lips against mine, claiming me with his tongue.

"I know you want it," he whispers in between kisses. "It's obvious, Kay. Why don't you just let it happen?"

Mr. Slate's molten-brown eyes flash in my mind, and I'm tempted to turn off the lamp again. It felt so incredible . . . so wickedly hot.

But so wrong.

I maneuver my way out of his grip and hop off the bed. My pants slide down my hip, and I scramble to tie the drawstring. "I'm sorry, but come on, my mom almost caught us. I don't want to take another chance."

His gaze wavers on my braless chest before lifting to my face. "Okay," he groans, standing up. "I guess I should go." He squeezes my backside and kisses me once more. "I'll see you in the morning, babe." A new flicker of light shines through his powder-blue eyes. His entire demeanor is different now . . . excited. If he was hard to fend off before, he'll be near-impossible now.

When he's gone, I climb into bed. Even though I'm way too wired to sleep right now, I burrow myself under the covers.

It's time for a reality check.

There's no more denying it. I've tried for weeks, but the truth is, I have serious feelings for Mr. Slate. I'm not entirely sure what these feeling are, but they are stronger than anything I have ever felt in my entire life. Maybe he isn't just a simple escape . . . maybe he's something more. I simultaneously feel ashamed and relieved as I finally admit the truth to myself.

Despite the impossibility of it all—whether it's The Blonde, the age difference, or the fact that he's my *teacher*—I just can't get Friday night out of my mind. My pulse quickens as the memories rush back all at once. My mind traces back to the school parking lot, and I smile to myself, remembering how the golden glow of the sun set around his handsome face . . . the way he leaned against my car: *How old are you, Kaley?* What was once an innocent question now has my head spinning. Why did he ask me that? Maybe he was just curious . . . maybe it was just a simple inquiry to fill the silence. But then, why was he so flustered when the custodian walked outside?

Butterflies swoop down into my stomach, flittering in circles, as my mind slips back to the darkened movie theater . . . when I caught his eyes on my legs. There was no mistaking *that*. I burrow deeper underneath the covers, blood burning through my veins. I can't forget the intoxicating scent of his jacket draped over me, giving me unexpected comfort. And as much as I've tried not to think about it, I can't let go of the ride home: *He's an idiot for letting you walk away in that dress tonight.*

Suddenly, restlessness stirs within me, and I am in dire need of his touch. I have never longed for anyone before, but feel a need for him that is so intense, I can no longer ignore the magnitude of my feelings. Heat creeps through my body, and I kick away the sheets in frustration. Before tonight, I figured my crush on him was partly because he's unattainable. I thought he was safe—I could never have him, so I would never have to worry about it going past my comfort zone, like I do with Tommy. But now I realize there's *nothing* safe about this man. Because given the opportunity . . . it's clear to me that I would let him have me . . . *all of me.*

The harsh truth is this: I want him. I need him. My body literally aches for him.

There's no going back now.

I desperately want my math teacher.

CHAPTER EIGHT

TOMMY'S FINGERS INTERWINE WITH MINE as we walk into the school. He still has that same look in his eyes from last night... enlivened, almost expectant. He kisses me good-bye with a fervency that's a bit too passionate for this early in the morning. Guilt drops into my stomach like a jagged stone as pangs of contrition threaten to overpower me. I try to shove the feeling aside as I continue on to class.

When I enter first period, Mr. Slate is sitting at his desk, and I make sure not to look his way as I take my seat. My nerves overwhelm me while he takes attendance, and I can't bring myself to meet his eyes. After using my boyfriend's body to make out with him last night, it's disconcerting to even be in the same room. I feel like it shows on my face or something.

My anxiety intensifies as he steps up to the front of the classroom and begins his lesson. I try desperately to pay attention to the board as he draws out his perfectly-lined graphs, but his enticing fingers wrapped around an innocent dry-erase marker have me distracted. It's almost as if I know what those fingers feel like against my body.... I know I don't actually know, but I'm now aware of how much I want to find out. It's impossible to focus on sleep-inducing ellipses when all I can think about is the way he felt on top of me... his hands against my bare skin... his lips tangled with mine.

The shrill ring of the bell makes me jump, and I realize my eyes were just closed. I glance around, but no one seems to have noticed, and I pack up my stuff. Mr. Slate quickly passes back our quizzes as the class begins to disperse.

"Excellent job," he says, handing over my quiz.

He grants me a half-smile, and the paper slips from my hand, falling to the floor. I scramble to collect it, feeling my face flush. *Why is his presence so unnerving?* He's already back at his desk when I finally glance down at my grade: 89.5 percent.

"Seriously?" I say, exasperated. "You can't round up? Aren't we taught to do that in like second grade?"

He shakes his head, his eyes twinkling with amusement. A small smirk plays at his lips as he rises from his chair. The classroom is nearly empty, and my heart sputters as he strolls over to me. There's barely any space between us when he stops at my desk. A hint of his tantalizing scent pulls on every fiber in my body, extending each thread until I feel my entire insides tighten.

"You got the highest score in the class," he says in a low voice. "You need to relax, Kay." He chuckles softly.

He's so close I have to crane my neck to peer up at him. When our eyes lock, the humor in his face vanishes. My breath hitches as his expression shifts to the one I recognize from Friday night. It only lasts for a second before he turns away, but I caught it. Flustered, I grab my things and rush out of the empty classroom, my heart pulsating.

THE DAY PASSES without anyone giving me a hard time about the altercation at Derek's party, and I am thankful. Other than feeling some distance from Emily, everything is going better than I expected. Tommy clings to me every chance he gets, squashing any rumors of a breakup. And although I have no doubt the details of our dispute are being discussed behind my back, I no longer care. I have bigger problems. Such as lusting after my math teacher instead of my boyfriend. I mean, why can't I just be content with him? Everyone else wants to have sex with my boyfriend, so why wouldn't I? But the only thing that thrills me is the thought of pretending he's Mr. Slate—and I can't keep doing that to Tommy. What I did was awful. And as much as I try to twist that experience into a positive one—like, maybe all I needed to do was wake up my sexuality—I know that's not the case. What I did was wrong, but what's even worse is . . . I woke up something else.

THE BOYS HAVE a home game late afternoon on Tuesday. I ask Emily for a ride, but she missed curfew last weekend and had her car keys taken away. Derek's been taking her to school. It feels weird that I didn't know that, but maybe I'm just being overly sensitive. Since we're both without transportation, we decide to hitch rides with our boyfriends. The downside to this is that they have to arrive an hour before the game, meaning Emily and I have to endure the bleachers for longer than usual. But at least it's a warm April evening . . . and I get to watch my favorite coach without anyone knowing.

We watch the boys warm up as the bleachers slowly begin to fill. My eyes automatically go to Mr. Slate anytime he moves. He takes a long drink from his water bottle, somehow making a simple action divinely sexy. I scan the crowd for The Blonde throughout the evening, but she never shows.

By the ninth inning, I'm exhausted. I didn't sleep well last night. My parents were fighting until the early morning again. It's getting worse.

"Baseball games are too long," I say to Emily with my elbows propped up on my knees, my head resting in my hands.

"We're here to support the boys, Kay." Her tone tempts

me to confront her, but then she smirks. "And appreciate how good their butts look in those uniforms." She watches Derek with admiration.

My eyes wander to Mr. Slate's uniform pants. "Yeah," I breathe, watching him walk up and down the third base line. "They *do* look good."

She smiles at me and I sit up straight, hoping she didn't notice where my gaze just was. I adjust my position and pull on my short denim skirt. Sitting on a metal bench for an entire baseball game is painful.

Literally and figuratively.

Emily breaks me out of my near-slumber when she jumps up cheering. I slowly rise and clap my hands. Apparently, we've just won.

Emily catches me in a yawn. "Why are you so tired?" she says, aggravated.

"Sorry, I haven't been sleeping very well."

That much is true. Between my parents fighting and my need for some Slate, it's hard to get a full night's sleep.

"Come on," she says, leading me down the bleachers. I hop down onto the grass after her, and Tommy lifts me into a giant hug, locking his lips onto mine.

"Not in uniform, Bradford!" Coach Miller bellows.

Tommy laughs. "I'll meet you by the truck."

He jogs off to the locker room, and I follow Emily toward the parking lot as she jingles Derek's keys.

"Wanna sit in the Beemer while we wait for them?" she asks.

Something pulls at me, and I glance over my shoulder, catching Mr. Slate's eyes on mine.

I thrust my gaze forward, suddenly rattled. "Uh, yeah okay," I say, rushing my hand through my hair.

She gives me a sideways glance. "You okay?"

"Yup," I say, trying to appear at ease. My body feels like

it's on fire—*is this how Tommy feels when he's next to me?* I feel like I should go apologize to the poor guy right now and let him have his way with me. How can he stand it?

Emily and I walk in silence until we reach the front of the school.

"You and Tommy seem to be doing better," she says. Her voice seems careful.

"Yeah, I guess," I reply.

"You guess?"

"I mean, yeah. Things are . . . fine."

"You guys seem so happy. What's wrong?"

"Nothing," I say. "I told you, I'm just tired."

She stops and turns to me, searching my eyes for answers like I'm in an interrogation room. "That's not it, Kay. Why are you so closed off?"

Wait. What?

"*I'm* closed off?" My buried vexation quickly rises to the surface. "You barely talked to me about the fight on Friday and once you heard my side of the story, I didn't hear from you all weekend."

"What did you want me to do? You guys had a fight. Tommy was wrong, but he was just reacting to the way you've been treating him. I tried to talk to you about it earlier that day, remember? I warned you."

"I went to the party to apologize," I say, feeling defensive.

"That's not what Jeff said."

"Jeff? I was the only sober one there; why would you believe anything other than what I tell you? *You're* my best friend—"

"We're *all* friends, Kaley," she spits out.

My simmering frustration quickly boils into anger. "So you're as close with Jeff and Tommy as you are with me?"

She sighs impatiently. "Of course not."

"Well that's what you made it sound like." The volume of my voice is starting to rise, and I try to pull it back. "I just don't understand you guys."

"Who?"

"You!" My voice rises again. "Tommy! All of you guys! I just got really crappy news about college. Which, by the way, you don't even seem to care about. I figured you guys would understand if I was a little depressed about it. Instead, you're mad at me."

Okay, so maybe college isn't my biggest concern right now, but it's my last ditch effort to validate my behavior.

"I can't believe you would say that to me," she says, her eyes wounded. "Of course I care!" People glance our way as they pass and she lowers her voice. "Don't be ridiculous."

"Well you have a funny way of showing it," I say. "According to you and Tommy, I'm apparently not allowed to have a bad day—or a bad week! You're only satisfied when I'm your little happy-go-lucky robot friend who will drive all your drunken asses home."

"That's such a load of crap, Kaley, and you know it." She turns away from me and sulks off toward the student lot.

I follow after her.

"Is it Ems? Really? Because I can't think of *any* other reason why you'd be mad at me right now."

She whips around, and I have to stop myself from crashing into her. "Because I don't believe you!"

I step back, her words catching me off guard. "W-what don't you believe?" The opposing team's bus turns onto the street, and the lot grows quiet.

"I don't believe it's just college," she says sharply. "There's something else. Something you're not telling me. So before you accuse me of not being there for you, why don't you ask yourself why I can't be?"

As soon as she says it, I know it's true.

"Am I right?" she says, her eyes narrowing.

Yes! Of course you're right! I want to tell you things . . . but I can't.

"What is it?" she says, softening.

"It . . . it's a lot of stuff, Ems," I say, defeated.

"So talk to me."

"I will, okay? Just not now. I really am tired."

She hardens. "Whatever," she says, storming off.

"Damn it," I whisper to myself.

She knows me too well. She would be appalled if she knew what was distracting me from our friendship. When *she* swoons over Mr. Slate it's all fun and games. She'd be furious if she knew a crush on my teacher was putting a strain on my relationship with Tommy. She doesn't want anything jeopardizing our precious foursome. Especially not a silly, childish crush. *But it's more than just that,* I realize. I haven't let her in on anything lately . . . the seriousness of my parents fighting, my lack of arousal toward Tommy, and my full-on arousal toward Mr. Slate—not that I would ever admit to that last one.

I watch her until she's around the corner and out of sight and decide to wait out here for Tommy. His truck is parked next to Derek's car, and I don't want the fight with Emily to continue. A cool breeze swirls around me as I stand on the deserted sidewalk, tugging on my long sleeves. I wish I had decided on jeans instead of a skirt. Scanning the faculty lot, I spy about five unattended vehicles . . . one being a shiny black Tahoe with oversized rims, polished to perfection.

Movement catches my eye as the hatch on the Tahoe slowly rises. Mr. Slate slings a bag of equipment in the back, then disappears from my view. I glance around the near-empty lot and hesitate before stepping off the curb. The Tahoe is facing the school, so he can't see me approaching. My brain screams at me: *Stay back!* But I'm drawn to him like a magnet to steel. I need to be near to him—even if for just a moment. I want his attention. I want him to reward me with that twinkle in his rustic-brown eyes. I no longer want to be his student . . . I want to be on his level.

I want to attract him.

I approach the SUV and round the corner, startling him.

"Oh! Hey there, Kaley." He glances around. "Car trouble again?" He hesitates. "Do you need a ride?"

I suppress a laugh at his unintentional innuendo. "My car's still in the shop," I say. "Don't worry, I have a ride." I smile. "Thanks again for helping me this weekend. You were right about the alternator."

He slides a baseball bat next to the bag of equipment. "No problem." His voice is stiff. He's no longer in uniform and wears a thin, dark-gray athletic shirt—leaving little to the imagination of what his upper body possesses—with a pair of black athletic pants. He still wears his baseball cap that threatens to hide his beautiful eyes in a way that makes him even more mysterious. The newfound ache swells below me.

"Do you mind if I sit for a second?" I ask.

Not waiting for an answer, I hop up on the back ledge next to the equipment and let my legs dangle before I cross them. His eyes flicker to my bare legs for a moment, sending a thrill across the back of my thighs. Uncertainty crosses his expression.

"This is okay, right?" I say with a timid smile. "It's not like we're alone or anything."

He stares at me without a reply—we both know we're pretty much alone. No one can see us back here. He seems guarded and takes a step back, continuing to watch me without saying a word.

"Sorry. Should I leave? I just wanted a minute to breathe. Emily's mad at me, and I'm not looking forward to going home." *Ugh, that sounded so juvenile.* "I still haven't told her about my parents, and I think she's misreading me," I add.

He crosses his arms, almost as if he is trying to hold onto himself. "I'm sure she'd understand if you just told her." His voice is low, and I start to wonder if he's annoyed.

I'm making a fool of myself.

"I'm sorry, I'll go," I say as I move to jump down.

He steps forward, pinning his body against the back corner of the Tahoe, blocking me. His arm stretches over my head, resting on the top of the vehicle, as he leans forward.

I freeze.

"It's okay, Kaley." His tone is like velvet. "I said you could talk to me, and I meant it."

He's so close, we're almost touching.

I try to find my voice. "I don't want to get you in trouble."

"You won't . . . you're not . . . it's okay—it'll be okay."

I blush. His words tumble awkwardly out of his mouth, but his eyes hold mine with a force that makes my whole body shiver, despite the warmth on my face.

"So, I take it you worked everything out with Bradford?" There's an undercurrent in his voice that I can't quite grasp. "That's good at least, right?" His impressive arm above me is distracting.

"I guess," I reply. His familiar scent is now mixed with his sweat. It's sensuous, and I wonder if this is what he smells like when he makes love.

His expression is impassive. "You forgave him for the other night?"

"I guess so," I say, running a hand through my hair. My elbow grazes his shirt. "Although, I somehow ended up apologizing to him."

"What did *you* have to be sorry for?" The edge to his voice surprises me. "He let you walk away in that dress, right?" His eyes darken. "That should be unforgivable."

I swear my heart stops beating, and I'm going to need a defibrillator. Energy charges the air between us as his intrepid words hang in the silence, dangling over me like forbidden grapes. A shiver ripples through me as my body recalls the sensation of his touch when I used Tommy's body, and I fight the urge to reach out for him. It'd be effortless to lean in and kiss him, he's so close.

"Are you cold, Kaley?" he asks, his voice barely audible.

I shake my head, stifling a nervous giggle. Dragging my gaze from his, I let my eyes slowly scroll down his toned body. When I look back up, there is an unmistakable hunger written all over his face.

Holy hell.

Anxiety grips me, and I break the silence. "So um . . . great game tonight."

Oh, real smooth. I'm at a loss for words, but there are probably a hundred thousand different things that would top "great game." Not to mention, I barely even watched the game—but we won so I assume it was great.

"Yeah," he says with a seriousness that makes me believe he isn't thinking about baseball. "We weren't expected to win, but we pulled it off." His inviting lips part slightly as his eyes rest on my mouth. "Kaley," he says softly. "I—"

"Kaley?" A third voice interrupts from behind him.

Mr. Slate jerks back in a flash, and I'm face-to-face with Derek.

"Derek! What are you doing here?" Yeah, that's probably the worst thing I could've said.

And I said it.

Anger flashes through Derek's eyes. "I was about to ask you the same thing. I was coming over to talk to Slate about the game."

"Yeah, me too," I fumble.

Mr. Slate folds his arms across his chest and squares his

shoulders to Derek. "What's up, Larson?"

I hop off the back of the Tahoe and adjust my skirt.

Derek watches me before turning his attention to Mr. Slate. "Just wanted to talk to you about that last inning . . . but you look a little busy."

"Not at all," says Mr. Slate. "We were just discussing precalculus."

Whoa. He lied.

"Really?" Derek challenges. "I thought you were talking about the game."

I look at Mr. Slate in alarm, but he doesn't acknowledge me. "Conversations progress, Larson," he says with authority.

"Wow. That looked like some heated precalc," Derek throws back at him. "No wonder she has an A."

"What exactly are you implying, Derek?" Mr. Slate's voice is severe. His entire body is tense, and I can tell he's struggling to keep his composure.

Derek smiles, but it doesn't meet his eyes. "Nothing at all, *Coach.*" He turns to me. "Tommy's looking for you. Why don't you go find *his* truck to ride in?" His glare rips through me, and he walks off before giving me a chance to reply.

I turn back to Mr. Slate and start to apologize, but he cuts me off.

"You should really try to talk about your problems with the school counselor, Kaley." He slams down the hatch, and I flinch. He climbs into his Tahoe without so much as a glance in my direction and drives off, leaving me alone in the darkened parking lot.

I try to ignore the hollow ache spreading through me as I trudge over to the student lot. What I wouldn't give to have my car here so I could just drive home myself. Just as I'm about to turn the corner, Derek steps out in front of me, and I yelp. He doesn't apologize for scaring me. Instead, he glares down at me with a fierceness I've never seen in him. He crosses his arms tightly against his chest, and I wait for him to speak, but he doesn't.

"What, Derek?" I spit out. I often hide my dejection underneath anger, but I never thought it would be aimed at him.

"What the fuck was that, Kaley? Would you like to fill me in?"

I have no idea how to react to this side of him. So I do what I always do.

Save face.

"Look, I don't know what you think you saw, but you're way off," I say to the best of my acting abilities. I try to remember everything I learned from the one semester of theater I took in eighth grade. Everyone knows I'm a terrible liar, but I'm not going to jeopardize Mr. Slate's career. Derek's ire crushes me, and I have to diffuse this fast.

"Do you think I'm a fucking idiot?" Derek only swears when he's really angry, and this is two in a row—and to the highest degree.

"No! Do you think *I* am? He's a teacher! That's insane," I say, trying to turn it around on him. "And I most certainly *will* think you're an idiot if you start spreading around false gossip that could cause a man to get fired. That kind of thing is serious, Derek. You shouldn't jump to conclusions."

His jaw clenches as he shakes his head at me. "Unbelievable, Kaley." He sighs and looks up at the night sky. A moment passes before he brings his attention back to me. The judgment in his eyes is sobering. "All right, fine. I don't know exactly what I saw. But it was something. And I'll be damned if I let you—"

"Derek!" Emily's voice interrupts his tirade.

"What?" he calls over his shoulder.

"What are you doing?"

"Talking to Kaley!" he hollers. Apparently, Emily can see Derek's back as we stand on the corner, but she can't see me.

"Well, let's go!"

Derek turns away, but I clutch onto his arm. "Please don't say anything," I plead. I've completely lost my bravado—I am desperate now. "You're wrong about what you saw and there's no reason to upset anybody—*anybody*." I know we're both thinking about our best friends.

He yanks his arm free and storms off without a word. *Shit.* I slip past his car, avoiding the sight of him and Emily, and knock on the passenger window of Tommy's truck. *Hold it together, hold it together.* He looks up from his phone and unlocks the door. I climb into the cab and he pulls me close to him.

"Sit in the middle by me," he says, grinning. He grips my thigh as I fasten my seatbelt. "We won," he says as soon as we pull out of the parking lot.

"Yeah, congratulations," I say, trying to sound upbeat. *What the hell just happened?* I'm still trying to catch my breath and register it all. "It was a great game," I say without inflection.

"Yeah, we weren't expected to win, but we pulled it off." He repeats the same exact line Mr. Slate said, but without the smoldering intensity.

How am I going to show my face in class tomorrow morning? What if Derek tells the whole school about what he saw? What if he tells Tommy? Emily? There's no way he'll keep this to himself, right? Most people I know would spread this juicy gossip like a wildfire.

Mr. Slate's cold voice plays in my head: *You should really try to talk about your problems with the school counselor, Kaley.* I feel the tears prick my eyes, but I push them back. Why does it feel like a breakup when there was never anything between us? But *there was something, wasn't there?* Unless I'm

94

completely delusional. It can't be all one sided—he wouldn't have reacted that way to Derek. And the way he was looking at me before Derek showed up . . . I can't be imagining everything, can I?

No, I decide.

We crossed some sort of line.

Tommy's wandering hand releases me from my tortured thoughts as it inches closer to the hem of my skirt. His hand is in an awkward position as he drives down the road, but it doesn't sway his determination. My legs are crossed, blocking any access, and I don't move them. When he pulls into my driveway, he shifts the truck into park and cuts the engine. Darkness washes over us, and I realize my parents forgot to leave the front porch light on for me—again. *Seriously?* I unbuckle my seat belt and give him a small kiss goodbye, but he holds on to me, slipping his tongue over mine.

When he comes up for air, he says, "What do you want to do this weekend?" With my legs now uncrossed, he slides his hand forward, boldly running his fingers over the front of my underwear.

"Not that," I blurt out.

He pulls back, moving away from me.

"I can't keep up with you," he says, starting the engine. I can't see his expression, but he's clearly upset.

"I'm sorry—I didn't mean for it to come out that way." *Am I seriously apologizing again?*

His eyes avoid mine. "Don't worry about it." His voice is terse. "I'll pick you up in the morning."

I lean in to kiss him, but he makes no effort to kiss me back.

"I love you," I say delicately. "I'm really sorry. I'm just . . . scared."

He faces me. "Why would you be scared with me? I thought we were closer than that."

"We are." But as soon as the words come out, I know it's a lie.

I don't feel close to anybody right now. I can't tell whether I've pushed everyone away, or if I'm being pulled in another direction. The guilt almost drowns me, flooding my heart. My actions are hurting everyone around me . . . even Mr. Slate.

Tommy lets me kiss him goodnight before I step out of his truck, but he doesn't wait for me to get inside the house before driving off. I make my way onto the porch and fumble with my keys in the black shadows. It's like the perfect metaphor for my life right now: a fumbling fool, alone in the darkness.

CHAPTER NINE

My STOMACH IS IN KNOTS as I get ready for school. Last night was a disaster, and I'm tempted to stay home, but that would only draw more unwanted attention. I want to look nice today, but in a subtle way that doesn't seem like I'm trying too hard, so I wear my dark-blue skinny jeans with my olive-green blouse that makes my eyes pop. Tommy's horn blares from outside as I down the last of my coffee. I take one last glance at myself in the mirror before running out the door, my stomach on edge.

Tommy smiles as I climb into his truck. "You look good," he says, leaning over for a kiss. He seems to have forgiven me.

"Thanks," I say, returning his smile. This also means Derek hasn't said anything to him about what happened, and I pray it stays that way.

Filled with trepidation, I grip my bag as we approach the main entrance. *I can do this.* I'm determined to stride into first period with my head held high. However, my pride quickly diminishes as I enter the building. After Tommy kisses me good-bye, I make my way down the hall and gather myself outside the classroom door. When I step inside, Mr. Slate is preoccupied at his desk, and I quietly take my seat.

Twenty minutes into class, he still hasn't looked at me.

"Does anyone have the answer yet?" he asks the class.

Looking up from my calculator, I raise my hand. I'll be damned if I am going to let him intimidate me.

He gestures to me without even glancing my way. "Kaley?"

"0.894?"

"Nope." His tone stabs me in the gut.

So much for my very last drop of pride.

"Anyone else? Andrew?"

My gaze drops to my book. I wish someone would pull the fire alarm so I could run out of here without looking like a crazy person. Mr. Slate writes Andrew's *correct* answer on the board and addresses the class.

"Look, if some of you aren't getting this by now, you're in trouble. I promise you this will be on the next test. If you can't calculate the eccentricity of an ellipse this late in the game, then you're not going to be able to finish the rest of the problem. You should have this down by now."

His words sting, and I want to chuck my book at his face. Why did I practically throw myself at this man last night? My grade is dropping and for what? I can't believe I let him knock me off my game. I sink lower in my seat. He's sending me a very clear message. A message that says: *Stay back, little girl.*

I don't pay attention for the rest of the hour.

AT LUNCH, I'M desperate for some light conversation and distraction from Mr. Slate. But as I take my seat at the table, Emily's in the middle of complaining about him. It seems as if I'm not the only one who had to endure his wrath this morning.

She finishes her rant and turns her attention to me. "Seriously, what's up his ass today? Was he pissed off in your class, too?"

Well, at least she's still talking to me.

"Um, yeah, he was actually."

Derek's eyes narrow in my direction, but I ignore him.

"Dude needs to get laid," says Emily.

Derek's stare is burning a hole through me, and it takes everything I have not to meet his eyes.

"I could help him out with that," says Avery, giggling.

Tommy appears next to me. "What's with this guy? Why do every girl's panties drop when he walks by?"

Everyone at the table laughs, except for Derek. He's quietly eating his sandwich, staring at the table. My appetite fades, and I push away my lunch tray.

Tommy turns to me and keeps his voice low. "You're not eating again? Should I be concerned?" Then he smirks. "I don't think I've ever seen you turn down pizza."

"What are you saying?" I snap. "That I'm some uncontrollable pig who can't turn down a slice of pizza?"

His eyes widen. "No—what the hell? You're perfect, Kay, I—what's up with you?"

"I'm just not hungry right now, okay?"

"What, are you seriously stressed about your math class? Are you worried your grade will drop to a B?" he ridicules, the crowd laughing along with him. *Yeah, Tommy's a real riot.*

"It *is* at a B actually." I did the calculations last night just to be sure.

"Oooooh," he taunts. "Not a B! Oh, the horror!"

Everyone laughs again.

"You should really start charging people for your little comedy act," I retort.

"You're just as bitchy as Mr. Slate today," says Emily.

Derek's eyes bore into me again, and my leg bounces uncontrollably underneath the table.

"Sorry," I whisper to Tommy. He has to be getting sick of this by now—I've really been testing his patience lately. Without making eye contact, I give him a quick peck on the cheek and stand up. I walk out of the cafeteria and spend the rest of the hour sitting in the library, literally staring at a bookshelf, with my earphones blaring.

WHEN THE WRETCHED school day comes to an end, Emily hops over to me with a wide grin on her face.

"Hey," I say cautiously. "Does this mean you're not mad at me anymore?"

She shrugs. "I refuse to waste my life with negativity. Besides, my mom sent me a text saying I get my car back tonight."

I manage a smile. "Awesome."

"Are you still coming over?"

I don't even remember making plans with her. I'm really not up for it, but since we're on thin ice, I know I need to go.

"Yeah, of course," I say.

She's still grinning at me. "Okay, good. Because Mr. Slate's taking us."

My smile goes stiff. "Come again?"

Emily beams. "Mr. Slate's taking us home."

Is she joking? For a second, I worry Derek told her about last night, and they're plotting some sort of cruel joke on me. But her face is genuine.

"I thought Tommy was taking me home. Or, us home. To your house," I stammer. I don't want her to think I forgot about our plans, and I don't understand what's happening right now.

"Nope. He ditched sixth period with Derek after they found out baseball practice was canceled—which is why Derek can't take us either."

I close my locker, dumbstruck. "And Mr. Slate is the only person on the planet that can take us home right now?"

This can't be happening.

"Of course not. But the boys left us here knowing we didn't have a ride, so I decided to have a little fun," she says.

"They probably figured we'd get a ride home with someone else. Can't they come get us? Let's ask someone else. I can't believe you're having a teacher take us home. Why on earth would he agree to this?"

I'm nauseated.

"Why wouldn't he? Kaley, it was like a sign from God. Derek had just told me they were ditching right before I walked into the office before fifth period. Mr. Slate was standing there in all his glory when I heard him talking to Donovan about giving him a ride home. So, I just went for it and totally put him on the spot. I poured it on thick—told him how Tommy and Derek ditched, and I acted like all of our other friends were too busy to help. I acted *super* sad about it. He resisted, but I finally wore him down. Mr. Bentley was even like, 'Take the poor girl home.' It was awesome!" She bounces up and down.

"Mr. Bentley said that? Isn't it against the rules or something? I thought teachers weren't allowed to be alone with students." I'm desperate now.

Emily laughs. "What are you talking about? The principal was cool with it, so it's obviously fine. I mean, if he can take home baseball players, he can take us home, right? Why are you being weird?"

I rake my hand through my hair. "I'm not." Emily's used to me being her partner in crime with things like this, so I do my best to act cool. "I just can't believe you got him to do this."

"Come on, Kaley, you know I always get what I want. And besides, I'm just having a little innocent fun." She gives herself devil horns with her fingers and sticks out her tongue.

I can't suppress my laughter. "I thought you were pissed at Mr. Slate today."

She drags me down the hallway. "I am determined to turn his frown upside down. *And* yours!"

When Emily pulls me through the door to his classroom, my laughter abruptly halts, and I fight the threat of a panic attack. Mr. Slate looks up from his desk, and I catch his hesitation for a split second before he regains his composure.

"Just give me a minute," he says, only making eye contact with Emily. Beads of sweat form on the back of my neck, and I try to act natural as Emily discreetly wiggles her eyebrows at me. We wait at the back of the classroom as he shuts down his computer. *This can't be happening.* At least Donovan will be a distraction—I can just hide in the back while they talk baseball, or whatever, and wait for it all to be over.

Mr. Slate rises from his desk and slings his leather messenger bag across his broad chest with ease. His tousled hair is as glorious as ever and his black dress shirt—with the damned sleeves rolled up again—is stretched taut over his upper body. Emily looks like she could sprout little pink wings and fly away as she gawks at him coming toward us. *Is that what I look like when I watch him?* How pathetic.

"Donovan isn't coming," announces Emily. My eyes bulge in her direction and she gives me a mischievous smile, then turns her charm on Mr. Slate. "He got a ride with Avery."

"Oh." Mr. Slate glances at me. It's the most contact I've had with him since last night. "Well . . ."

I interrupt before this turns disastrous. "I'm going to Emily's, so you don't have to take me home," I say, sheepishly. Emily's forehead creases as she regards me. "You know, so you only have to make one stop," I rush, hoping Emily doesn't catch on and that he gets the message.

His face contorts slightly like he's in pain, and he takes a moment before speaking. "All right," he says to Emily instead of me. He adjusts his bag and walks out the door.

Emily nudges me as we follow him outside. I shoot her a

warning look, and she smothers a giggle with her hand.

"Did you have something to do with Donovan not show-ing?" I whisper as soon as I'm out of earshot.

A small smile crosses her lips. "Maybe," she says in her most innocent voice. I sigh and shake my head, then stop at the shiny black Tahoe that is becoming all too familiar to me by now.

"Shot gun," Emily whispers, and I roll my eyes.

"By all means," I say. She couldn't pay me to sit in the front seat right now.

Mr. Slate unlocks the doors, and Emily hops up into the front seat. I open the rear passenger door, only to find my-self blocked by boxes of travertine tiles.

"You'll have to sit on my side, Kaley," instructs Mr. Slate as he gets in.

Oh, are you acknowledging me now, Mr. Shit?

I slam the door and trek around to the driver's side, tak-ing my seat behind him. He turns in his seat and sets his leather bag on the floor beside my feet. I catch his familiar scent and try to breathe out of my mouth.

"Shoot," he says. "I forgot something. I'll be right back, girls, sorry." He jumps out and rushes back into the build-ing.

Emily looks around the interior. "Man, he *is* a neat freak, isn't he? Look! He even has a litter bag." She laughs. Then she opens up the console and starts exploring.

"Emily, don't!" I say, panicked.

She takes out his iPod.

"Ems, put that down! He's going to catch you snooping!"

"Chill, I just want to see what kind of music he listens to." She scrolls down the list and frowns. "There's a lot of Aer-osmith and Def Leppard on here." She turns to me. "He's not *that* old, is he? My parents listen to that junk."

"We like Aerosmith," I reply.

"Yeah, but—"

"He's coming!"

She throws the iPod back in the console and slams it shut, giggling. She lets out a dreamy sigh as she watches him approach. "Damn, he's gorgeous."

"Sorry about that, girls," he says, sliding into the driver's seat.

"No worries, Mr. Slate," says Emily.

I ignore the irrational stab of jealousy as I recognize Emily's flirtatious tone. I buckle my seatbelt, refusing to acknowledge him, and stare out the window.

"Hey," he says, tapping the back of his seat. I turn my gaze from the window and find a folder in my face. He's holding it behind his head as he sits forward in his seat. "Will you set this back there?"

I snatch the folder out of his hand and set it next to me.

Emily directs him to her house and chats nonstop. She even asks him about a few algebra problems from her homework before turning the conversation to baseball. Mr. Slate and I make brief eye contact through the rearview mirror when she brings up last night's game. I focus out my window as the two of them discuss the details. I hate being trapped in this backseat—I want to be somewhere else. *Anywhere* else. Yet, deep down, there is nowhere else I'd rather be. The regret of my foolishness last night is eating away at me, and I flip my hair to the side, attempting to hide my face.

We come to a stop, and I realize we're already at Emily's. She thanks him for the ride, and I steal another glance in the rearview. My heart springs into my throat when I see that he is already looking at me. He casts his gaze away, and I push open my door and jump out. I close it gently behind me and follow Emily into her house without looking back.

EMILY GLANCES UP from her phone. "Change of plans Saturday night."

"Why, what's going on?" We're sprawled out on her bedroom floor, going through magazines and eating cookie dough. Well, Emily's eating it, I'm nibbling. The ride home still has me queasy.

"Well, if the boys win Friday night's game, they'll make it to the playoffs. And if they do, the coaches are going to throw a barbecue for the whole team—girlfriends are invited."

Coaches . . . Mr. Slate.

"Uh, yeah I think I'm going to bail on that."

Emily waves her hand disregarding my statement. "You're going. It'll be fun. And all the other girlfriends will be there—you're *not* humiliating Tommy."

Her concern for Tommy irks me, but I try to let it go. "I can't believe you're excited about a party with supervision. Where's it being held?"

"Coach Miller's house," she says, retrieving another text from Derek. "And bring your bathing suit."

You have got *to be kidding me.*

"We're swimming?! It's only April. I need the temperature to hit at least ninety-five before I swim."

"It's supposed to be ninety on Saturday, princess. And if that's still too cold, he has a spa," she says, smirking.

I'm silent.

"Kaley, you cannot turn this down!" She sends Derek another text. "I told him we'll be there." She reads his reply and hesitates before looking up at me. "We want to have a couple drinks before we go. Will you drive us?"

I roll my eyes and toss a magazine aside. "Fine. But this is weird, isn't it? Hanging out at a teacher's house on a Saturday night?"

"You know how close the team is with the coaches. And

they all say that Mr. Slate's a really cool guy. It'll be fun!"

Right.

"Fine," I say.

It's bad enough having to face Mr. Slate during first period, but to hang out with him socially? No thanks. Hopefully it won't be too difficult to avoid him. I'll just be sure to socialize with whoever is farthest away from him. Probably won't be too hard, since he'll most likely be the one avoiding me.

WHEN EMILY PULLS into my driveway, I'm relieved to see my car parked on the side of the house. *Finally!* As she drives off, I unlock the front door and step into a shouting match between my parents.

Just when I didn't think this day could get any worse.

They're in the kitchen, so I make sure to slam the front door closed as hard as I can.

Silence.

Yep, I knew that'd do it.

What I really want to do is hide upstairs in my bedroom, but I'm sick of this. I drop my bag at the bottom of the stairs and march into the kitchen.

With my hands on my hips, I stand in the entryway, my face hard. "So what are we going to do about this?"

My mom's face is streaked with red blotches. "We didn't know you were home, sweetie. I'm sorry you had to hear that."

"You're sorry I had to hear that," I repeat coldly, folding my arms. "Are you both certifiably insane?"

My dad turns to me. "Excuse me?"

"Do you think I live in a soundproof bedroom?"

"Watch your tone," my dad warns.

"It's okay," my mom assures him. "We're sorry, Kay."

"I hear you every damn night," I say, enunciating each

word slowly.

My dad's face inflames, and he raises his voice. "Watch your mouth. You don't talk to us that way, do you understand?"

I raise my voice to match his. "Do *you* understand that I can't get a good night's sleep in my own house? Do you even care that it affects me?" I pivot and storm off to my bedroom, hollering as I stomp up the stairs. "I can't wait to move out of this house and away from this fucked-up family!"

My dad charges up the stairs after me, but I slam the door in his face. When he swings open my door, I hear my mom yelling after him, but he ignores her. He's wearing a face that I once feared. But he doesn't scare me this time—I'm too livid.

"Kaley . . ." He keeps his voice low, but the vein on his forehead swells as he points his finger in my face. "Don't you *ever* use that language again. You are so out of line, young lady." His voice shakes with controlled rage, and I know he's trying to restrain himself.

I feel my chin tremble as his intense glare strikes my armor . . . and I start to break. Tears well up in my eyes, and I collapse on my bed with my head in my hands.

His arms are around me in a flash and my body stiffens.

"We'll be fine, Kay," he says, rubbing my back.

"I can't take this," I cry.

"Everything will be fine. It's just a little bump in the road." He holds me for a moment as I choke back tears, then squeezes me tightly before letting go.

As soon as I hear the door click behind him, I break down.

I don't know how long I sob into my hands, but I eventually force myself to stop. If I don't, I'm afraid I'll cry forever. I send a text to Tommy telling him I don't need a ride tomorrow. Then add: And thanks for ditching me today.

I couldn't help myself.

My mom pokes her head in and treads lightly to my bed.

"I want to talk to you," she says with a gentle voice. She sits next to me and strokes my hair the way she always has since I was a little girl.

She slips me a tissue, and I wipe my nose.

"What's going on with you and Dad? I've never heard you fight—now that's all you do. I don't understand."

She takes a deep breath. "You know, Kay, lately I've been noticing how much you're growing up. You're a young woman now. So, I'm going to be honest with you." She pauses. "Your father and I have never had a great relationship."

I turn to her. "You haven't?"

Her eyes become glassy, making them appear almost doll-like as she struggles to steady her voice. "We've just always been able to ignore it, I suppose . . . until recently."

"So what's changed?"

"I think it's because you're eighteen now and growing up, getting ready to spread your wings. We've always had you as a distraction, I guess, but now it's like we have to face each other, and it's been . . . difficult." She takes a breath. "Your father and I married right out of high school . . . after we found out I was pregnant with you at the end of our senior year."

"What?" It feels like the air has just been suctioned out of the room.

"We wanted to do the right thing, so we got married right away."

I spring off the bed. "You got married because of me? So . . . this is *my* fault?"

She grabs my hands. "Of course not, sweetie. You are the best thing that has ever happened to us. This is just life, Kaley. It's not perfect."

I'll say.

I slip my hand through my hair and pace the room.

"I'm sorry, Kay. But I thought you deserved to know."

I stare at her. I want to ask her why I deserve to know. Why she feels the need to tell me this. I'm trapped somewhere between wanting to be an adult and still wanting to be sheltered from reality. But her troubled eyes deflate me, and I flop back into my desk chair.

"I'm sorry, Mom," I say. "I didn't mean to swear at you guys. I don't want you guys to be unhappy; it's just been hard on me."

"You had every right to say what you did, Kay. I'm sorry we've been selfish."

"So what now? Are you going to go to counseling?"

She pauses. "Your father has been going, actually."

"But not you?"

She shakes her head. "I'm just not ready yet."

"It's important, Mom."

"I know. Don't worry about that now. I'll see you in the morning." She hugs me before kissing me goodnight and slips out of my room.

My phone chimes with a text from Tommy: Looked like u needed space.

I send him a hasty apology and turn off my phone. I scrub off what's left of my makeup and change into my pajamas, then crawl into bed. My once seemingly perfect life is unravelling at the seams faster than I can comprehend.

The house is silent, and I am quickly pulled into a heavy slumber.

CHAPTER TEN

SATURDAY ARRIVES WAY TOO FAST—probably because I'm dreading it. The boys won their game last night, which means the team's celebratory barbecue is on for today. Mr. Slate has been icy to me all week, and I'd rather be getting a root canal than going to this miserable party. I wear my plain black bathing suit underneath my pink halter top and jean shorts—not that I plan on swimming. I imagine The Blonde sitting poolside as all the boys gawk at her, while Mr. Slate rubs her down with sun tan oil.

This is going to suck.

I drive to Derek's house where Emily and Tommy are already on their second drinks.

Derek is pounding a third.

Are they capable of celebrating an event without alcohol? Or a Saturday night for that matter?

I lean against the counter and fold my arms. "You guys ready?"

"Don't be like that," Tommy teases. "It's just a couple of beers—we're celebrating!"

"If you get caught, you're off the team, you know."

"It's fine, Kaley, chill," says Emily as she slurps the last of her beverage.

"I'm serious. We're going to a teacher's house."

Tommy slips his arm around my waist. "They're just coaches. They're not like normal teachers, we'll be fine."

"I know how much of a stickler you are for the rules, Kaley, but let it go," says Derek with a sarcasm that only I can detect.

Biting my lip, I ignore him and turn to Tommy. "Let's go," I say, leading him out to my car.

He lets Derek and Emily cram into the backseat before climbing into the front.

"Wow, your car is super clean, Kay. I don't think I've ever seen it like this," Tommy says in astonishment.

I give a weak smile. "I just thought I'd give her a little TLC."

"Are you going to finally cave in and let me and my dad restore this thing for you?"

"I don't know . . . maybe."

"Nice!" He gives me a kiss on the cheek. I'm thankful he's in a good mood—maybe today won't be a total bust.

Derek directs me to Coach Miller's house and seems to be in a decent mood as well—maybe alcohol isn't always a bad thing. I park on the curb behind a shiny black Tahoe that is all too tempting to rear-end. The street is lined with cars, and it appears as if most of the team has already arrived. I normally wouldn't mind going to a teacher's house for a barbecue with the baseball team—it might even be fun. But knowing Mr. Slate is here leaves me feeling insecure and anxious to flee the scene. And with Derek casting suspicious stares in my direction for the past week, it makes the whole situation that much more tense.

My anxiety spikes as we step outside into the backyard. I spot Mr. Slate near the grill, talking to Coach Miller, who is grilling hotdogs and hamburgers for the team. Several of my classmates are in the pool, but most are standing around, drinking sodas and talking. Derek and Tommy join the group by the grill and greet everybody with their customary head nods and cryptic handshakes. Mr. Slate glances my way, but seems completely unaffected by my presence. Emily stands next to Derek and Tommy while they start up a conversation with him, so I make my way over to Avery and a few of her fellow cheerleaders on the other side of the yard. I attempt to match Mr. Slate's indifference while listening to the latest gossip amongst the girls. A quick scan around the yard reveals no sign of The Blonde.

Good, one less aggravation to deal with today.

After about an hour, everyone is sitting around the picnic tables, indulging in burgers, hot dogs, and other traditional barbecue fare. I stare at my potato salad, letting the multiple conversations around me morph into a far-off drone.

Tommy turns to me and proceeds with caution. "Are you sure you don't want any meat, babe?"

"No, I'm fine, thanks," I reply.

He slings his arm around me, giving me a quick peck on the lips, and I notice Mr. Slate's eyes on us. I turn my gaze downward, taking a bite of my potato salad.

After several hours of awkward inner tension and endless amounts of mind-numbing baseball talk, the crowd starts to thin out. Jeff's parents are out of town, and everyone's heading over there for beer pong. Derek and Tommy are still in deep conversation with the coaches, discussing tactics for the upcoming playoff game. I sit at the edge of the pool with Emily, chatting, while our legs dangle in the water. The sun sets as we reminisce about the school year that's soon coming to an end, and she even manages to make me laugh and take my mind off things. This is what I've always loved about her. It feels good to laugh with her again.

Derek joins us. "What's so funny, ladies?"

"Nothing," we say in unison.

"Miller said we can go in the spa."

My heart catapults into my throat. I've avoided stripping down to my bikini in front of *him* the entire afternoon, and thought I was home-free.

"Will Mr. Slate be joining us?" Emily teases.

"No," Derek replies straight-faced. Ever since he found me in the back of the Tahoe, he's lost his sense of humor with all things Slate-related. "He's helping clean up, and Miller said we can go in for a while if we want. 'Just so long as we act appropriately.'" He says, using air quotes and a mocking voice.

"Let's go!" Emily squeals. Before I can object, she drags me into the house, down the hallway, and pulls me into the bathroom. She takes her bathing suit out of her bag and strips off her clothes. "See? You get your spa time after all."

"I never wanted spa time, Ems. Especially at a teacher's house." *There has to be a way out of this.*

"It's cool, Kay, they'll just be cleaning up. And besides, I was talking to Slate and Miller a lot today, and they really are chill guys."

Then why does one of them make me so hot?

"Slate and Miller?" I cock an eyebrow at her. "So, you're on a last-name basis now?"

"Everyone calls them that."

"Are you sure you don't want to go play beer pong?" I suggest. "Sounds like fun."

She stops mid-change. "*You* want to play beer pong?"

Yeah, that's not going to work.

"No, not really," I admit.

"Didn't think so." She turns around so I can tie the back of her top.

WE MAKE OUR way back outside and find "Miller" laying out a stack towels out for us.

"I'm not kidding," he cautions the boys. Tommy and Derek are already in the spa with Seth and Donovan. "I can see you from my kitchen window—no fooling around." He walks back into the house just as Avery returns, prancing around in her skimpy bikini without a care in the world—I envy her confidence sometimes.

Emily and Avery join the boys in the spa, and I glance at the kitchen window. Coach Miller and his wife are talking to Mr. Slate and part of me wonders why The Blonde never showed. *Hmm . . . trouble in paradise?* I reluctantly slip off my halter top and shimmy down my shorts. Tommy lets out a whistle, and I give him a feeble smile as I step into the spa. The scalding water bubbles against my skin, sending a jolt through my body. I fasten my hair into a high bun and slowly ease my way into the water. Feeling eyes on me, I look up at the kitchen window.

Mr. Slate is watching me.

If it were any other teacher it would creep me out, but instead, heat courses through my veins that has nothing to do with the temperature of the water.

Tommy loops his arm around me, bringing my attention back to the group. Everyone is cracking up as Seth retells the story of how Emily got Derek and Tommy in trouble for ditching, and how the coaches punished them by making them run laps until they both puked.

When the boys change the topic back to baseball, I join the conversation with Emily and Avery, discussing our plans for college and exchanging gossip acquired throughout the party. But I'm only half-listening. I continue to glance at the house every so often, but never catch him staring again.

Avery moves over to Donovan's lap, and Coach Miller bangs on the kitchen window, startling everyone. With a hard expression, he points at Donovan and Avery and shouts "No!" His voice is so powerful, it's even intimidating through the glass. Avery giggles and slides off his lap.

After a while, everyone is fed up with the supervision and ready to head over to Jeff's party. Emily and I slip into the bathroom to change.

"Is it cool if I just drop you guys off at Jeff's and go home?" I ask her as we touch up our makeup. I somehow managed to keep most of my hair dry, which is shocking.

She turns and looks at me with a somber face. "Why don't you want to hang out anymore? You're always moping around." Her concern touches me. "And you're crazy if you think Tommy's going to put up with it much longer. No offense, but he can get any girl he wants."

And there it is again.

Her words sting, regardless of how true they are. Is that the real reason he puts up with me? Because I'm the only girl who won't sleep with him? He's always been a good friend to me, but I'm starting to wonder if I'm just some sort of prize. I push the thought away.

"Honestly Ems, I'm stressed about the future, my grade in math is plummeting, and my parents' fighting has gotten really bad."

There, I did it. Finally pulled the "fighting parents" card.

Her expression is sympathetic. "How bad?"

"Really bad. They keep me up almost every night. . . . It's why I'm always tired."

"I'm sorry Kay, why didn't you tell me?"

"I don't know. It's embarrassing for some reason." I look down. "I feel like it's my fault."

She touches my shoulder. "Why would it be your fault?"

"I finally confronted my parents about everything the other night, and my mom told me they've just grown apart. She confessed they were never really great together, but got pregnant senior year and chose to do the 'right thing.' I guess they focused on me for most of their marriage, but now that I'm older, they're forced to face each other again." A lump forms in my throat. "I'm the reason they got married. *I'm* the reason they're miserable." My voice cracks, and I press the back of my thumbs under my eyes to stop the tears as the reality of my words cut into me.

"I can't believe she said that to you," says Emily in a soothing voice.

"Yeah, it pretty much made me feel like crap."

She strokes my arm. "You poor thing. Thank you for finally telling me. I'm so sorry. Are you sure you don't want to come with us? You can stay the night at my house. Someone else can drive—you deserve to blow off a little steam."

"No, Ems. I really need to just go home. Please."

"Okay," she says. "Hey, we'll grab a ride with one of the guys, okay? Just go home from here. And call me if you need anything."

"Thanks."

After a long hug, we step into the hallway and join everyone in the living room.

Emily addresses the crowd. "Hey, can we get a ride with one of you to Jeff's party? Kaley needs to go home."

All eyes fall on me, including Mr. Slate's.

Tommy rushes to my side. "You okay?"

I appreciate his genuine concern, but it makes me feel guilty as well. The situation with my parents is weighing heavily on me, but it isn't the main reason I want to crawl into my bed right now.

"Yeah," I reply. "I'll talk to you about it tomorrow, okay? Have fun tonight, you deserve it."

He kisses me, then takes me by the hand and leads me outside. I wave good-bye to everyone, but they're all talking amongst themselves. Mr. Slate is the only one looking my way, but he doesn't wave back.

"You're not mad?" I ask Tommy as he takes me to my car.

"No, it's okay. Do you want to talk about it now?"

"Not really. Just go to the party."

He leans me against my car and pulls me in for a kiss. I

can't believe he's being so chill about me bailing. He hasn't had *that* much to drink, and it was hours ago. He wraps his arms around my waist, kissing me slowly. His tenderness pulls at my guilt-ridden heart.

"So, prom's coming up," he says after ending the kiss. His arms are still tightly wrapped around me. "A bunch of us are getting hotel rooms in downtown Phoenix."

"Oh yeah?" *Ah.* Now I know why he's being so sweet.

"Yeah." He says, kissing me again—as if his kiss has magical powers that are going to convince me. "You interested?"

His eyes remind me of a puppy dog begging for table scraps. In fact, he's making me feel like table scraps right now as he paws at me.

"Tommy, I'm not losing my virginity on prom night. That's so cliché."

He releases his hold on me. "So when exactly do *you* have it planned?"

"I *don't* have it planned. I'd prefer it to be spontaneous."

He scoffs. "How can it be spontaneous when you never allow us to be in a spontaneous situation?" His voice is starting to rise. He's gone from puppy dog to pit bull in under six seconds flat.

"Well, *this* behavior isn't going to get you what you want, I can assure you."

"What do you expect, Kaley? Am I supposed to wait forever?"

"What is *that* supposed to mean? I can't believe you're saying this right now! You know I'm—"

"Everything okay?" Mr. Slate's voice slices through the tension as he strolls down the driveway. I didn't even hear him come out of the house.

"Yes," I say without looking at him.

"Why don't you call it a night, Bradford," he warns.

When Tommy doesn't budge, he stops at the end of the driveway and faces us.

Tommy drags his eyes from me and pins them on Mr. Slate. "Everything's cool, Slate." His words don't match his defiant tone.

Mr. Slate's expression hardens as he folds his arms.

"Can we have some privacy?" Tommy says, his voice crisp. "I'm talking to my girlfriend."

Mr. Slate's eyes flash to mine for a split second before returning to Tommy's. "No, I think you should go cool off."

Tommy turns his body away from Mr. Slate, focusing his attention back on me. I meet Tommy's eyes, unable to look anywhere else. My throat tightens as the pressure builds between them.

"Bradford, I'll give you two choices," cautions Mr. Slate. He relaxes his stance. "You can either walk away right now, or you can stay with me after practice on Monday and run stairs until you can't see straight."

Tommy sets his jaw, keeping his back to Mr. Slate, and I chew on my inner lip, wincing when I accidently draw blood.

Just when I think Tommy's going to mouth off again, he quickly spins around, causing me to flinch, then charges up the driveway and into the house. I look back at Mr. Slate, but he's already stepping into his Tahoe. I stand under the streetlamp for a moment, feeling an empty space burgeon inside of me. Mr. Slate pulls onto the street, and I glance back at the house, half-expecting Tommy to return. Not wanting another encounter, I slide into the Chevelle as the Tahoe disappears around the corner.

Tears roll down my cheeks as I drive home, the engine's roar serving as a backdrop for my thoughts. My life feels like it's being shattered to pieces, and I'm the one holding the hammer. *I'm* the cause of every disaster in my life. Tommy and I constantly bicker. Why? Because of me. My parents exchange verbal blows nearly every night, and their marriage is falling apart. Why? Because of me. With Emily, Derek, and Mr. Slate, there have been fights, tension, and anger. Why? Because of me. I just want everything back to how it used to be. Back to when my parents were happy, and I wasn't a walking tornado. Back to when I was content with surface-level Saturday nights and light-hearted conversations. Back to spring break when Tommy was my whole world, and I was headed to California for college . . . back when life was easy, and I was in control.

When I pull into my driveway, I cut the engine and lean back in my seat. Somehow, I have to set the hammer down and glue the pieces back together. . . . *Is it too late for that?* Taking a deep breath, I draw my phone from my bag and send Tommy a text:

I'll think about prom night, ok? Call me later. I love you.

CHAPTER ELEVEN

I'M TRYING. I REALLY AM. But the week drags on as I hide my despondency underneath mechanical smiles and empty laughter. Emily and I are getting along great—even Tommy and I have made up, but we're still fragile. Derek is still cautious around me, however, and Mr. Slate continues to act as if I don't exist. He doesn't even look at me when I hand in my test on Wednesday.

Relief greets me Friday morning, promising an end to a tiresome week. I'm anticipating the weekend more than usual because the boys are busy with extra baseball practices as they gear up for the playoffs, and the team is staying at Derek's all weekend. Emily will be gone as well. Her parents are taking her up to Flagstaff for the weekend to check out NAU. She's still positive about getting into USC, but her parents are making sure that she explores all of her other options. The four of us have plans to hang out tonight, of course, but other than that, I'll be enjoying a solitary weekend alone where I won't be required to perform.

Mr. Slate passes back our tests at the end of class, and there it is, written in harsh red ink.

An actual D.

If I'm not mistaken, this brings my overall grade down to a C. I know I've been struggling, but this is getting out of hand. Underneath the D, is a note from Mr. Slate in his annoyingly perfect handwriting:

YOU ARE BETTER
THAN THIS!

It's such a slap in the face. I overhear some of my classmates freaking out over their grades and talking about going to tonight's study session. I'd rather perform naked cartwheels in the cafeteria during lunch than go to Mr. Slate's study session, but this is getting serious now. I need to pass this class to graduate, and once you fall behind in math, it's nearly impossible to catch up.

I have to go.

Even though it's the only night our group can hang out this weekend, no one argues with me about going to the study session when I show them my grade at the lunch table. They're giving me a free pass tonight. The sick and twisted irony is not lost on me. I'm finally free to attend his study session—*guilt free*—when it's the very last place I want to be.

I DON'T BOTHER looking my best for the study session. It's obvious I overstepped my boundaries with Mr. Slate, and even though it's been almost two weeks since I made such a fool of myself in the back of his Tahoe after the baseball game, he's clearly still keeping his distance. As much as I hate to admit it, his brush-off still leaves me feeling hollow—it seems unreal that not that long ago, he was admiring my dress and we were sharing our favorite candy at the movie theater. I throw on a pair of ripped jeans and a plain navy-blue T-shirt, then pull my hair back into a ponytail and head out the door.

When I arrive back at school, a wave of nausea rolls over me. I apply my bubble gum lip balm, then pop a peppermint in my mouth, hoping it will settle my stomach. I try to keep my legs steady and my head held high as I enter the building. His classroom door is propped open, and I'm thankful to see four other students already seated at the back table. *Safety in numbers.* I join them without looking in the direction of Mr. Slate's desk. Avery is the only student I'm acquainted with, so I sit next to her. Shortly after, Mr. Slate pulls up a chair and sits across the table from me.

"Okay, let's get started," he says. "First of all, I just want to say that I'm happy you all showed up. It shows me that you care about improving your grade. It won't be easy, but it's possible if you're willing to put in the work."

And so it begins.

He reviews the last chapter and answers every question that is asked. I remain silent throughout the session, but try my best to pay attention. I really do need to improve my grade, but I'm too intimidated to ask him anything. Luckily, the other students are asking the same questions that I have, so I just follow along . . . or attempt to. The way Avery gushes over Mr. Slate's every word distracts me. Does she not realize how obvious she is? Memories of my own boldness in the back of his Tahoe flash through my mind, immediately humbling me. Can't get more pathetic than that, I suppose.

But wasn't he a little bold, too?

I shove the thought out of my mind and scold myself. *Clearly, he's not that into you, Kaley. I think he's made that pretty damn obvious.*

As if he can read my mind, he breaks my train of thought. "Kaley?"

"Huh?" I look up at him, making eye contact for the first time tonight.

"Do you know the answer?" he asks. It feels like a challenge. "I've heard from everyone but you tonight."

I have no idea which problem we're working on and my cheeks flush with heat. "Um . . . no, I'm not sure."

He drops his pencil on the table and leans back in his chair. "Why are you even here?"

Everyone's eyes swivel in my direction as his stare turns me to stone.

I gape at him. "W-what?"

"Why are you even here?" He folds his arms. "It's one thing to not pay attention in class, but this is my free time, and it's not to be wasted." His words carve into me like a rusty, serrated knife.

A lump builds in my throat, and I push back my chair, bolting out of the classroom. He calls after me, but I charge down the hall, not stopping until I'm safely in the bathroom. I rip a paper towel out of the dispenser and blot my eyes, putting all my strength into stopping the flow of tears. I'm sick of crying. I want to hide. I want to leave the building. I want to go back in time and grab my damn car keys so I can just go home. Actually, if I *could* go back in time, I would never have let him play with my mind, and I sure as hell wouldn't have approached him in the parking lot after the baseball game.

I don't know how long I stay in the cold, desolate bathroom. . . . Minutes? Hours? It feels like years. *Screw it.* I can't stay in here forever. I'll just go get my stuff and get the hell out of here. Maybe someone else can help me with my math—I'll figure something out, but enough is enough. I'm not going to let this jerk have power over my emotions anymore.

I swallow what's left of my pride and step out of the bathroom. When I near the classroom, I'm relieved to see that the session is over and everyone is leaving. Avery is the last to leave—*of course.* Her mock concern as she passes by only fuels the growing anger within me. I watch her stroll down the hall and start to wonder if she's ever thrown herself at him, too. She's always hanging on his desk and is often the last to leave his classroom. *Geez, am I no better than Avery Jenkins?* I shudder at the thought. I slip quietly into the room, grab my stuff off the table, and rush back to the door.

"Kaley, can I talk to you?"

Damn it.

I grudgingly turn around—but only half way—and meet his eyes. "I wouldn't want to get you into trouble by being alone with a student," I snap.

His expression remains impassive. "Shut the door, please. I want to talk to you."

I hesitate before doing what I'm told. My heart pounds against my ribcage, but I'm not going to let him intimidate me anymore. Squaring my shoulders, I stare at him with ice in my veins.

He gestures to the back table, his voice gentle. "Sit down for a minute."

I set my belongings down on a nearby desk and meet him at the table. He waits for me to take a seat, but I refuse, leaning against it and crossing my arms. I remain motionless, staring straight ahead at the door.

"Well?" I say impatiently.

He steps directly in front of me, forcing me to look up at him. "Are you okay?"

I scowl. "What do *you* care? I'm *fine*."

He pulls his hand out of his pocket and carefully places it on my arm. "I'm worried about you."

Whatever bravado I've been holding up vanishes, and I struggle to meet his eyes. "Why? I'm fine, really." His touch burns through my arm, quickly thawing my icy façade.

"I'm sorry if I've been cold to you." His warm copper eyes peer down at me, melting me into the floor. *Why does he have this power over me?*

"No problem," I mumble.

"It *is* a problem. I don't like seeing you upset."

"Why do you care if I'm upset?" I ask, my voice barely audible.

That familiar unreadable emotion crosses his expression as several moments of silence pass between us. He slides his hand down my arm, locking his hold onto my elbow. My pulse beats into my eardrums, but I don't move a muscle. I can't.

"I care about you, Kaley."

I try to swallow over the dryness of my throat. "What do you mean?"

His deep chestnut eyes surge into me, and he gently tugs on my elbow, causing my arm to fall to my side. My breathing halts as he slides his hand around my waist, awakening every inch of my body, and slowly erases the distance between us. My heartbeat is deafening, and I'm sure he can hear it reverberate through the silence. He lifts my chin, and before I can process what's happening, he leans down and presses his warm lips tenderly against mine.

If I could combine every kiss I've ever shared in my entire life, it still wouldn't compare to this one delicate kiss upon my lips.

He pulls his head back, his penetrating eyes burning into mine, questioning, searching. He leans forward again, this time pressing his entire body against me. His invigorating scent wraps around me, pulling me under. A small gasp escapes my throat as his lips take hold of mine, kissing me with an animal-like aggression. His hypnotic mouth is delicious, tasting minty and sweet.

Grabbing my waist, he lifts me onto the table with ease and presses his hips between my legs. I run my hands through his tousled hair, then clutch the back of his neck. His lips are soft, but fearless. He leans me back, cradling me in his arms, so I'm almost parallel to the table. His body feels strong around me, and I wrap my legs around his waist. My body rouses as his commanding lips travel down to my neck, simultaneously shutting down all coherent thoughts. I inhale sharply when he bites at my collarbone, then kisses the dip between them. He trails his mouth back up my neck, and his lips return to mine with new urgency.

"Kaley," he whispers.

Hearing my name sends shivers down my spine, and I kiss him back with a magnitude I've never experienced before. I feel him pull away, but I don't want him to stop. I can't let him stop. I need this. Nothing else matters right now, except his mouth on mine, his body flush against me. I tighten my hold, and he chuckles, his breath tickling my lips.

"The night-shift custodians will be here any minute," he murmurs against my mouth.

He pulls back again, but I clutch onto him tighter.

"Damn it, Kaley," he whispers. But he gives in to my demands, securing his lips over mine once more. This time he teases me with a slow, deep kiss sending electric shockwaves down to the deepest part of my belly. He pulls me forward into an upright position, but remains wedged between my legs.

He finishes with a succulent kiss on my bottom lip. "We really do have to go."

I try to catch my breath as I open my eyes. "Mr. Slate, I—"

He winces, cutting me off. "Elijah."

"Huh?"

"Kaley, my name is Elijah."

I quiver at the reveal of his name.

"Elijah Slate," I whisper, trying it out for the first time.

He rewards me with a gorgeous grin, showing off his perfect teeth, and kisses me again with authority. His hands slide down past my waist, and my blood boils as he slowly caresses my inner thighs. *Holy hell.* I feel like I could pass out. I press my body against his—I can't seem to get close enough. His muscular back feels even more amazing than I imagined, and I explore as much of it as I can, running my hands over every curve of muscle. His breaths become uneven as his hand slides up the base of my neck, grasping underneath my ponytail and pulling it slightly, forcing my head to tilt back as he kisses me deeper. I circle my arms around his hips, pulling him closer.

"Please," I beg in between kisses.

"Please what?" he whispers.

"Please don't stop."

His breath catches, and his hands leave my hair and travel down my back, his masculine fingers clutching my hips. He slides his hands farther down, and his thumbs tease my inner thighs, expanding the ache below me. The sound of keys jingling outside the door interrupts the sensation, and he jerks me off the table faster than I can make sense of. He tosses me my books, and it's all I can do to remain standing as the custodian opens the door.

"Oh, I'm sorry," says the gray-haired man. "Am I interrupting?"

His question is innocent; still, panic shoots through me.

"No, not at all," says Mr. Slate, flashing a confident smile. *How does he do that?* I marvel at how calm he appears after just having his lips on my neck . . . his hands on my thighs. "We just finished a group study session. Perfect timing, actually."

"Okay, great," says the custodian, pushing the door against the wall and into the door jamb.

I pass through the doorway in a daze and turn down the hall. I hear footsteps behind me, but don't look back—I'm too paranoid. When I make it outside, Mr. Slate falls into stride next to me.

"Let me walk you to your car."

"Are you sure?" My voice is shaky.

"Yes, of course. It's dark out."

I walk in stunned silence until I reach my car and lean against it for support.

"I'm really sorry," I say.

"For what?" He seems to still be catching his breath.

"We almost got caught."

He laughs, rubbing the back of his neck. "That's no reason for you to be sorry."

I'm not sure what to say or do now. The parking lot is empty, but it feels unsafe. Like we're being watched.

"I'm sorry I had to pull you up like that. How's your arm? Did I hurt you?"

"No, I'm fine," I assure him. I don't want to tell him that my entire body is on fire, and at the moment, I probably wouldn't even know if he had ripped my arm completely off.

"Okay, good." His eyes dart around the parking lot.

"We should probably go, huh?" I say, sensing his apprehension.

"I don't want us to look suspicious, Kaley, I'm sorry. I don't want to leave you like this, but I'm not going to get either of us in trouble."

I nod. "It's okay, Mr. Sl—Elijah."

His eyes smolder after I say his name. His gaze rests on my lips, and I'm thankful to have my car to steady me. He shoves his hands in his pockets and clenches his jaw. "I really should go." His voice is strained.

I nod and open my car door. He puts his hand on top of the door frame as I climb in.

"Drive safely," he says, peering down at me.

"I will."

After he's sure I'm all the way in, he shuts my door. My hands shake from the adrenaline pumping through my veins, and it takes me three times to get my seatbelt secured. He waits until I start the engine, then waves good-bye as he heads to the employee parking lot. The sound of my breathing fills the interior of my car, and I flip on the radio to drown it out. My legs are wobbly when I press on the gas, and my arms feel like rubber as I grip the steering wheel.

I turn onto the street in a stupor. I can still taste the minty flavor of his lips, reminding me that I'm not in a dream—this is real. *This really happened.* And it was nothing like I imagined it would be . . . nothing compared to the night I used Tommy's body as a vessel to fantasize about him. That fantasy is a small flame compared to the real thing. It's like Elijah doused me with gasoline, igniting my sparks into a carnal explosion. My body still burns from his touch, and I'm not sure if the embers will ever cool.

When I reach my driveway, I don't even know how I got home. I enter the dimly lit foyer and try to sneak past the living room to the stairs.

"Kay?" my dad calls.

Damn.

I edge into the light of the family room, hoping my demeanor doesn't reveal the fact that I just made out with my math teacher.

"What's up?" I say in an octave higher than my normal voice.

"Everything okay?"

I clear my throat and try to lower my voice. "Yeah, of course."

"How'd your study session go?"

Oh, it was pretty much life-changing.

"It was all right," I say.

"Well, keep at it, honey."

If only he knew what he was suggesting.

"Sure thing, Dad." I say, trying to wipe the grin off my face.

I head to the kitchen, not realizing how thirsty I am until now. I fill up a glass of water and gulp down the entire thing in one breath. I repeat this action once more before filling up the glass a third time, taking it with me.

"Where's Mom?" I ask, stopping at the bottom of the stairs.

"She's at her book club," he says, his gaze never leaving the TV.

Sure, keep your book club meetings, but refuse to go to counseling, Mom. Priorities.

I say goodnight and head up the stairs. My legs are a little stronger as I climb, but I still feel a bit like a newborn fawn struggling to walk for the very first time. When I enter my bedroom, I flick on the lamp and toss my stuff onto my desk. I set the glass of water on my nightstand and flop onto my bed. I wish I kept a diary, because boy do I have one for the books. It would put all other diary entries in the free world to shame.

Feeling wired, I bring my pillow to my chest and curl into a ball, wondering what the hell I'm going to do all weekend. It's not like I can call him up, or we can go on a date tomorrow night. I literally have to wait until Monday morning to see him. And then what? What am I supposed to say to him?

I wish we hadn't been interrupted. I wish we would've laid some ground rules, or maybe planned a secret date. Something! I know nothing, except that I have never felt such intensity inside my body before . . . and I want more. I miss his lips already; I miss his powerful body against mine . . . but I'm trapped here all weekend. Sure, I know where he lives, but he doesn't know that I know. Not only do I want to avoid looking like a stalker, but I also want to avoid getting us caught.

I touch my fingers to my lips . . . I can still smell him on me. I lay on my bed for a long time, wishing I could call up Emily and gush over every detail, but I can't. I can't say or do anything. This is going to be a torturously long weekend.

CHAPTER TWELVE

THE WEEKEND GOES BY JUST as painfully slow as I anticipated. I spend all of Saturday writing an English paper, rearranging my closet, and organizing my dresser drawers—anything to keep my mind occupied. My clothes are now color coordinated, and my socks are even alphabetized by hue. On Sunday, I study for math and help my mom clean the house. Like I said—painfully slow.

Tommy calls me Sunday evening, recounting his entire weekend, and sweetly tells me how much he misses me. He keeps me on the phone for two hours, allowing the realization of my indiscretions to finally hit me. The fact that Tommy didn't even cross my mind until the morning after the study session has me shocked and disappointed in myself. But I can't do anything about it just yet. I need to talk to Elijah before making any rash decisions.

Almost immediately after hanging up with Tommy, the phone rings again. It's Emily, asking if I want to drive up to Scottsdale after school on Friday to shop for prom dresses. She's been searching for the perfect dress for weeks, whereas I haven't even thought about it. Whether I like it or not, prom is right around the corner, and I can't procrastinate any longer. Although, in the back of my mind, I'm no longer sure if Tommy and I will still be together by prom—but of course I can't tell *her* that. We discuss the details for Friday, but it's hard to focus on what she's saying. My thoughts wander to Mr. Slate wrapping his sculpted arms around me, kissing me . . . caressing me.

Emily's voice interrupts the heated memory. "You sound

so giddy. I was starting to worry you were gonna be mopey about prom, too."

I wish I could tell her the real reason I'm bubbling with euphoria, but I play it off. "Um, yeah. I mean, no! I'm totally excited." I'm thankful she can't see my ridiculous grin. I know I should be feeling nothing but remorse, but my yearning for Elijah silences my conscience.

I WAKE UP before my alarm goes off and spring out of bed. I hop in the shower, taking extra time to use my favorite scented body wash and shave my legs—twice. I don't want to look like I'm dressing up for him, but I want to look hot, so I keep my outfit subtle, slipping on my white denim skinny jeans and an aqua T-shirt that complements my eyes. I take my time perfecting my makeup and curling my hair.

By the time I notice the clock, I realize I'm out of time. I down some coffee and steal a piece of bacon from my dad's plate while he's talking on the phone. Anticipation creeps into me as I drive to school. What's he going to say to me? Are we going to talk about Friday night? Obviously, I'll have to act natural during class, but I can't ignore what happened. What if he doesn't say anything? Should I ask to meet after school? There is *no* way I can survive another day without knowing where we stand, or what's going to happen next.

If he doesn't address it, then I will, I decide.

My nerves magnify as I make my way into the building, and I fight the urge to grin like a baboon when I walk through the door of his classroom. Refusing to look at his desk, I take my seat.

Avery is at my side before I even set my bag down.

"Are you okay?" she asks.

I look up at her, confused. "Yeah, why?"

"Mr. Slate *totally* humiliated you Friday night," she says, condescension drowning out her attempt at compassion.

Actually, he made me feel like a woman, stupid little girl.

"I'm cool, Avery," I say, pulling out my notebook.

Her golden locks spill over her shoulder as she peers down at me, her voice dripping with synthetic concern. "I felt *so* bad for you."

"I'm sure you did," I say, straight-faced. "Thanks for your concern, but I'm fine. He even apologized."

"He did?" She lingers at my desk, waiting for me to dish out the details. She's like a bumble bee hovering over an open soda can, thirsty for artificial syrup.

"Yeah, so don't worry about it." I give her a hard look, making it clear that our conversation is over, and she hesitates for a moment before heading back to her desk.

I glance over at Elijah's desk as he shuffles through a stack of graded assignments. He clears his throat and tugs on his tie, unbuttoning his collar.

Good. I'm not the only one on edge.

As he explains the graph on the board, my gaze falls to his lips. Those succulent lips were on my neck just three days ago. Watching him write out equations on the board and listening to him give a quick review on logarithms, you'd never guess he just made out with a student less than sixty hours ago. Either he's done this before, or he's just as confident as he portrays.

I hope it's the latter.

He doesn't make eye contact with me once, and I continue to admire his ability to keep his cool. The bell sounds, prompting noisy chatter as everyone gathers up their things and rushes out the door.

Elijah's voice captures me through the ruckus. "Kaley, can you stay back a minute?"

My breath catches in my chest. *This is it.* The moment I've been craving all weekend. I thought I prepared myself, but my body tells me differently as I float to his desk, where he stands waiting. I rake my hand through my hair. Is he going to ask me out? Does he have a plan set in place? Is he going to sneak a passionate kiss? My lips burn at the thought. He waits for the last student to exit before facing me. The swirling butterflies in my stomach remind me we're alone. Again.

"Kaley," he says, dropping his gaze. "I'm sorry . . ."

"For what?"

When he looks back up at me, the pain in his eyes alarms me. "For Friday night. . . . I lost control, and I'm sorry."

"What?" is all I can manage. But his face tells me all I need to know. A lump rises in my throat. "Well, I'm *not* sorry," I blurt out. Maybe he just needs reassurance that I can handle this.

"It never should have happened," he says quietly. "I took advantage of you, Kaley, and it won't happen again—I promise."

Pressure plows into my stomach, ripping the air from my lungs. *No, no, no.* I take a moment to process his words. There are way too many things wrong with those two little sentences. "Look, if you're worried I'm—"

A group of prattling students burst through the door, and he hastily takes his seat, turning his attention to his computer.

"Are we understood, Kaley?" he says in his teacher's voice, loud enough for everyone to hear.

The entire world slows down as I try to grasp the situation. My feet are imbedded into the floor, my entire body immobilized. His eyes remain fixed on his monitor as the classroom fills around me. I finally tear myself away, pushing past clusters of students, and dash out the door.

My pace quickens with each step as I rush down the hallway. I round the corner toward the exit and charge out of the building. The security guard hollers after me, but I stride past him across the parking lot without regard. He shouts again, and when I don't answer, he follows me to my car.

"Hey!" he bellows as I open the door to the Chevelle. "Where do you think you're going?"

"I'm eighteen," I say in a dead voice. I toss my bag in the back and plop down in my seat.

"Excuse me?" he says, haughtily. "I don't care how old you are when you're on *my* grounds. You need to come with me . . . now!"

Why do security guards always seem to have an inferiority complex? His cocky attitude makes me want to ram him with my car. Instead, I slam my door and crank the volume on my stereo. My car sputters to life, and I mash on the gas pedal, praying it doesn't stall. As I peel out of the parking lot, I watch him flail around in my rearview mirror. I'll probably pay for that later, but I don't care.

MY DAD IS just leaving when I pull up the driveway.

"Kay, are you all right?"

"I don't feel well," I say as I brush past him into the house.

"Do you need to see the doctor?"

"No, I just need to lie down."

"Well, call me or your mom if you need anything, okay?"

I don't respond. When I reach my bedroom, I grab my iPod and slide my headphones over my head. I set the volume on full blast and drop to my bed.

I don't cry.

I don't move.

I don't feel.

WHEN THE BATTERY on my iPod dies, I pull myself up and grab my old CD player out of my newly organized closet. I plug my headphones into it, set a random CD to repeat, and

135

collapse back on the bed.

The next thing I know, someone is shaking me, and I fling open my eyes and am greeted by a dark figure. Deep-purple shadows fill my room and the smell of dinner wafts from downstairs. I must've fallen asleep, but I don't feel rested. I slide off my headphones when I recognize his face.

"What time is it?" I ask. "What are you doing here?"

Tommy's voice is gentle. "It's five o'clock."

"AM or PM?"

He laughs quietly. "PM. Are you okay? You weren't at school today, and Emily and I have been trying to call you."

"I think I left my phone in the car, sorry." *Not that I would've answered it.*

"Your dad said you were sick and that I could come up and wake you."

"I'm fine. I left school after first period. I don't know what it was; I just didn't feel well."

He sits next to me, resting his hand on my arm. "How do you feel now?"

Like someone just stabbed me in the chest and left me for dead.

I sit up. "Better," I lie.

"Emily told me about your parents. Is that what's really going on with you?"

"She wasn't supposed to say anything," I say, switching on my lamp. That irritates me a bit. Emily is supposed to have *my* back, not Tommy's. But maybe she's just worried.

"Well I'm glad she did—I've been worried about you, Kay. I couldn't figure out what was up with you lately. You can tell me anything, you know."

Oh, can I? Can I tell you that I think I'm in love with my math teacher, and he's all I think about? Can I tell you that he made me feel like a woman for the first time in my life? Can I tell you that he just tore my heart out, and it hurts far worse than I'd care to admit?

I gaze into the beautiful ice-blue eyes I've known since I was thirteen—eyes that care about me. And even though I'm sensitive to Emily always siding with Tommy, I know she cares about me, too. I'm lucky to have such great friends, especially when I haven't been fun to be around lately.

I pull Tommy in for a kiss and slide onto his lap. With one leg on either side of him, I push him down on the bed, kissing him forcefully. He grabs my hips, pulling me against him. A little voice in my head tries to remind me that it's nothing compared to the make-out session with Elijah, but I push it down. We wrestle around for a while before I break away. Still on top of him, I sit up and smile down at him. I bite my bottom lip, hesitating.

"What's wrong?" he asks, breathless.

"I want you to book that hotel room."

He props himself up on his elbows. "Seriously?"

"Seriously," I reply. I kiss him again with the same aggression, and he grabs my backside eagerly.

"You got it," he says between breaths.

"Kay, dinner!" my dad calls up the stairs.

"Okay!" I holler back.

I climb off Tommy and smooth my hair. He lays there smiling at me.

"Wanna stay for dinner?" I ask.

"Only if I can have you for dessert," he says with a wide grin.

MY PARENTS ENJOY Tommy's company as usual, putting on their perfect little act they've honed for the past—well, eighteen years, apparently. Tommy helps my mom with the dishes, and I suppress an eye roll—parents are so easy to please. Afterward, I walk Tommy out to his truck.

"I'm glad you came over tonight," I tell him.

"Not as glad as I am." He wraps his arms around me,

drawing me in for a kiss.

That stupid little voice in my head tries to grab my attention, but I strangle it, kissing Tommy harder. That infuriating voice has done nothing except get me into trouble, and I refuse to listen to it anymore. I've been an idiot for being so devastated over Elijah—*Mr. Slate.* It's mortifying that it wasn't just a physical thing for me. It's clear that was all it was for him, which is why he just "lost control." I've been so foolish.

Tommy, on the other hand, actually cares about me. Yeah, he's put some pressure on me lately, but is that really his fault? He's the hottest boy in school, yet somehow hasn't slept with the entire student body—clearly, he values intimacy in *some* way. Why would I want to jeopardize what we share? I have to lose my virginity sometime, right? So, why not with Tommy? We have a history together. It makes perfect sense that he'd be my first. It's an ideal situation.

After we wish each other goodnight, I run upstairs to get ready for bed. I rush through each action, humming a random tune to keep my thoughts at bay. As I climb into bed for the night, I slip my headphones back on and turn up the volume.

That pesky little voice can kiss my ass.

CHAPTER THIRTEEN

My big wavy curls bounce in perfection as I march up the pavement in my bright fuchsia summer dress and nude wedges. My favorite perfume permeates my sensory as I wave my wrist over my nose and give my hair a toss. When I reach the entrance of the school, I remain imperturbable as several whistles call after me. I slow my pace for a moment and glance at the cluster of boys, rewarding them with a wink before stepping inside.

With model posture, I strut down the hall and into Mr. Slate's classroom. My books slap against my desk, piercing the silent room. I didn't intend on that, but manage to keep my composure as I take my seat.

"What's up with you, girl?" asks Avery from her desk.

"Wouldn't *you* like to know," I say, my voice cutting. She turns away, and a sly smile crosses my lips. *Yeah, that was bitchy of me, but I'm not in the mood today.*

Elijah—er, Mr. Slate—or *Slate*—whatever the hell he wants to be called—glances my way. This annoys me to the point of having to restrain myself from flipping him off in front of the entire class. My gaze locks onto him as he goes through the new chapter, but he never returns my stare. I ask several questions throughout the morning—forcing him to acknowledge me—and spring out of my seat as soon as the bell releases class.

Avery engages him as I gather up my books. "So Mr. Slate, I hear you're going to be one of the teachers chaperoning the prom."

My stomach flip-flops against my will.

"Yeah, I am," he replies, rubbing the back of his neck.

Seth snickers from the back of the classroom. "How'd you get stuck with that gig, Slate?"

"Well, I'm the newbie around here, so they sort of signed me up without my consent," he says, chuckling.

I hate that he's able to laugh with such ease. I hate that he's just going on with his life without a care in the world.

Avery squeals. "Are you going to dance?"

I roll my eyes so hard it almost hurts. I can practically hear her eyelashes batting, and I want to rip them off her stupid face.

"Uh, no. You do *not* want to see me dance," he replies, laughing again.

Yeah, laugh one more time, asshole, I freaking love it.

I storm out of the classroom and continue on with my life. I flirt with Tommy throughout second period and even high-five Duncan during gym class. At lunch, I keep my hand on Tommy's thigh, and we exchange a few kisses while everyone at the table talks enthusiastically about prom. Emily pulls out a magazine, showing me pictures of dresses she likes and reminds me of our shopping trip on Friday, like I've already forgotten. Deep down, I think she's worried I'll cancel.

At the end of the school day, we meet at our usual spot and hang out for a while. After parting with Emily and Derek, Tommy and I stroll hand-in-hand as he escorts me out to the front of the building. He's late for baseball practice, but we share a long good-bye with our bodies interlocked.

"Get a damn room, you two!" shouts Jeremy, a fellow teammate, slapping Tommy on the back before running off to practice.

"Soon enough," I say to Tommy, flashing a devilish grin

at him. He smiles and quickly draws my mouth to his.

Mr. Slate brushes past us as he heads to the parking lot. "Hey Bradford, can you help me out with the equipment?"

Tommy breaks from my lips, turning to Slate. "You got the new bats?"

"Yep." He stops and faces us, acknowledging only Tommy. "You're going to be late."

I shoot him a frosty glare. "He'll be there in a minute," I snap.

Mr. Slate's eyes flash to mine for a split second before turning away.

Tommy's eyes widen. "Wow, you really *do* want to fail his class, don't you?" he says as soon as Mr. Slate's out of earshot.

"No, but I need to kiss you good-bye, and he rudely interrupted."

He laughs. "He would kick my ass if I talked to him like that. You're lucky you're so cute."

With a nonchalant shrug, I loop my arms around his neck and press my body against his, kissing him with vigor. He wraps his arms around my waist, and I force that infuriating voice further down with each vehement kiss.

When I break away, I plaster a smile on my face. "Have fun at practice."

"I'll call you tonight."

He releases his grip, and I turn around, catching a glimpse of Mr. Slate next to his Tahoe. His eyes are on us, and a pang twinges in my chest. Tommy jogs over to him, and I straighten my posture as I swagger off to my car.

EVERY MORNING, I dress to kill. I continue to ask endless questions throughout first period, unintentionally improving my grade in the process, and Tommy and I are more solid than ever—on the outside at least. My alter ego has taken up

permanent residence, forcing me into autopilot. I keep myself as busy as possible, making sure I always have something to focus on. *No idle time.* It gets me through, and before
I know it, the school week is finally over, and Emily and I
are driving up to Scottsdale in search of the perfect prom
dresses. This is the last weekend to settle on something, so
we are determined to make it happen. To my surprise, I'm
actually looking forward to it—maybe even feeling a little
excited.

"So the limo is set to pick us up from Derek's house,"
Emily says as she coasts up the 101. She talks so fast, I have
to try to keep up. "I'm coming over in the morning and we'll
get ready at your house—is your mom still doing our hair?
Then I'll take you to Derek's. You told your parents that
you're staying the night with me, right? The limo will pick
us up from Derek's and take us to prom. Derek wanted to
pick us up, but I want to hang out as his house, which will
be way more fun. Oh! And we can leave our bags in the limo, and they'll keep them secure while we're at the dance.
Then the driver will pick us up and take us to the hotel," she
exclaims. I'm surprised she isn't out of breath.

"Sounds perfect," I say, trying to match her excitement.
Prom *is* starting to sound fun, but I'm still uneasy about
what's taking place afterward.

We arrive at Kierland Commons in the north end of
town, just after four o'clock. Emily pulls into the upscale
outdoor shopping mall that's buzzing with Barbie-esque
Scottsdale housewives. She parks the car, and after a quick
discussion, we decide to eat after we shop. No girl wants to
try on dresses with a belly full of food, and we want to enjoy
our dinner. We browse a few stores and boutiques before
hitting the jackpot. Emily falls in love with a lacy black
strapless number that looks stunning on her. It has a built-in
corset, and the skirt puffs out playfully, echoing her person-

ality and showing off her long, gorgeous legs. It's *so* her, and I insist she buy it. Still feeling unsatisfied in my own quest, I continue to shuffle through rack after rack and start to feel hopeless . . . until I see it.

Red.

I snatch it off the rack and rush into the dressing room. I slip into the silky satin and admire my reflection in the full-length mirror. It's a beautiful, fire engine red that hugs my body as if it were custom designed for me. It's short, but not too short. It doesn't show as much cleavage as I expected, but the way it embraces my body makes it quite suggestive. It glorifies my tan legs, while the thin spaghetti straps almost make it look strapless—it's *immaculate*.

Emily gasps when I step out of the dressing room.

"What do you think?" I ask, trying to hide my glee. I need her honest opinion.

A small smirk plays at her lips. "I think you might be breaking some school rules in that dress."

"Why?" I turn around in front of the mirror. "It doesn't show anything."

"And yet, it shows *everything*," she says, deadpan.

I tear myself away from my reflection and turn to her. "Tell me the truth."

"You saw my reaction! I had to pick my jaw up off the floor, Kay."

After a final turn in the mirror, I say, "Okay. This is the one."

Emily laughs and shakes her head. "Tommy is going to explode."

We pay for our dresses, then walk to dinner, chatting about the boys, school, and our summer plans. Twinkle lights line the streets of the shopping center, illuminating the walkway as the sun sets against the desert-orange sky. I breathe in the dry air of the balmy evening and exhale. It feels like old times with her tonight, and a flutter of emotions fills my chest. I miss my best friend. And even more, I miss my carefree life. We gab about everything—well, almost everything. A pang in my heart reminds me our friendship still isn't quite what it used to be. . . . I long to tell her about Mr. Slate, but swallow the temptation, causing a small knot to form in the pit of my stomach.

"You found the perfect dress to lose your virginity in, Kay," says Emily, taking a bite of her ravioli.

"Shh!" I glance around the restaurant.

"Chill, no one heard me," she says. "So, are you nervous? Excited?"

"Um, yeah. Both."

Her expression softens. "Are you ready?"

I let out a sigh. "I am. I really am," I say, trying to convince the both of us. "It's time, and Tommy's a great guy. I love him, you know?"

"You guys are great together, Kay. And he really loves you, too. Maybe we'll have a double wedding one day." She laughs.

"I . . ." Speech evades me, and I stare at my salad. I wonder if she would hate me if she knew what I did last Friday.

"I'm *kidding*," she says. "Besides, who else would be my maid of honor?" She waves a hand in my face, breaking my daze. "Wow, you *are* nervous. Don't stress about prom, Kay, you'll be fine. And even if the sex isn't that great, it will get better—I promise."

I squirm in my seat. If I can talk about sex to anyone, it's Emily. She's the closest thing I have to a sister, and she's experienced . . . but I can't bring myself to ask her any questions.

Taking a sip of my iced tea, I look at my best friend, listening as she goes on about the different ways we can do our hair and makeup now that we know what our dresses look like. I nod along, intermittently giving my opinion, but the urge to tell her about Slate is building inside me.

Tell her. She won't tell anyone. Who else do you have to confide in?

"Kay?" Emily's concerned voice pulls me back to her. "Are you okay? You look like you're in pain."

Tell her!

I can't.

"Yeah, I'm good," I say. "Sorry, I just didn't chew enough before I swallowed that last bite. Hurt going down a little." I fake a cough and take a sip of my tea.

Emily's eyes scrutinize me. She doesn't seem to be buying it, but drops it in the end.

THE NEXT DAY is the semi-final game for the high school baseball state championship. Emily picks me up, and we drive to the game early, securing ourselves front row seats. I ignore Slate as he paces up and down the sideline and focus my attention on Tommy. Emily and I cheer for the guys and yell at the umpire every time he makes a bad call—or just a call we don't like. It ends up being a close game. We're up until the last two innings, but end up losing the game by three runs. But the good news is: No more baseball. And no more Mr. Slate disrupting my free time.

Emily and I wait for the boys outside of the locker room, anticipating their sullen moods, determined to cheer them up. The crowd of rowdy students makes it hard to hear much of what Emily is saying, and I have to rise on the tip of my toes to see the locker room door. My stomach drops when Tommy and Derek step out of the locker room . . . with Mr. Slate.

Can a girl get a break around here?

The three of them are carrying huge bags of equipment and are deep in conversation. Tommy's face brightens when our eyes meet, and he trots up to me.

I throw my arms around him. "I'm sorry you lost."

"That's okay," he says. "With you next to me, I feel like a winner." A pain pricks my chest, and he pulls my face to his, giving me a soft kiss. Then he leads me out to the parking lot with Derek, Emily, and Mr. Slate in tow.

Kill me now, please.

Tommy steers me toward the Tahoe, and I feel myself panic. "Where are we going?"

"This is Slate's car," he says.

Yeah, I'm well aware of that.

"We're just dropping off some equipment real quick, then we'll go, okay?"

I try to smile. "No problem."

The boys toss the bags in the back, and I step aside. Mr. Slate and I don't make eye contact—not that I'm looking his way. His unexpected presence nearly shakes the barrier I've built between us, and I have to steal myself for a moment. I slip around the corner and lean against the side of the Tahoe, wrapping my arms around my waist. I can hear Slate thanking Derek and Tommy, and the slaps of their typical bro-handshakes, as I focus on my shoes, wishing they'd hurry. I glance at the shiny rim next to me as memories beg to be let back in. I squeeze my eyes closed, pushing them out.

"Excuse me, Kaley," a silky voice meets my ear.

I jerk my head up and see Mr. Slate standing directly in front of me. He peers down his nose at me, but his expression is soft. I glance to my right and notice the slim space between me and the truck parked next to the Tahoe and quickly straighten up to give him room to pass. He squeezes past me, and I hold my breath, intentionally blocking his captivating scent from filling my airways.

Tommy pokes his head out from around the back. "Coming, babe?"

Exhaling, I take his hand as I hear the driver's door of the Tahoe shut. We follow Derek and Emily out to the student lot in silence.

Don't look back at him, don't look back at him.

My resolve weakens, and I can't resist peering over my shoulder.

He's staring right *at* me. . . .

Damn it.

AFTER A LOVELY dinner with Derek's parents, Tommy takes me home just before midnight. My headphones keep me up late before my brain shuts down, and I finally drift off. Sleep is my new best friend, granting me temporary escape from my life.

THE DOORBELL RIPS me out of a dreamless slumber. Confused, I slide off my headphones and shuffle down the dark stairs, with only the moonlight shining through the windows to lead the way. I peek out the shutters and see a black Tahoe parked outside. I rush to the door and swing it open. Elijah stands before me, still wearing the same athletic pants and shirt he wore after the game tonight.

"What are you doing here?" I ask him.

His eyes are soft. "I wanted to apologize. I'm sorry, Kaley," he says, stepping into the house, "but I can't get you off my mind." I take a step back, but he grabs my arms and pulls me close to him, lowering his lips to mine. Unable to resist, I wrap my arms around his neck, and his mouth moves with urgency as he pushes me back into the living room. The back of my knees hit the edge of the couch cushion, and I fall into a sitting position.

"My parents are home," I whisper, looking up at him.

His eyes twinkle as an alluring grin spreads across his face. He pins me down on the couch, pressing himself on top of me and brushes his mouth against my jaw line. His scent is like a drug, and my body calls out to him.

"Elijah," I murmur, "I thought you said—"

His tongue suddenly invades my mouth, quieting me instantly as he slides his hands underneath my shirt, skimming his fingers up my sides. My body shivers. He pulls his head back and studies my face.

"Did you tell Tommy about us?" he asks.

I try to speak, but can't.

He smirks. "He probably wouldn't like it too much if he knew."

"It was just a one-time thing . . . I thought."

"Yes," he breathes, kissing my lips. "Although this makes two."

I want to ask him about his girlfriend. I bet *she* wouldn't "like it too much" either. *Why do I feel angry all of a sudden?*

"No, she wouldn't like it either," he says, reading my thoughts.

A salacious grin spreads across his face, and his lips return to mine, my body trembling beneath him. He breaks away too soon, and I touch his face, tracing the outline of his jaw.

"I love you," I whisper.

His body stiffens, and I instantly regret my words. Panic grips me as he pulls away.

"No, please," I beg.

Anger grows in his eyes, and his voice is hard. "You said you wouldn't tell anyone."

"I didn't. What are you talking about?"

"I'm sorry, Kaley," he says, his jaw tightening. "But you're a child."

"I'm a *child* to you? Why did you even come here then?" I shout as angry tears burn in the back of my eyes. "Why would you come to my house and *apologize*?" I pound my fists against his solid chest. "Why do you do this to me?" My cry is desperate, and I grasp at his shirt as he breaks away. "No! You have to tell me *why*." I demand.

He steps away from the couch and walks out the front door without looking back. I try to run after him, but my body won't budge.

"No!" I yell after him.

I hear the Tahoe's engine, then tires spinning against the gravel.

"No!" I yell again. *Why won't my body move?*

The engine grows louder, and the room starts to shake, but I'm still stuck to the couch.

"Kay," says a voice.

I clutch the sides of the couch as the shaking becomes violent.

"Kay," the voice says again.

I fling open my eyes and squint at the early morning light trickling in through my bedroom window. My mom is leaning over me, her face struck with concern. I'm gripping the sides of my mattress, and it takes me a moment to realize it was only a dream.

"Kay, are you all right? I heard you screaming. Did you have a nightmare, sweetie?"

"Yeah, I guess," I croak.

Her face relaxes. "Do you want to talk about it?"

"No . . . I don't remember it," I lie.

"Well that's good." She's quiet for a moment. "Do you want to go back to sleep, or get up?"

I peer at the clock and groan. It's too early for a Sunday morning, but I don't want to stay in my bed. Even my beloved sleep has betrayed me. I can't even trust my own subconscious anymore.

"I'll get up," I tell her. I need to stay awake.

She brushes away a few strands of hair that are stuck to

my moist face. My entire body is damp.

"Okay. I'll start breakfast then."

"And the coffee," I say.

"You got it." She exits my room and goes downstairs.

I relax into the mattress. The dream felt so real. . . . I can still feel him, even smell him. Impending emptiness begins to engulf me, and I try to push it away, but the hollowness slowly fills me with desolation . . . building, expanding, un-relenting until the pain in my chest floods open.

No!

I will *not* let it win. I climb out of bed, turn on the radio, and get ready for the day.

CHAPTER FOURTEEN

THE DISTRACTION OF MUSIC IS wearing off. My iPod has been on shuffle for two weeks straight, and I can only take so much of the same compilations. Even the random songs on the radio no longer offer any solace. I kill the Chevelle's engine, and the stillness almost destroys me.

Silence is cruelty in my world.

My efforts of studying, staying up late, and drowning myself in music are becoming futile. No matter how hard I try to divert my thoughts, I'm hanging on by a thread.

My door swings open, nearly causing me to fall out of my car. Tommy's smiling face beams down at me.

"Hey, babe," he says, taking in my appearance. "Damn, you look hot."

"I do?" I ask, surprised.

I didn't put much effort into my appearance this morning. I'm wearing my black cropped yoga pants with a black razorback tank top and neon-pink sneakers. My hair is pulled back into a high ponytail.

He smirks. "Everybody loves yoga pants, come on."

I grab my bag and step out of the Chevelle. Tommy slips his hand over mine and leads me into the building.

"I'll walk you to class," he says, with a bounce in his step.

"Really? That's sweet." I wonder how long the chivalry will last after prom night. Is he just trying to seal the deal? Or does he truly love me? More importantly, do I love him? *Of course I do*, I demand before the nagging voice has a chance to retort.

We stop just outside Mr. Slate's classroom, and I fix my eyes on Tommy. I watch his lips move as he chats away about something, but I don't hear a word. I have to accept this. . . . I have to accept the fact that my moment with Mr. Slate was just that: a moment. A *mistake*. He simply lost control, nothing more. We both did.

Maybe I've been confusing my *own* feelings with lust. I've never really experienced lust before—maybe I just convinced myself that my sexual desires were actual feelings for him. Maybe I didn't know how to separate the two. I just need to refocus. Tommy's not only one of my best friends, but he and I make sense. *Way* more sense. We don't have to hide; it isn't complicated.

But what if *Tommy* is just feeling lust? What if *he's* confusing *his* libido for love? His lips suddenly seize mine, cutting off my thoughts. His hands slide down past my waist, squeezing his favorite part of the yoga pants.

"Tommy!" I squeal, giggling. "People can see you."

He laughs. "So? They're all jealous." He kisses me again, then heads to class.

And there it is.

That faint whisper, suggesting I'm just something to be conquered—that I still have yet to find real love. I shove it down and turn toward the door, running smack into Mr. Slate as he tries to enter the classroom. I bounce off his solid shoulder and step back, catching my balance.

"Sorry," we say in unison.

Did he see Tommy grabbing me?

"You okay?" he asks.

I give a slight nod and attempt to keep my expression neutral. His, of course, is impenetrable. So maddening.

Let it go, Kaley . . . let him go.

He steps aside, letting me walk in ahead of him. When I pass by, I catch his glorious scent, and a pang of longing threatens to shake me. I take my seat just as the bell rings, and he begins class before I even have my book open. I continue to focus on him and ask questions throughout the period, but not with the same aggression as before. My hardened shell is cracking.

WHEN CLASS IS over, I sling my bag onto my shoulder in one slow movement. Even my actions are less antagonistic today. Avery leans on Mr. Slate's desk, asking him a question about the assigned homework, and my gaze shifts to his face. He's chewing the tip of his pen, staring off into the distance . . . but I soon realize that distance is my desk.

"Mr. Slate?" Avery repeats herself, speaking louder this time. Her perky voice jerks him out of his trance, and we share brief eye contact before he acknowledges her. I trudge down the aisle, and our eyes meet one more time before I step out of his classroom.

Why does he have to do that to me? I'm trying so hard to move on and let him go. I almost want to go back in and yell at him. Instead, I plod over to my locker to exchange my books. As I'm grabbing my English textbook, a pair of hands slip around my waist, and a hard body presses against me. Little wavelets of electricity flow down my spine as my mind is still fixated on Mr. Slate. I feel a soft nibble on my neck and imagine it's him.

I close my eyes and lean into the kiss. "Mmm . . ."

Tommy then makes his way to my lips, snapping me out of it. "I'm dreaming about you like every freaking night," he murmurs in a lustful tone.

"You are?" I don't know what else to say. I can't exactly tell him who's invading *my* dreams. I wish I could dream about my actual boyfriend—it would make my life so much easier.

Tommy is like static cling throughout second period and

even walks me to my next class, which is in the opposite direction of his. He continues to walk me to each class, meet me at my car every morning, and grip my hand all week like a monkey fearful of losing his banana. It's obvious he's excited about prom and where our relationship is finally going, and I do my best to match his enthusiasm.

My contact with Mr. Slate stays at a minimum the rest of the week, which makes things a little easier. Emily is eager for Saturday and her spirit is infectious. I feel myself go in and out of several emotions: anticipation, enthusiasm, nervousness, and exhilaration. It's like I'm on a bipolar merry-go-round, unsure where to get off.

IT'S FRIDAY NIGHT. The Big Day is only hours away. Tommy is over at my house while we watch a movie—and when I say watch a movie, I mean make out on the couch, obviously. My parents are out on a *date*—no weirdness there or anything. But at least they're making an effort. Tommy, of course, is taking full advantage of the lack of parental control. We take a few breaks to talk about prom, but for the most part, he's like a piranha in heat.

The TV screen has been blank for a while now. I don't even know when the movie ended.

"My parents will be home any minute," I say, trying to break away. Hard to do with an extra seventy pounds on top of you.

He sighs. "All right. I should get going anyway." He lifts himself off me and pulls me to my feet.

"I can't wait for tomorrow night, babe," he says, standing up and stretching. "A place *all* to ourselves. No interruptions." He gathers me into a big bear hug, momentarily lifting me off the ground, squeezing a laugh out of me.

"Yeah, me too," I say, muffled in his neck.

I follow him out to his truck, and he turns to me before

climbing into the cab. "Are you really ready for tomorrow, Kay? I want to be sure." His imploring eyes peer back at me.

"Yes," I promise. "More than ready." I reach up and kiss him with assurance.

He smiles, his bright eyes skimming my body. "You are so damn sexy, Kaley. You have no idea how happy you make me." He squeezes my hip, then hops into his truck. "See you tomorrow for the best night of our lives," he says before shutting his door.

After his truck disappears down the road, I bolt upstairs into the bathroom and rip off all my clothes. I turn on the shower, rotating the faucet to the colder side as I brush my teeth. My lips are raw. I shove my iPod into the sound dock and scroll down to an album I recently ordered and set it on repeat—apparently I'm in the mood to torture myself. I don't know what I'm anticipating as Def Leppard flows through the speakers, but in some hopeful way, I'm determined to transfer my feelings for Mr. Slate over to Tommy. He is the *right* guy for me, and I'm desperate to have that same feeling toward him as I do for Mr. Slate.

I step into the cool shower and let the icy water run down my back, goose bumps springing up over every inch of my body as I listen to the music. The songs aren't too bad actually, but of course all I can think about is Mr. Slate. I wonder which tracks are his favorites and imagine him driving in his Tahoe listening to this album.

I lower myself onto the floor of the bathtub as the arctic stream pelts my body. A new song comes on, and it catches me—it's as if the words were written about him. . . . I close my eyes, recalling Mr. Slate at the study session—his body over mine with that raw hunger in his eyes and how he whispered my name. I haven't allowed myself to think about that night for weeks, but I finally let my mind go there as the music echoes through the bathroom. Fire burns inside me despite the frigid water, and I force myself to picture Tommy's face. I imagine Tommy holding me and kissing me at the study session instead of Mr. Slate . . . I imagine us in a hotel room. Pain throbs in my veins as I try desperately to hold on to the sensation, but it slowly dissipates, and I give up. The water turns unbearably cold, forcing me to open my eyes and stand up. *So much for that.* Feeling dizzy, I throw the faucet onto hot, nearly scorching myself, and rush to wash my hair and body. Just as I turn off the shower, a knock on the door startles me.

"Just letting you know we're home," my mom shouts through the door.

"Okay," I holler back. I turn off my iPod and wrap myself in a towel and head back to my bedroom.

Slipping into my pajamas, I stare at my prom dress hanging on my closet door and try to will myself to feel something. *Anything.* The harsh reality is that Mr. Slate doesn't want me. Clearly, he's attracted to me, or at least *was* for a moment, but that's the extent of it. He doesn't want an eighteen-year-old senior in high school—he just got caught up in the moment. He's a man. A typical, red-blooded man. No different than Tommy, or any other boy I know. Hot coals of frustration burn inside me, quickly sparking into small flames.

I've been holding this man on a pedestal.

Here I am listening to an album just because I know he likes the band. What am I *doing*? Why do I think he's so sophisticated and distinguished? Because he's older? Because he has a career and fancy clothes? *Please.* You could put Tommy in designer outfits, give him a briefcase, and the dude would still want to bang me in an elevator—he'd probably even give the security camera a thumbs-up while doing so. Mr. Slate made out with a student in his *classroom*—how's that any different? Underneath the designer suits is just another boy who can't control himself. The small flames of fury burst into a blazing wildfire.

That's it.

I'll be damned if I let him ruin my senior prom. This is *my* time. I can't let some stupid schoolgirl crush destroy my life. Prom—and losing your virginity—is like a rite of passage. And I'm sure his attraction for me never stopped *him* from going out on dates, or pounding the sheets with The Blonde every night. I bet he stopped bringing her around so she wouldn't mess up his game. After the way he handled *our* situation, I have no doubt he has dozens of beautiful women at his disposal. There's no way he'd ever put his life on hold for me. So why am I letting *him* stop me from living *my* life?

I'm going through with it tomorrow night. I love Tommy. He's fun, sweet, and gorgeous—I bet I would've slept with him already if I hadn't let this selfish infatuation get in my way. I know I can find pleasure with him if I just block this stupid man from my mind. I'm going to have the time of my life with my friends tomorrow. We're going to laugh, party, and make it unforgettable. This is going to be one of the best nights of my life—I will make sure of it.

CHAPTER FIFTEEN

TODAY IS THE LAST DAY I will see myself as a virgin. Staring into the mirror at my reflection, I examine every inch of my face. *Will I look any different after tonight?* Of course not. But I can't help wondering if I'll be able to notice a change in me. Red catches my periphery, and I turn to my closet door. Running my fingers over the silky fabric, I feel a grin stretch across my face. My beautiful prom dress stares back at me, full of hope, full of promise. I let out a deep sigh. It's going to be a perfect day . . . and an unforgettable night.

The coffee aroma calls me out of my introspection, and I obey. I wander out of my bedroom and glide down the stairs. My mind feels freer this morning. Peaceful. When I reach the bottom of the stairway, I halt. My dad sits slumped over in his favorite recliner, staring out the window, cupping his coffee mug. He looks like he belongs in some sort of dystopian Folger's commercial. Something about his behavior, and the stillness of the house, sets off my internal alarms.

"Dad?"

He jerks out of his haze and turns to me, revealing a reddened face.

"Hi, kiddo," he says, cracking a strained smile.

Kiddo?

"What's going on? Where's Mom?"

He turns away from me, focusing out the window again. "She's at Tammy's."

Tammy is my mom's best friend, and her boss. She must be grabbing some extra hair supplies for Emily and me. But what's up with my dad?

When I realize he's not going to divulge any further, I ask, "Why?"

He takes a moment before speaking, and I realize he's trying to hold his composure. He sets his mug down and rubs his face before resting his elbows on his knees. He folds his hands beneath his chin, his gaze never leaving the window.

"We're separating, Kaley."

It takes me several seconds to process his words before they slowly seep into my gut, wrenching my insides.

"What?" I whisper.

My parents' fighting has been intense, sure, but this can't be happening. The house has been quiet the past few nights. It's too sudden; where was the warning? I mean, there are way more steps to take before a separation, right? Like, counseling and dates and—

"Wait," I say. "You went on a *date* last night. You seemed fine—you weren't even fighting. You seemed *good*!" My voice rises to a pitch I don't recognize.

"Kaley," he says with patience. "We didn't fight last night, you're right. We had a calm discussion over dinner and stayed up late talking over everything. It was a rational, peaceful conversation. She's just . . . done."

"*She's* done?" I say, my voice cracking. "And what about you, Dad? Are *you* done?" A sharp ache in my hand startles me, and I realize I'm gripping the banister with all my strength. I release my hold and shake it out just as he rises from his chair. He's by my side in three long strides, wrapping his arms around me.

"Yes, I am, Kay. I'm sorry." A pain in my chest swells, and I break away.

"I can't cry right now," I say, stepping back. "I'm sorry, but this is an important day for me."

Realization crosses his face. "Oh, Kay, it's your prom to-day."

"Yup."

"I'm so sorry."

"Don't worry about it," I say, repelled by his pity. Slipping by him, I rush into the kitchen and pour myself a large cup of coffee in my favorite mug. It has a picture of my parents and me at the state fair several years ago. They look so happy in the photo. How long have they been living this charade? Tears spring up, and I frantically wipe them away. *No. This is* my *night.* I can cry about it tomorrow, I just need this *one* night. My dad enters the kitchen as I'm pulling a carton of hazelnut-flavored cream out of the fridge.

"Is Mom coming back soon?" I ask over my shoulder. "I need to let Emily know what time to be here."

He leans against the counter. "I just told you she left. . . . Are you okay?"

I turn to him, confused. I guess it was a stupid question. "Yeah, I just . . . I mean . . . well, she was supposed to do our hair."

"Oh," he says, grimacing. "I didn't realize. She didn't say anything about it. But she probably just forgot; I'll call her." As soon as he picks up the phone, I snatch it out of his hand and slam it back down.

"Don't," I warn.

"It's fine, Kay. I'm sure she wants a picture of you and Tommy and all that. She'll be upset if she misses this."

"*She'll* be upset?"

"Kaley." He pauses. "Don't let problems between me and your mother ruin your day."

A sharp laugh escapes me. Like their problems aren't my problems—are my parents for real?

"I'll even leave the house," he continues, "and let you girls have your day."

"No, Dad," I say, exhausted. "Just *please* . . . leave it alone. It's no big deal."

The kitchen falls silent, with just the lonely sound of my spoon scraping the edges of my coffee mug as I stir in the cream. I watch the dark liquid slowly transform into a light, warm caramel, causing the image of Elijah's eyes to flash in my mind. . . . *Mr. Slate, not Elijah,* I remind myself.

My dad's brittle voice breaks through the uninvited image. "Are you sure you don't want me to call her?"

With my gaze transfixed on the steaming liquid, I give a sharp nod. "I'm sure," I say, trying to sound convincing.

"Okay," he says, giving up and switching topics. "I'm going to a poker game tonight at Bob's house. What time will you be home?"

I let out a humorless laugh. I don't understand how he can just separate from his wife and then go play poker, but that's just me.

"I won't be," I say. "I'm staying the night at Emily's. I'll be home sometime tomorrow."

"All right. Well, have fun. Here's some cash for tonight." He drops a wad on the counter.

"Thank you," I say quietly.

"You're welcome. Don't let this put a damper on your night, Kay," he says, patting my shoulder. The small gesture makes my next breath rattle from my chest. "Please, have fun."

I swallow down the urge to cry. "I will," I assure him as he leaves the room.

I can't believe she walked out on us—on *me*. My own mother. Just like that. Without warning. She didn't even have the decency to write me a damn note. And of all days. Was she really that unhappy? Is my dad really that bad? Today, most parents will annoy their kids by taking too many photos and gushing over them, while mine are too wrapped up in their own issues to even *remember* my prom. I wash down my dejection with a sip of coffee, determined not to break. I'll be damned if I let my parents ruin my night.

It's time to take action.

I send Emily a text, making up a story about my mom having the flu and that we're on our own in the hair department. She's disappointed, but understands. I'm not trying to hide another facet of my life from her; I just can't tell her the truth today—she'll want to talk about it, and I refuse to ruin our special day. She says she'll pick me up in a couple of hours, and I use the time to get ready. Nothing is going to stop me. My problems will still be here when I get back, so why not enjoy tonight?

The stereo blares on full volume as I take a lengthy shower, the steam calming my lungs, the hot water relaxing my muscles. The fast beat of the music echoes against the bathroom walls, quickly pushing out the negativity in my head. I take extra care in prepping myself—lathering myself with my favorite body wash and shaving three times, even using an expensive hair conditioner on my legs to make them extra soft.

By the time I'm packing my bag, energy courses through my veins. Okay, and a little anxiety. But the good kind . . . I think. I sift through my drawers and fish out a pair of bright pink shorts—that are *super* short—and a thin white tank top. Cute *and* comfy. I don't want to sport my raggedy pajamas the first time I stay the night with a guy, but I'm not exactly up for sleeping in pasties and a G-string either—a girl's got to be comfortable. I pack up my cutest undergarments, the essential toiletries, and a pack of condoms. Emily was brave enough to buy them for me last week, although she assured me Tommy would be well-prepared. My pulse quickens as the intimidating box stares back at me, and I'm reminded to take my birth control pill.

When I turned eighteen, I was able to get a prescription without my parents' consent. After Tommy and I became exclusive, I wanted to be prepared. Much to my humiliation, I didn't think about it showing up on my parents' insurance statement. Thankfully, it was my mom who saw it and promised not to tell my dad; however, that didn't stop her from giving me "the talk." A little late at my age, but she meant well.

A pang swells in my heart as I recall her uneasy face while she gave me that awkward, yet important, talk. She's always been able to find the perfect balance between mother and friend—which is why it's such a blow that she forgot about my prom. It makes me realize just how miserable she's been. The realization weighs heavily on my chest, but I force it aside and zip up my bags. Emily's horn sounds from the driveway, erupting a thrill in my belly. *Can't think about my parents now. Nothing but the present moment from here on out.* I swing my overnight bag over one shoulder, then my other bag filled with hair supplies over my other shoulder, and grab my garment bag. I yell good-bye to my dad and shuffle out the door, trying not to topple over.

This is it.

HIDDEN AWAY IN Emily's bedroom, I set up a mock hair salon and take charge. My mom may be the talented professional in the family, but I'm not so bad myself. Taking my time, I give both of us my best rendition of what I like to call "cat-walk locks." I despise prom updos and vehemently talk Emily out of one.

"Trust me," I say. "There's a reason you never see models on the runway like that. Guy's love long, flowing hair. It's a *fact*."

After about three hours, we're admiring ourselves in the mirror.

"We're knock-outs," says Emily, her eyes sparkling.

And she's right. Our hair turned out amazing, if I do say so myself, with long wavy curls and volume to die for. Emily played up her lips in a vixen-red, while I gave myself an intense smoky eye and natural, kissable lip—my signature look. It always baffles me when girls feel the need to change their appearance to the point of making themselves unrecognizable for prom. I'm a firm believer in going as your sexy self, just intensified. It's way hotter. And in *these* dresses? Please. We know we look incredible.

Emily's reflection stares back at me through the glass. "Ready to go?"

Her simple question almost knocks the air out of my lungs. Suddenly, I'm petrified.

"I need a shot," I blurt out.

Her eyes widen in the mirror, then she turns to me. "A shot? Like a *shot* shot?"

"I think so. I mean, I'm not asking for immunizations," I say with a nervous giggle.

She purses her lips together. "Well, I still have to drive. We'll take shots at Derek's."

Pushing down my parents' separation feels like a rock in the pit of my stomach, and now I'm facing sex for the first time in a matter of hours. I need a shot of alcohol.

"Can I have one now?" I plead. "I need to take the edge off, Ems."

She's contemplative as she regards me. "Okay," she says finally, "but *promise* me we can take one together at Derek's, too. I never get to drink with you!"

"I promise," I say, laughing at her poutiness. And I mean it. Suddenly, I'm ready to drink the night away.

A giant grin blooms on her face. "Yay!" she says, squealing and jumping up and down. "Okay, let's go," she says, hustling me down the hallway. "Mom! Go get the camera, we're ready," she hollers as we pass the living room.

Mrs. Kirkwood gasps. "Oh! You girls are breathtaking! Okay, I'll be right back," she says scurrying down the hall.

As soon as she's out of sight, Emily whispers "Quick!" and leads me into the kitchen. She jumps up on the counter, resembling some kind of stork in heels, and snatches a bottle of vodka out of the cabinet. She's all business as she pours me a drink. "Hurry and take it; we have *no* time."

I down the shot and scrunch my face. She has the liquor bottle and shot glass back in the cabinet before I even open my eyes. Just then, Mrs. Kirkwood rounds the corner, and I do my best to straighten my face. After a few fun poses in front of the camera, and reassuring her we'll get copies of the photos we take at Derek's, we grab our bags and rush out the door.

My body loosens as the alcohol makes its way down my limbs. Emily cranks up the stereo in her car, and we sing along, constantly checking out our stunning reflections in the mirrors. When Derek's house comes into view, my adrenaline accelerates to the point of nausea.

"I'm ready for another shot," I announce as we come to a stop.

She giggles. "You got it."

CHAPTER SIXTEEN

A BEAMING MRS. LARSON OPENS the front door as we step up the walkway. "Oh my goodness! You ladies are drop-dead gorgeous!"

Tommy and Derek are descending the stairs when we enter the foyer, looking exceptionally handsome in their tuxes, and I laugh at the backwardness of it all—aren't the girls supposed to walk down the stairs with the boys admiring them? In the boys' defense, they wanted to pick us up, but Emily insisted. There's nothing like the breezy atmosphere of the Larson house. And tonight, I'm extra appreciative.

"Damn!" Derek howls, swooping up Emily and spinning her around.

Tommy approaches me, his eyes wide, and he fumbles for words. "Wow, Kay . . . wow."

I can't help but grin. "Do you like my dress?"

After a long pause, he drags his gaze from my dress and settles on my eyes. "You have no idea. You're a goddess, babe." He kisses me on the cheek, and I flush.

Derek's parents never hover, so we're left alone in the great room with a plethora of hors d'oeuvres. I scan the table of gourmet cheeses, sandwiches, sushi, and delicate little chocolates, and realize I haven't eaten today. My nerves have diminished any sort of appetite, but I grab a fancy-looking cheese on the end of a toothpick and pop it into my mouth, knowing I need something more than just coffee and booze in my stomach. After a short while, Derek whips out a small squatty bottle of alcohol and pours three shots. His parents often turn a blind eye, but they would never condone us drinking in front of them, so we need to be discrete.

"Do you have another shot glass?" asks Emily. "Kay wants one, too."

Derek turns his eyes to me, pressing his lips together. "You don't drink."

His fatherly tone strikes a nerve, and an unexpected anger flares up inside me. "Yeah, well, things change." I grab a shot glass and toss the liquid down my throat.

Emily gasps. "Hey! That was mine!"

My eyes latch onto Derek's, and my voice is hard. "Lighten up, buddy. This is supposed to be one of the best nights of our lives. Besides," I say, giving a careless shrug. "I've drank before."

His eyes drill into me, and I know what he's thinking—that I've only consumed alcohol once in my life, and it was a disaster. But who does he think he is? He's still punishing me for the night he saw me in the back of Slate's Tahoe, and it's about time he lets it go.

Tommy takes his shot and slips his hand around my waist. "Just don't get sick this time, babe. That's expensive tequila." He gives me a playful smirk.

Emily pours herself a shot, then another round for everybody. We nibble on some snacks, and eventually, Derek eases up. Before long, everyone is laughing and having a great time. I force a sushi roll in my mouth, knowing I need the food to counteract the alcohol. Tommy may have been joking, but he's right. Getting sick tonight is the last thing I need.

After a while, I excuse myself to the restroom. The floor feels like a moving sidewalk as I make my way down the hall. Closing the bathroom door behind me, I stare at myself in the large mirror above the double sinks. Butterflies twirl around inside my stomach, and I press my hands against the cool marble counter and release a deep breath.

"Don't be scared," I whisper to my reflection. "It's normal to be nervous."

But nothing about this day is normal. My mom walking out on me isn't normal. The alcohol coursing through my blood stream isn't normal.

I don't even remember normal.

Unsure of how long I've been in here, I run my hands underneath the faucet, lathering them with a delicate rose-scented soap. I take a deep breath in. This is a monumental occasion, and it's meant to be enjoyed. The third shot hits me as I make my way back down the hall, and my edginess slowly evaporates. Tommy greets me with his boy-next-door grin—it has me noting how heartbreakingly handsome he is, and I greet him with a kiss. He encircles his arm around my waist, and I snatch the tequila, pouring myself another shot.

"Kay," warns Emily. "We haven't eaten much today, be careful."

"I just want one more," I say, tossing it back just as Derek's parents enter the room. Emily grabs the bottle and slides it behind the couch—I swear, my best friend is some sort of alcohol ninja.

Mr. and Mrs. Larson gather us in the backyard near the waterfall that cascades over a rocky grotto into their enormous lagoon-style pool. A kaleidoscope of colors burst from the flowering bushes, providing the perfect backdrop for a photo shoot. The outdoor fireplace is blazing like the bright orange twilight skyline. Mrs. Larson directs us while she snaps what seems like a thousand pictures. Some traditional, some fun, and several goofy. Before long, we're all shuffling into the limo, and it feels like the old gang again as we fool around, laughing with each other as we reminisce. Tommy's hand is glued to my thigh, but my anxiety is long gone, and I lean in to kiss him. His hand slides higher, and I giggle.

"Hey now," teases Emily. "At least wait till you're in your room."

I pull back and gaze at him for a moment. "Your eyes are *so* blue," I say in awe. "They're *really* beautiful."

Tommy lets out a boisterous laugh. "Okay, you *are* drunk."

"No I'm not! They're beautiful." I grab his face, squishing his cheeks and turn him toward Emily and Derek. "Aren't his eyes beautiful?" The three of them laugh, but I don't know what's so funny. "I'm serious. They remind me of the water in Bora, Bora."

"When did you go to Tahiti, Kay?" says Emily.

"Hey, I've seen pictures!"

They all laugh again, and the sound fills my heart. This is my old life. The life I miss. The four of us goofing around without a care in the world. This is all I want, and I try to savor the moment.

The limo comes to a stop, and I peer out the window.

"We're here already? The drive felt like ten minutes."

"Because it was," says Derek.

I forgot the venue was so close. Okay, so maybe I did have one too many shots . . . but something in me wants one more. After everyone files out, I swing my legs out the door. Tommy holds out his hand, but I catch Emily's eye and giggle, then slowly fall back on the seat.

"Kaley!" Emily says, laughing. She pushes Tommy aside and pokes her head into the limo and leans over me. "You're about to have a major wardrobe malfunction. Get up!" She pulls me out of the limo, both of us doubled up in laughter.

Tommy rushes to my side. "Are you sure you're okay?"

I grab hold of his arm, grateful as it steadies me. "Never better," I say, a bit too loud. I note his concerned expression and lower my voice. "Really, I'm fine," I assure him. "Just feeling happy and relaxed."

He smirks. "All right . . . come on, sexy, let's go inside."

Gas lanterns flicker, moving shadows against the rock walls as we approach the stone rotunda of the Villa Siena, where all the prom dates are shuffling inside. After handing a woman our tickets, Tommy leads me down the dimly lit hallway, adorned with wall-mounted candelabras, and I clutch his arm for balance. A tall, marble archway provides a dramatic entrance into the main ballroom. Tommy stops abruptly, and I almost trip.

"Slate! What's up man?"

"Hey, Bradford," replies Mr. Slate, shaking his hand in the way that only guys know how to do. His simple black slacks and navy-blue dress shirt are tailored to perfection as always.

"Hey, Professor McHottie, looking sharp!" I say, giving him a theatrical thumbs-up.

Emily bursts into laughter behind me and a flash of uneasiness crosses his features, but he remains poised.

"Kaley!" says Emily, attempting to chastise through her laughter. "Oh, my gosh," she says, trying to gather herself, "I'm so sorry, Mr. Slate—it's just an inside joke kind of thing."

"Yeah, I think he can crack that code," says Derek, deadpan. He slides past me, engaging Mr. Slate in a bromance handshake. A new song blares from inside the ballroom, and I squeal in delight.

"I *love* this song, come on!" I say to Emily, pulling her through the entry before anyone has a chance to stop us. I shove my way through the crowd, leading her to the center of the dance floor.

"I love Drunk Kaley!" Emily shouts, twirling me around.

We laugh, and suddenly I'm without a care in the world. Just fully content, moving to the beat with my best friend as everything else fades into the background. The crowd tightens around us, and we sway our hips to the music, raising our hands, my inhibitions melting away. Emily beams at me, and I grin back at her, the thumping base pulsating through me.

After several more upbeat songs, a disappointing slow song interrupts the flow, forcing us to stop. Just as we turn to leave the dance floor, someone grabs my waist, and I shriek. I whip around to Tommy's smiling face and giggle. He pulls me close, and I circle my arms around his neck as we sway to the music.

A golden hue emanates from the circular chandeliers hanging above our heads, casting a warm glow on Tommy's face.

"You are such a lightweight," he teases, pressing his body against mine. He leans down to whisper in my ear, and I catch Mr. Slate's eye over Tommy's shoulder. He's on the other side of the room, leaning against the wall . . . staring at us.

"Kay?" says Tommy, pulling back. "Did you hear what I said?"

"Huh?"

"I said I love you, Kaley."

His ardent blue eyes peer down at me, and I push a smile to my face. "I love you, too," I say in a rush. "Sorry, it's just loud in here." The empty pit in my stomach nudges through the numbness of the alcohol.

"I need to use the restroom," I say, weaving out of his grip.

"Are you okay?"

"Yeah, totally." My smile is strained. "I'll be right back."

He gives me a quick kiss. "Okay, I'll be over there." He nods to his buddies around the refreshment table.

As soon as I turn away, my smile drops. I slip through the crowd, keeping a focused stare on Mr. Slate. He's still leaning against the wall with his hands comfortably in his pockets, no longer looking my way. With my shoulders back, I step in front of him, sliding a hand on my hip.

"What the hell was that about?" I shout through the blaring music.

"Kaley," he says, glancing around the ballroom. "What are you doing?" His voice is firm, but quiet.

"What am *I* doing?" I spit out. "I'm dancing with my boyfriend at prom, what are *you* doing?"

He lifts a shoulder. "I'm chaperoning."

"Is that all?" I ask.

"I have no idea what you're talking about," he says, peering down his nose at me.

I step closer, meeting him squarely in the eye. "Really? Because it looks like you're enjoying my dress, *Mr. Slate.*"

Anger flashes through his eyes as he steps forward, away from the wall. "Kaley, stop," he warns. He folds his arms and scans the room over my head. "Just walk away."

I take a step back. "I've been trying to walk away."

His features soften, and he meets my eyes. "I said I was sorry."

I let out a sharp laugh. "For the love of God, just leave me the hell alone—*please.*" I turn on my heel and catch Derek's judgmental stare over Emily's shoulder as they dance.

Perfect.

I storm off to the ladies room and lock myself in the second-to-last stall. Pressing my hands against the door, I lower my head and fill my lungs with air. *Shake it off.*

Snickers from the stall next to me grab my attention, and I straighten up. I hear "Shh," and I flush the toilet to appear normal before unlocking the door. Just as I step out, Avery and a few of her sycophants tumble out of the large stall. My eyes lock onto Avery's lumpy velvet satchel, and she giggles, noticing my gaze.

"You wanna drink?" she asks.

The alcohol gods must be smiling down on me.

"Hell yes," I say, grinning. She pulls me into the stall, locking out her cluster of cronies, and pulls out a small bottle of red liquid.

"What the hell is that?" I ask.

"It's cinnamon, you'll love it," she says, handing me the bottle. "And the best part—no one will smell alcohol on your breath."

I take a whiff of the potent liquor before taking a swig. It tastes like liquid cinnamon candy, and I hesitate before handing it back to her.

"Can I have one more?" I ask.

She smirks, then nods. I take two more sips and give it back. She tucks it back into her sack and exits the stall without a good-bye.

Well, that was odd.

Hoping I didn't just get roofied, I step out of the stall and stop at the mirror to freshen up before heading back out to the dance floor.

I ignore Derek's hard stare as I pass him and make my way through the crowd to where Tommy is standing around the snack table with his buddies, devouring a plate of food. Meanwhile, their dates sip on diet sodas and look as if they haven't eaten in weeks.

Guys have it so easy.

I tug on Tommy's elbow, and he slides his arm around me as he finishes up his conversation. After he downs the rest of his drink, he leads me out to the dance floor.

"Everything okay with you?" he asks.

"Yeah, why?"

He pulls me close. "Just making sure."

I tighten my grip on him, and the room blurs as we slowly spin around. He leans in for a kiss, and I sink into it, latching onto his neck.

When he breaks away, he says, "You taste like cinnamon."

"Yeah? You taste like alcohol."

He grins. "Seth spiked our drinks."

"Why didn't you give me any?" I whine.

"Because I can handle my liquor, babe. And I don't want you passing out on me later."

I glare at him, and he laughs.

The rest of prom goes smoothly. Tommy has to steady me a few times, and because he thinks I've only had a couple shots, he watches me with hawk-like eyes for the rest of the evening. I almost get Seth to hook me up with a Coca-Cola "concoction," but Tommy is quick to intercept. Emily and I dance to our favorite fast-paced songs throughout the evening, and the night lives up to its promise. I never catch Mr. Slate's gaze again and soon forget all about him. By a quarter to eleven, we're ready to leave.

WE STEP OUTSIDE, and a warm gust of wind catches our dresses and threatens a brief moment of indecent exposure. Luckily, my dress is pretty tight, but Emily shrieks as she struggles to hold hers down. The smell of rain fills the moist air, and I'm hoping we make it to the hotel before the skies open up. Tommy holds me close as our limo pulls up and helps me in before climbing in after me—or should I say on top of me. He hovers over me, embracing me in a heated kiss, and runs his hands over the back of my dress.

"Hey, wait until you're in your room, tiger!" says Emily as she smacks the back of Tommy's head. Derek climbs in after her as Tommy and I sit up, readjusting ourselves. Derek opens up a compartment and tosses everyone a bottle of water. I consume mine in a few gulps, and Derek tosses me another. The drive to the hotel takes about forty minutes, but Emily keeps us entertained—she has us roaring with laughter as she imitates the creepy guy who took our photos.

Tommy squeezes my leg when we pull up to the hotel, and my stomach flips. I down the rest of my water and take Tommy's hand as he helps me out of the limo. My hair whips around in the wind, and Derek carries Emily's bag so she can hold her dress down.

The gigantic cherrywood front desk of the hotel stretches the entire length of the lobby, and several prom-goers hang around an ornate stone fountain that serves as the hotel centerpiece. It feels just as cliché as I imagined. I fight the urge to plunk down in one of the plush chocolate-colored arm chairs while Tommy checks in.

With room keys in hand, we stroll to the elevators, and Emily grins at me. We step inside the elevator, which is decked with floor-to-ceiling mirrors, and Emily and I admire our reflections. As far as I can tell, our amateur work is holding up. My stomach rolls as the elevator comes to a stop, and I grip my bags as we make our way down the hall.

Emily stops at her door, which is across from ours. "Do you guys want to hang out in our room for a while?"

I prop my hand on the wall to steady myself. "Sure—"

"No, we're good," Tommy interrupts, sliding the key card and opening the door.

Emily laughs and hugs me goodnight. "See you in the morning. . . . Have fun," she says, giving me a knowing look.

Tommy flicks on the light, and I follow him inside, setting my bags on the enormous king-sized bed. The room is nice, but pretty basic. It reminds me of a room I stayed in with my parents when they took me to Sea World several years ago. I quickly push the thought out of my mind. Now is *not* the time to be thinking about my parents. I plop down on the bed and the room sways.

"I think I need to eat something," I say, clutching my

stomach.

Tommy hurries to my side. "Do you want me to call room service?"

"Yeah, that'd be great."

He snatches the menu from the table. "What would you like?"

"Anything." I grab a bottle of water from the mini fridge and notice an array of snacks. I hold up a bag of animal crackers. "Do you mind if I take these?"

"No, go ahead." He's already on the phone ordering a burger and fries.

After munching on a few zoo animals, I take a few sips of water and step into the bathroom. As I freshen up, the room slowly steadies and my stomach calms. Relief washes over me. When I come back out, Tommy's pouring himself a drink.

I lift an eyebrow. "Where'd that come from?"

"Derek," he says with an enticing smile. "How are you feeling?"

I smile back. "Better, actually. Can I have some?"

He hesitates before handing me his glass and pouring himself another. "Are you sure you're okay? Room service will be another twenty minutes or so." He kicks off his shoes and shrugs out of his jacket.

"I'm good," I say, climbing onto the bed. I take a sip of my drink and rest my head on the headboard. "I had fun tonight."

"Me too," he says, untying his bow tie and throwing it on the table. "Do you want to watch TV while we wait?" He grabs the remote and slides next to me.

"No," I say. My hands tremble as I set my glass on the nightstand.

I turn to him, my heart pounding. I kick off my heels and swing my leg over him, causing my dress to hike up. The

176

room spins for a moment as I gaze down at the blue-eyed boy whom I've known since I was thirteen years old. Deep down in my heart, I know he would do anything for me, and he deserves this moment. I want this for him—*for us*. It's time to take control and show him how much I love him—show him how sorry I am for all the crap I've put him through lately. I can trust him with my life—he isn't perfect, but neither am I.

"What are you thinking about?" he asks, his voice gentle. He sets his drink beside mine.

"You."

His familiar eyes glitter with anticipation as they peer into mine. He smiles at me, and I know I can make this work with him. Maybe I've just been nervous about taking things to the next level, and my subconscious used Mr. Slate as a barrier—as a way to protect myself. Maybe it felt safer to focus on someone unattainable. Sex has always scared me. . . . I know how boys are about this sort of thing—it's never kept a secret, and it's degrading. I never open up to him in the way he deserves because I'm scared of being hurt, of ending up like my parents, of feeling trapped. If I give myself to him, if I open my heart finally, he can give me everything I need. And he'll grow up eventually. . . . He has the potential to become a mature man one day—be a true partner.

If only I would let him.

I start with his shirt, unbuttoning slowly. He stares into my eyes as I slip it over his shoulders, revealing the hard body that makes every girl swoon—he really is a sight to behold when I'm not so focused on fending him off. My legs tremble as he hikes up my dress past my red lacy thong.

"Damn," he sighs. "You are so hot." His gaze is fixed below my waist, and I snatch my glass from the nightstand, sucking down the rest of the drink before slamming it back down. My fingers shake as I unbutton his pants.

His eyes widen. "Room service will be here soon."

"Who cares?" My lips are on his, and I pull down his zipper.

He hesitates before following my lead and soon falls into the moment. His breathing amplifies as his hands slide up my thighs, and I flinch as his fingers graze me underneath the lace. *You're such a coward, Kaley.* I slam my eyes shut and let him touch me. *I can do this.* I just need to get out of my head. I *want* to be in this moment. I *need* to be in this moment.

I *am* in this moment.

He scoots down the bed, and I lock my thighs around him, our lips never separating. He slides down his boxers, and I feel him yank the delicate lace aside and press himself against me. My body jolts, and I gasp as he grips my hips tight, pressing me against his bare skin.

I pull back and spring off the bed. I hold my head as the room spins.

"I can't do this," I breathe, tugging down my dress.

"Kay, wait." He sits up, and I catch sight of him before he pulls up his pants and stands next to me. "Hey, we can go slower, babe. I'm sorry. You've just been killing me in that dress all night."

A loud knock at the door interrupts, and a man's voice calls through the door, "Room service!"

Tommy fastens his tuxedo pants and shuffles to the door. My heart feels like it's going to spasm, and my throat tightens, restricting the air to my lungs. As I watch Tommy retrieve the tray, my vision blurs. The man in the hallway looks over Tommy's shoulder and smiles at me. I squint at him, but his smile morphs into a distorted smirk, and suddenly there is two of him. My heart stops beating, then pounds irregularly. I rush to the bathroom, the short hallway stretching beneath my bare feet, and flick on the bright light, locking the door behind me.

In the mirror is a girl with wild eyes and a blood-drained face. I squint at the hazy reflection and press my hand to my chest, feeling the sporadic thumps of my heart. *What the hell is my problem?* The walls close in around me, and I hunch over, steadying myself on the counter before sliding to my knees. *Breathe, Kaley.* I force my shoulders back to allow more oxygen into my lungs. *Am I going to pass out?* A tingling sensation runs down my right arm, and I can't remember which arm signals you're having a heart attack. . . .

"KAY?" TOMMY'S VOICE sounds like a distant echo. I didn't hear the bathroom door open, but he's at my side, lifting me up onto the toilet seat.

"How did you get in here?"

"Through the door," he says. I can't see his face, but his tone alerts me.

"I thought I locked it."

He sighs. "The door wasn't even all the way shut, Kaley. I knew I shouldn't have given you that last drink." He's quiet for a moment. "Are you sick? What's wrong?"

I open my eyes. "I don't know. I can't breathe and my arm is going numb."

"Hey," he whispers, kneeling in front of me. "It's okay . . . don't freak out. I'm sorry, I really am. We'll go slower. You probably just need to eat."

"This isn't right," I mumble, using his shoulders to push myself onto my feet. I pause to let the room steady before moving past him.

"Kay!" He follows me out to the bedroom. "You can't seriously be mad at me right now—*you* were taking the lead there."

"I'm not mad at you," I say, forcing myself to meet his

eyes.

His toned shoulders slump as he slides his hands in his pockets. He really is handsome—all of him. And I *do* love him . . . as far as I know what love is. But the pain in his face is *my* doing, and I feel like a monster.

"You know what?" I say, my voice breaking. "I think I need to go home." I drop down on the bed and slip into my heels.

"Kaley, don't be ridiculous." He steps in front of me and rests his hands on my shoulders. "This is why you shouldn't drink—you can never handle it."

I whip my head up and narrow my eyes at him. "It's not the alcohol," I spit out, breaking his grip. I grab my bag and head toward the door, ignoring the sway of the room.

"Kaley, wait," he says with a sigh. I turn around, and he takes a step forward. "It's okay. We don't have to do anything. We can just eat and watch a movie or something, go to bed. It's cool . . . don't leave."

The tightness in my chest won't let up, and I stand up straighter. As much as I want to take him up on his offer, I have a sneaking suspicion he'll continue to paw at me all night long. I know he's sincere, but I don't know how much he can take with me lying in bed next to him all night. My mind flashes to the skimpy pajamas I packed, and I shake my head. I know I need to go home.

"I'm sorry," I say, turning away.

I yank open the door and stagger down the hall. I glance back, wondering if he'll follow me—I don't want him to, but it feels wrong leaving him like this . . . and yet it feels wrong if I stay. When I round the corner, Avery and her squad of skanks spill out of the elevator.

Fantastic.

Her eyes light up when she sees me. "Where are you going, girl?"

"Nowhere," I mutter.

"We're having a party in room 304 if you're interested."

"Yeah, maybe I'll check it out." I give her a quick nod and step into the elevator—I can't tell if she's too drunk to notice me leaving with my bag, or if she's just a complete idiot.

The elevator doors slide closed, and I'm left alone, my spineless reflection staring back at me. My lungs struggle for air, and I can't wait to get outside. My hands shake as I clutch my bag, and I suddenly long for my mother.

Leaning back into the corner, I breathe out a shaky sigh. I don't know if Tommy will forgive me this time. What am I going to say to him tomorrow? What is there to say? How am I going to face Emily and Derek after they find out I left?

And what am I going to say to my dad when I come home early tonight? I have to think of a reason why I'm no longer staying the night at Emily's without him being suspicious. There's no way I can make curfew, but maybe he'll still be at the poker game. They usually run pretty late. Technically, I do feel sick, maybe I can play up that angle . . . but what if he smells the alcohol? When I reach the lobby, I hurry over to the concierge's desk.

"I need a cab," I tell the young man.

He hesitates, running his gaze over my dress. "Uh, actually, there are some cabs outside waiting. Would you like me to walk you out?"

"No, thank you," I reply.

I hurry across the lobby, slowing only when the floor sways. The glass doors slide open, and a gust of wind meets my face. It's intense, but at least I can breathe again. I wave at a cab, and the driver steps out and takes my bag, opening the rear door for me. I'm thankful my dad gave me extra cash tonight, but I'm pretty far from home and hope I have enough.

"Would you like your bag with you or in the trunk,

miss?" asks the driver as I slide into the backseat. His Jamaican accent catches me off guard.

"With me is fine," I say. A burst of thunder erupts, causing me to jump.

He chuckles, handing me my bag. "Yeah, it's a little stormy out tonight." He shuts my door just as the rain begins to fall. Tears sting my eyes as I squint through the droplets on the cab window, peering back at the hotel. *How could I do this to Tommy?* My chest tightens, and I crack open the window. The open-air calms me, helping my head clear a little.

"Where to, miss?" asks the driver after closing his door.

Another crack of thunder rumbles as pellets of rain strike the cab. I check the time on my phone—already half an hour past my curfew. No matter what excuse I give my dad, I'm going to be in trouble. I cringe at the thought of coming home to his angry face and pray that he stays out late.

"Miss?" says the driver.

"Sorry," I say. I give him the address and slump down in the seat, shuffling in my bag for my mints. I know I must reek of booze.

We hop on the freeway, and I relax in my seat. *So this is how my prom night turned out.* I wonder if I'll be able to laugh about it one day . . . not any time soon, that's for sure.

"No date tonight?" asks the driver, breaking the silence.

"Uh . . ." It's a bold question, but for some reason his accent and kind eyes make it feel nonthreatening. "He's still at the hotel."

"Ah, I see. Looks like he doesn't know how to treat a lady," he says, chuckling.

"Something like that," I say, although it's not exactly true. Tommy's intentions aren't wrong, but they just aren't right for me. I lean forward and rest my head against the seat in front of me. *How could I have done this to him?*

I turn and lean against the door, pressing my cheek against the cool glass. We ride the rest of the way in silence, my thoughts straying in every possible direction as guilt permeates through me. I long for this disastrous night to be over with. The cab slows down, removing me from my tormented thoughts, and I open my eyes. When we come to a complete stop, I pay the man his fee, plus a tip—the very last of my cash supply.

He smiles at me. "I will wait here until you're safely inside."

"Oh, you don't have to do that. My dad's home, it's okay," I assure him.

"I insist." He steps out of the cab and opens my door.

I pop another breath mint in my mouth and step out of the cab. The rain bombards me, and I clutch my bag, trotting up to the front porch, under the shelter of the roof.

"Well, that sobered me up," I say to myself.

I run my hand through my dampened hair and exhale as I press the little glowing disk on the side of the house and wait.

No answer.

I count to ten before knocking on the door—I don't want to have to go back to the cab and explain to the driver why I'm locked out. Praying for a miracle, I count again—when I reach six, I hear the deadbolt unlock. My heart races as Mr. Slate slowly opens his door. He's barefoot, wearing jeans and a white T-shirt that look like they've been thrown on in a hurry—his hair is damp and disheveled.

He squints in the dim light, then his eyes widen. "Kaley?"

"Can I come in?" I ask.

His eyes dart behind me, and he hesitates before opening the door wider and stepping aside. I turn and wave to the cab driver, and he waves back before driving off.

I look Mr. Slate in the eyes as I step into his house.

CHAPTER SEVENTEEN

MR. SLATE CLOSES THE DOOR behind me and faces me in the entryway. The state of his appearance has me already regretting my arrival.

"Am I interrupting anything?" I ask. If The Blonde pops out from behind a corner, I will die, just *die*.

He shakes his head slowly, still clearly befuddled. "I mean . . . not exactly."

What does that mean?

"Are you alone?" I ask more directly.

He chews on his full, bottom lip, and I imagine biting it.

"Yes," he says eventually, crossing his arms. "What's going on, Kaley? Are you okay?"

"I'm fine," I say, shivering. I rub my arms as I take in my surroundings. The décor in his house is reflective of his wardrobe. Rich, earthy colors run throughout the open floor plan. A large island separates the kitchen and living room, and there's a hallway to my left. It's cozy, yet masculine, and I'd be having another panic attack if it wasn't for the alcohol silencing my anxiety.

He presses his lips into a fine line. "Okay . . . well, you just took a cab to my house, and you're carrying an overnight bag."

"Um . . . yeah," I say, dissolving into a nervous giggle.

He grabs my bag and sets it down next to the hunter-green sofa. I watch him step into the kitchen and pour a glass of water as I remain rooted to the floor. On his way back to the living room, he gestures for me to sit.

"Here," he says, handing me the glass. "Drink this." He sits on the opposite end of the couch, his posture rigid, and clears his throat.

"I'm not completely plastered or anything," I say, crossing my legs.

"You're *something*," he says. "Drink up."

I take a sip of water. "I'm okay, really."

His disapproving eyes and five o'clock shadow remind me of his age. He slips a coaster on the coffee table just before I set my glass down, and I smile. *Ruggedly handsome neat freak.*

I shiver again, and he tosses me a blanket off the back of the couch. "Here, dry off with this."

His eyes dart across my dress as I pat myself down. "Do your parents know where you are right now?"

I smirk and toss the blanket beside me. "What are you, an after-school special?"

His unblinking eyes remain humorless. "Where do they think you are?"

I swallow. "Emily's house."

"And where does Emily think you are?"

"Um . . . in a hotel room across the hall from her."

His jaw tightens, and he waits a moment before asking, "And where does Bradford think you are right now?"

I bite my bottom lip. "Home."

He sighs. "Why did you take a cab to my house, Kaley?" His inflection is too close to his teacher tone, irritating me.

"I didn't really think about it," I confess. "I planned on going home, but when the driver asked where I wanted to go . . . I just gave him your address."

He leans back against the couch. "I'm not even going to ask how you know my address."

"I appreciate that, thanks," I say, stifling more nervous laughter.

"Drink your water."

I roll my eyes. "Yes, Mr. Slate," I say teasingly as I pick up the glass to take another sip.

He winces. "Don't call me that, please."

I set down the glass and tilt my head. "So, what—you want to be on a first-name basis again?"

He runs his hands through his damp hair and locks his fingers behind his head. I linger on his protuberant biceps as he speaks. "I don't know, Kaley. This hasn't been easy for me, either."

I scoff. "Really? Could've fooled me."

"Good. That was the whole point."

I realize the liquid courage will eventually wear off, leaving me embarrassed and humiliated for my candor, but I can't live with this tug-of-war in my mind anymore.

I came here for a reason.

"Okay, look," I say, folding my arms across my waist. "You're kind of ruining my entire life, and I need to move on. Either you want to do something about this or not. I'm graduating in four and a half weeks; I'm eighteen years old—what's the problem?"

He lowers his arms, resting his elbows on his knees and leans forward. "I'm going to assume that's the alcohol talking."

"It's not just the—" I start. And then it happens. My words are past my lips before I can stop them. "You can't kiss me like that and then just tell me you lost control. Maybe I'd believe you if I didn't always catch you staring at me in that . . . *way* of yours. I mean, what are you afraid of? Obviously, you are—or *were*—attracted to me, so what do you want? Are you worried I'll get too attached or something?"

He springs up from the sofa. "I should take you home."

I mirror his action, standing up too fast for my inebriated state, and the room starts to sway.

"I don't want to go home," I say, trying to steady myself. "I want you to at least answer my question first." As much as I hate my transparency tonight, I know I need an answer—I need to move on for good.

"And what's that?" he says, turning to me.

"If you're attracted to me—and I swear I won't tell anybody—what are you afraid of? Getting into trouble? I mean, I get that, I do. I'm sure you get laid all the time, so I'm not worth the risk."

His eyes tighten. "That's who you think I am?"

"Well what else is it? Don't you have some beautiful girlfriend or something? What am I supposed to think? You said you cared about me, and I get it—you said that in the heat of the moment. Look, we all make mistakes. But I'm a big girl, I can take it. I just want the truth for once. I—"

"I *do* care about you," he says, cutting me off. He takes one long stride and grabs my arms, his face inches from mine. "The truth is I care *too* much about you. And it isn't right. You're a *student*—I'm a *teacher*—that's *not* okay. *Get it?* You're young, Kaley, you have college ahead of you, a boyfriend, and I could lose my *job*—there are a million reasons why I *shouldn't* care about you!"

Time suspends as the full impact of his words hit me.

"But you *do* care?"

He breaks his hold, stepping away. "Look, it's more serious than you think. Even if I caved in to my feelings and we tried this out after you graduate, I could still get in serious trouble."

Feelings? Regretting the last few shots of alcohol, I'm not sure I heard him correctly, and it takes me a moment to process.

"Even *after* graduation?" I dare to ask. Now that I know he might actually have feelings for me, my guard comes crashing down before I can stop it.

His expression is solemn. "If we went public soon after graduation, or if someone found out about us, I could still be reported to the school board and be blacklisted from the district. Every district, in fact."

I know he's telling me bad news, but I'm too enthralled over his use of "we" and "us."

"It's kind of difficult to get another teaching job if you're known for dating students," he says, allowing a slight smirk.

"Oh," I say, defeated. "Have you dated other students before?"

He jerks his head back. "*What*? Of course not! Honestly, is that what you think of me? I've *never* felt this way about a student. Look, Kaley, I'm really sorry I put you through all of this. But like I said, you're young with so much ahead of you. Our relationship would be too complicated. Trust me. I want to do the right thing here—just please forgive me for everything, and I promise I will treat you like a normal student and leave you alone."

"No," I plead. "Please don't leave me alone; I don't want to be left alone." My pride is long gone, and I step forward, cupping my hands around his face.

"Kaley, please," he says, grabbing my wrists. "You're overestimating my self-control."

I gaze at him. "Don't you get tired of being so perfectly disciplined all the time? Don't you ever just want to let go?"

He clenches his jaw, and my gaze falls to his mouth. *I miss this mouth.* ... I never thought I'd be this close to it again. He continues to peer down at me, his eyes darkening as I rub my thumb against his scruffy chin.

In one fluid motion, he grabs my waist, pulling me close, and parts my lips with his. He tastes even better than I remember, and my thirst for him deepens. I wrap my arms around his neck, and I'm suddenly very aware of the fact that we're completely alone. There's no danger of Derek, or a custodian, or anyone interrupting us this time, and everything I've been pushing down the last month comes flooding to the surface. My body is starved for his touch, and I kiss him with a ravenous hunger. He lifts me up, and I lock my legs around his waist. After three quick steps, he slides me on top of the glossy kitchen island and tangles his masterful fingers into my hair, gently tugging it. We claw at each other with an uncontrollable desperation.

I reach down to the hem of his shirt and yank it up.

"Kaley," he warns, breaking away from my lips.

"*No*," I say, abhorring the loss of his kiss. "Don't you dare do this again."

"You've been drinking. I don't want to take it too far."

I smother his protest with my lips. "What did you expect when you lifted me onto your counter top?" I murmur between kisses.

"I know, I'm sorry." He pulls back for a moment, his gaze flashing to my legs. "You're just hard to resist," he says, sliding his hand up my thigh.

"So don't," I say, my breaths ragged.

"Kaley, you're not sober," he chides, but his words don't match his actions.

I tug on his shirt. "I'm good, Slate."

His eyes burn through me, and my dress is forced up higher as he wedges himself farther between my legs, his mouth locking onto mine. We're in the same position as that fateful study session and a well of emotions spring up inside me. I slip my fingers underneath his shirt and run my hands up his back, greedily exploring the muscles that have teased me all semester.

"I need you," I whisper.

He pulls back with force. "Don't say that," he warns. "I can't take advantage of you."

"No, I'm good," I say, clutching onto him. "Take advantage, please!"

A deep chuckle escapes his throat. "Okay, okay. I have to do the right thing here." He pries my hands loose and tries to step back, but I tighten my legs around him. "Kaley," he cautions, but I sense a trace of amusement. "This isn't easy for me—I *am* a man. Don't push it."

"So, what now?" I say. "You're just going to make out with me in your kitchen and then make me go home?" I grin as I squeeze his hips between my thighs.

He sighs, brushing the loose hair out of my face. "I should, but you're making it very difficult to stay away from you."

"Then *don't* stay away from me," I implore. "You're all I think about."

Somewhere underneath the confidence-inducing alcohol, I fear his reaction to my transparency. He lifts my chin, anguish filling his eyes. My stomach clenches, and I brace myself for rejection.

"You have no idea how crazy you've made me," he says, his voice strained. Silence falls over us as he stares at me. "I can't believe you're here right now. You took quite a risk, Kay." He leans forward and brushes his lips against mine, and the last of my coherent thoughts vanish. He nibbles my bottom lip and peers down at me with those warm, intoxicating eyes. A shiver vibrates through my body, and I hear a deep, low laugh against my lips.

"Are you cold, Kaley?" His eyes twinkle with mirth.

I slowly shake my head, and he tilts my chin to the left, grazing his lips down the side of my neck, and the familiar ache rises to a new level. He slides his fingertips across my thighs, goose bumps forming at his touch. With his mouth skimming along my collarbone, his fingers stretch underneath my dress, but stop just before the thin wall of lace.

I inhale sharply. "Just how do you expect me to take it

slow when you do things like that?"

"Sorry," he says, his voice edgy. He lifts his head and gives me a lopsided grin, rendering me senseless in my already intoxicated state.

He pulls away, my body suddenly abandoned and cold. He slides me off the countertop, and the room spins as soon as my weakened legs hit the floor. I can't tell if it's because of the alcohol or him—probably a little of both. I follow him back into the living room, but he stops in front of the couch and turns to me.

"Actually, let's get you out of that dress."

I perk up and release a wicked grin.

"I mean into something else," he says, emphasizing his words. "You brought clothes with you, right? I can't take any more of . . . *that*." He gestures to my attire.

"Wait," I say. "You're not taking me home?"

He hesitates. "Do you want to go home?"

I struggle to keep his gaze. "That's your call."

He rubs his jaw as he regards me, and I watch the conflicting thoughts race behind his eyes. After a while, he exhales, dropping his hand.

"Stay," he whispers.

Stay!

He lifts a hand in a "stop" gesture, reading my reaction. "I want you to stay, but I'm still not taking advantage of you."

I nod. "Okay."

He releases a relaxed grin, and I dissolve into the floor.

"Um . . . can I use your bathroom?" I ask.

"You're not going to throw up, are you?" he says, horrified.

"No!" I laugh, picking up my bag. "I need a place to change and freshen up . . . unless you want me to change right here," I say with a mischievous grin.

"Definitely not." He takes my bag from me and leads me down the hallway. I hesitate when he passes the bathroom and leads me to the end of the hallway, into his bedroom.

"Um, wow. I thought you wanted to take things slow, Mr. Slate," I jest.

He whips around so fast that I'm forced to step back.

"Don't do that," he says in a stern voice. Noting my reaction, he softens. "I'm remodeling that bathroom, so you need to use this one, okay?"

I nod, wide-eyed, and he guides me through the dimly lit master bedroom. I scan the area, spying a large, mahogany-framed bed. Matching nightstands adorn both sides of the bed, and a dresser rests along the wall, a large mirror hanging above it. The walls seem to be painted dark gray, but it's hard to tell in the soft light spilling from a single lamp on one of the nightstands. His bedding is dark as well, but the bed is turned down, exposing crisp white sheets—he must've been getting into bed when I rang his doorbell, and I imagine crawling into that big bed with him. Suddenly, I slam into a hard surface, breaking my reverie.

"Ow!" I cry out, pressing my hand to the side of my face.

Laughter erupts next to me, and I take a step back. Apparently, I walked right into his back when he stopped to turn on the bathroom light.

Real smooth.

"Oh, yeah. You're sober all right," he mocks.

"Shut up!" I say, still holding my face and joining him in laughter.

He tries to regain his composure, but his shoulders still shake. "Are you okay?"

"What the hell do you have under that shirt, Slate? Are you made of steel?"

He roars into laughter and leads me inside the bathroom. Bronze light fixtures provide a soft glow that bounces off the rich chestnut walls. The shower is enclosed by spotless glass, showing off the intricate travertine tile work. A large bathtub sits in the corner next to the shower, also surrounded by stone.

"Wow," I say. "This is beautiful. Did you remodel this one, too?"

He rubs the back of his neck. "Yeah."

"Quite the handyman, are we?" I take another step inside. "Hmm . . . this tub looks kind of big. Is it made for two?"

He rolls his eyes playfully. "Just hurry and get dressed before I take you up on that. I'll be in the living room."

He leaves me alone, and his words echo through my head. Just hearing him tease me about having me in the tub rouses me. And I kind of love seeing him flustered. He's so cool and collected in class all the time—it's a nice change when I can throw him off. I brush my teeth and freshen up before taking off my stilettos and slipping out of my dress—there is no way I'm sober, or I'd be hyperventilating right now as I stand naked in Mr. Slate's bathroom.

Elijah Slate.

Elijah Slate's bathroom.

I dig through my bag and pull out my bright pink shorts. Insecurity paralyzes me as I lift them up, realizing just how short they really are. This is all I brought with me, though—I can't exactly sleep in jeans. It's one thing to plan my sleep attire knowing I'll be sleeping next to Tommy; it's a whole other situation with Elijah. *Am I seriously spending the night at his house right now?* A thrill runs through me, snapping me out of my fear.

I slip on my shorts and pull my tank top over my head. When I catch my reflection, I realize it leaves very little to the imagination—I don't want to sleep in a bra, but I can't exactly walk out there like this, although it's tempting. I pull a bra out of my bag. It's neon-pink. *Great*. It'll show right through, but it's better than nothing. After putting it on, I check myself in the mirror one last time before stepping out of the bathroom. I drop my bag at the end of his bed and steal another quick glance around the room, running my hand across the sturdy bed frame—his bedroom is so sexy, and I can't believe I'm standing in it.

As I creep down the hallway, I find him sitting on the couch next to a neatly folded stack of blankets and pillows, watching ESPN on low volume.

When he notices my approach, he does a double-take, and his eyes widen. "You have *got* to be kidding me."

I freeze. "What?"

"*That's* what you're wearing? It's almost worse than the dress!"

"Oh, sorry," I say, feeling heat spread across my face. "It's all I brought."

He lets out an exasperated sigh, mumbling something incoherent, and rises. "You can sleep in my bed, I'll sleep out here."

"I can't take your bed," I say, horrified. "I'll sleep out here, it's cool."

"No," he says as he sets up a makeshift bed.

"Seriously, *I'll* sleep out here. You'll be so cramped on this thing."

He tosses a pillow at the end of the sofa and sits down on the opposite side. He pats the spot beside him, avoiding my appearance at all costs, and I drop down next to him.

"Do you want to watch a movie or something?" he asks, flinging a blanket over my legs.

"Weren't you about to go to bed before I knocked on your door?"

"Yeah, but I'm not tired anymore."

"Okay then," I say, snuggling closer to him. "Let's watch

a movie."

How differently this night has turned out. Guilt pulls at the back of my mind, reminding me of how terrible I am for abandoning Tommy, but elation mixed with booze trumps my shame for now, and I push it back.

He shuffles through the movie channels before settling on a romantic comedy that has already begun, but that I don't think either of us cares about. He clicks off the lamp and wraps his arm around me.

I can't believe I'm in his house, on his couch, wrapped in his arms.

Taking in his scent, I relax into his chest. I try to shuffle through my muddled thoughts and take a moment to process where I am and the events of the night. He's right, I *did* take a big risk tonight . . . and it was worth it—even though I'm still unclear about where he stands with me. I'm itching to ask him about The Blonde, but the way I left Tommy tonight, I have no room to talk. This moment is all I need right now, and I'm so thankful I gave the cab driver his address. *Best decision I made all night.* After a while, I break free from his embrace and swing my legs up onto his lap as I lay back on the sofa, resting my head against the pillow.

"See?" I say, smiling at him. "I fit perfectly on this couch. *I'm* sleeping here."

The blanket slid off me when I moved, and his gaze drifts to my legs. He traces his fingers along my calf and our eyes lock. His hand glides up my leg, and he shifts his body toward me. I pull my knees apart as he crawls in between my legs and brings his face to mine.

He kisses me so deeply that fire spreads throughout my entire body. If this is infatuation, I could never handle love. I wrap a leg around him, and he runs his hand up the back of my thigh and over my backside, slipping his hand underneath the back of my tank top. I tug at his shirt, expecting him to stop me, but he doesn't. Instead, he lifts his body off me and pulls it over his head.

He lowers himself back down, and I rush my hands up to stop him.

"Wait."

He freezes.

I strain my eyes. "It's hard to see in this light, but . . . is that an *eight* pack?!"

He bursts out a laugh, only accentuating his abs even more, and quickly returns to me. His skin is smooth underneath my hands as I eagerly explore his miraculous upper body.

"Seriously, Slate, do those actually exist?"

"Apparently," he says, his eyes glimmering. "I don't normally have an eight pack, though. It's new."

"It's new?" I ask. "What, did you buy it off Amazon or something?"

He barks another laugh.

Even his laugh is sexy.

"No, I've just been working out more than usual. You know, trying to stay busy—keeping my mind off . . . *things*." His features shift to something more serious and my stomach flutters.

"You've been working out to keep your mind off *me*?" All this time I thought I was going insane by keeping myself occupied, assuming he couldn't even spare a thought about me. This new insight has me reeling. I feel myself falling fast, and it scares me.

"Pretty much," he says. "I work out, golf, remodel bathrooms . . . you know, whatever's necessary," he says with a chuckle.

I can't speak. I'm waiting for someone to wake me up and ruin the best dream I've ever had. My eyes wander to his chest, and I drink in his strong, wide shoulders that feel so protective around me. When I pull my gaze back up, I recognize the hunger in his eyes, and I lean up to kiss him. He slips his hand up the back my shirt and unhooks my bra with ease. I slide it off from underneath my tank top and toss it on the floor. Admiration washes over his face as he looks down at my body and leans into my neck, his lips causing me to forget the world that exists outside of these walls. His hands wrap around my rib cage as his thumbs lightly trace the sides of my breasts. I start to lift up my shirt, but he stops me.

"Kaley, I can't." His voice is muffled in the curve of my neck, and I let out a heavy sigh.

"Please," I whisper in his ear. "I want you, Elijah."

I feel the weight of his body as he buries his head in my neck, letting out a loud groan, crying, "Oh, God!" He lifts up his head, his eyes wild. "I have to stay in control. You're not sober, and it's not right."

"I feel fine, I promise." I touch my nose, alternating my right and left fingers, like they do for DUI tests, and he laughs.

"See?" I say, smiling.

"Yeah, you almost poked your eye out, but nice try."

I pull him in for a kiss, then slide my hands down the sides of his naked torso and trace my fingers along the top of his jeans. When I reach the front, I unbutton them.

He jumps back.

"Shit," he gasps.

I have a better view of his body as he kneels before me, and the aching pressure below me escalates. He refastens his jeans, and I catch a glimpse of a black waistband that tortures my curiosity.

"Are you going to make me beg?" I say.

"Please, don't," he says with his eyes closed. He stays there for a moment and steadies his breathing. When he opens his eyes, his expression is wary. "Kaley, I have a hard time controlling myself around you, I'm sorry. I'm only human . . . but I know my limits. And it's not just your intoxicated state that's stopping me; although, it's really helped my conscience tonight."

"Honestly, I'm fine," I say, hoping to assure him.

"It's not just that," he says as he lowers himself over me, his face inches from mine. "You're worth more than that, Kaley. I want to take this slow."

My heart sputters. "So, you want to take this somewhere?"

"I don't think I have a choice anymore," he whispers.

I can't suppress a grin, and he eyes my mouth. I bite my lip, trying to hold in my delight, and he presses his lips to mine. But the kiss ends before I can even begin. I want more, but don't push it. He turns me on my side, facing me toward the TV and wedges himself between me and the couch. I have no idea what the movie's about, but it doesn't matter—if you've seen one romantic comedy, you've seen them all. He wraps his sturdy arm around my waist and slides his arm between my breasts, gently clasping the base of my neck. He holds me close as he nuzzles my neck and kisses me below my ear, sending a shiver down my spine.

"Hey," I warn. "Don't start something that you aren't willing to finish, *Slate*."

I feel him shake with silent laughter. "Fair enough, beautiful."

Warmth floods my chest, and I relax into him, feeling his breath against my neck. My eyes become heavy as I listen to the rhythm of his breathing, and my body eventually gives in to sleep.

CHAPTER EIGHTEEN

A THUNDEROUS BOOM STARTLES ME awake as the walls shake around me. My eyes spring open in the darkness, but I can't tell where I am. A flash of lightning pierces through the shutters on the window, giving me a brief view of my surroundings, and I sit up as another rumble vibrates the bed.

I'm in his bedroom!

He must've carried me in here after I fell asleep and took the couch for himself.

"It's okay," says a soft whisper.

I flinch and notice a shadowy figure lying next to me. My body trembles from the panic that tore me out of my peaceful sleep—I realize now it's just a thunderstorm, but my body still needs to catch up with my brain. And lying in my math teacher's bed alongside him isn't exactly helping.

He secures his arm around me, pulling me close. I burrow my face into his bare chest and press myself against him, wrapping my arm around his firm torso. He kisses the top of my head, then rubs my back as another flash of lightning penetrates the bedroom. I brace myself for the delayed rumbling, and he tightens his arm around me as it comes to pass. I'm too tired to process the intimacy between us and relax in his sturdy embrace. The sound of the torrential downpour striking the roof eventually coaxes me back to sleep.

I CRACK OPEN my heavy eyelids to a soft glow filtering through the slits of the shutters. The tiny beams of sunlight sting my eyes, and I wait for my vision to adjust before scanning my surroundings. I squint at the empty space beside me, and the dam in my chest breaks loose, flooding me with wonderment. *It's not a dream. I'm in his bed . . . Elijah Slate's bed!*

I realize the shower is running and slowly sit up, my head throbbing. He looked like he just showered before I showed up on his doorstep last night. . . . *Is he really that freakishly clean?* I really need to pee, and although the toilet is in its own private room, I know there is no way I'll be able to slip in without seeing him naked. Flipping the covers aside, I jump down from the bed and clutch the edge of the dresser to steady myself. My stomach rolls, and I close my eyes to shut out the sway of the room. *Ugh. Too fast.* I hear the shower turn off, and I catch my reflection in the mirror. I fell asleep before washing my face and my eye makeup is smeared, making me look raccoonish. I attempt to wipe it away, but it won't budge. *Great.*

As I slide my fingers through my tangled hair, his reflection stops me as he steps out of the bathroom wearing jeans and a black cotton T-shirt. I study his bicep as he ruffles a towel through his damp hair, causing his T-shirt to rise, revealing just a bit of his toned stomach. My breath catches in my throat. I remember my raccoon eyes and an uncontrollable heat surges through my cheeks.

"Good morning, beautiful," he says with a heart-crushing smile.

My stomach flutters against the nausea.

"Good morning," I croak, hoping he won't kiss me before I get a chance to brush my teeth.

He grabs his phone from the nightstand and glances at the screen before sliding it into his pocket. "How's your head?"

"Kind of sucky," I admit.

He offers his hand. "Come out to the kitchen, I'll make you feel better."

My mind flashes to last night's event on the island, but I know that's not what he means. "Um . . . can I meet you out there?"

He drops his hand to his side. "Sure. You okay?"

I nod, forcing a smile. As soon as he leaves the room, I rush into the bathroom to relieve myself, and the dizziness forces me to hold onto the wall. Once the room stops spinning, I carefully make my way to the sink and splash water on my face, scrubbing off the mess of dried makeup. I sweep the mouthwash off the counter and gargle for as long as I can handle without gagging. My stomach threatens me, and I pray I don't throw up in his immaculate bathroom.

After pulling my hair up into a sloppy bun, I make my way down the hall. As I pass the living room, I notice he's already put the blankets and pillows away, and I smile. *Everything in its place.* When I step into the kitchen, he pulls out a chair that's tucked underneath the side of the island and gestures for me to sit. I catch him glance at my chest as I walk over to him and look down. *Crap.* My heartbeat quickens, and I feel myself blush.

"Sorry," I mumble, sinking into the chair. In my state of grogginess, I forgot to put on a bra, and my thin little tank top allows more than a suggestion. "Please tell me you have coffee."

"Oh," he says, hesitating. "I don't drink coffee, sorry."

I sigh, leaning my elbows on the counter and rubbing my temples. He drops two effervescents into a small glass of water and slides it in front of me.

"Here," he says with a smile. "Drink this, you'll feel better."

I bring the glass to my lips and as soon as the medicinal taste hits my tongue, I nearly choke. "Ugh! What the hell is this?"

"Just trust me."

I force another sip and try not to gag.

He leans against the counter. "Do you want breakfast?"

"Do you shower twice a day?" I ask.

He clamps his lips together, and his eyes dance at the random question. "Um, no. Not normally. Why?"

I shrug and look down at my fizzy drink. "Just wondering. Your hair was wet last night. It looked like you had just showered before I came over, and you just showered this morning."

"Oh, yeah I did, but that's because I went for a quick run this morning."

Of course you did, Mr. Perfect.

"So, you were just going to let me wake up all alone wondering where you were?" I tease.

"I left a note. And you seemed to be sleeping pretty well."

I don't even want to know what he means by that. The image of him watching me drool on his pillow flashes through my mind, and I cringe. I take another sip of the wretched drink and make a face.

"How's your stomach? Do you want some eggs or anything?"

I wince. "Ew. I can't handle eggs right now. I need carbs. Like toast, or hash browns, or something."

He frowns. "Oh . . . I don't really have anything like that. The only carbs I have are vegetables . . . well, and brown rice and quinoa."

"Right," I say. "The whole eight-pack thing."

He laughs. "Something like that. Oh! I have oats—do you want some oatmeal?"

I stare at him for a moment. "No, thanks." The thought of wiggly, mushy oats make me want to wretch.

"Finish your drink, and I'll run out and get you something real quick."

"No, you don't have to do that. Honestly, I'll be fine. My stomach just needs to settle."

"I want to." He kisses the top of my head. "I'll be right back," he says, slipping on his shoes. He grabs his keys and disappears through the garage door.

I finish the last of my revolting drink and head back into the bedroom to take a shower and get dressed. My bra is on top of my bag, folded in department store quality, and I shake my head, amused.

Feeling too queasy to be anxious over using his shower, I drag my bag into the bathroom, and I'm thankful to see he laid out a stack of towels for me. I admire the beautiful stone tile surrounding me as I wash up and take a moment to relax underneath the hot, penetrating stream of water—it's like a gift from God.

After I force myself to turn off the shower and step out, I dry off and pull out my jeans and gray cotton T-shirt. I search for my hair dryer, only to realize I left my bag full of hair products at the hotel. Awesome. Taking a chance, I peek in his cabinets and eventually find a pink hairdryer way in the back, on the bottom shelf. Either this belongs to a woman, or I have bigger problems. My mind flashes to The Blonde as I plug it in and get to work. I'll have to ask him about her eventually, but I can't handle that today. Hopefully, they're broken up and she just left this behind. . . . Unless he has it here for his endless string of women he brings home. *Will you chill out? You don't know that!*

After I'm done, I set the hairdryer back in its place and apply a minimal amount of makeup—just enough to look a little less dead. I spread my bubble gum chap stick across my lips and feel my headache starting to dissipate.

As soon as I open the bedroom door, the smell of breakfast wafts through the house and my stomach rumbles. Seems the repulsive drink has some merit. When I reach the kitchen, he's frying up some hash browns and my chest swells. His face brightens when he notices my presence, and he flashes that incredible smile of his.

"All right, Kay, I've got hash browns, toast, and waffles—will that suffice your need for carbohydrates?" he says with a smirk.

"I think that will do." I notice a waffle maker on the counter. "Waffles from scratch? Like, homemade?"

"Yep," he replies. "Belgian. I don't like that frozen junk."

"You are a *god*," I say, walking to the island. He laughs, and I sit down at the counter, finding a fresh steaming cup of coffee. "You got me Starbucks, too?" I ask in disbelief.

"I wasn't sure what you liked, so I just got you a latte, is that okay?"

"Yes, of course," I say in awe. He winks at me and returns to his cooking.

I sip my coffee, trying to let the fact that I just spent the night at "Mr. Slate's" house resonate with me. And now he's cooking me breakfast—and even bought me coffee. The whole scenario seems too good to be true. I wish I could stay in this moment for the rest of my life.

He presents me with a large Belgian waffle, a plate of hash browns, toast, and sausage.

"Breakfast is served," he says.

My eyes take in the overwhelming display. "Sausage, too? I'm not going to be able to eat all of this."

"Don't worry about it. I'll help you out," he says, sliding in the chair next to me. "But first things first." He grabs my face and draws me in for a kiss. "Good morning."

"Good morning," I say, an uncontrollable grin spreading across my face. He releases me, and I butter my waffle, then cover it in syrup. Not only am I hungover, but I ate like a bird yesterday. This is pure heaven.

We enjoy our smorgasbord, all the while feeling like I'm in a magical dream. Right now it's just us. No school, no parents, no complications. Just the two of us, talking, laughing, and enjoying a beautiful breakfast together.

"I don't want to take you home until it's dark out, is that okay?" he says, setting down his fork.

"That's fine with me." I don't want to go home at all.

"This is going to be hard, Kaley. Especially for the next month. I can't call or text you—I can't leave any evidence. I hope that doesn't upset you."

I lean back in my chair. "No, I understand. I don't want you to get in trouble."

"You can't even tell Emily," he warns.

"I know," I say, nodding.

"She doesn't know anything about us, does she? Be honest."

I lift my eyes to his. "No, I swear! Don't worry. It's difficult, yes, but it's fine. I understand the seriousness of it." I lean over and trace my fingertips along his jawline.

His lips part as his gaze falls to my mouth.

"I won't say anything," I whisper.

He leans in and kisses me deeply, tasting like syrup.

AFTER CLEANING UP the kitchen, we make our way into the living room.

"Maybe you should call Emily real quick," he says as we sit down on the sofa.

"Why?" I ask.

"You're going to be staying here all day. I don't want her showing up at your house or something and have everybody start wondering where you are."

He's right. I should at least feel her out. Maybe I can tell her that I'm home sick with a hangover.

"Okay," I say, running back to his bedroom. I grab my phone from my bag and slide my finger across the screen as I make my way back to the living room. "Crap."

His posture stiffens. "What?"

"I have four missed calls from Emily."

"Call her." His voice is firm.

"I'm so sorry, I should've texted her last night or something," I say, cradling the phone to my ear.

She picks up in less than a ring. "Hello?"

I try to keep my voice casual. "Hey. Sorry I missed your calls this morning,"

"Kaley, where are you?" she says panicked.

"I'm at home," I say, hoping she hasn't already checked there.

"I had no idea where you were, and you weren't answering. You freaked me out!"

"I'm sorry, Ems. Everything's okay."

"Everything's *not* okay," she says, her voice stiff. "Have you talked to Tommy?"

I squeeze my eyes shut and pinch the bridge of my nose. *Here comes the "Poor Tommy" speech.* "No, I haven't," I say, dropping my hand to my side, "and please spare me the lecture. I changed my mind about last night, and I'm not going to feel guilty about it."

Silence penetrates the other end of the line, and I check my phone to see if we're still connected. When I see that we are, I snap.

"Hello?"

"You should call Tommy, Kay," she says, her voice barely above a whisper.

I sigh. "I will. Eventually. Maybe tonight or something. I don't want to deal with it right now." I glance at Elijah. "I'm sorry I pissed everyone off, but I'm not going to let you guys make me feel bad for changing my mind."

A heavy sigh sounds through the phone.

"Are you seriously mad at me, Ems? Because that really hurts if you are," I say. I've never really told her how much it bothers me when she always takes Tommy's side. Maybe it's time I do.

"Kaley," she says quietly. "Tommy slept with Avery last night."

Air sucks out of my lungs, and my limbs go cold. "He . . . *what*?" I whisper, slowly sitting down on the couch. I faintly feel Elijah slide over next to me.

"He slept with Avery. Trust me—I'm not mad at *you*."

I clutch my throat. Sure, I'm guilty of sleeping over at my teacher's house—and even trying to have sex with him; okay, and technically cheating on him a month ago—but Tommy doesn't know that. He thinks I was just too scared last night and went home.

"Avery had a party in her room," Emily continues, "and somehow Tommy ended up there. I'm not sure how it all went down, but when Derek knocked on his door this morning he saw Avery in his bed."

"Holy hell, Emily. Well, are you sure they didn't just pass out or something?"

"I'm sure. Tommy confirmed it with Derek."

"I-I don't know what to say . . ."

"I know. I'm sorry, Kay. Do you want me to come over?"

"No!" I yelp. "Uh—no. Don't come over," I stammer, trying to recover. "I really don't feel well. Maybe you can stop by tonight. I just need to sleep this off."

"Are you sure?"

"I'm sure. I'll text you tonight when you can come over, okay?"

"Okay," she says through a sigh. "I really wanted to make Tommy confess directly to you, but I just wanted you to know."

"No, I'm glad you told me. I just need some time to . . . process this."

"Okay, text me later and I'll come right over."

"I will." We disconnect, and I lower my head.

"Kaley? What's wrong?"

I lift my gaze to Elijah's concerned face.

"Tommy slept with Avery last night," I say. Even as I re-peat Emily's words, shock courses through me like I'm hear-ing it for the first time.

His head jerks back. "Seriously?"

I snap out of my daze and stand up. "Look, I know I'm not innocent in all of this, but he thought I just went home. It's not like he *knew* I was cheating on him, so he just decided to bang some stupid skank!"

"Come here," he says softly. He takes both of my hands and pulls me down next to him, shifting his body toward me. "He never deserved you, Kaley. Trust me." The sincerity in his voice is heartening.

"I'm so glad I didn't sleep with him last night," I say, slumping back against the couch. "If he's capable of this, he doesn't deserve my virginity."

Elijah's body goes rigid. "Your . . . *what*?"

Shit.

"Um, my virginity. . . . I was going to lose my virginity to him last night," I confess, wishing for a giant hole to bury myself in.

Anger flashes through his eyes, and he jumps off the couch. "You're a *virgin*?"

I cower in my seat. "Yes," I say, bracing myself. "Why, does that turn you off?" *Of course it does. Why would he be interested in a young girl with no experience?*

"Kaley!" His legs are planted wide, his arms crossed. I've seen him in this stance a few times while coaching a game. "First of all," he says, lowering his voice a little, "don't be

ridiculous. It does the opposite of tu.
that's beside the point." He rubs the
pauses. "I just assumed you and Bradfol
You guys come off that way, so I'm just b.
And truthfully, you seemed to know what
last night." I suppress a smile as he contin
all," he says, his voice turning cold, "Brad
know he's just a typical, immature high scho   y, but I
always thought he was a complete dick. I hated seeing you
two together."

"You did?" I say, scrambling to understand. I can't recall
anyone referring to Tommy as anything negative—*ever*. Everyone I know practically worships him. Kind of refreshing,
to be honest.

"And third of all," he says, interrupting my thoughts. "I
cannot believe that you were going to let me take your virginity without me even knowing!"

I put my hands up. "Please calm down, Elijah."

"I'm serious, Kaley. I'm *so* glad I didn't sleep with you
last night."

His words prick my heart.

"Hey," he whispers as soon as he notices my reaction. He
kneels in front of me. "That's not what I mean." He cups my
face, forcing me to meet his eyes. "I just mean that I would
hate myself if I slept with you so early on in our relationship—and it would've *killed* me if I'd stolen your virginity
last night without having known. You are worth so much
more than that, Kaley. Bradford sure as hell doesn't know it,
but I do."

A lump builds in my throat. "I never wanted to sleep
with Tommy," I say through gritted teeth. "I wasn't being
careless with you last night. I haven't wanted to be with *anyone* in that way . . . until I met you." I cringe at my honesty.

He draws closer, his warm brown eyes piercing into

want to be with you, too, believe me. But I want to
. I'm not in this to just sleep with you casually. I hope
you know I would never risk my career for some meaningless sex. . . . I want to make love to you, Kaley."

Holy. Hell.

"Is that okay with you?" His gaze pins me to the couch,
and I nod, unable to formulate a response. He grants me a
crooked smile and shifts his body next to me, pulling me
into his arms. I sink into his chest.

"Can I ask you something?" I say after a long silence.

"Sure," he says, kissing the top of my head.

"Are you . . . single?"

He cranes his neck back and looks down at me from the
corner of his eye. "Yes . . . are *you*?" He smirks.

I bite my lip and ignore his playful quip.

"Are you sure?" I ask. "You don't have a gorgeous supermodel girlfriend that you need to tell me about?

He cocks his head. ". . . Do you model?"

"Slate!" I say, softly punching his chest.

He laughs. It's a fun, carefree laugh, and I think it's my
new favorite sound.

"I'm serious!" I say.

He grins. "So am I."

I stare him down, trying not to laugh.

"There's no one else, Kaley," he assures me.

"Then why are you smirking?"

He laughs again. "Because I find it hilarious that *you* are
asking *me* that question."

"Trust me, I'm single," I say bitterly.

He eyes me intently, his smirk morphing into that ravenous look of his that makes me forget what day it is.

"Not anymore," he says, flipping me on my back and
hovering over me. His lips cover mine, and I'm lost once
again.

WE SPEND THE rest of the afternoon talking, intermittently watching movies, and even falling asleep on the couch. Neither of us need lunch after that hefty breakfast. We kiss off and on throughout the day, but he's taking it even slower now, which of course drives me absolutely crazy. As we sit talking, I hang on to his every word—it still feels unreal being alone in his house, conversing casually. I end up telling him about my dad announcing my parents' separation right before prom, and it's comforting having someone to talk to about it. He's a great listener, and I don't feel any judgment from him.

The sun is now completely sunken below the skyline, alerting us both that our time together is almost over.

"I'm going to miss you like hell tonight," he confesses.

"Me, too," I say.

We indulge in one last deep kiss that has the potential to spark another heated exchange, but he pulls away before things get too far. It takes all of my willpower to get off the couch and follow him out to the garage. He carries my bag to the Tahoe and opens the passenger door for me. My heart feels heavy, and I'm already longing for more uninterrupted time with him—I don't feel like I've learned enough about him yet. The day ended too quickly. I climb in, and he sets my bag by my feet. We already discussed the fast getaway needed when he drops me off—I need to grab my bag and jump out as quickly as possible. He hops into the driver's seat and just as he's about to start the engine, I yell "Wait!"

He halts, alarmed. "What's the matter?"

"Nothing," I say. "I've just always wanted to kiss you in this thing." I graze my lips against his, and he shifts toward me, grabbing the back of my neck. I rest my hand against his upper thigh, and he pulls me closer, kissing me with the same intensity he held last night. When he breaks away, I almost whimper. He presses his forehead against mine, our rapid breathing penetrating the silence.

"Promise me you'll make love to me in the Tahoe one day," I say with a grin.

He chuckles. "Anywhere you want it, Kay." He shifts back to his seat. "When the time is right," he warns.

"Yeah, yeah," I say, sitting back.

He slips the key back into the ignition, then hesitates.

"Here," he says, grabbing my phone out of my lap. "Just in case we need to communicate."

My eyes widen as I watch him enter his phone number.

"I thought that was too risky," I say in a hushed voice. As excited as I am to have his personal phone number, it still makes me uneasy.

"It is," he says, handing it back to me.

I tilt my head, noticing the name he entered. "Garrett?"

He shrugs. "It's my middle name. If anyone sees it, just say it's some hot guy you met at the mall," he says with a wink. He pulls his phone out of his pocket and hands it to me.

"Why, Mr. Slate," I say in my best Southern belle accent, "are you asking me for my phone number?"

He winces, and I laugh, retrieving the phone.

"You are going to be the death of me, Kaley," he groans.

I enter my number, then give him a playful kiss as I hand it back to him.

He peers down at his phone. "Christine? Nice."

I make a face.

"What, you don't like it? Kaley Christine is cute."

"Kaley Christine Kennedy? A little *too* cute if you ask me."

"It's perfect," he says, hitting the garage door opener. "At least they didn't spell your middle name with a K."

I shove his arm as he starts the engine with a laugh.

He backs out of the garage halfway when his face grows serious, and he stops.

"I only want to use this when we absolutely have to, okay?" He gestures to my phone. "You probably think I'm too paranoid, but even code names are dangerous. But I'd rather take this risk than have you show up at my house randomly when I have some teacher luncheon here or something."

"No, I totally get it. I won't do that, I swear."

"And when we *do* have plans for you to come over, use this." He takes a garage door opener out of his pocket and hands it to me. "Keep it in your glove box. That way you can just drive right into my garage, okay?"

"This is all feeling really risky," I say.

"Everything we do is risky. We'll only have you drive in at night and hope for the best," he says.

I like the sound of coming over at night—I miss his bed already.

"And if I do text you," he says, "promise me you'll delete it as soon as you read it. I know it's a fake name, but still."

"No worries, *Garrett*." I smile, and he leans down to kiss me, and I take a final whiff of his glorious scent. I dread going home to my small, empty, callow bed.

He holds my hand the entire way home. His grasp is warm and protective, and I never want to let go. When we pull up to the house, dread washes over me. In our earlier discussion, we decided not to risk a good-bye kiss, either.

"You're not going to change your mind Monday morning, are you?" I ask, only half-joking.

His expression is sober, reminding me of the night he dropped me off from the movies. "Not a chance. I'll be thinking about you the entire time we're apart. Remember that."

"Me too."

He squeezes my hand before letting go, and I jump out of the Tahoe. I rush up the driveway, glancing over my shoulder when I reach my door. He gives me a small wave before driving off, and I step into the house. As I close the door behind me, I'm instantly lonely, yet alive at the same time. Ironically, even though my boyfriend banged another girl last night, prom still ended up being the best night of my life.

My dad is sitting in the family room, and I greet him before marching straight to the kitchen in search of food—suddenly, I'm ravenous.

He appears in the entryway as I rummage through the pantry. "How was prom, Kay?"

The edges of my mouth curve into a grin, and I keep my back to him. "It was actually pretty great."

"That's good to hear," he says. "There's leftover pizza in the fridge if you want some."

I rush to the fridge and grab a slice from the box, not bothering to reheat it, and bite off a large portion.

"Your mom wants you to call her."

I stop mid-chew.

"I'm really not up for that tonight, Dad," I say with my mouth full.

"She feels awful and wants to talk to you, Kay."

"Emily's coming over," I say.

"Didn't she just drop you off?"

I almost choke, and I'm forced to swallow a big chunk. It hurts going down. "Uh, no. I got a ride from Tommy. He and Derek came over today," I say, realizing how easy it is to get caught in a lie.

"But you were just with Emily. Why is she coming over?"

Heat prickles my skin, and I feel myself start to perspire. "Um . . . she just texted me. I have her favorite shirt, and she wants to wear it tomorrow." *Holy shit, I'm going to have to get better at this.* I pretend to be interested in my pizza to avoid eye contact.

"Well, okay. But that will just take a minute. You should still call your mother."

"Why?" I snap, glaring at him. "You guys don't care about *my* time table, so why should I care about yours?"

"Kay, I'm really sorry about your prom," he says, sounding less than remorseful. "Your mom is, too. She wants to apologize about everything. Just talk to her."

"Fine," I say, cramming the box back into the fridge.

I run upstairs and text Emily that I'm still not feeling well. I can't handle any more lies tonight—they're already catching up to me. How am I going to keep track of them all? She is insistent on coming over, but I pacify her by agreeing to let her give me a ride to school tomorrow so we can talk. I'm not looking forward to lying profusely to my best friend, but it's imperative that I pull this off. At least I've bought myself another twelve hours.

One down, one to go.

I text my mom and tell her I'm not up for talking tonight, but that we can talk another time. She's adamant about it, so I agree to meet with her after school. There. Everyone is satisfied—well, except for me. It's a lot to handle in one day. After such a euphoric time with Elijah, tomorrow's going to be a bitch.

He's worth it.

My phone chimes, and I half expect it to be Tommy, but the screen reads "Garrett." Adrenaline pumps through my veins, and I sit up to read his text:

Have a good night, beautiful. I'll see you in the morning.

My chest flutters, then fills with warmth, melting away my angst. In the midst of all the drama with my parents, Tommy, and lying to everybody, I can't help but feel content.

I text him back: Aren't you breaking your own rules, Garrett?

He replies instantly: What can I say? You always make me lose control. Now delete this and have sweet dreams.

I imagine my dreams will be the sweetest they've ever been. After staring at the screen for longer than I'd like to admit, I force myself to press delete and drop back on my bed with a wide grin plastered to my face.

CHAPTER NINETEEN

"You look happy." Emily's watchful eyes peer over her coffee mug as she leans in the doorframe.

"Huh?" I attempt a cool glance her way as I curl the last section of my hair, but it's no use. When I turn my attention back to the mirror, my grinning reflection stares back at me in betrayal. No matter how hard I try to suppress it, it's glued to my face.

Her eyebrows squish together as she regards me. "What are you smiling about? Did you make up with Tommy or something?"

My smile dissolves into a hard line. "No. I haven't even spoken to him."

"Okay, good," she says. "I mean, not that you haven't spoken to him, just that I don't think he should be let off the hook so quickly."

"Definitely not," I agree. "What did Derek say about everything?" I give my hair a quick spritz of hairspray and toss my makeup into the drawer.

She shrugs. "Not too much. I think he's torn. Tommy's his best friend, so they have that stupid 'bros before hos' concept, or whatever. I mean, he's upset about it, but they still hung out yesterday."

I flick off the bathroom light, and we head to my room. "I don't expect him to hate Tommy or anything."

"Me neither," she says. "But it's just so weird now. The four of us are so tight, it just feels . . . strange."

"I agree," I say.

Emily babbles on about Tommy and the demise of our

foursome, and I tune her out as I slip on my wedges. I'm wearing a soft-yellow summer dress with the intent of driving Elijah a little crazy today. The dress is flowy, but short. I know my legs are a weakness of his, and I just can't help myself. I grab my bag and follow Emily downstairs.

Emily continues her vehement monologue about Tommy and Avery the entire way to school. I try to convince her I'm fine, but she isn't buying it. Since I can't tell her the real reason I'm not distraught over Tommy, I have to let her vent about him and "The Slut Bag," as Emily now refers to her.

"Tommy made his own decision," I say as soon as I can get a word in. "It's not all Avery's fault."

"Oh, I'm pissed off at Tommy, too," she says. "But Avery knew you guys were together. That's totally breaking the girl code. She's a bitch."

"Well, she's always been a bitch," I say with a laugh. "But who knows what Tommy told her that night. Maybe he told her we broke up."

"I can't believe you're not more upset about this!" she says, practically punching the air with her fist.

"Um, I think you're upset enough for the both of us," I say with a wry smile.

She glances at me, frowning. "I'm serious, Kay. Are you in shock or something? I mean, aren't you devastated?"

I'm silent as I mull over my next words carefully. "Honestly? No. Hurt, yes. But I'm not *devastated*. If I really wanted to be with Tommy, I would've stayed with him that night."

"Really? But I just thought you left because you're not ready to go all the way yet."

"I feel ready," I say, without skipping a beat. "But not with Tommy."

She turns to me, and I drop my gaze, pretending to smooth out my dress. *Crap, I shouldn't have said that.*

"Then with who?" she asks, her eyes darting back and

forth between me and the road.

"No one. Watch the road!" I say as the car swerves. When Emily's focus is back on driving, I continue. "I just know I don't want to sleep with *him*, that's all. Honestly, I think it was more about Tommy than it was my willingness." I didn't plan on being so honest with her, but I don't know what else to do. The faster we can all get over this, the faster I can be allowed to be happy.

She pulls into a parking space and cuts the engine. "Wait," she says, just as I grab the door handle. "So you're saying it *wasn't* about you being scared?"

I give a slight shrug. "I don't know. Maybe a little ... but I don't think so."

Her eyes search mine as if trying to read my thoughts, and my guard immediately rises.

"Why?" I ask.

She chews her lip. "Well ... I didn't want to say anything, but Derek's kind of mad at you."

A small jolt goes through me. *Shit, did he reveal his suspicions about me and Slate?* "Me? Why?"

"Well, according to Tommy—whatever *that's* worth— you were all over him these past few weeks. And it was *you* who wanted to book the hotel room."

"Ha! Right. The hotel wasn't Tommy's idea, not at all. That was *all* me," I say sourly. I lean against the door. "So, wait. Derek's mad at me about *that*?"

"He thinks you led Tommy on."

The comment is like a hard poke in the ribs.

"I stood up for you, of course," she says quickly, noting my reaction. "I told him that's complete bullshit and that you were just freaked out about going all the way."

"First of all," I say slowly. "Tommy has been like a dog with a bone since the day we became exclusive. And second of all, I have every right to change my mind."

"I agree, Kay. But you just told me that you *weren't* scared . . . so they're kind of right."

I glare at her and sit up straight. "So what are you saying? That I led poor, innocent Tommy on, therefore his actions are completely validated?"

"No!" she says. "I just—I can see both sides, that's all."

"Yeah, you're great at that," I say, my voice rigid.

"It's not okay what he did, Kay, and I'm super pissed off at him. I'm just saying—"

"I get what you're saying, Emily," I spew out her name as I grasp the door handle. "Just promise me you'll never work for a rape-victim hotline. You're like the poster child for coercion."

That pushes her over the edge.

"What the hell, Kaley! I'm just trying to show you both sides! I *am* on your side, but we're all friends and this really sucks," she says, slamming her fists on the steering wheel.

"I know it sucks!" I shout back. "And I'm sorry!"

I take a deep breath as I watch students pour into the building. First period is about to start.

"Look," I say, lowering my voice, "I don't want to fight with you."

She collapses back in her seat. "Neither do I."

"Great. My mom's picking me up from school, so don't worry about taking me home." I step out of her car without another word.

Donovan whistles at me as I enter the building, and I stop myself from giving him the finger—I'm ready to explode at the next person who makes a wrong move.

I storm into Slate's classroom and throw my bag down on my desk. I'm too livid to be nervous anymore. This whole mess has gotten way out of control, and I wish I could just run away with him and forget all the drama of high school.

"Kaley!" calls Avery from her seat. Her chipper voice

twists my nerve endings into spasms. *Is she seriously going to act like she didn't just bang my boyfriend?*

Emily's right, she is a slut bag.

I ignore her as I lower into my seat and open my textbook.

"Kaley!" she says again, this time with a squeal. "You won Best Eyes in the yearbook!"

"Awesome," I say flatly, without looking her way.

I hear snickers behind me and Avery huffs, folding her arms in my periphery. "Too bad there isn't a Biggest Bitch category," she says, hissing. "You'd probably win that, too."

Several people say "Oooh," and I roll my eyes, sitting back in my chair.

"I'm pretty sure you've cornered the market on that one," I say with callous.

"Ladies," says Elijah, cutting through the laughter behind me. "Cool it."

"Sorry, Mr. Slate," I say with a smirk.

His expression is neutral, but I sense a twinkle hiding behind his eyes. Avery flips her hair, and he takes roll. When he calls my name, I smile at him, but he flicks his glance away. My eyes glaze over as he steps up to the board, reviewing a bit of what we learned last Friday and introducing a new chapter. Last week feels like it was years ago. A different lifetime. Visions of him serving me breakfast and ravishing me on his kitchen island replay in my mind. Memories of lying in his arms during the thunderstorm tease me, and I feel myself flush. My pulse races as I think about where his lips were this weekend—and his hands—knowing that no one in this classroom has a clue.

I'm mindlessly chewing my pencil eraser, fantasizing about his powerful shoulders hovering over me as we make love on his desk when the piercing bell jolts me out of my daydream. Everyone gathers up their belongings and rushes out of the classroom, but I take my time—I'm dreading next period. Elijah is routinely cleaning the whiteboard, and I watch his back muscles with a newfound knowledge that makes it almost impossible not to jump on him right here. He sets down the eraser and scans the room before settling on my legs. For a brief, precious moment, we're alone.

"You're killing me, Kay," he says.

I grin in triumph. He nods for me to come near, and I saunter over to his desk, half-hoping he'll fulfill my recent fantasy.

He leans forward, his deep caramel eyes sparkling. "You look beautiful today."

A shock of electricity strikes my throat, sending a line of fire down to the deepest part of my stomach, and it takes every ounce of self-control not to lean in and kiss him.

"Not that that's different from any other day," he says with a killer smile.

I open my mouth to speak just as the door swings open. A group of chattering students fills the silence, and Elijah turns to his computer as I rush to my desk and grab my bag. Without glancing his way, I scurry out the door, my body humming.

When I reach my locker, it's as if an invisible force field zaps away my joy and replaces it with dread. I switch out my books and take my time, strolling to second period.

Please say he's absent today.

No such luck. When I arrive to class, Tommy is already seated. He stares straight ahead as I approach my seat next to him, and anger floods my vision. *Coward.* I know I'm guilty of my own indiscretions, but his blatant disdain sparks an unexpected rage in me. Even as I slide into my seat, he gives no inclination that I'm even there. I look his way ten minutes into class, still nothing.

Slate's right, he is a dick.

From the disaster in the hotel room, to the pure ecstasy of Slate's house, to fighting with Emily and Avery—and then my brief moment with Elijah this morning—it's a challenge to stay focused. It's easy for me to slip into the weekend memories, though, and I'm soon back at Elijah's house, watching him pull his shirt off and drinking in his perfect statuesque body. I want so desperately to be back in that moment. I watch his breathtaking smile in my mind's eye and hear his beautiful laughter in my ear . . . remembering how perfectly his lips fit with mine . . .

"Kaley?" Mrs. Taylor's voice ripples through my sweet reverie.

"Yes?" I reply.

"I would like to think you were deep in thought about our discussion, but since we're talking about the tragedy of *Frankenstein*, your goofy smile says otherwise."

About thirty heads turn in my direction, and I'm reminded of why I prefer sitting in the front of class. Even Tommy is looking my way, and I feel a flush of heat.

"Sorry," I say.

"Must've been a good prom," says Mrs. Taylor, smiling. "I'm happy for you, but it's imperative you pay attention to this section—it will be on your final. In fact, why don't you read the next paragraph."

"Um, sure," I say panicked. I have no idea what page we're even on.

The bell rings, saving the day, and I blow a grateful breath from my lungs. I snatch my things and rush out the door.

Tommy soon falls into stride with me. "Can we talk?"

I stop in the middle of the hall, causing a minor traffic jam, and turn to face him. "Really? *Now* you want to talk?"

"Well, we couldn't talk in class."

I scoff. "Oh, my apologies. I didn't realize you were such

a dedicated scholar. Besides, you haven't exactly called me." Not that I wanted him to.

He sheepishly draws up his shoulders. "I know, I'm sorry. Derek said Emily told you what happened, and I wanted to explain myself in person."

"What's to explain?" I say coolly. "You slept with Avery, who hasn't? I think I've pretty much got the gist."

His body tightens. "You *don't*."

"Fine," I say, turning away. "We'll talk later."

"When?" he calls through the crowd.

"Later!" I holler over my shoulder.

WHEN THE LUNCH bells rings, the thought of the cafeteria nauseates me. I think about the tension between Emily and me and the disapproving glares I'll receive from Derek—and I definitely don't feel like dealing with another snide comment from Avery, or sharing another awkward moment with Tommy. So instead, I decide to catch up on some homework in the library. I find a table in the back, hidden by a large book shelf, and settle into some homework.

I SUCCESSFULLY DODGE my friends for the remainder of the day, and I'm actually thankful my mom is picking me up so I don't have to deal with Emily. I stop at my locker after the final bell to grab the books I need for tonight's homework. I'm almost in the clear when Tommy leans against the locker next to mine.

Damn it.

"Hey," he says in a gentle tone.

I avoid his gaze. "Hey." My voice is even.

"Why weren't you at lunch?"

"I was busy."

"Come on, Kay. Talk to me."

I turn to him, unleashing a rancorous stare. "I don't have

anything to say to you, so if you have something to say to me, you'd better hurry because my mom's picking me up."

He takes a deep breath, and his drooping posture somehow infuriates me more. "I just want you to know that I'm sorry. You have no idea how sorry I am. I was so mad after you left, so I went to a party down the hall. I got really wasted and—"

"Yeah, I know what happened," I say, cutting him off. "What do you want from me?"

His ears flush red. "I want you to forgive me."

An edgy laugh bursts out of me. "Are you *insane*?" I can't believe his narcissism. He wants me to get over it in less than twenty-four hours? If he knew where I spent Saturday night, there's no way he'd even *speak* to me. Part of me wishes I could tell him. Just end this now.

He springs forward, his voice escalating. "I was drunk. You *left*. I barely even remember it!" Traffic slows around us as people start to congregate.

I look him hard in the eye. "That's too bad," I say, my voice low and level, "because you would've remembered it with me."

He kicks the locker below mine, and I flinch. "What the fuck, Kaley?" His voice reverberates through the hallway. "You left! I made a fucking mistake! *You chose to leave!*"

My body shakes with anger. "And *you* chose to sleep with a whore! So deal with it!" My voice is vicious—I barely recognize it.

A group of students come to a complete stop to watch the spectacle, and I turn my wrath on them. "Walk away!" I shout. They begin to disperse, but too slow for my liking.

I turn back to Tommy and deepen my tone. "So this is *my* fault? I chose to leave, and you barely remember it, so I'm just supposed to get over it and act like nothing happened, right?" I shake my head in disgust and spit my next words out like venom. "You know, it's really pathetic what happens to a boy when he's lived his entire life on a pedestal."

His lips curl, and he swings his fist into my locker door, slamming it shut. I recoil, trying to step away, but back into the wall of lockers.

He glares at me, inches from my face. "That's bullshit, Kaley!"

"Bradford!" Elijah's voice roars through the hall. He pushes past the ring of onlookers and grabs Tommy with force. "Let's take a walk." He yanks him by the collar and drags him down the hallway with authority.

"What the hell, Slate?" Tommy cries out, trying to break loose. Elijah releases him just before opening the door to the office and pushes him inside.

What. Just. Happened.

The size of the crowd has now tripled, loud murmurs filling the hall. Spectators look my way as they whisper to each other. I want to run the hell out of here, but I'm incapacitated. My feet are glued to the floor, my brain struggling to keep up with my racing thoughts. My phone buzzes against me, and I robotically pull it from my bag. I tear my gaze from the office door and read a text from my mom saying she's waiting out front. *Crap.* I desperately want to talk to Elijah, but I know there is no way it's going to happen. I force my shaky legs down the hall, my eyes skirting the captious stares from other students.

My mom's car is near the curb, and I summon the best smile I can manage.

"You look pretty today," she says as I slide in next to her. "Everything okay?" she asks when she gets a closer look at my face. "You look like you've seen a ghost."

My clammy hands struggle to buckle my seatbelt. "I just have a lot of homework . . . and I'm not really in the mood to talk." The last part is true at least. Silence permeates the car as she drives off campus and after a minute and a half, guilt convicts me. "Sorry, Mom. I'm willing to talk. I'm not trying to punish you; it was just a horrible day at school."

"How come? Is everything okay between you and Tommy?"

"Um, not really," I admit.

"Really? What happened? Your dad said you had a great time at prom."

I play with the zipper on my bag. "I did. It's a lot of stuff. I don't really want to talk about it right now."

"Well, you kids will work it out. He's perfect for you."

I give her a sideways glance. "He's perfect for me?"

"Yes. He's a great kid. And you two look so cute together."

I roll my eyes and gaze out the window. I wish I could introduce her to Elijah.

She pulls into the parking lot of a little café, and I peer through the windshield. The place is packed with old people. "This is where you want to talk?"

"Yeah, is this okay? I figured we could get a bite to eat."

I shrug and follow her inside. It's a cutesy little place, plastered with doilies and frilly tablecloths, and I feel like I've been transported to a tea party in the 1800s. A tall, gray-haired woman leads us to a tiny table that reminds me of something that belongs in a dollhouse and hands us our menus. There's an entire page dedicated to the tea selections, so I'm not far off about the tea party vibe. I close my menu and set it aside.

"You already know what you want?" asks my mom.

"I'm not hungry," I say.

When the woman returns to take our orders, my mom smiles. "We'll share a platter of the cucumber sandwiches and a side of fruit kabobs. I'll have an iced tea, and Kaley?"

"Water's fine," I say.

"Lemon?" says the woman.

I shrug. "Sure." She gives me a disapproving look before turning away. It's clear my manners aren't up to her standards.

My mom leans her elbows on the table. "Look, Kay. I can't tell you how sorry I am that I forgot about your prom. I will never forgive myself for being absent on your special day. It was the worst timing to walk out on your father."

"So you really walked out on him?" I ask. "Dad almost made it seem mutual."

"Well . . . it's complicated."

The woman drops off our beverages, and my mom takes a sip of her iced tea before continuing.

"Your father and I got together very young," she says.

"Yes, you've told me this story," I say. "You got pregnant with me, and I ruined both of your lives. Got it."

She lowers her brows. "You did *not* ruin our lives. You are my joy. Your father adores you and would do anything for you. So would I. This is not your fault."

"I know it's not, Mom, but you make me feel that way when you say crap like that." I sit back and chase the lemon wheel with my straw. I can't even drink this. I despise lemon in my water and don't know why I said yes to it.

"I'm sorry," she says.

The woman returns with our food and asks if we need anything else. I shake my head and she leaves us alone. I watch my mom pick up a delicate cucumber sandwich between her fingers and stare at it, her eyes glossing over.

I lean forward. "Look, Mom. I'm sorry. I know you must've been really unhappy with Dad. I just wish you would've at least tried. I mean, you wouldn't even go to counseling."

"It was too late by the time he started going," she says, almost in a whisper.

"What does that mean?"

"Never mind. It's complicated."

I let out an exasperated sigh and lean back. "I am an adult, Mom. If you say it's complicated one more time, I'm going to lose it. I'm graduating in a few weeks; I'll be nineteen this summer—I'm not a child. What is so complicated that I wouldn't understand? That you just fell out of love? That you were never *in* love? What?"

"Kaley," she says, her face solemn. "I had an affair."

"You . . . what?" The air is pulled out of me, and I cup my mouth.

"Your father and I have had issues for years, and I had an affair six months ago. I finally told your father . . . although I think he always knew."

I drop my hand in my lap. My stomach churns, and I'm grateful I decided against eating. "Wait. He always knew? You said that *you* walked out. Are you saying he still wanted you to stay after that?"

"Yes. Well, he wanted me to stay until I told him it was an ongoing affair, and that . . . that it's still ongoing."

My queasiness transmutes into anger. "Are you telling me you're still with this prick?" I say, glaring across the table. She doesn't bother reprimanding my language. "What does this mean? Are you in a relationship with him?" Hot, furious tears invade my vision, and I try to blink them away, but they quickly overflow. I snatch a doily off the table and wipe my eyes.

She nods. "Yes, Kaley, I am."

My chair scrapes against the floor as I stand up. "I can't do this here. I need to leave."

She tosses a wad of cash on the table and follows me out to the car. I crumple into my seat, unable to look at her.

"Please don't hate me," she says once we're on the road. "I was just so miserable for so long—I know that's not an excuse. But, I just wish you could understand."

I push back the tears and stare out the window. "I don't hate you, Mom. But how can you expect me to understand? This is my father we're talking about."

"I know," she says. "I just hope someday you will." Her voice is so quiet, I'm not sure it was meant for me to hear.

"I can't believe you thought taking me to a public place was a good idea to break the news."

"I hadn't planned on telling you today, sweetie. I'm sorry."

Suddenly, I feel torn between my parents. She wants me to understand, but I can't help feeling loyal to my father. It would be the same if it were the other way around, and it was my dad who cheated. I know she's expecting me to understand her as a woman, in the same way I understand Emily. But it doesn't change the fact that I'm her daughter, and I just found out she's been cheating on my father. I feel like I'm being ripped in two.

"I'll be moving back into the house soon," she says, breaking the silence.

I turn to her. "What?"

"Your dad will be getting a condo, and I'll be staying in the house."

"And where will I be?"

She glances at me. "Well, I hope you'll be staying with me while you go to ASU."

Unbelievable.

She pulls into the driveway, and I have my door open before the car comes to a complete stop.

"Kaley!" she calls out.

My chin trembles as I force myself to meet her pleading eyes. "I don't hate you, okay?" I say, my voice cracking. "I just need some time."

I slam the door and bolt into the house.

CHAPTER TWENTY

I SPRINT UP THE STAIRS as fast as my legs will allow, slamming my bedroom door behind me. My limbs become jelly, and I crumple to the floor like a deflated balloon. I cry out from the deepest part of my being, pulling a pillow from my bed to muffle my sobs. I let my agony release into the pillow as I clutch my stomach, wanting to claw out my insides to alleviate the pain.

I never knew I could feel this way about my parents. It's not like I didn't have some warning, but they're the only family I really have. My dad's family lives hours away, and my mom's family is out of state. Up until recently, my parents have been my whole world. But this is more painful than I anticipated—in my gut, I knew they'd been headed for a divorce, and I've been trying to accept their separation, but I never predicted this from my mother. It devastates me that she's done this to my father. He's far from perfect, but at least he tries. He doesn't deserve this—our family doesn't deserve this. I always wondered why she wouldn't consider counseling. Now I know it's because she doesn't want it to work.

She wants someone else.

My bedroom door squeaks open, and seconds later I feel a gentle hand on my shoulder.

"She told you, didn't she," says my dad.

My shoulders quake as I wail into my soggy pillow. He sits beside me, rubbing my back.

"I'm sorry, Kaley," he says. "I asked her not to say anything."

I snap my head up and wipe the tears and snot off my face with the edge of the pillow. "Why would you want to protect her like that?"

"I was trying to protect *you*, Kay. I knew it would hurt you too much. And I didn't want you to think less of your mother; she's a good person."

"How can you sit there and be so rational about this, Dad? What about you? Aren't *you* hurt? Are *you* okay?" I burst into tears again and lay my head in his lap.

When I'm with my mother, I'm a woman. When I'm with my dad, a little girl. . . .The real me is stuck somewhere in between.

He strokes my hair as I gasp for air between sobs.

"I'm okay," he says. "Of course it hurts, but I'll be fine. It's not solely on your mother for the fall of our marriage. It's more complex than that."

"I hate this."

"I know you do, Kay."

"Why are you letting her keep the house?"

He sighs. "I want you to stay in the house you grew up in, and you need to be with your mom."

I sit up and scowl at him. "Why would I want to stay in this house with *her*?"

"Because a girl needs her mother."

"You expect me to stay here when she brings that asshole over? She told me they're in a relationship! You're just as crazy as she is."

"Watch your mouth," he warns.

"No!" I say. "I'm legally an adult. I'm not staying here!"

His voice is even. "Well, you can live with me, but I'm not taking the house. And I don't know how much you'll like the area, but I'm probably moving near Grandpa and Grandma."

My grandparents live north about three hours away, near Flagstaff. I only see them on birthdays and Christmas.

"So, you're leaving me too?"

"No one is leaving you, Kay. I'll just be a few hours away, and your mom wants you to stay with her."

I rise to my feet and straighten my dress. "You both left me a long time ago."

"Kaley," he says, pushing himself off the floor. "You just need a little time to get used to the changes. Do you want to go see Dr. Sekelsky?"

I let out a harsh laugh. "Your shrink? No. I don't need a shrink right now; I need to get out of this house." I grab my necessities out of my bag and shove them in my purse before storming out of my bedroom and down the stairs.

"Kaley Christine," he calls after me. "You are not driving anywhere when you're this upset. Do you hear me?"

"I'm eighteen, Dad, and I don't belong to either of you anymore."

"Excuse me, young lady? You have *no* job, pay *no* rent, and live under *my* roof. You are not driving right now."

"It's not your roof anymore, remember, Dad?" I say with a sneer.

"Watch your tone. You know what I mean, Kaley."

"I'm sorry," I say in defeat. I know I'm not getting out of this house by being disrespectful, so I soften my tone. "I'm fine to drive, just please let me get some air." It pains me to put more stress on him, but I need to get away.

His posture sags. "Where are you going?"

"I don't know. I'll probably see if Emily's home."

"It's a school night," he reminds me.

"I won't be gone long," I say, holding back a new wave of tears. I know if I start crying again, he'll take my keys.

"Fine," he says. "Please don't be out late."

I step forward and give him a tight—but brief—hug. I

want him to know that I love him, but I'll lose it with anything longer than that.

I'm not sure how long my dad let me cry in my room before coming up to console me, but it's already nightfall when I step outside. As soon as I get into my car and turn on the engine, my tears spill out. I weep as I back out of the driveway, frantically wiping my face to see the road. I drive down the street until my house is out of sight and pull over.

I shuffle in my purse for my phone and pull it out. I scroll down to Emily's name as teardrops fall onto the screen. As I wipe them off, it scrolls down to "Garrett." I glance at the time before tapping the screen.

Elijah answers on the first ring. "Hello?"

I try to steady my voice, but can't catch my breath. "Hey," I choke out. "I'm so sorry for calling."

"What's the matter?" I hear the alarm in his voice.

"Are you alone?"

"Yes. Kaley, what's wrong?" The concern in his voice is like a tiny flame, flickering warmth underneath the ice in my heart.

"I'm so sorry to call you like this." I try to take a deep breath and hope he doesn't think I'm some young, piteous girl.

"It's okay. Tell me what's going on. Where are you right now? Did Bradford do something to you?" he says, his voice becoming protective.

"No. I'm in my car," I say.

"You shouldn't be driving this upset, Kay."

I groan. "I know."

"Come over."

A twinge of excitement nudges through the throbbing in my chest. I pause, trying to form words over the swelling in my throat.

"It's okay, I don't have to come over," I say at last. "I was on my way to Emily's, I just—I don't know. I just wanted to hear your voice. I'm sorry; I know I'm being irresponsible by calling you."

"Just come over, baby."

Hard to say no to that.

"O-okay."

"I'll see you in a few."

I hang up the phone and pull back onto the road, continuing to wipe the tears that compromise my vision. What am I going to say to him when I get there? I'm a wreck. I should've just gone to Emily's; I'm a blubbering mess.

Then it hits me. What the hell am I going to do with my life? My future keeps changing. Just when I was getting used to the idea of staying home and going to ASU, my parents blindsided me once again. Home no longer feels safe. I can't live there with *her*. And I know I can't handle seeing another man in my house. I'm queasy at the mere thought of him pulling up the driveway to pick her up for a date. I suppose I could live in the ASU dorms, but it's so close to home it feels silly. And without Emily as my roommate, it doesn't sound like much fun anyway.

As I turn onto Ironwood Drive, I open my glove box and pull out his garage door opener. But when I turn into his driveway, the garage is already open. I pull into the left side and cut the engine. The garage door closes behind me as he opens my car door. He's wearing a black cotton T-shirt with thin, gray athletic shorts—delicious as usual. I climb out of my car, and he pulls me into him. I throw my arms around his waist as the sobs flee my chest.

"My mom had an affair and my dad's moving away," I say, muffled into his chest.

"Oh, shit," he whispers.

My knees give way, and he supports my weight as he slowly guides me inside to the couch. He sits down, leaning against the armrest and gathers me into him. I melt into his hold, his mouth pressing against the top of my head as I cry. His presence soothes me, and I eventually regain my breath.

"I'm sorry," I say, finally looking up at him. *Oh, he's painfully handsome.* I cringe at the thought of what I must look like. "I'm a mess. I should've just gone to Emily's. You don't need to deal with this."

"Kaley, you're never a bother to me. I'm glad you came over." He kisses a tear that caught on my cheek, and I giggle.

"Taste good?" I say, smirking.

"Mmm, salty." He grins, and I laugh. "There's my Kaley," he says softly as he brushes the hair out of my face. "Talk to me, baby."

My heart flutters against the ache, and I wipe away the remaining tears. I catch him up on everything, from my mom announcing the affair at an elderly tea party, to my dad revealing that he's moving up north, and how I can't fathom living with my mother.

"How come?" he asks.

"I can't handle it, Elijah. Can you imagine her boyfriend coming around? I just can't."

He smiles.

"What?" I ask.

"I love hearing you say my name."

I rest my hand playfully on my hip. "Are you even listening to me Elijah Garrett?"

"Yes, I promise," he says with a sheepish grin. "I'm sorry, you distract me sometimes."

"I swear, you are the only person on the planet who could cheer me up right now."

His expression sobers, and he gives me a light kiss on the lips. "Good."

"Thank you," I whisper.

"I'd do anything for you, you should know that."

"Apparently," I say. "Why don't we talk about the day *you* had, mister?"

He belts out a laugh. "Kaley, you make me do crazy things."

"Oh, so it's *my* fault?"

He runs a hand through his hair. "I wanted to punch that kid in the face. He's lucky we were on school grounds."

"Nice," I say, wincing. "You call him a kid when he's only five months younger than me."

"Oh, you're all woman, trust me." He squeezes my thigh. "I won't let anyone talk to you like that," he says, his face hardening. "And any hint of violence toward you? I'd lose my job in a heartbeat to protect you."

"Don't you dare," I warn.

"Well then, he better stay away from you."

I run my hand across his solid chest and lean in to kiss him. He explores my mouth with intensity, grabbing a fistful of my hair. I rearrange my body so I'm straddling him. I'm still in my little yellow dress, and the only thing between me and the thin fabric of his shorts is my scanty underwear. He traces his fingers up my thighs, slipping his hands underneath my dress, gripping my waist and edging me closer to his hips. I inhale sharply when I feel him against me and kiss him with urgency. His breathing becomes rapid as I slide my hips back and forth against him, the familiar ache building beneath me. He breaks from my lips, releasing a husky groan. A small whine escapes me, and I lean in for more.

"Kaley," he says out of breath. "I can't—you make me too crazy."

I force my lips onto his anyway. He kisses me back with fervor, jerking my hips against him once more before breaking away again.

"Please," I whisper.

"Kaley, don't," he cautions. "If you don't stop, I won't be

able to do the right thing."

I trail my fingers across his chest. "But what if it *is* the right thing?"

He shakes his head, giving me a lopsided smile. "Not yet, baby."

I sit back in a huff. "Okay, calling me 'baby' isn't helping the situation."

His brow rises. "Oh?"

"It's driving me insane."

He flashes a wicked grin. "Good to know."

I take that as a challenge and press my mouth to his ear as I whisper in my best throaty voice, "I need you, Elijah."

He lets out a frustrated groan and with gentle force, slides me off his lap. I dissolve into laughter as I sink into the couch.

"You are so beautiful," he says, watching me.

My laughter subsides. "Are you kidding me right now? I'm a mess!" I wipe under my eyes, and the realization of him seeing my cry face makes me want to hide.

"You're always beautiful," he says, pulling my legs across his lap. "But you have too many dresses that should be illegal." I smile, and he laces his fingers with mine. "Are you feeling better?"

I nod. "*You* made me feel better . . . and more sexually frustrated than I've ever been in my life."

"Right back at ya, Kay," he says. "Seriously, are you going to be okay to drive home tonight?" He fiddles with the hem of my dress. "Because we'll have to burn this dress and put you in a potato sack if you plan on staying the night."

I laugh, a thrill running through me. "Don't worry, I have to go home. My dad is freaking out as it is."

He's quiet for a moment. "You know, if you can't live with your mom, NAU is a good school. If you'd be happier living with your dad.

"Don't be ridiculous," I say.

"It *is* a good school."

"I'm not putting down your school," I say. "I'm not leaving you." As soon as the words leave my lips, I cringe internally. *Why do I have to be so transparent around him?*

"Kay, don't make any decisions based off me."

I feel a tight pinch in my chest, but I know he's right.

"I'm not," I say, dropping my gaze. "It's not just that. Sorry, I don't mean to imply that we're in a serious relationship or anything, I—"

"Hey," he says, lifting my chin. "I don't want you to leave. But I'm not going to be selfish here. I don't want you to be unhappy." He shifts me around so my legs slide off his lap and wraps his arm around me. "I want you to live your life, baby." He kisses me on my temple.

"I *am* living my life," I say. I lean against his chest and notice his cluttered coffee table. His grade book is propped open with stacks of papers covering the entire surface. "Oh my gosh. You were busy when I called. I'm so sorry; I should go." I spring forward, but he latches onto my waist, pulling me back.

"Hey, don't worry about it," he says, holding me tight. "No big deal."

The scene reminds me he's an adult. Like, a real adult with real responsibilities. It also reminds me he's my teacher.

"Wait," I say, craning my neck. My gaze locks onto the stack near the back. "That's *my* class. Are those our tests from Thursday? Can I see my grade?" I feel his chest shake with laughter.

"*I'll* grab it," he says, releasing his hold on me and sitting up. "You're not allowed to see other students' grades." He kneels on the floor in front of me and searches through the stack.

In a playful, yet seductive tone, I say, "Since when are we

following the rules, Mr. Slate?"

"Kaley," he says sternly. "Don't."

I giggle and take advantage of his position, looping my arms around him from behind and nibble on his ear. He tosses the stack of papers, and they fall in a haphazard pile as he whips around and reaches up to kiss me. My hair falls around his face, creating a private cave just for our lips. I wrap my legs around his chest, and he slides his hands up my thighs, grabbing my backside and grunts as he yanks me forward with force. I grip his back as he lifts me up and sits back on the coffee table. My knees press against the stacks of papers, and I'm pretty sure he's sitting on his grade book. He lets me push him down on the table, and two more stacks fall to the floor.

"Sorry," I murmur, pushing up his shirt. I kiss his neck and slowly make my way down his well-muscled chest, listening to his staggered breathing. I think I hear him whisper "Kaley," but I'm not sure. When I'm almost to his belly button, I slip my fingers under his waist band and start to pull.

"Kaley-Kaley-Kaley," he says panicked. He pulls me to his face as he sits up, causing more papers to slide off the table. He shakes his head as he tries to catch his breath. "You . . . I can't. Don't—" He lays back down, his hands resting on my thighs, and whispers, "Shit."

I lean forward over his heaving chest, pinning my gaze on him. Lowering myself, I place my lips softly against his, and he moves his tongue like honey across mine, his arms wrapping around my back. As I start to slide my hips against him, he grabs hold of my arms, pushing me back.

"Kaley," he says, his voice raspy. He sits up and slides me farther back, so I'm sitting almost to the edge of his knees.

I bite my lip. "Sorry." I glance around at the mess of papers spread across the floor and try not to laugh. "Ooh, *really* sorry. This has to be killing you."

"Ha! You'd think. But if I have the strength to stop this," he says, gesturing to me. "Then I can handle a little mess."

I slip my hand through my hair. "Well . . . thanks for getting my mind off things, big guy," I say with a laugh.

An impish smile curves his lips upward. He rises from the table, lifting me with him, and flings me onto the couch. I squeal, then break into hysterics.

"Glad I could be of service, Kay," he says dryly, turning back to the mess.

He doesn't let me help him gather up the assignments—he's serious about me not seeing another student's grade—and tosses them in a sloppy pile on the coffee table, then joins me on the couch with my test.

"Promise me you'll stay calm when I show you this," he warns.

My laughter vanishes, and I sit up as panic washes over me.

"You're not calm," he says, noting my expression.

"Well, you're obviously about to deliver bad news," I exclaim. I snatch the paper out of his hand, revealing my grade. "I got a *C*?" I slump back on the couch. "It's not even a high C."

He grabs the test and tosses it on top of the pile before I can dissect it. "Do you realize the average grade in this class is a 67.9 percent?"

"Seriously? That's *average*?"

"Yes. You're still near the top of the class, Kay. You're smart and beautiful—you need to calm down. Okay?"

I nod, then groan. "I absolutely hate what I have to say right now."

His body stiffens. "What?"

"I have to get back home before my dad's blood pressure rises any more than it already has."

"That might help my blood pressure, too," he says with a wink.

"Hey, that's all you, buddy. I'm more than willing to release the pressure."

He shakes his head. "You *are* going to be the death of me." He pulls me off the couch and leads me back out to the garage.

"Drive safely," he says, opening my door for me.

"I will," I reply. "And thank you."

"Anytime."

He wraps me in a tight embrace, and I inhale deeply.

"Damn," I say, breathing him in. "I'm going to miss this smell tonight.

He steps back, pulling his shirt over his head.

"Here," he says, handing it to me.

I burst out laughing. "Are you serious right now?"

"Anything to put a smile on that beautiful face." He leans down to kiss me, and I take full advantage of his nakedness, sliding my hands across his mountainous chest and ripped abs. I hear his breath catch in his throat.

"Sorry," I say, pulling back.

His eyes burn through me. "Don't be."

"Thank you for tonight . . . and today with Tommy. Do you think you'll be in trouble?"

He clears his throat. "I'll be okay." He sounds confident, but I catch a trace of uneasiness beneath his eyes.

"I better head back," I say.

"Okay," he whispers. He holds the door as I slide into the driver's seat.

"Unless you're *absolutely* sure you don't want to strip me out of this dress and throw me on your bed," I say, with a playful grin.

He rests his arm on the door frame and ducks his head inside, his eyes darkening. Fitting his fingers underneath my chin, he presses his thumb against my bottom lip, parting it slightly, his gaze fixed on my mouth. Excruciatingly slow, he leans down and skims his lips against mine. *Mmm . . .* When his tongue finally meets mine, I feel it in the core of my belly, crawling lower, deeper. I'm dizzy when he releases me.

His eyes twinkle. "What. You don't think I'm worth the wait?"

It takes me several seconds to speak. "Um . . . most definitely."

He winks and gives me a light kiss before stepping back, and I drink in his massive upper body.

I hold out his shirt. "Are you sure you want me to take this?"

He lifts a shoulder. "Only if you want it."

I grin and drop it in my lap.

His lips curve into a half-smile. "Text me when you get home so I know you're safe."

"I will."

He closes my door, then opens the garage for me. He sends me a wave as I back out of the driveway, and I etch the vision of his sculpted torso into my mind.

As I turn onto the street, I lift his shirt to my face and inhale my favorite scent, sending my entire body into a near-hypnotic state. No one else could've relieved my pain tonight, and I'm so thankful he's in my life now.

I've always judged girls who completely lose themselves in a relationship, but he's the only thing holding me together, and I feel myself falling fast. And even though my brain is screaming at me to slow down, my heart and body want to charge ahead at full speed. I know I should be careful, but I'm already in way over my head. He has the power to completely shatter my heart into a million tiny fragments. . . . But if someone is going to break my heart, I'd rather it be Elijah Slate than anyone else. He's worth the risk, and I can only hope he feels the same about me.

I pull into the driveway and shove his shirt into my purse. The front door swings open just before I slide my key into the deadbolt. My dad fills the doorway, and even under the dim porch light, I can see his neck vein straining against his skin.

"Emily called."

My heart stops. "She did?" I suddenly realize I didn't take my purse into Elijah's house. I fish in it for my phone and find I have two missed calls and a text from Emily.

"Where were you?" he demands.

This can easily be a trap.

I squeeze past him into the house and take a risk. "Uh, Tommy called, so I went over there for a while." He has no idea we broke up, and I pray Tommy didn't call the house while I was away.

His eyes slice through me. "Were his parents home?"

I force myself to hold his stare and swallow hard. "Of course."

He studies me for fifteen agonizing seconds.

"Okay," he says at last. "Well, I'm going to bed."

"Goodnight," I say cheerfully through gritted teeth before darting up the stairs. This is getting out of hand. If I'm not more careful, I'm going to get caught in a lie—and soon.

I send a text to "Garrett," letting him know I'm home. Then I call Emily and plop down on my bed.

"Where have you been?" she says.

"Well hello to you, too," I say.

"Kaley," she groans.

"Sorry, I went out for a drive."

Another white lie I'll have to remember.

"Your dad said you told him you were at my house, so I freaked out not knowing where you were. Why did you lie to him about taking a drive? I thought I blew your cover or something."

Oh, you absolutely blew my cover.

"I was going to call you and come over, but then I just felt like driving. I had a rough night after meeting with my mom."

"What happened?"

As much as I don't feel like it, I tell her the story.

"No!" she gasps when I finish.

"Please don't say anything."

"I won't. I swear. I won't tell a soul, not even Derek."

"Thanks," I say. "I'm beat, Ems. Talk tomorrow?"

She pauses. "Okay. Call me if you need anything."

"I will," I say. "Hey, wait. Was there a reason you called me earlier?"

"Oh. Well, it doesn't seem very important now after hearing about your mom," she says, "but I just wanted to talk to you about what happened with Tommy today. I called you as soon as I found out. *Everyone's* talking about it."

My stomach drops. "They are?" *Great.* "I think Mr. Slate did what any teacher would've done," I say, diplomatically.

"I heard he manhandled Tommy," she says wryly.

"No," I say, trying to downplay it. "He grabbed him by the shirt because he wouldn't listen. I mean, Tommy was kind of losing it. He punched my locker."

"Still though, I don't know if he's allowed to do that. I hope he doesn't get fired."

Every muscle in me tightens. "Yeah, me too," I say. "Honestly, Ems, if you hear people talk about it just play it down. I don't want him getting fired because of me. Actually, I was glad he was there. Tommy was in my face and getting a little scary."

"Okay, I will," she says. "If anyone deserves to be reprimanded, it's Tommy."

I'm thankful she's supporting me for once instead of him.

Even more thankful we're not fighting anymore.

"Oh! I have something that's less depressing to tell you," she says.

"I would love that."

"You won Best Eyes in the yearbook."

I clamp my lips together, fighting the urge to make a sarcastic remark. I feel completely indifferent about it all. I just want to graduate and be free.

"Yeah, I heard that," I say, sparing her the details of my encounter this morning with Avery.

"We all won, actually."

She seems excited, so I indulge her. "Really? What did you win?" It takes every ounce of effort to sound upbeat.

"Most Outgoing," she says with pride.

"Oh, that fits," I say.

"Tommy won Best Looking," she says mockingly, no doubt for my benefit. "And Derek actually won two categories. Best Smile and Best All Around."

"Wow. Didn't even know that was possible. Well, let's hope it doesn't go to his head," I say. She laughs and we chat a few more minutes before saying goodnight.

I slip off my wedges and check my messages, reading Elijah's reply:

Goodnight, beautiful.

A flutter tickles my belly, and I stare at the screen, soaking in his words before I delete them. I make a silent promise to myself that if we're ever allowed to go public, I will put his number under "Sexy Slate." It's much more fitting than "Garrett." I long for the day I can call him freely and never have to delete his messages.

As I wash my face and get ready for bed, I think about how my life has changed in such a short period of time. Everywhere I look, things appear so perfect, but are rarely what they seem. Our tight-knit group wins trivial popularity contests that will go down in high school history, yet we're all on edge with each other. And as far as anyone else can tell, my parents have had the perfect marriage. On top of that, *no* one has any idea I'm dating my math teacher. . . . *Is everything in this world just a façade?*

I slip out of my clothes and pull Elijah's shirt out of my purse. I slide it over my head, letting his delicious scent envelop me, and climb into bed. As I lay my head against my pillow, I pull the collar of his shirt to my face, inhaling deeply, and imagine him lying next to me. My entire soul aches for him, and I try to ignore the disquietude of him being punished for today's incident. I snuggle into his shirt as I bury myself under the covers. I'm not going to worry about that now. Exhaustion soon takes over, and instead of fearing my dreams, I pray for Elijah to be the star of the show.

CHAPTER TWENTY-ONE

I SUCK AT LYING.

I know this about myself. And it's not exactly helping my nerves right now. *Okay, there's no need to panic.* I don't have to *lie*. I just have to tell the truth . . . just not all of it.

Lord, help me.

I stare at the ominous door and wipe my moist palms on my jeans. The shades in the window are drawn, so I can't see inside. With my elbows resting on my knees, I bury my face in my hands. I have no idea what I'm going to be asked, so I can't prepare my answers. A buzzing sound interrupts the silence, followed by Mrs. Miller's chipper voice.

"Ms. Kennedy?" she says.

I peer through my fingers and meet her smiling face.

"Mr. Bentley's ready for you; go right in."

I open my mouth to say thank you, but nothing comes out, so I just give her a weak smile before dragging myself to the principal's office. Wrapping my fingers around the cold metal handle, I take a deep breath, then exhale as I press the handle down.

"Hello, Ms. Kennedy," says Mr. Bentley as I enter. "Have a seat."

Two intimidating men in suits are seated off to the left with briefcases and legal notepads. *What am I walking into?* Mrs. Miller rushes through the door with her own notepad and sits to the right of Mr. Bentley, just as I take the hot seat, front and center. Suddenly, I feel insignificant as I peer over Mr. Bentley's overpowering desk.

"Kaley, this is Mr. Davis, our district lawyer," says Mr. Bentley, indicating the man closest to me.

District lawyer? I swear I can feel the blood draining from my face. Mr. Davis nods to me, and I attempt a polite smile.

Mr. Bentley gestures to the man next to him. "And this is Mr. Alvarado, our superintendent."

Shit!

I do my best to return a nod, but all I can think about is running out of this room screaming.

"They are here to witness this meeting and gather the information you provide for us," he continues. "You of course know my secretary, Mrs. Miller, who is also here to record the meeting and serve as a witness. Everything you say is confidential; we just need to collect all the facts so we're prepared if this case goes any further."

Case? . . . Any further? The air around me turns stale.

Why didn't I demand more answers from Elijah last night? Why didn't I ask for advice on what to say in this situation? I saw worry in his eyes last night, but I just ignored it. Why did his stupid, sexy face and phenomenal physique have to distract me from the seriousness of what went down yesterday?

Idiot.

Yet another ominous yellow notepad makes its appearance as Mr. Bentley pulls one from his desk, and I'm pretty sure my ass is sweating. I keep glancing at the door, wondering if Tommy or Elijah is expected.

"So, Ms. Kennedy," begins Mr. Bentley. He clicks open his pen, but it feels like he's cocking a gun. "Please tell us what happened yesterday after school."

All eyes swivel in my direction.

Really? He can't begin with something smaller? How am I supposed to answer such a loaded question?

"Kaley?" says Mr. Bentley. "Everything said in this room

is strictly confidential, understood?"

Goodness knows what expression I'm wearing. I glance around the room again. It seems the meeting is starting; hopefully, that means I don't have to state my case in front of Tommy or Elijah. Four gazes patiently wait, holding their pens ready. Locked and loaded.

Perspiration trickles down my neck, and I clear my throat. "Sorry, it's hard to know where to begin."

Mrs. Miller's comforting smile catches my eye, slightly lowering my anxiety for a moment. I'm glad she's here.

"Just start at the beginning," says Mr. Bentley. "Before Mr. Slate intervened."

I feel my face flush at the mention of his name and drop my gaze, knotting my fingers together. "Um . . . well, Tommy and I were in the middle of an argument." My voice sounds small. Like it belongs to somebody else.

"And for the record, this is Tommy Bradford, correct?" says Mr. Bentley.

"Yes," I say. Everyone scribbles on their notepads, and I clam up.

"Go on," says Mr. Bentley. "What was the argument about?"

The room feels like it just shot up fifty degrees. "Well, I . . . I mean, it's complicated." *Am I supposed to bring Avery into this and reveal my life drama?* Everyone stares, waiting for me to continue. So, I do. "We were fighting about something that happened after prom." The room of eyes burn through me, and I feel like a baby seal surrounded by sharks. "T-that's all I want to say about the fight."

Mr. Bentley shifts in his seat. "Kaley, you don't have to tell us what the argument was about if you're uncomfortable. But you do need to tell us what happened during the altercation."

I hate this. I hate what I have to do.

"Tommy got really upset with me and punched my lock-er. And that was after he kicked another locker."

"He punched *your* locker?" says Mr. Bentley, clarifying.

"Yes."

"Where were you standing?"

"I was right next to my locker. On the right. He kicked the locker underneath mine, then he punched my locker. There's a big dent in it now. I didn't realize that until this morning. It was jammed and the custodian had to help me get it open."

More scribbling on notepads.

"Okay, so he punched your locker, damaging it, then what happened? Did he get physical with you?"

"No!" I burst out. "Just with the lockers." I squeeze my eyes closed and hold my breath. "And he was yelling."

I feel like an asshole.

"And is that when Mr. Slate intervened?"

I open my eyes and rub my lips together. *Intervened.* That sounds like a positive way to put it. I run with it. "Yes. Well, almost. Tommy got in my face and was shouting. I was trapped between the lockers and the people around us, and I was getting scared, to be honest. That's when El—uh, Mr. Slate stopped him." My hands tremble after my slip-up, and I shove them under my legs.

"Mm-hm," says Mr. Bentley as he jots something down. My eyes dart around the room. No one seems to have caught it. "And then what happened?"

I hesitate. Everything I say is being recorded—and I've already slipped on his name. *I suck so badly at this.* I grit my teeth and sit up straight.

No, I can do this.

"Mr. Slate asked Tommy to come take a walk, but Tom-my refused." I pause and meet my principal's eyes. "Tommy was still in my face, and I was really afraid. He wouldn't let up. He wouldn't leave." I choose my next words carefully. "That's when Mr. Slate took Tommy by the shirt and ... walked him to the office."

I sit back as the group vigorously scrawls on their legal pads.

"When you say Mr. Slate 'took' him by the shirt, how do you mean exactly? Please elaborate."

I pull my hands onto my lap and squeeze them together. "Is Tommy pressing charges?"

"We are not at liberty to discuss details regarding any other party. Just answer the question, Ms. Kennedy."

I swallow hard. "He just grabbed him by the shirt collar, I think." *Crap.* I shouldn't have said "grabbed." That sounds too aggressive. "He didn't hurt him or anything," I rush. "Tommy wouldn't listen to him."

No one replies, or even looks up from their notes, and I decide to keep my mouth shut. The less I talk, the less possibility for more slip-ups.

Mr. Bentley is still writing as he asks the next question. "Did he have him by the shirt the entire time he walked him to the office?" He looks up, meeting my eyes.

"Um ... I'm not sure," I lie. "There was a crowd of people, and I couldn't see."

"Did you see Mr. Slate handle Tommy in any other way?" His eyes search mine, and I feel like he can read my deepest darkest secrets.

My mind flashes to Slate pushing Tommy with force into the office. *So many witnesses.*

I shake my head. "No, not that I saw," I lie again.

After more torturous note-taking, he addresses me.

"Okay, Ms. Kennedy. Is there anything else you can tell us? Anything you would like to add?"

Should I tell them I was glad Slate was there? That Tommy was out of control? I don't want to overdo it ... but I don't want to underdo it either.

"That's everything," I say.

WHEN I'M BACK in Slate's classroom, I feel the weight of several eyes on me, but I ignore them. The only eyes I'm interested in are his, but they don't meet mine. The bell rings shortly after, and I linger as the class disperses. He catches my eye and gives a quick shake of his head, then turns his back to me and resumes cleaning the whiteboard.

Not good.

I grab my things and walk out the door.

THE ENTIRE WEEK sucks. Big time. Tommy and I aren't speaking. The stares and whispers are obnoxious, but quickly fade by Wednesday. Every lunch period is the same and goes something like this: I sit next to Emily as she leans an elbow on the table and picks at her food, ignoring the mindless chatter. I never ask her what's wrong—I know it's the breakup of our group. Once in a while, I catch Avery staring wistfully at Tommy, but he continues to give her the cold shoulder. I almost feel bad for her.

Almost.

But none of this compares to the lack of contact with Elijah. He's distant in class. He never looks my way and never sends a text at night. I know he said we couldn't communicate unless it's an emergency, but he's already broken that rule twice. Why would he leave me in the dark now? It certainly feels like an emergency to me. I sustain a brave face in front of my schoolmates and friends, while every fiber of my being yearns to speak to him. I'm finding myself more and more apprehensive about our relationship and even more stressed about the status of his job. Is his career in jeopardy? Why won't he tell me what's going on? Is he sending me hidden signals that I'm supposed to decode? He *has* done this sort of thing before. But that was before we ... we what? What are we *really*? My insecurity gathers into the pit of my stomach, and I start to contemplate the unthinkable: is it possible our relationship is over before it even began?

CHAPTER TWENTY-TWO

STILL NOTHING.

It's Friday and I'm in hell. To make matters even worse, I'm without my car again. My dad took it in for an emergency tune-up first thing this morning. Emily is kind enough to pick me up, but I'm taken aback when I climb into her car and find her more docile than I've ever seen. When I ask her if she's okay, she gives me a weak smile and a nod. I guess she's taking the split of our group pretty hard, but I don't indulge the conversation. I love my best friend, but there's too much on my mind. Too much I can't talk about. I can't find the capacity to hold a normal conversation with anyone. . . . I *need* to speak to Slate.

BY THE END of first period, panic has overtaken me. He still hasn't made the slightest bit of eye contact—not even during roll call. I decide to swallow my fear and initiate the conversation. There is no way I can go an entire weekend without knowing where we stand, or what's going on. I take my time as I pack up my stuff, waiting for Avery to leave the room.

I hate her face.

She's discussing the homework, as usual, but she doesn't fool me. She may have fornicated my boyfriend's brains out last weekend, but there is no way she's touching Slate. His eyes briefly touch mine as he answers her long-winded questions, and I feel like I might go into cardiac arrest. After zero contact in four days, it's like my first glorious sip of water after crawling through a desert.

As Avery leans into his desk, I imagine yanking her golden hair back and punching her in the throat. When she can't procrastinate any longer, she picks up her books, observing me. I hold her stare until she's the first to break away. She glances at Mr. Slate, then back at me.

"What?" I snap.

"Aren't you going to be late for second period?" she says in her irritating little princess voice.

"What the hell do you care?" I retaliate. "I have a question for Mr. Slate, and if it didn't take you so long to comprehend what he was saying to you, neither of us would be late."

She huffs and marches out the door. I roll my eyes and approach Elijah's desk just as someone else comes through the door. *Damn it!*

I let out a loud, exasperated groan.

"What's wrong, Kay?" I hear Emily's voice behind me.

I spin around, feeling my face flush.

"Nothing," I squeak. "Just, you know, I hate math with a passion. Nothing new here."

She scrunches her brows in confusion.

Yep, I still suck at lying.

I grab my things and give her an exaggerated smile. She's still wary as she watches me leave, and I pray she lets it go by lunch.

BUT SHE DOESN'T.

"What's up with you and Slate?" she whispers.

I almost spit out a mouthful of soda.

I cough, trying to finish my swallow. "What?"

She shoots me a glance while she pours dressing over her salad. "Did you get in trouble because of the Tommy incident or something?"

"No, why would I?"

She shrugs. "I don't know. I didn't think you did, but Avery said you were called into the office on Monday, and you still haven't mentioned it to me. And today . . . I don't know. You seemed upset when I walked in, but . . . he almost seemed . . . *amused*. It was weird."

"Amused?" *That was his expression when I turned around?* "I was just talking to him about the homework." It's becoming much more difficult to lie to her. Physically painful.

"That's all?"

"Yes. Why? What did you think was going on?" It's a dangerous question, and I'm afraid of her answer, but I have to feel her out. If she suspects something, I need to put a stop to it right away.

She glances around the table and lowers her voice. "I don't know. The whole interaction just seemed odd . . . and intense. I'm just making sure everything's okay."

I rake my hand through my hair. "Everything's fine, Ems. Sorry I didn't mention the office thing; it was just so awful. I felt caught in the middle."

I want to ask if she knows if Tommy is pressing charges, but I figure she'd tell me if she knew. But with all the stuff I've been keeping from *her*, who knows? Maybe she's doing the same. I take a swig of my soda and pray she doesn't convey her suspicions to Derek.

AS SOON AS the final bell rings, I'm hauling ass to Slate's room. I need to be quick before Emily comes looking for me. After the last student leaves the room, his eyes greet mine as I stride up to his desk.

"Sorry," I whisper, a little out of breath. "I just wanted to know . . ."

I suddenly don't know how to finish my thought. There's so much I want to know. Where do I begin? We really need time to talk about everything that went down this week, but do I just invite myself over? It's not like I can ask him to meet me somewhere.

"You wanted to know . . . ?" He blesses me with that twinkle in his beautiful brown eyes as he waits for me to finish.

It comes out in a jumbled haste. "Emily's going to be looking for me, so I have to hurry. I just want to know what's going on. And . . . when can I see you again?" I cringe at my lack of cool and study my shoes as I run my hand through my hair.

When I lift my gaze, he's smiling at me.

"I'm busy Sunday, but you can come over any time before that." He appears entertained by my jitteriness and leans back in his chair. Is this the expression Emily caught? *Damn him.* He is pure confidence, and I want to crawl over this barrier of a desk and rip the suit right off his strapping body.

"Okay," I breathe. I don't want to seem too eager, but it comes out anyway. "Um . . . tonight? Or tomorrow if that's better."

He chuckles. "See you tonight. Come over after dark."

I immediately break into a grin, unable to suppress my glee. "Okay. I better go."

As I turn and head for the door, he calls after me. "Kay," he says, leaning forward, his expression serious. "I know the lack of communication has been hard, but after what happened I'm just trying to be extra careful."

"I understand," I say.

I hurry out the door and am met by Emily and Derek as they stroll down the hallway, hand-in-hand.

My heart palpitates. "Hey, guys!" I say a little too loud.

"Hey," they say in unison.

"Everything okay?" Emily asks.

"Uh, yeah," I fumble. "Totally. I just um . . . forgot something."

They both stare at me blankly.

"About the homework. I just had a question about the homework," I finish. *Shit.* I clear my throat. "So, you ready to go?" I spin around, not waiting for an answer and take off for the parking lot. I burst out of the building ahead of them and focus my gaze straight ahead as I march to Emily's car.

Just when I think I've made it to safety, I hear Derek behind me. "Sup, Slate!"

I whip around and see Elijah and Derek embraced in their familiar bromantic handshake as they engage in conversation.

"I want to wait to say good-bye to Derek, is that cool?" says Emily when she meets me by the car.

"No problem." I pull on the passenger door handle, but it's locked. When I look up at her, she's leaning on the roof of her car across from me with suspicious eyes.

"What's up with you?"

"Me?" I ask, peering over the roof of the car.

"You seemed really . . . excitable back there."

"Oh, I did?" I glance at Derek and Elijah still immersed in conversation. My mouth goes dry as I try to think of a good excuse. "Well . . . I didn't want to say anything in front of Derek, but I was talking to Slate about the incident."

She perks up a little. "Oh, really?"

"Yeah, I was just . . . thanking him. And I'm so relieved he isn't in any trouble," I lie.

I can only hope that's true. If he were getting fired, he'd be gone by now, right? If I'm wrong, I'll have some explaining to do, but it's the best I can do for now.

Derek comes up behind Emily and gives me a quick nod. "Avert your eyes, Kennedy," he says, twirling Emily around to kiss her.

She tosses me the keys, and I turn away, opening the passenger door, then slink down into the seat. I reach over and start her car so I can roll down the windows. When I look up, Elijah's eyes find mine as he walks across the lot. He winks at me before disappearing out of sight, and an uncontrollable grin spreads across my face.

He's still mine.

Emily opens her door and pokes her head in. "What are you smiling at?" she says, plopping into her seat.

"Huh?" I turn to her. "Oh, nothing."

She drives around to the exit, pulling into the turn lane, right beside Slate's Tahoe. He discreetly shifts to his left, peering down at me, his eyes magnetic. I bite my bottom lip, attempting to tone down my feverish grin. When Emily starts to pull out onto the road, he flashes me a sexy smile before turning in the opposite direction.

"What are you so happy about?" asks Emily. "No offense, but I figured you'd be moping around this weekend."

"Screw that," I say. "I'm moving on."

She sighs. "I wish I could say the same."

"I know you're upset, Ems. I'm sorry. But you still have *me*. And you still have Derek. That's more important than the four of us still hanging out together. Right?" I wish she was handling it better.

"Yeah, but aren't you sad we don't meet after school anymore? You and Tommy aren't even speaking. It's just depressing. High school's almost over, and our group is a wreck. I just thought we'd be savoring the end of the year right now. . . . I thought it would be so . . . *different*."

My heart sinks as she opens up. Here she is heartbroken over the collapse of our group, whereas I'm too enraptured with Slate to give a damn about repairing things with Tommy. I don't think she expects me to forgive him, but I think it's also what's making her feel hopeless about it.

"Well," I say softly. "Maybe it's better this way."

"How's it better?" Her voice sounds abnormally bitter.

"I don't know, Ems. Maybe it'll be less sad when we all have to part ways."

"Maybe less sad for you. I imagined all of us getting together when we're home on breaks. I didn't think this would be the end."

"I'll still hang with you and Derek. And you and I can still have fun on our breaks," I say, trying to cheer her up. "I'm sorry, but you don't expect me to hang around Tommy, do you?"

"Of course not," she says. Her voice cracks, and I turn to her.

"Ems, don't cry. It'll be okay, I promise."

"I didn't get in to USC," she blurts out.

My mouth falls open. "You didn't?" I realize I haven't asked her about it in weeks.

She shakes her head, letting a tear fall down her cheek. "No . . . I haven't even told Derek yet."

"Oh my gosh, Ems. I'm so sorry." I rest my hand on her shoulder. I've been so wrapped up in my own life, I had no idea what my best friend was going through. "When did you find out?"

"I got the letter on Tuesday."

So that's why she's been extra gloomy.

"When are you going to tell him?" I ask.

She shrugs. "I don't know. I can't seem to bring myself to do it."

"Do you want me to tell him?"

She pulls into my driveway, wiping a tear. "No, I can do it. Please don't tell anybody yet."

"I won't." I pause. "Do you want to come in? Talk about it?" I'm meeting Elijah, but that's not for another few hours.

"No, thanks. I'm going to Derek's. But what about you? I know you're going to ASU now, but have you thought about

NAU? I mean your dad's going to be up there now and that would solve living with your mom. We always dreamed of dorming together."

Crap. That technically would solve the problem. She looks at me like I'm her last bit of hope.

"I didn't even apply there," I say. "And it's too cold. Have you thought about ASU?"

She shakes her head. "No, I want to do the teacher education program at NAU. It's really good."

"So is the one at ASU."

"Just think about it," she pleads. "Maybe just do your first semester at ASU, then transfer to NAU in the spring. We'd have so much fun together. And you'd be free from your mom and her boyfriend."

I almost flinch at the unsettling reference. *My mom and her boyfriend.* It sounds so absurd out loud. I shake off the disturbing label, bringing my focus back to Emily.

"I'll think about it," I lie. She doesn't reply, and I reach over to give her a hug. "Call me if you need anything, okay?"

I ATTEMPT SOME homework, but my mind is useless, so I decide to get ready instead. I take a shower, straighten my hair until it's nice and sleek, and pack my bag. Just in case, I search my drawer for the pack of condoms, but they're nowhere to be found. I must've left them at the hotel.

You're welcome, Avery.

I hear my dad's car pull into the garage, and I bounce down the stairs, meeting him at the door.

"You ready to go get my car?"

He hesitates. "Oh, uh, it's not ready yet."

"What do you mean it's not ready yet?"

He sets his stuff down on the kitchen table. "There are some things wrong with it, and they want to keep it a little longer."

"How long?" I whine.

"I think they said a week or two."

What?

"A *week* or two? What the heck is wrong with it? I need my car!"

"It's the carburetor mainly," he mutters, grabbing a beer from the fridge. "Can't Emily take you to and from school for a while?"

I follow him out to the family room as he sinks into his chair. "Well, yeah, but what about the weekend? I have plans."

He grabs the remote and clicks on the TV. "Where are you going?"

"I—uh. Nowhere . . . *now*," I say.

"Can't someone pick you up? I would offer you my car, but I need to load it up tonight. I guess I could drop you off first."

"Uh, no. That's okay." What I wouldn't give to have my best friend in the know so she could take me to Elijah's. I feel defeated. "Why are you loading up the car?"

"I'm heading out early tomorrow morning to scout some places out, so I'll be gone all weekend."

I gloss over the miserable thought of my dad trying to find a place to live on his own and focus on the positive part of his answer: *I'll be gone all weekend.*

"Really?" I say, hopeful. My mind flashes to Elijah coming over tomorrow night. It'll be risky, but he could park the Tahoe in the garage.

"Your mom will be staying here, so you won't be by yourself," he says, quickly slaughtering my fantasy.

"Dad, I'm eighteen."

"I know. It's not about that. I think she wants to spend some time with you. She's upset about what happened between you two. She loves you, Kay."

If she really loved me, she'd let me have my math teacher over for a little rendezvous.

I trudge upstairs to my room and pull out my phone. With how strict Elijah's been this week, it's uncomfortable sending him a text. But I have no choice. I let him know I'll be without my car for possibly two weeks and have to cancel tonight's plans. I cringe. *How embarrassingly juvenile.*

My screen suddenly lights up with the name "Garrett" across the top. *Holy crap!* I can feel my heart beat in my fingertips as I tap the display to answer.

"Hey," I say softly.

"Hey, baby," he croons.

"You're calling me?"

"Thought it'd be easier."

I can't keep up with him. He's so careful one minute and breaking rules the next.

"I don't think it's a good idea for me to be picking you up."

I sit on my bed and sigh. "I know."

"Can you borrow your dad's car?"

"He's loading it up for a trip this weekend. And my mom's coming to stay with me." Everything I tell him about my life makes me feel like a child. "She wants to spend time with me, but she'll probably let me have her car tomorrow."

"No, you should stay with her."

I'm quiet. I want him to want me to come over as badly as I do.

"You need to patch things up with her. Next weekend, okay?"

Next weekend feels like a million years away.

"Okay . . . hopefully I'll have my car back by then."

"Let me know when you get it back, and we'll have a sleepover."

My heart flutters. "Okay."

"Have a good weekend. I'll see you Monday, baby."

I SPEND THE rest of the weekend like a caged animal in the zoo. I go for a run first thing Saturday morning in hopes of relieving the tension of captivity. My mom and I never continue our conversation regarding her affair. Instead, we eat an awkward dinner together—well, awkward for me; my mom seems a little too serene for my liking. I can tell she's happy, but it only escalates my anger. That, and she's treating me like I'm an egg about to crack. Everyone thinks I'm distraught over Tommy, and I feel myself becoming more and more fractious with every sympathetic gesture.

That evening, my mom and I lounge in the family room for a movie marathon. Sitting still is the last thing I want to do, but I oblige. After rejecting all my violent movie requests, she forces me to watch romantic dramas. *Thanks, Mom.*

Every cell in my body misses Elijah. The advice he gave me rattles around in my head: *You need to patch things up with her.* But I can't talk about it. With my irascible mood, I know it won't turn out well.

I catch her texting throughout the evening, and I know she's talking to *him.* Why else would she be sitting by herself, grinning like a schoolgirl? It's hard to watch for multiple reasons. The breakup of our family, for one—and my mother's oblivion to the pain it's causing everyone. But it's also a harsh reminder of the restrictions in my relationship with Elijah. *I* should be texting *him* with a stupid smile on my face. I should be able to lie in bed and talk to him all night if I please. He should be able to come pick me up for a date. A *real* date, not a house date where I have to sneak into his garage after sundown.

My mixed emotions weigh heavy on my mind, and I toss

and turn most of the night, finally falling asleep after two in the morning. I awake at sunrise, just as restless as the day before, and force myself into my running attire. While I'm stretching, I try to stay in the moment, not letting myself feel anything but my muscles expanding. I go out for a long run and finish off with a cold shower.

I'm turning into Slate.

Fantastic.

CHAPTER TWENTY-THREE

IF LAST WEEK WAS HELL, this week is purgatory—which I always thought would be way worse. The whole "not knowing" thing would be its own kind of hell. Either way you look at it, this week is worse than the last. Every day, I ask my dad about my car. And every day, he tells me it'll be done in a day or two.

Every day is a disappointment.

I can't even distract myself with Emily's company. Ever since she broke the news to Derek about not attending USC with him, she's been spending every waking hour by his side. We barely even talk during lunch because she's so focused on his every word. Can't blame the poor girl, but I've never felt lonelier.

I don't even care when Friday arrives—my dad told me again this morning that my car will be ready soon, but I don't believe him. You can only dangle a carrot in front of a person for so long. It's been almost two whole weeks since I've had Elijah's lips on mine, and I've been taking it out on my pencil erasers, one by one, during each math class. If I don't get some Slate soon, all the erasers within a ten-mile radius are going to suffer a brutal homicide.

"Kaley, can you see me after class?" Elijah's voice pierces the silence as he passes back our quizzes.

He and I haven't communicated since last Friday, and I literally have to press my lips together to hold back a grin. After ten painstaking minutes, the bell finally dismisses class. When the last student leaves, he boldly approaches my desk.

"Is your car back yet?"

He's so close to me, I catch his delicious scent and clutch my notebook to refrain from grabbing him.

I shake my head. "No. My dad said it will be ready soon, but he's full of it. He's been saying that since Monday."

"Okay," he says, clearly disappointed. He glances at the door. "Text me if you get it back this weekend, okay baby?"

Baby? He's not playing fair.

His eyes linger on my mouth before he steps away, and it takes everything I have to maintain my equanimity. My arms feel frail as I fumble with my books, cradling them to my chest. Just as I turn around, Emily enters the room alongside a girl I barely know, her eyes locking with mine.

"Hey," she says softly.

She glances at Elijah, then back to me.

"Hey," I say with a careful smile and walk out the door.

"WHAT'S UP WITH you?" I ask Emily as she's driving me home. Her wide grin has me guarded. She never asked me about what she saw this morning—or thought she saw—much to my relief. But since she hasn't exactly been smiling the past two weeks, this mood swing causes my fear to jump to the worst case scenario: She talked to Derek and has put the pieces together.

Calm down. There's no evidence of anything.

"Nothing," she says in a sing-song voice.

"Yeah, right," I say, laughing. "What's going on?"

"You tell me," she says as we pull up to my house.

My jaw drops.

Tommy is standing in my driveway next to a sleek, shiny, pitch-black Chevelle.

"What the hell?" I exclaim.

Emily laughs in delight, and I step out of her car in a

daze. Before I can turn back to her, she drives away, beeping her horn while waving good-bye. I'm too stunned to be mad at her for leaving me alone with Tommy.

I gape ahead as I walk up to the car. The windows are rolled down, and I poke my head inside. "Is this my car?"

Tommy hands me the keys, smiling. "My dad and I did some work on her. Well, with the help of his crew."

I run my fingers across the new glossy paint. My old beater gleams back at me like she just rolled off the assembly line.

"Are you for real right now? You guys painted it?" I turn to him. "And my dad knew?"

He nods, looking quite proud of himself for pulling this off.

"Dang! He told me it was the carburetor or something. I can't believe you were all in on this."

"Oh, we did way more than paint it. We pretty much re-built the entire thing. Runs great now. She's fast, so be careful. I can take you out the first couple of times until you get used to it." He grins at me. "Do you like it?"

"She's gorgeous," I say. Tommy and I haven't spoken in almost two weeks. The awkwardness of it all has me unsure of what to say next.

"You'll look hot in this thing, babe. Not that you didn't already."

Babe?

My temper instantly flares, and I turn to him, crossing my arms. "So, what now? Did you think I would just come running back to you because you fixed up my car? I didn't ask you to do this."

He glances down, shuffling his feet. "No," he says quietly.

Not the reaction I was expecting. Silence grows like a poisonous weed around us. When he looks back up at me, his face and neck are flushed.

"I just want you to know how sorry I am."

I release my arms, letting out a sharp breath. "Thank you," I say, trying to take the edge off my voice. "For the car. You didn't have to do this." I glance at my glistening Chevelle. "How much do I owe you?"

"What?" His eyes are tender, but he seems almost offended. "It's a gift, Kay. No strings, I promise."

And he goes for the kill.

"Wow . . . I don't know what to say." I can't look at him. He's still the reigning King of Guilt.

"Look," he says. His voice breaks, demanding my attention. When I meet his watery eyes, I'm stunned. "I really do love you, Kaley. You're not like the rest of the girls at school. I don't want anybody else . . . I don't want to lose you."

His words are like a switchblade to my heart. I've never seen Tommy break down. Ever. A sharp pain pierces the back of my throat, and I strain to hold it together. I don't want to hurt him any more than I already have, but I don't want to lead him on either. I know it's best if he just moves on.

"Tommy," I begin. "I *cannot* believe you did all this for me," I say, motioning to the car. "I can't thank you enough. I care about you so much. . . . I always will, you know that. But the truth is . . . I'm not in love with you. And frankly, I don't think you're in love with me either." I think about the way Elijah treats me, carrying my bags, his gentle touch, respecting my virtue—almost to a fault—and I add, "In fact, I'm positive that you're not."

"I am, though," he says, his voice gruff. "I swear to God, I'm in love with you, Kay." The muscles in his neck are stretched taut, and I know he's holding back a real cry.

I keep my voice calm. "You *think* you are." I can't stand seeing him like this, but I have to do the right thing. I'm no angel either, and he wouldn't be saying these things if he knew the truth. If the other man wasn't my teacher, I'd confess right now. He deserves to move on. He deserves to be happy with someone else.

His shoulders sag as he slips both hands into his pockets. I take a step forward and wrap my arms around him, my own tears pricking my eyes. He encloses his arms around my waist, holding me tight.

We have a history together. Nothing can ever change that.

Nor do I want it to.

"I'm sorry," I whisper.

"Me too," he whispers back.

I don't know how long we hold each other, but long enough for a painful tingle to spread through my arms. I step back and wipe the stream of tears off my face. "Thank you for my car. It's too much, though. I don't deserve it."

"Yes, you do. I've wanted to do this for a long time, and I want you to at least know that I'm sorry. I really am."

I look into his reddened-blue eyes. "I know you're sorry, Tommy." After his over-the-top gesture, I can only imagine what people will think of me when they find out I didn't take him back. I sigh as my eyes slide over my slick new car. "But people are going to think I'm a total bitch."

He shrugs. "Fuck 'em," he says. He gives me a half-smile, pulling a laugh out of me.

"That's excellent advice."

He gazes at me for a moment. "So, what are you doing tonight?"

Elijah's handsome face flashes through my mind.

"Um," I say, struggling to think of something. "Plans with my mom!" I burst out.

He tilts his head, scrutinizing me, then lets out an uneasy laugh. "Okay, then. Well, can you give me a lift? I sort of need a ride home."

"Oh!" I say. "Sure, hop in."

"Take the long way to my house. I want you to take her for a spin and make sure you're good."

I roll my eyes. "I think I can handle it, dude."

He begins to tell me everything they did to my car, and the pangs of guilt start all over again as I slide into my newly restored Chevelle. I turn the ignition, and it roars to life, startling me.

Tommy laughs at my reaction. "Nice, right?"

I nod as I shift into reverse. I've never felt so undeserving in my entire life. When I tap on the gas, my car lurches backward, and I slam on the breaks.

"Shit," I breathe.

"Told you," Tommy says, gratified. He leans back in the seat and rests his arm on the window frame. "Just ease into it."

I baby the gas pedal as I back out of the driveway and turn onto the street. The engine rumbles along while I get a feel for her, and it isn't long before I'm hauling ass down a back road. My old Chevelle feels smoother, sturdier—like it won't choke to death every time I press the gas pedal. But most of all, it feels *powerful*. I can see now why people talk the way they do about American muscle. This thing is still a beast—but in a good way now. I almost feel invincible.

I thank Tommy over and over. At least we're talking again. The silent treatment between us has been awful, and I'm grateful to have him back in my life. It gives me hope that maybe one day we can be friends again.

We stop at a light, and my nagging curiosity gets the better of me. "Can I ask you something?"

"Sure," he says, pulling his gaze from the window, fixing his eyes on me.

"Did you press charges against Slate? Or are you going

to?"

"Slate?"

I pretend his stare isn't burning a hole into the side of my face and keep my eyes straight ahead.

"No," he says finally. "Why?"

I try to keep my voice light and casual. "I was just wondering. I got called into the office last week and wasn't sure what all was going down. I don't want him to get fired or something crazy."

He scoffs. "Why do you care so much?"

"I don't," I say defensively. "I just don't want him getting into trouble for me. I mean, I feel like it was my fault."

He studies my face for a moment, but I refuse to look at him. "Slate's going to be fine, don't worry about it." He pauses. "*I'm* fine, by the way."

Heat stings my cheeks. "I didn't mean for it to sound like I'm not worried about *you* getting into trouble," I say. "But you did go a little bat-crap crazy on me."

He turns toward me. "Aw," he says, his voice dripping with contempt, "but you had your little Slatey-boy come to the rescue, didn't you?"

"What?" I risk a glance at him.

"Oh please, Kay," he says, slumping back into the seat. "Going to his study sessions? Blushing whenever Emily jokes about him at the lunch table? You're so obvious."

I open my mouth to defend myself, but nothing comes out.

"You really think I didn't see you talking to him at prom when you were on your way to the bathroom?" he continues. "I could tell you were making him uncomfortable by standing so close. I told myself it was just the alcohol, but . . ." his words trail off.

"But *what*? I have no idea what you're talking about," I practically growl.

He flicks his gaze out the window. "It's cool, Kaley. Everyone's entitled to have a little crush. But don't embarrass yourself."

I pull up to the curb in front of his house and slam on the newly sensitive breaks, adrenaline pumping through my veins. "What the hell does that mean? And you're *way* off base."

He lets out a harsh laugh, and his crystal-blue eyes pierce into mine. Any trace of the earlier sadness is gone. "It's just pathetic to watch you around him. That's all."

"Get out," I order.

He doesn't hesitate, slamming the freshly painted door, and stomps up the walkway.

"No strings, my ass," I mutter to myself as I slam down on the gas. My car howls as I accelerate down the road, the engine mirroring my anger. *I don't feel too pathetic when he kisses me until I'm weak in the knees, asshole.*

Just when I start getting used to the idea of being in a relationship with Elijah, I'm reminded of how risky it all is. Graduation can't get here soon enough.

I'M RELIEVED TO find my house empty when I return. I need to get a hold of my rage before I end up taking it out on an innocent bystander. I pull out my phone and text Elijah that my car is back in my possession. *Hopefully, he'll help me release some of my rage tonight.* The thought has me eager to start my evening with him, and I begin packing my bag. My phone chimes, and I swipe it off my desk. I read Elijah's reply with anticipation:

Have to cancel, baby. Have plans I forgot about. Tomorrow night, I promise.

I fall back on my bed and groan. "You have *got* to be kidding me," I say to myself.

As disappointment wraps around me, Tommy's words

slither into my mind: *Don't embarrass yourself. . . . It's just pathetic to watch you around him.* Uncertainty trickles in, and I spring from my bed. I can't sit here all night; I'll go insane.

I text Emily: Are you free tonight?

She replies right away: Going 2 dinner with D. Wanna come?

Sure. I despise being the third wheel, but I'm desperate.

Cool, we'll pick you up at 7.

I CLIMB INTO the backseat of Derek's alpine-white BMW and apologize for intruding on their date.

"No worries, Kay," says Derek. His infectious smile warms me. "Are you up for Scottsdale?"

Emily twists around in her seat. "I'm making him take me to Mastro's."

"Uh . . ." Mastro's is amazing, but insanely priced. I've only been once when Derek's parents took us all out after his brother's graduation.

"It's on me, Kay," says Derek.

"Are you sure?"

"Of course he's sure," says Emily.

Derek glances back at me with a smile, and I'm touched.

"Thanks," I say. "Sounds great."

I actually feel relieved to be getting out of town—even if it means having to intrude on a night out with another couple. My heart aches for Emily, though. How many more dates with Derek will she have before he leaves for USC?

"How'd it go with Tommy?" asks Emily.

"Not that great," I admit. "Don't think I'm horrible, please. I didn't know he was going to do all that for me—I can't just forget everything that happened and—"

"It's okay," Emily says. "We're not judging."

Derek glances back at me, his eyes sincere.

I smile. "Thanks."

The sun begins to set as we cruise up Loop 101, and I let

them chat away as I gaze out my window, watching the pink desert sky contrast the rustic Superstition Mountains.

When we pull up to the steakhouse, Emily lets me out of the back seat, and I raise my arms above my head, giving my body a good stretch. Derek takes Emily's hand, and I follow them inside.

While Derek checks in at the host desk, I take in the décor. I was practically a child the last time I was here and incapable of truly appreciating the ambience. Piano music softly penetrates my ears as the hostess shows us to our table. The gray stacked stone walls guide us into the dining area where wrought iron sconces glow against the brilliant-white table cloths. We take our seats at a corner table near an intimate rock fireplace.

"Okay, this is way too romantic to be dragging me along," I say sheepishly.

"Don't be silly," says Emily, smiling.

I check Derek's expression for any sign that I'm a bother, but he doesn't seem to mind at all.

Our server greets us, introducing herself, and takes our drink orders. As soon as she leaves, I dive into the menu, trying to ignore the slight awkwardness of interfering on what should be an intimate and romantic date for them. I hear Emily's breath suck in, and I glance up from my menu. Her eyes are fixed on something over my shoulder, glinting with intrigue. Her gaze slides to me and she gives a quick nod, indicating where I need to look. I follow her line of vision and peer over my shoulder, scanning the dining room.

And then I spot her.

The Blonde!

She is stunning in a sleek black jumpsuit that I thought only runway models and celebrities could pull off. The red bottoms on her stilettos catch my eye as she struts away, just as a man joins her, looping his arm around her bare shoulders. An older gentleman, who appears to be the restaurant manager, stops them and the three of them engage in conversation. The Blonde's date laughs, then kisses her on the side of the head, revealing his face for a split second, and I feel a sharp stab of pain assault my chest.

The man is Elijah.

The Blonde pats Elijah's stomach, then wraps her arms around him as the three of them erupt into laughter again.

"What are you two gawking at?" says Derek, his voice sounding miles away as the intimacy I'm witnessing sinks into my heart.

I spin back around, my mind reeling.

This is it. This is the reality.

He lied to me tonight.

Emily's hawk-like stare examines my face, and I try to switch my expression to a smile that's excited about the "juicy gossip," but I know I'm incapable of pulling it off.

"What's wrong?" she whispers.

"Nothing," I say.

"What's going on?" asks Derek. He leans into Emily, straining his neck to look over my shoulder. His eyes shift from curiosity to recognition. "Oh, geez," he says relaxing back in his seat. "Slate and his girlfriend? Really? You two are pathetic."

He said "pathetic" with friendly fire, but the word shoots into me like a poisoned dart.

"You know I only have eyes for you, babe," Emily gushes, leaning in to kiss him.

"Whatever," Derek says. "I'm going to call him over here. Maybe you two will stop pining over him when you meet his girlfriend."

"So you've met her, then?" I ask. The question comes out a little more aggressive than I planned.

"Yeah," says Derek slowly, his eyes searching mine.

"She's really nice."

Emily scoffs. "When did *you* meet her?" She sounds un-characteristically jealous.

"She was outside the locker room after a game, chill. Some of the guys were talking to her. I just met her for a second," he says defensively.

Emily gives a tight nod, then sinks into her seat, sulking. I've never seen her like this. Derek leans in, giving her a light kiss that quickly turns deeper. I take their distracted state to dare another peek over my shoulder and see Elijah leaving with her.

"I'll be right back," I say, but I don't think they hear me.

I slip out of my chair and rush down the aisle. I peek around the corner and see Elijah holding the front door open for The Blonde. He turns back to wave at someone, and I duck back behind the wall, my heart pounding. I wait a few seconds before poking my head back out. When I see that he's gone, I rush to the front door. Elijah is sliding into the passenger seat of her Mercedes, and I feel bile rising in my throat as I watch them interact. He's laughing at something she's saying and rests his arm against her headrest. He seems so carefree and relaxed.

"Miss?" a man's voice says behind me.

Startled, I whip around.

"Can I help you with something?" he asks.

It's the manager. The one Slate and Blonde Bitch were talking to. I point to the Mercedes.

"Do you know them?" I ask boldly.

His gaze follows my finger, then he says, "Yes, they dine here frequently."

My limbs go numb. *Of course they do.*

"Is there something I can help you with?" he asks again.

"No, no thank you." My voice is hoarse over the ball of emotion hardening in my throat. I want to bolt to the restroom, but I know I'll lose it. I make my way back to the table, trying to conceal my distress.

Keep it together, Kaley.

"You look pale," Derek comments as I return to the table.

"Thanks, Larson. You really know how to stroke a girl's ego."

He laughs. "I do what I can."

"Everything okay?" asks Emily.

"Yeah, I just went to the restroom."

They continue to stare at me.

What are they, detectives?

Our server arrives, presenting us with our delicately prepared dishes, and I'm left alone.

I CONSUMED ALMOST every bite of my meal, and now I feel sick as I climb into the backseat of the Beemer. Eating was the last thing I felt like doing, but I wasn't about to be rude when Derek was treating me to such an extravagant meal. I did my best to act natural throughout the evening, but with every affectionate exchange between Derek and Emily, it became more and more arduous to sit calmly across the table.

By the time I'm buckled in and Derek's back on the road, I pull my phone from my purse and scroll down to "Garrett," my hands trembling as I text him:

Will you be free later tonight? I can tell my dad I'm staying over at Emily's.

It's almost fifteen minutes later when he replies:

Not free tonight, baby. Keep texts to emergencies only. See you tomorrow.

Air is involuntarily ripped out of my chest. My vision blurs as I toss my phone aside, and I frantically wipe my eyes before the tears spill over. I fix my gaze out the back window and have to cup my palm over my mouth to stifle a sob.

"Kay." Derek's alert voice jolts me from my desolation.

I look up at him as he's glancing back at me repeatedly while still trying to keep his eyes on the road. When we pass under a street lamp, I can see his face full of concern.

"You okay back there?" He reaches his arm back, giving my knee a tight squeeze.

The small gesture is like a sledge hammer to the tiny dam I'm holding together, and I crumble forward, a sob fleeing from my chest as I drop my face into my hands. I feel a delicate hand on my leg, and I know it's Emily.

"Kaley." Her voice is alarmed.

"I'm sorry," I cry out. "I'm just so . . . *confused.*"

"About what?" she asks.

I try to control my breath, but my lungs spasm. My voice quivers as I try to speak. "D-does everyone ch-cheat?"

It's quiet for a moment.

"No," Emily says softly. "I don't think so."

"I-I just f-feel like everyone cheats . . . *everyone.* M-my mom . . . Tommy . . ." —*even me,* I want to add.

Even Slate.

"Your mom?" I hear Derek ask.

"Her mom had an affair," Emily whispers to him.

After a moment, I lift my head, wiping my face with my sleeves.

"I'm fine," I say, sniffling. "I'm sorry. I know you guys have your own thing you're dealing with, I don't mean to—"

"Shh," soothes Emily. "It's okay."

She waits, her eyes compassionately patient.

I nod. "I'm okay," I assure her, managing a weak smile. "I promise. It's just been a rough couple of weeks . . . for *all* of us."

She gives me a gentle smile, then faces forward in her seat, and I go back to gazing out the window, letting the tears flow as I try to steady my breaths. I feel Derek look back at me again, but I don't meet his eyes. I can't.

I can't believe he's seeing her tonight. And behind my back. I've been such a fool. He probably went to Scottsdale thinking he wouldn't get caught.

So, is this what I get? Is this karma biting me in the ass?

I put my friends through hell the last couple months, and all for what? A stupid, naïve infatuation with my math teacher. Damn, he's convincing. He should be teaching theater instead. Our relationship is a joke—*I'm* a joke.

I pick up my phone, tempted to text him again. *Just cancel plans for tomorrow and be done with him*. I blow the air from my lungs and toss my phone aside—I've already made such a fool of myself; I don't want to text him when I'm this upset. Especially when he's with *her* doing God knows *what*.

His text keeps flashing in my mind: *Keep texts to emergencies only*.

And finally, it all comes together. He can call and text me whenever he wants, but I can't do the same. He can go a *week* without giving me the slightest bit of contact, acting like it's all too risky—yet, when Friday rolls around, he approaches *my* desk asking me to come over. And calls me *baby*! His mercurial nature had me fooled into thinking he was just being cautious and then losing control at times. But now I know what it really is: power. He's in charge . . . and I just played right into his game.

CHAPTER TWENTY-FOUR

I'M READY TO DUMP SLATE. I'm ready to dump his lying, cheating, stupid, sexy, perfectly sculpted ass.

Okay, I'm totally not, but that's what I keep telling myself.

Everything is set into place. My dad thinks I'm staying the night at Emily's—I know she'll be at Derek's late tonight, so I'm pretty certain she won't blow my cover. I need my dad to think I'm staying the night so he won't wait up for me. That way, if I come home "sick," he'll be in bed and I can slip into my room unbothered. If things go the way I imagine they will, I won't feel like doing much besides lying in bed anyway, so it shouldn't be too difficult to pull off.

I'm wearing my best jeans and a purple blouse—a more adult look. My hands shake as I pack my bag. *Why am I even bothering?* While I don't know for sure how this night will go, both possible outcomes have my stomach in knots. First, I have to confront him. The thought of it makes me nauseated. And if for some miraculous reason he has a reasonable explanation for what I saw—*yeah right*—I will be spending the night. This is different than spontaneously showing up to his house intoxicated—this time, it's planned. I push the butterflies down, positive it won't be a happy ending.

My phone chimes with a text from Elijah:

Bring your bathing suit.

My heart skips a beat. *Bathing suit?* Last time we were together, he could barely handle my dress and wanted to hide my body in a potato sack. . . . Does he expect tonight to be the night? Blonde Bitch flashes before my eyes. *Did he have her in a bikini last night?* Okay, I'm ready to cancel the entire evening. Maybe it's not such a good idea to be face-to-face. Maybe I should just text him and cancel. *No, you're doing this!* I take a deep breath and open my dresser drawer, fishing for the perfect suit. I doubt the evening will even get this far, but if it does, I need to look my best. As I shuffle through the drawer, my phone chimes again:

The one you wore at Miller's.

My mouth goes dry. Okay, he's after something. I'm tempted to text back asking how exactly a bathing suit constitutes as an emergency. *Controlling dick.* With my pulse racing, I snatch up my black bikini and shove it in my bag. If I don't leave now, I'll chicken out. I grab my bag and fly down the stairs, hollering good-bye to my dad as I dash out the door.

"Hey!" he calls after me. "What's going on?"

I spin around. "I'm going to Emily's, remember?"

"You look like you're running from a fire."

"Oh, sorry. I'm just excited."

"Excited to drive your new car, I bet," he says, smiling.

"Uh, yeah. Definitely." I clench my teeth as I pin a phony smile on my face.

"You know, Kay, Tommy's a really nice boy." His smile fades. We never talk about boys, and I squirm inside. "You should give him a chance."

I silently count to three before speaking. "Yeah. Maybe."

That seems to pacify him, and his smile returns. "All right, Kay, have a good night—be safe."

"You got it."

I bolt to my car, toss my bag in the passenger seat and slam the door shut. "Arghh!" I scream, releasing my pent-up frustration as I start the engine. "Did you know he banged some other girl on prom night, *Dad*?" I shout as I press on the gas. The deep throttle of the engine satisfies my adrenaline as I continue to yell into the empty space. "But, hey!" I let out a humorless laugh. "He made my car all shiny and new, so I should just take him back, *right, Dad*?" I laugh harshly again at the craziness of my life—I am literally driving to my math teacher's house for a sleepover and have to confront him about a gorgeous blonde chick. Suddenly I miss the days of Barbie dolls and Nickelodeon.

I pull into Slate's garage, my heart thumping. After the door closes behind me, my car door opens and he pulls me out, wrapping me in his arms. I inhale the best scent in the entire universe, and all my doubts fizzle away. His lips seize mine, diffusing my anger like he just doused it with water. *How is it possible I've forgotten how amazing his lips are?* He releases me, and I try to regain my bearings.

Stay strong, Kaley. Remember where his lips were last night.

"This looks like a little more than a tune-up," he says, leaning back to admire the Chevelle.

I groan. "Um, yeah. It was a surprise."

"From your dad?"

"Not exactly. I mean, he was in on it, but it was Tommy," I say, mumbling Tommy's name.

"Really . . ." His brows rise. "Hmm." He presses his lips together, sliding his fingertips over the sleek exterior.

"Yeah," I say. "His dad owns a shop and he and the crew rebuilt the engine. And painted it, obviously."

He walks to the front of my car and steps back, leaning on his workbench. "Hmm," he says, rubbing his jaw.

"It was sort of an apology gift. I guess."

He crosses his arms, his eyes locked onto the Chevelle. "Interesting." Heavy silence falls over us as I watch him stare at the car. His voice is careful. "Did you forgive him?"

I shift my stance. "Kind of . . ."

His eyes flick to mine. They feel lethal.

"But uh . . . I-I basically told him that I didn't love him and that he should move on."

"Ouch," he replies, unable to shield a delighted smirk. He walks to the other side of my car, lifting my bag out of the passenger seat. "Let's start our night, shall we?"

Spit it out, Kaley. Do it now.

"Okay," I say.

Fool!

I follow him into the house. I've missed this place so much; it feels like months since I've been here. I still don't understand how he can decorate so well and be a math teacher. How is he so perfect at everything?

Like a perfect liar?

He leads me down the hall and sets my bag at the foot of his bed while I lean in the doorframe—suddenly, I'm not feeling so bold. He stands facing me in his sensual bedroom, wearing a relaxed pair of jeans and a white button-down shirt—but knowing him, I'm sure the simple ensemble cost a small fortune.

He tilts his head. "You okay?"

I give a tight nod, but can't muster a smile.

"I wanted to relax in the spa tonight. You interested?"

I realize I've never even seen his backyard.

"Sure," I say quietly.

"Let's go then."

"Now?" I consider dashing back out to the garage to the safety of my car.

He gives me a crooked smile, and my knees almost buckle. *Why does he have to be so devastatingly handsome?*

"Yeah, is that okay?"

I nod.

Confront him!

He kisses me on the side of the head and exits the room.

Exactly where he kissed *her* last night. Suddenly, all I can think about is the harem of women that must traipse through this house every weekend. Women that he kisses "sweetly" in the same spot. Women that use the pink hair-dryer under his sink . . .

Where the hell is my willpower?

I close the bedroom door and try to stay calm. How did this happen? I haven't even confronted him yet, and he already has me changing into my bikini. I'm putty in his hands . . .

I bet all the girls are.

I toss my hair into a messy bun and give myself a once-over in the mirror. When I wore this suit at Coach Miller's house, I had purposely chosen a boring one, and I'm surprised Elijah requested an encore. Just as I'm about to leave the room, I realize I didn't bring a cover-up, or a towel or anything. I check his bathroom, but only see one used towel hanging on a hook. I feel myself start to panic. I didn't take much care in what I packed because I didn't really think I'd be getting into my bikini tonight. I pause at the bedroom door.

Just go out there. He's pretty much seen it all, already.

My mind goes to Blonde Bitch, and my stomach rolls. I cringe at the thought of him comparing my body to hers. I force the air out of my lungs and open the door.

I inch down the hallway and find him leaning against the kitchen counter, staring at his phone, his thumbs moving swiftly across the screen. He has on a pair of swimming shorts, showing off a body that would make even a Greek god jealous, but all I can think about is who he's texting.

When he lifts his gaze, his eyes greedily soak in my appearance. "Finally, I get that bikini all to myself."

A shiver runs down my back. A comment like that would've flattered me a couple weeks ago, but now it feels like nothing more than a cheap line he uses on every girl—I no longer feel special.

I feel played.

He wraps my hand in his and leads me outside to a serene little oasis. There's a moderately sized in-ground pool in the corner of his yard with a spa attached, adorned with beautiful rockery and white oleander flowers. It's a quaint backyard, with manicured trees providing privacy from the neighbors. There's even a string of small twinkle lights along the covered porch area, giving off soft lighting.

"It's really lovely back here," I say in awe.

He steps into the spa and faces me. "It's even lovelier now." He winks at me and holds out his hand. I swallow down the disobedient flutters swarming inside of me, and I place my hand into his, stepping into the warm, silky water.

I wonder if he realizes how kind he is with the small things. Is it just the way he is? Or is it a game? He always carries my bag, opens my doors, and now he's assisting me into the spa. I've never experienced such gallantry with a high school boy. It's hard not to be captivated by him, but now I'm just curious about why he's so good at this.

I sink into the relaxing water. "You keep your spa at a nice temperature."

He chuckles. "Yeah. I don't like it when it's blistering hot. I prefer bath water." He sits across from me and leans back, resting his brawny arms on the ledge. His face becomes serious as he regards me. "Are you going to tell me what's wrong?"

I surrender my hands in the air and groan. "Do I seriously wear my emotions on my sleeve? I feel like everyone can read me like a book."

He smirks. "You're a little expressive, yes. But I like it."

I exhale and look at him. This is the last place I want to bring up Blonde Bitch. I hate the idea of having to storm off in a bikini, sopping wet, but this is it. *It's now or never.*

"Where were you last night?" I blurt out.

He cocks his head. "Why?"

Strike one, Mr. Slate.

"I'm just wondering. Am I not allowed to ask that question? Or is that against your *rules*?"

Careful, Kaley. Play it cool.

"You can ask me anything." His expression is unreadable. "Mastro's. In Scottsdale."

He catches me off guard with the truth, and I play with the jet stream as I ponder what to say next—I don't want to sound foolish.

I stare at the bubbling water and burst out with it. "I saw you last night with Blonde Bit—er, the blonde girl—*woman*! Whatever." I can't bring myself to look at him, so I keep talking. "The one that came to one of your baseball games. I just want to know the truth, okay? I'm not some ditzy little high school chick who's cool with getting played. That's not me." I feel a sense of release when I'm finished. I wait for him to reply, but he never does, and I finally peer up at him.

He's grinning at me.

Oh, he's much too good at this.

"What?" I snap.

"Come here, baby."

Unsolicited butterflies flitter around in my chest.

"*No*, Slate," I say, ignoring his charm. "Just tell me."

"Okay." He sighs, and I brace myself for his explanation.

"Her name is Audrey," he says evenly.

His admission is a blow to my stomach, smashing the butterflies into smithereens, practically knocking the wind out of me, and I drop my gaze.

"Audrey Slate," he adds.

My head snaps up.

"She's your *wife*?"

He belts out a laugh.

"No, Kaley . . . she's my *sister*."

What?

My ears start to pound. If this is true, I look like a moron. If it's not true, it's the lamest lie that's ever been told in the history of the free world. I don't know which to believe.

"That didn't look like your sister," I say.

He stretches an arm out to me. "Come here, baby."

"No!" I shout.

His eyes widen at my reaction.

"I'm sorry, but you two looked . . ."

"What?"

I shrug my shoulders, unable to meet his eyes.

"I wasn't even sitting next to her, Kaley, I don't know why you jumped to that."

"What do you mean you weren't sitting next to her?"

"My brother was between us."

"Your . . ." I blink at him. "I didn't see your brother."

"Who did you see then?"

"You! And The Blonde! Your arms were wrapped around each other. You were laughing with the manager. It was just the two of you. And I watched you leave! I saw you open the door for her and get into her Mercedes and . . . *leave* with her."

"My entire family was there, Kay. I just finished up my classes this week, and I forgot we were celebrating. You're right though, they left before us. And Audrey drove me home."

"And then your text!" I stand up, the water bubbling against my ribcage. "You practically scolded me for texting you."

"Oh, shit." He laughs, flaring my anger. "Baby, I'm sorry." He reaches out for me again.

"No," I say, my throat straining against unshed tears.

"Audrey almost saw that text," Elijah explains. "I'm sorry

you misinterpreted it. She would've seen 'Christine' and started interrogating me."

I nod slightly, looking down at the water. "Okay." I'm so confused. Embarrassed.

"Hey," he says, and I lift my eyes to his. "Come here."

This time I step forward, taking his hand. He pulls me onto his lap, settling my legs on either side of him, and I bury my face in the crevice of his neck, mortified.

He chuckles. "Don't be embarrassed. You had every right to ask me about it. I probably would've had the same reservations."

"I'm sorry," I say. "I was already having a bad day, and then I saw you with Little Miss Perfect, and you . . . Wait." I lift my head, my eyes widening. "You *kissed* her!"

His eyebrows shoot upward. "I can assure you, I did not." He looks like he's holding back more laughter.

"You kissed her on the side of the head."

He shrugs, his face turning serious. "I love my family, Kay."

"You do that with me, though, so I just thought—"

"Yeah, and I"—he seems to catch himself—"care about you, too."

The wall around my heart crumbles a tiny bit, and I glance down. "I'm sorry."

"It's okay, baby."

Wait a minute.

"But last night Derek said . . ."

"Said what?" he asks.

"That she was your girlfriend. He said he met her." I think back to the colorful dialogue between the boys at the lunch table describing all the things they wanted to do to "Slate's girlfriend," and I scrutinize his face. "Actually, *all* the boys refer to her as your girlfriend."

He scrunches his eyebrows. "I don't know why. I never

introduced her; I guess they all jumped to the same conclusion you did."

He leans in, brushing his lips against mine, and my pulse speeds up.

I pull back, just enough to look him in the eye. "You swear to me, Elijah Garrett?" I demand.

"I'm more than willing to show you my family photos, if you need. Birth certificates and finger prints may take a little longer though," he jokes.

I shake my head, struggling to keep his gaze. "I'm such an idiot."

"No, you're not." He slides his hand beside my jaw, pressing his thumb against my bottom lip, pulling it down as his gaze drops to my mouth. "God, I love these lips." He takes his time leaning forward, his eyes never leaving my bottom lip, and gently covers my mouth with his.

Still immersed in humiliation, I'm dying to flee, but his incredible lips—and the fact that the infamous blonde is his sister—has my heart leaping in celebration.

"Swear it again," I whisper against his lips.

"I swear, baby," he whispers back.

I sink into his arms, and he moves his mouth with an intention that sparks my body with fire. *This kiss is different.* It's as if all the pent-up frustration during our weeks apart are exploding into this one kiss. We're the only two people in the universe, and all the previous doubts and negativity dissolve into the sultry water, setting me free to drown in his kiss. His lips break from mine as he makes his way down my throat, and I tilt my head back allowing him full access. He grabs my waist as his lips travel down my chest and every ounce of my being melts into him. I reach around my back, pulling on the string of my bikini, but he clutches my hand, abruptly stopping me.

"You've *got* to be kidding me, Slate," I groan.

"There is no way I will be able to control myself if you take your top off right now," he says gruffly.

"So *don't* control yourself," I plead. "Not only did you request a sleepover, but you also requested this bikini. You didn't exactly ask for a 'potato sack,'" I tease. "I haven't seen you in *two* weeks; it's been torture."

He laughs. "Oh, you don't have to tell me that."

"So what's stopping you then?" I ask.

"Well, for one thing, I don't have any protection. So we can't anyway." He seems proud of himself for finding a solid argument.

"What kind of guy doesn't have a stockpile of protection?" I ask.

"The kind who's trying to do the right thing," he retorts.

"Well, I'm on birth control," I say with a sly grin. "So, I kind of have my own built-in stockpile."

Check mate.

He tilts his head in disapproval.

"Hey! I'm disease free. I'm a virgin, remember? Wait—" I pause. "Unless I'm about to find out that you actually have a flaw. A *big* one."

He drops his head back and belts out a laugh. "I have many flaws, baby, but that isn't one of them." His eyes twinkle in the dim lights. "Trust me. I got tested for everything under the sun last year . . . twice."

Oh . . .

Okay, that doesn't exactly help my earlier suspicions. Images of supermodel skanks dance in my head, but I push them aside. I'm too preoccupied with desire to give a damn right now.

"Okay, then let's go," I say, tightening my legs around him.

"Kaley," he warns.

"Come on," I moan.

He sighs. "I want to wait."

Insecurity knocks on the door of my heart, begging to be let back in.

"I want you," he says. "Trust me. You're all I think about."

"Then, what are you waiting for? I mean, why'd you invite me for a sleepover?"

"I'm sorry if I gave you the wrong idea. I just thought it'd be easier this way. We wouldn't have much time together if you didn't stay over, and I wanted more than just a few hours with you. I've missed you."

"I've missed you, too," I say, wrapping my arms around his broad shoulders. "I've just never known a guy to want to wait, sorry. It messes with my head."

"We need to at least wait until after graduation."

I sulk in frustration, knowing I can't argue with that. I know he has to protect himself.

"Fine," I say. He kisses me on the curve of my neck, and I moan. "No one's ever caused me to take cold showers before," I whimper. "This sucks."

He pulls back, his eyes dancing. "You've been taking cold showers?"

"It's not funny!"

"It's hilarious!" He laughs and kisses me on the lips. "I promise I will make it worth your wait, baby," he says. A wide grin spreads across his handsome face. "But I'm starting to wonder if you only want me for sex."

"Oh no, you're on to me," I say dryly.

His hands are still around my waist, distracting me. I slide off his lap and reclaim my spot across from him—I need a little space. I'm beginning to feel like a high school boy myself.

"So," I say after a while. "You said I could ask you anything?"

"Anything," he says, running his hands through his hair, dampening it. Water pours over his face, his glistening biceps flexing, and I'm suddenly launched into my own personal men's cologne ad.

"Well," I begin, my thoughts completely erased. "Um . . ."

He cocks his head, completely oblivious to what his simple actions do to me. I struggle to rein in my hormones, tearing my eyes away from him.

"I feel like you know a lot about me," I say, "but I don't really know that much about you."

"Shoot," he says.

"Last night you went out with your family."

He nods in agreement.

"Tell me about them."

"Well, I have two sisters and a brother. I'm the youngest in the family . . . and the disappointment," he says with a laugh.

I'm taken aback. "Disappointment? How so?"

"I didn't become a lawyer at my dad's firm."

"Wow. Okay, so your dad's a lawyer."

"So is my *sister*, Audrey"—he pauses to wink at me—"and my brother. My mother also used to be an attorney before she stayed home to raise us. Now she has her gardening club and society functions to keep her busy."

"So what does your other sister do? Why isn't *she* a disappointment?" I tease.

"She's a nurse practitioner. They're fine with that," he says, chuckling.

He seems so light-hearted about being the "family disappointment." I wonder if it's his way to cope, or if he really is okay with it.

"Why did you become a math teacher instead of a lawyer?"

He rubs the side of his jaw, and I almost lose my focus again. "I grew up always thinking I'd join my dad's firm, and even went to school with that intention, but I honestly didn't enjoy law. It's so boring."

"Okay, I can respect that," I say, "but math *isn't* boring? You must really love it."

"It's not that I love it so much, I'm just good at it. That's why I like to teach it. After I changed my major, my parents urged me to do something else with math besides teach, but I refused, clearly."

"Is that why you want to teach at the college level? To feel more respected?"

He shrugs. "Maybe that's part of it. I feel like I should be lying down on a couch for this, Dr. Kennedy," he ribs, pushing a playful splash in my direction.

"Okay, I'm sorry," I say, returning the splash. I lean back and try to relax as a jet stream massages my back.

"What?" he says eyeing me.

I let out a nervous giggle. "Okay, okay. I do have another burning question. . . . What's the deal with your wardrobe?"

He laughs louder than I expect. "Do you not like it?"

"I love it, actually," I admit. "But . . ." I hesitate before continuing. "No offense, but you're a math teacher. Not only are they known for their lack of style, but they can't afford half of what you wear."

He's grinning as if he's enjoying some kind of inside joke. "I know, it's kind of outrageous. It's my sister, Audrey. Well, I guess both my sisters—and my mom sometimes—but it's mainly Audrey. She's always shopping for me, and over the years, has completely taken over my wardrobe."

"Wow," I reply. "I wish she were *my* sister."

His smile drops and my muscles tense.

What did I say?

I try to push past it. "Is your family close?"

"Yeah, we are." His voice is tight. "Very close."

"What's the matter?" I ask, hoping I can handle the answer.

He sighs and shakes his head. "Nothing . . . I wish I could introduce you to them."

I'm touched he wants me to meet his family, but crushed by the reminder of our situation.

"Maybe after graduation," I suggest.

He doesn't respond, and I instantly regret my words. "Never mind," I say quickly. I don't want him feeling like I'm pressuring him to rush our relationship.

He rises as droplets of water cling to his torso. His hard body glistens in the twinkle lights, and I drink him in. He glides forward and grips the ledge on either side of me, leaning in. I tear my eyes from his gleaming muscles and peer up at him.

"What is it?" I whisper.

His features remain inexpressive. Clearly, it's *something*. I want to ask him what he's thinking, but something in his eyes makes me fear his response. That, and I don't want to be one of those girls who pester. He leans down, his lips arresting mine, and he kisses me with a roughness that has me dying for him to hold me prisoner. I slide my hands up his strong, sleek arms as his mouth consumes mine. Brusquely, he pulls away, and I gasp for air.

"Sorry," he whispers. "Come on. Let's go inside."

He never answered my question.

CHAPTER TWENTY-FIVE

I WAKE UP TO ELIJAH'S hard expression as he glares at his phone, his thumbs gliding vigorously across the screen. He sighs, tossing it carelessly onto the night stand, and it clatters against the wood.

"Everything okay?" I ask.

His hair is damp—from the shower, I presume—and he's wearing nothing but a pair of black boxer briefs. I silently curse my morning eyes for providing me with blurry vision.

"Sorry, did I wake you?" He sounds irritated.

I prop myself up onto my elbows. "No, but I think you may have broken your phone."

"It's fine," he says curtly, disappearing into his closet.

I slide off the bed, tension charging the room, and sneak into the bathroom to brush my teeth and relieve myself. When I step out, he's back over by his nightstand, wearing a pair of jeans, with his back to me as he types on his phone again. My vision is now perfectly clear as I tip-toe across the room, admiring his well-sculpted back. I timidly pull my bag onto the bed and dig through my clothes.

"Hey," he says softly, slipping his phone in his pocket. He's now facing me.

I freeze. "Hey."

"You hungry?"

"Actually, I think I'm gonna take off. I know you don't want me leaving during the day, but I think it'll be fine."

I don't want to be here if I'm not welcome. He's been sort

of aloof since we got out of the spa last night, and now he just seems downright irritated. He's either dealing with something personal, or he's about to break up with me, and I'd rather be somewhere else. Anywhere else.

He walks around the foot of the bed, meeting me on the other side. With an impish smirk, he slides his warm, strong hands underneath the back of my T-shirt, pulling me close.

"Why do you want to leave?" He squats down and teases my lips with his. "What's the matter?"

"Nothing's the matter with *me*," I say.

He cocks his head, his face still inches from mine, and looks at me like he has no idea what I'm referring to.

"The phone, Slate. You seem . . . pissed off."

"Oh," he says. "That's nothing. I forgot to cancel my golf game, so they were wondering where I was. They're not too thrilled when I miss, and this is twice in a month." He rolls his eyes.

"That's it?" I ask. "I'm sorry; you didn't have to cancel for me." *Especially if it's going to put you in a bad mood*, I add silently.

"You're much better than golf, Kaley." He draws me in for a kiss, and I clutch onto his solid back. "Mmm," he sighs. "I wish I could wake up to you every morning."

My chest tingles inside of the guarded cage I've built around it. I know his behavior last night had nothing to do with golf, and I'm not about to trust this mood swing.

He trails the back of his fingers across my cheek. "Will you stay?"

I nod and his lips twitch into a crooked grin.

"Breakfast?" he asks. "I bought a coffee maker."

"You did? Oh my gosh, that is so . . . *sweet*. Thank you."

"I aim to please, baby." He leads me out to the kitchen and pulls the coffee maker out of the cupboard for me. "I have no idea how to make it, but I figured you could handle that."

"No problem," I say with confidence.

As we putter around the kitchen, me in my braless attire and Elijah sporting the jeans-only look, I have to admit I could get used to this. His phone chirps a few more times as I'm setting up the coffee maker, and I try to decipher his expression as he reads the texts. It's clear he's now ignoring whomever it is, but I don't ask any more questions. Instead, I start the coffee, trying to ignore the urge to flee. I've never felt so paranoid in a relationship before. It's unfamiliar territory, and I don't want to feed into it. He's pulling a carton of eggs out of the fridge when the doorbell rings.

Our eyes immediately lock across the kitchen, both of us temporarily immobilized.

"Let me see who it is," he whispers. He creeps toward the front door and peers through the peephole. "You've got to be kidding me," he mumbles, turning away and walking back into the kitchen.

"Who is it?"

"No one." His sharp reply is like a sliver, piercing into my insecurities.

A knock raps on the door, and I look to him, panicked.

"Just ignore it, they'll go away."

"Okay," I say slowly, unsure of what to do now.

He pulls out a pan and places it on the stove, and I attempt to follow his lead. I pull a mug out of the cupboard and hear the deadbolt unlock. I spin around to face him, my heart leaping into my throat.

"Shit!" He takes hold of my arm and yanks me into the hallway. "Hide in my room!" he yells in an urgent whisper. "Closet!" he adds as I plunge down the hall and into the master bedroom, closing the door tightly shut. My hand is gripping his closet door when I hear a woman's voice.

I drop back to the bedroom door, cracking it open. *Why*

did he tell me to hide in the closet? Does he expect this woman to come into his bedroom? My stomach twists as old suspicions flood my mind with uncertainty.

Maybe it's just Audrey. He made it clear last night that he can't introduce me to his family yet; maybe that's all this is.

I have to find out.

I strain to hear what they're saying, but can't make anything out. I poke my head out and notice the door to the garage is open and creep down the hallway. I know he'll be furious with me if I get caught, and my heart pounds against my chest as I make my way to the garage entrance. I inch my way over to the door. It's cracked open, but I can't see her.

But I can hear her.

"You look hot right now, babe," she gushes. "You've been hitting the gym hard."

I stop breathing.

Not Audrey.

I hear him reply, but can't make out the words. Why is his voice so low? Is he making sure I can't hear him? My mind races with anxiety.

"Is this your new car?" says the mystery woman. "Are you restoring classics now?"

He's closer to the door now, and I hear his reply this time. "No, this is just a buddy's of mine. He needed me to store it over here this weekend."

He said it so matter-of-factly. I try not to jump to conclusions—I mean, he can't exactly say it's his student's car and she stayed over last night.

But he lied with such ease.

I finally catch sight of him through the small slit. It takes me a moment before I realize he's walking toward me, and I dash back across the house and into the bedroom as silent as a deer in the woods. I slip into his closet, shutting the door behind me. As I try to regain my breath, I flick on the light.

His wardrobe is nothing short of intimidating—designer suits, shirts, pants, shoes, even bags—all meticulously organized. I spy a messenger bag on one of the shelves and peek at the label: Gucci. I sift out a random suit and glance at its label: Dolce & Gabbana. *Seriously?* If this room wasn't so small, I'd swear I was in David Beckham's closet. I feel like his wardrobe is mocking me. *Am I the biggest idiot on the planet?* Of course this guy is a player. Telling me he's not ready to have sex with me yet is probably part of his game. The man wears designer clothes and constantly tests himself for STDs—have I been a complete fool this entire time? He's so damn convincing!

Tommy's sardonic words replay in my head: *Don't embarrass yourself. . . . It's pathetic to watch you around him.*

The faint sound of the automatic garage door opening yanks me out of my thoughts, and I reflexively flick off the light. *Is he leaving with her?* I have to see what's going on. I step out of the closet and grab my bra from my bag. If I'm going to get caught, I at least want my damn nipples to be hidden. I sneak out of the bedroom and back down the hallway. Adrenaline pumps through my veins as I peer through the crack of the door once more. This time, I see her, but her back is facing me. She watches Elijah as he backs the Tahoe out of the garage and parks it in the driveway. She's blonde.

Of course.

And she's leaning on the hood of my car.

Self-righteous bitch.

Elijah hops out of the Tahoe and walks back into the garage, out of sight. Her head swivels in his direction, reminding me of an owl stalking its prey, and I take in her pretty profile. I don't like the way she's watching his movements. And I especially don't like that she's as pretty as he is—they look like a couple. They obviously know each other well, since she has a damn key to his house.

A key to his freaking house!

Suddenly, I don't feel like staying here a minute longer. I dart back to the bedroom and strip off my sleepwear. I throw on my yellow tank top, then slip into my white denim skirt and slide into my sandals. I can't believe I've been lying to my best friends for *weeks* over this stupid, sexy, jackass. Just as I hear the automatic garage door close, I storm down the hallway, my bag in tow. As I round the corner, Elijah steps into the house, and I push past him.

"Whoa-whoa-whoa—*Kaley*," he says as I stomp off to my car.

I stop to see if the wench scratched my new paint before tossing my bag inside. I try to slide into the driver's seat before he can catch me, but he grabs my arm before I can get in.

"Kaley!"

"What?" I snap. I try to pull away, but my strength is no match.

"It's not what you think," he says.

I let out a jarring laugh. "Right! You need a new line, Slate, I think I've heard that one before." I continue to try to yank my arm free, but he just tightens his grip.

"Let me at least explain!"

I relax my arm and stare him dead in the eye. "Was that Audrey?"

"No—"

"Was it your other sister?"

"No—"

"Then, no!" I say, jerking my arm back. "Let me go, you're hurting me!"

He loosens his grip, but refuses to release me. Instead, he grabs my other arm, tugging me forward, and slams my car door shut with his knee, then pushes me against it.

"Listen to me," he demands. His eyes darken as he looks

down at me. "You can't just hop in your car and expect me to come chasing after you like some damn movie! *I don't have that luxury!*" His booming voice reverberates through the garage.

I grit my teeth. "I don't *want* you to chase me, I just want to leave. I've seen and heard enough, *Slate*," I say, spitting out his name.

"I'm not letting you leave," he says. He doesn't appear to be using much of his energy pinning me down like this. I, however, am beginning to sweat.

"Do I need to call the cops?" I threaten.

He sighs and lowers his voice. "Would you really call the cops on me?"

I jut my chin forward in defiance. "If you hold me hostage."

"Kaley," he begs. "Please hear me out. And then if you still want to leave, you can."

He waits to see if I'm going to fight him before slowly releasing me.

"Fine," I say, rubbing my arm. "But I can't handle any lies, Slate. I'm serious."

"Come on," he says, taking my hand and leading me back into the house.

I notice a house key on the coffee table as I sit on the sofa across from him.

He follows my stare and regards me with caution. "Is your arm okay?" His face looks pained.

I cross my legs and arms, ignoring his question. "Is she your girlfriend?" I ask, my foot bouncing uncontrollably.

"I thought *you* were my girlfriend," he says with a slight smirk.

"*Don't* play with me right now," I warn.

He sighs. "No, not anymore."

"How long has she been your 'not anymore?'"

He shrugs. "A while. Kaley, it was a rough breakup, I—"

I put my hand up. *Screw this.* I give an unfriendly nod before standing up and turning toward the door.

He springs up after me. "You promised me you'd hear me out."

I whip my body around and all my doubts spew out in one rage-filled stream. "So, what am I to you then? Am I just a rebound? Your mid-life or quarter-life crisis or something? Let me guess—you lost the love of your life, so you thought you'd just score some little high school student! Or are you just trying to make her jealous? *What*?"

My own voice startles me. I don't think I've ever heard it in such hysterics. I don't even know what I just said, or if it even made sense—all I know is I can't believe I threw my entire life away for this guy. Between Tommy sleeping with Avery and my mom's affair, it's impossible for me to trust anyone anymore. Nausea wrenches the pit of my stomach, and I feel the acid rising in my throat. I am *not* going to get sick in front of him. I clutch onto my keys and bolt back toward the door.

He grabs my arm, twisting me around. "Damn it, Kaley!"

I tug my arm back, but it's no use. When I try again, he pulls back even harder, grabbing both of my wrists. He lugs me over to the sofa and holds me down, pinning my wrists behind my back.

"Listen to me," he says, out of breath. "Yes, she's my ex. But we broke up over a year ago. She was my girlfriend in college. We fought all the time. I wanted to break it off so many times, but we had been together for so long, I felt guilty."

My mind goes to Tommy. I can definitely relate to that. I relax my body a little, and he loosens his grip on my wrists, but doesn't let go.

He regains his breath. "Our relationship was at rock bottom, Kay . . . about to shatter at any moment . . . and that's when she told me she was pregnant."

I squeeze my eyes shut and wait for the air to return to my lungs. I can't swallow the image of him being with another girl, let alone *that* girl—*woman*—carrying his child. Jealousy slithers like a venomous serpent around my heart. I picture her perfect little frame and luscious blonde hair, with that beautiful profile. My stomach churns, and I pray it settles quickly before I blow chunks all over him.

"It changed everything," he continues. "Well, for me anyway. It wasn't the way I had planned on bringing a child into the world, but it was already done, and I wanted to do the right thing. I went back to school right away and started working on my graduate degree. They allowed me to take extra classes because of my academic reputation. I wanted to teach college-level courses as soon as possible and make more money. I took out a loan and bought this house, I traded in my Audi A5 that I *adored*, and bought the Tahoe. I was completely focused on providing for my child and being a good father."

Oh great, even the beloved Tahoe is tainted. I can't take this. I sink into the couch, too numb to struggle. He takes note of my defeat and releases his grip from my wrists and sits next to me. He holds my hand, rubbing the back of it with his thumb. I barely notice. He takes a deep breath and continues.

"I was at home," he says, his voice distant. "I had just finished up some homework and was preparing my next lesson when Jasmine came home. I was extremely sleep deprived and stretched beyond my capacity. I could tell she had been crying, so I got up to ask her what was wrong, but she put her hands up like she wanted me to stay back. I asked her what was going on, but she wouldn't tell me anything. When I asked her if something was wrong with the baby, she burst into tears. Kaley, I can't tell you what I felt in that moment. It was pure agony—I was scared, honestly."

I notice his eyes are red as he stares through the coffee table. "Before I could ask her what had happened, she confessed that she aborted the baby."

I gasp. "Without telling you?"

He gives a slight nod, and I squeeze his hand.

"She just blurted it out and fell to the floor crying." His face is haunted as he relives the story. "But then my devastation quickly turned into outrage. I get that it's not my body, Kaley, but to have no control over what happens to your own child is a kind of pain I wouldn't wish on anybody.

"I yelled at her. I mean, I *really* yelled at her. It was bad. I threw my glass of water against the wall and it shattered everywhere, scaring her." He sighs heavily. "I smashed the lamp, too. I'm not proud of it; I was completely out of control. She begged me to stop, but it only infuriated me more." He lowers his head, his shame palpable.

"I finally calmed down enough to ask her why she would do that to me, but she just continued to cry, so I just sat and watched her. I didn't know what else to do.

"Soon after, I heard a truck pull into the driveway and saw that it was my best friend, Reed. I told her to go to the bathroom and clean herself up. I assured her that I wouldn't tell him what was going on. Even though I hated her at that moment for what she'd done, I still wanted to protect her. I wanted to give her a chance to explain herself before I divulged this information to anyone else.

"I hurried to pick up the pieces of broken glass and porcelain to hide the evidence of my temper. She was still on the floor, so I stopped to lift her up and urged her to get cleaned up. Then she looked up at me and whispered, 'He wasn't supposed to be here yet.'

"At first I didn't know what she meant. Then I realized

Reed was still sitting out in his truck. I started to put the pieces together and asked her why he wasn't coming up to the door, and she said, 'Because he isn't here to see you. . . . He's here to pick me up.' I asked her why, and she cried, 'Because we're together, Elijah! We have been for six months!'

"That's when I really lost it. I shouted for her to get out and she practically ran to the door. To be honest, she looked like a pathetic whore to me as she struggled with the door handle—I was disgusted by the sight of her. But when she finally opened the door, I stopped her. She had fear in her eyes when she looked up at me—I hated that she was scared of me. But I had to ask the question that I think anyone would've asked, even though no answer would've made me feel any better. I asked her if the baby was even mine."

He swallows, taking a moment.

"I'll never forget that look in her eye right before she told me she didn't know. She turned away from me, and I watched her walk out to my best friend's truck as my whole body started to shake with rage. I was livid. I followed her outside—I didn't want to, but I was beyond self-control at that point.

"Reed and I had been best friends since we were twelve years old, mind you. He didn't even get out of the truck to face me man-to-man. He just cracked open his window like a chicken-shit as she climbed into the cab. I was about to rip into him when I noticed Mrs. Chapin outside watering her lawn. Tearing Reed out of his truck in front of my neighbors and beating him until he was paralyzed wasn't going to solve my problems, or relieve me. I'd been working my ass off for my reputation, and I was not going to let the two of them take anything else away from me. My career was all I had left.

"He looked like an idiot as he spoke to me through the

crack in the window—he had the gall to say, 'I'm sorry, man. It just kind of happened. You said you weren't happy anyway—' I cut him off and said, 'Don't! Don't you dare tell me about my relationship like you know a damn thing.' Mrs. Chapin was still watching us, so I gave her a smile and a wave. Then I turned back to Reed—I was sure to keep my voice low this time—and I said, 'You are a fucking coward. Have a great life; the two of you deserve each other.' I turned and went back into the house, and he drove away. We haven't spoken since."

After a moment, I clear my throat. "Holy hell. And is this the first time you've seen her since?"

"Not her, no," he says, and the pit in my stomach solidifies. "I've seen her a few times since, but briefly. She's still friends with my sister."

"She's friends with your *sister*?" I ask. "Which one?"

"Audrey."

Great.

"Doesn't that upset you?" I ask.

"That they're still friends? Audrey knows I don't like it. We just don't talk about it. But she knows not to bring her around me."

I shift in my seat. "Forgive me if this is too personal, but is she why you got tested for STDs? Or is that just something you do often?"

He chuckles and shakes his head. "No. I got tested right after I found out she had been cheating. And a second time to be sure."

Relief stretches through my chest, and I take a deep breath. "Okay. So you lost your girlfriend, your best friend, and possibly your baby in the same day?"

He leans his head against the couch, his face is raw, and looks into my eyes. "I was only sad to lose the baby—if it was even mine—and my best friend. It was over with Jasmine way before any of that went down."

"I'm just confused by you, Slate," I say. "I mean, you seem so sincere right now, but she was just about to come into your house—with her very own *key*."

"Kaley, I didn't realize she still had a key. Let alone the gall to use it. But look," he says nodding to the coffee table. "I made her give it back."

I chew on the corner of my lip. "What was she doing here? Were you texting her this morning? Were you lying to me about golf?" *Why can't I trust him?*

"No, Kay," he says, rubbing my hand. "I haven't lied to you about anything. The first text I got this morning *was* about golf. I really did forget to cancel. Then she texted me a few times asking for her snowboard." He rolls his eyes. "I didn't say anything to you about it because why would I? I don't care about her. Anyway, I guess Audrey told her I still had it, and that's how it all got started. Jasmine's crazy like that. It makes me hate her even more—the fact that she would just text me about her snowboard, instead of going through my sister. And then come into my house uninvited."

"Are you dense, Slate?" I ask.

His brows rise, and he almost laughs. "What?"

"It's almost summer," I say. "The snowboard was an excuse to see you. She wants you back; I heard her. You don't have to play dumb with me. She called you 'babe' and said you looked hot. And I saw the way she was looking at you."

"Damn, I guess that looked bad. I'm sorry you got the wrong idea," he says, leaning over to kiss me on the forehead. "But you heard my reply, so you should've known that I wasn't interested."

"No, I couldn't hear you."

"Oh. Well, that's probably better. I wasn't very nice."

"So, I guess I'm just a stupid drama queen then?"

He sighs. "You've dealt with a lot of infidelity lately, baby. And honestly, I would've felt the same way. I can't say I would've *reacted* the same way," he says with a wink, "but I understand. . . . And if I'm being honest, I can't stand the sight of your car now, knowing it looks like that because of Bradford. It drives me insane."

"Really?"

"Really," he replies.

"I'm sorry you went through all of that. I don't know what to say."

He turns toward me, resting his hand on my thigh. "I don't want you to say anything, Kay. Believe me when I tell you that I didn't want to be in another relationship when I met you—it was the last thing I was looking for. And I sure as hell wasn't looking for a high school student—no offense—but I doubt you were looking for a teacher," he says, smiling a little. "But the day you walked through the door of my classroom, my whole world stopped. Actually, it had been stopped for over a year. It's like the world started spinning again." He drops his head back against the sofa and laughs.

"What is so funny right now?"

"I am so bad at this," he says, still laughing. "I'm sorry. I have trouble explaining how I feel. I'm better with numbers than I am with words."

"I think you're better than you think you are," I say with a soft smile.

"I tried to ignore you, Kaley," he says. "I tried to stay professional and get you out of my head. My graduate classes weren't enough to distract me. You have no idea how much golf I played just trying to focus on something else. I tried to keep busy—even coaching the baseball team. But that quickly backfired when I realized you'd be at every game watching your boyfriend play. I did everything I could to stay away from you." He lifts my chin, forcing me to keep eye contact with him. "I know hearing about my last relationship, and the seriousness of it, is hard for you. But trust me when I tell you that I have *never* felt this way about anyone before in my entire life."

Holy . . . I draw my legs underneath me, my guard faltering as I try to let his words sink in.

"I'm sorry if this is too soon for you to handle," he says quietly, "but I feel like I need to speak my truth. Especially after seeing how freaked out you got this morning. This is out of my control, Kaley, and I've stopped trying to fight it. I'm risking everything for this. For us. Do you think I'd do that for just anybody? Believe it or not, I do get offers from women"—he pauses with a smirk—"I've turned everyone down . . . until you came along."

He leans in and kisses me. Not his usual slow, teasing kiss. This is a hungry, urgent kiss. It feels like a continuance from the last kiss he gave me in the spa. A raw, burning, fervent kiss. The wall I've been trying to secure around my heart comes crashing down, and I wrap my arms around him.

He takes me from my waist, pulling me on top of him, and I sit astride him as his hands slide up my back. He moves his lips down to my neck, and I let out a soft moan. He hoists me up as he rises from the couch and carries me, my legs wrapped firmly around him. Our lips never break from each other as he makes his way down the hallway and into his bedroom. He lays me down on his luxurious bed, pinning himself on top of me. My hands explore his bare chest, and his hands graze my thighs, hiking up my skirt, his virile fingers brushing the sides of my panties.

A well of emotions surge through me, and he lifts my tank top over my head. His eyes run over my white lace-trimmed bra before he leans in, kissing the spot on my neck that sends tremors down my sides. His lips make their way down my collarbone, then down the center of my chest, continuing down to my stomach. Butterflies spring into action as his lips skim past my belly button. He stops when he reaches the hem of my skirt and reaches around behind me, deftly unhooking my bra. The small action has me spinning. He's always warning me that if I take my bra off, he won't be able to stop himself. I eagerly slip it all the way off, and he feasts his eyes upon me.

After a few beats, he leans forward and whispers in my ear, "Your beauty is unreal." His lips are then fierce against mine, and I fumble with the button on my skirt before sliding it down.

He doesn't stop me.

"Are you sure, baby?" he whispers.

"Yes," I breathe. *Please!*

I know the smart thing to do is wait until after graduation, but I don't want to think rationally, I only want to feel. He just revealed a piece of his soul, confessed his feelings for me, and I want him. All of him. Now.

My fingers find the top of his jeans, and I unfasten them, revealing the black boxer briefs that teased me earlier this morning. My hands tremble as I timidly slip my hand over him, and he kisses me with a new thirst, thrusting his hips forward. I pull on his boxers, inching them down. I want him more than I've ever wanted anything in my life. And after months of yearning, of craving, of longing, I'm finally going to have him.

He starts to slide down the last garment separating my natural state from his covetous eyes when the doorbell rings.

He lets out a groan that sounds closer to a whine. "You can't be serious."

"Pretend you're not home," I urge.

His lips return to mine just as the doorbell rings again. He continues to kiss me until an urgent knock strikes the door.

"Damn," he whispers. "The Tahoe's in the driveway, they know I'm home. He stands up, and I instantly mourn the loss of his body. He peeks through the shutters.

"Shit!"

I sit up straight. "What's wrong? Is she back?"

"No," he says, slipping on his jeans. "It's Stan."

"Who's Sta—Principal *Bentley*?"

"Shh! Yes," he whispers. "Get your clothes on and hide."

"What the hell is he doing here? Does the principal make random house calls often?"

"We golf together, and he's probably not happy I bailed without warning. *Twice.* He's going through a nasty divorce, so he's a little needy lately."

"He is? Oh, that's kind of sad." I'm not exactly a big fan of the guy, but after witnessing what my parents have gone through, it makes me pity him. I wouldn't wish that on anybody. "So you're like his confidant?"

"Kay," he says, throwing on a thin gray shirt. "We don't have time to discuss this right now, hurry."

I realize I'm still sitting on his bed, almost completely naked. "Right, sorry!" I jump up just as the doorbell rings again. "Geez, talk about eager." My lightheadedness makes it difficult to function at a normal speed.

He draws me close and tastes my lips once more. "Please hurry and put your clothes back on, or I'm never going to be in a position to answer the door."

I look down at his jeans and grin.

"I'm serious Kay," he says, rushing me into the closet. Another knock pounds on the door, and he waits another moment before leaving the room.

I scramble to put my clothes on, my body still quivering. I try to process what just happened. It's a lot of information to take in this morning, including the "big rule" of his we were just about to break.

I figure I'll be safe coming out of the closet and waiting on his bed, but I can hear my principal's voice through the wall, and it makes me too nervous, so I sit on the floor of his closet instead. It smells like him in here. I rest my head against the wall and close my eyes. I've never experienced this kind of passion before. I can still feel exactly where his lips were on my body, and my skin tingles at the thought of his warm, masculine fingers.

But as my body starts to settle, my thoughts take over. . . . Hiding in his closet feels degrading, but jeopardizing his career is the last thing I want to do. Graduation is on the horizon, and I can't wait to be free.

But will we be free? I wonder.

Let's say after I graduate, my principal knocks on the door—which now seems highly likely—would I be able to show my face in this house? I'm free to do as I please, but is Elijah? Mr. Bentley will still be his boss. I don't want Elijah to risk his reputation and be blacklisted from the community, yet at the same time I know I don't want to run to his closet every time there's a knock at the door. I'm surprised it bothers me so much—I figured I'd be content to live the rest of my life in his closet, if it meant I could feel his body on mine and be wrapped in his arms every night.

But I think I was wrong.

I was just about to have sex for the first time in my life, only to be rushed into a closet. What if we had been in the middle of it? Would that have been my first experience? That's more demeaning than losing your virginity in the back of some guy's van. I replay his words in my mind: *I have never felt this way about anyone before in my entire life.*

I should be euphorically happy. But instead, I'm hiding in his closet for the second time today. I know it's not his fault, and I know he doesn't *want* to hide me, but no matter how I look at it, it leaves me feeling inadequate. The realization of the impossibility of our relationship hits me like a block of ice. I try to remind myself that he really does care about me. Maybe even loves me. But as I listen to the voices through the wall, I feel almost worthless.

Embarrassed.

Maybe even . . . *pathetic.*

CHAPTER TWENTY-SIX

WHEN ELIJAH RETURNS TO THE bedroom, he finds me lying on the floor of his designer closet with tears streaming down my face.

"I'm sorry, Kaley," he says, easing himself onto the floor beside me. "I didn't think he'd stay that long. I kept trying to get him out of here."

"How long have I been in here?" I ask, sniffling.

He's silent for a moment. "Over an hour."

I look up at him. His eyes, laced with penitence, rest on mine.

"An hour and a half," he admits. "I'm sorry, baby."

"Don't apologize," I say, sitting up. "I feel like an idiot right now, crying in your damn closet. This is probably confirmation that I'm too young for you, right?" I smile through my tears and wipe my face.

"No, Kay." He runs a reassuring hand over my bare leg. His hand feels strong, warm. "I knew this would be complicated, but I didn't realize to what extent. I've expected a lot from you, and I haven't been fair. I can't imagine it feels good to be hidden away in a closet like this."

"It's not just that." I squeeze my eyes closed. "I was about to lose my virginity, Elijah . . . only to have you—"

"Kay, I—" He exhales. "Oh, God," he whispers quietly to himself.

I open my eyes. "I'm not trying to make you feel bad, it's just . . . a lot to take in."

"I'm so sorry," he says, his face twisting in anguish. "I'm

316

being selfish."

"I don't want you to have to choose between me and your career." I bring my knees up to my chest, making more room for him on the cramped floor.

"I know you don't," he says softly.

"Okay, let's be real here," I say, resting my chin on my knees. "I graduate in two weeks. Where does that leave us?"

He presses his lips together as if mulling it over, then proceeds with caution. "Truthfully, I'd feel a little better about getting caught, or going public, sometime after your graduation. We'll still need to be cautious for a while."

I inhale. "How long is a while?"

He hesitates. "I don't know. . . . I want to say six months, but honestly, I'd rather wait at least a year."

Reality smacks me in the face like a stinging snowball.

"At *least* a year?"

He doesn't reply.

"Look," I begin.

"Before you say anything," he says, cutting me off. "I'm going to be real with you, Kaley. I thought you and I would have a few dates and it would move along slowly, allowing more time to pass. I thought if things ever became serious between us, it would happen way down the road. And by then it would be a safer time for us to take that next step." He takes a deep breath and slowly releases it. "I've tried to take it slow with you. . . . I thought I had it all planned out, that the timing would work to our advantage. But that's not what happened. I care about you a lot . . . much more than I anticipated this early in the relationship."

My heart warms, throbs, and shatters at the same time.

"I care about you, too," I say. "But what are we supposed to do? Your timeline didn't go as planned. Math doesn't work for everything—not for human emotions, Slate. And I don't want to be selfish, but I *hate* lying to everybody. It's slowly killing me. I can't even fathom lying to my family and friends for another *year*. This is affecting my whole life, and I wasn't expecting it to be this difficult, either." I pause as the daunting truth swells in my throat. "I can't believe I'm about to say this, but with how strong my feelings already are . . . I don't think I can handle losing you later on, when my feelings are even more intense. I think I've had all the heartache I can handle this year."

"Baby," he breathes. He leans forward, taking my hand in his. "Look, I—" He slams his eyes shut for a moment, then fixes his gaze on me. "I know. And you're right. It's too much to ask of you, I know that. You're about to start college; you deserve to live your life and be in a relationship with someone who can take you out to dinner for hell's sake."

"I don't want anyone else, Elijah, but it's going to be too painful losing you down the road . . . whether it's weeks from now, or six months from now. I feel like I'm better off starting the grieving process *now*." As soon as the words tumble out of my mouth, I want to take them back.

"Kaley," he whispers. He scoots over to me and pulls me into his arms. "Why are you so sure you're going to lose me? I'm not going anywhere. Let's try this, okay? I want to try to make this work."

"I can't be in a relationship where I'm stuck in your closet," I say, my voice cracking.

With my head pressed against his chest, I listen to his heartbeat, counting each one—measuring the silence between us. *One . . . two . . . three . . . four . . .*

"I should go." I unravel myself from his hold and stand up.

"Kaley," he says, but it almost sounds like a distant echo.

He follows me out to the garage in silence, and I stop in front of my car door. I meet his despondent gaze, and it instantly guts my insides.

"Don't give up on me, Kay. We can figure this out. I promise I won't break your heart," he says, brushing a stray hair out of my face.

"It's already breaking."

He touches my cheek, then wraps his hand behind my neck, kissing me softly on my quivering lips. "Let's just see how things are after graduation, okay?"

"Will things be different?" I ask. "I mean, can I at least be open with my close friends? Emily at least? My mom?"

My heart cracks as I read the hesitation on his face. "I don't know, Kay. I just need some time. I can't risk it."

I nod and stare at the floor. "No, I understand. I'm sorry, I don't want to put you in that situation."

He doesn't deserve to risk his entire career for me. He just got done telling me it was all he had left after everything he went through last year. It's not right for me to demand such a thing.

But it's not right to ask me to live in a proverbial closet, either.

Maybe if he said a few months—maybe even six months—I could handle it. But at least a year? I have to protect my heart as well.

"I want to see you next weekend," he says. "I know you have finals to study for, and I have my graduation, but Friday night works for me. Will you come over? Please?"

"Your graduation is next weekend?" I ask. "That's great, Elijah. Congratulations. I'm sorry, I didn't even realize."

"Not your fault. We haven't seen each other in a while," he says with a half-smile.

"I'd love to see you walk," I say.

"Oh," he says, stepping back slightly. He shrugs, shoving his hands in his pockets. "Well, my family will be there, so . . ."

I swallow hard. "Right. No, I was just thinking out loud, sorry."

And there it is again.

The secrets.

The lies.

The closet.

I've been anticipating my *own* graduation day for so long, naively thinking we'd finally be free, only to realize we'll still be trapped. We'll still have to lie to everyone we know. This amazing man who supposedly cares about me more than any other girl, golfs with my principal. They're buddies. He can't even introduce me to his family. And he's expecting me to continue the lies to *my* loved ones for at least another year.

I need a preemptive strike—take myself out of the game now before I'm in even deeper. My feelings for him are stronger than anything I've ever felt before, and I cannot imagine losing him months from now, when my feelings are even more intense. I don't think my body is capable of bearing such pain.

But that's the inevitable future for us. I can see that now. He's everything I want and everything I can't have.

I switch to autopilot. It's the only way I can attempt to survive this.

"I really should go," I say. "And you're right. I have finals, and it sounds like you're busy with your family. Maybe we'll meet up after my graduation and see where we're at." I didn't mean for it to sound like a business deal, but that's how it came out.

He doesn't speak as he opens my door. I slide into the driver's seat and reach into my glove box, pulling out his garage door opener.

I hold it out to him. "Here."

His features go slack with shock, then winces as if in

physical pain. "Kay—" he breathes, cocking his head to the side.

"Just in case I don't see you." My eyes dart around his garage. "I don't want to have to return it later if this doesn't . . ." My voice falters. "Just take it, please."

Don't look at him. You'll break.

I feel him take it out of my hands before he gently closes my door. I back out of his driveway, glancing up when my tires meet the asphalt. He stands in the garage, his face ashen, not seeming to care that it's daylight. I tear my gaze away, his forlorn expression etched into my mind as I drive down the road, turning left off of Ironwood Drive.

I AM AN emotionless zombie by the time I make it home, refusing to let my pain reach the surface. But it won't last long . . . my outer shell is seconds away from cracking. I slip past my dad in the kitchen and bolt up the stairs, tackling two steps at a time and lock myself in the bathroom. It's the only room in the house with a lock, and I'm desperate for privacy. I turn on the shower, the numbness in my chest beginning to tingle the same way Novocain does when it starts to wear off.

My body shakes as I peel off all my clothes and step into the tepid stream. I turn the temperature as hot as I can stand and collapse onto the porcelain tub floor. *Please, God, say I didn't just make a terrible mistake.* As I slump over on my knees, the wound in my chest frees itself and a desperate cry comes pouring out of me—an open-mouthed, silent cry that rips from the innermost part of my being.

CHAPTER TWENTY-SEVEN

"KALEY?" MY DAD HOLLERS FROM the kitchen just as I am leaving for school.

I hesitate at the door. "Yeah?" He used my full name. Not a good sign.

He steps into the living room, his eyes doleful. "I found a place near Grandma and Grandpa." He pauses. "I'll be moving soon."

The dull pain in my chest nudges awake.

"How soon?" I say, my voice almost a whisper.

"I'll be leaving right after your graduation ceremony."

My body goes cold. It's too fast. Too soon.

"Okay," I say, my voice brittle.

He steps toward me. "Kaley—"

I put my hand up, halting him.

"It's okay, Dad. I'm fine. I just have to get to school," I say, turning for the door.

"Your mom's moving back in on Saturday," he rushes.

I turn back around. "What? Where will *you* be?"

"I'll be here," he says. His vacant eyes seem to gaze right through me. My heart breaks for him. I guess I'm not the only one on autopilot. "She wants to have dinner with you. I told her you would."

I clamp my lips in a hard line and stare at him for a moment before walking out the door.

MY GAZE IS glued to my desk as Elijah uses a popcorn metaphor to explain hyperbolas, but I am only half-tuned in.

Whenever I find the courage to look his way, his eyes never find mine.

The memory of his shattered face after I handed him the garage door opener continues to haunt me. I've hurt him, I know I have. He opened up about his painful past, revealed his feelings for me, and was about to make love to me . . . and I broke it off.

But it's not like he's sent me a text, or given me a call—he isn't exactly fighting for me. I'm not trying to play games or anything, but his actions are as clear as mine. His career is more important than me. And I respect that. I can't expect him to throw his life away for me. Nor can I throw away my own.

It seems we've reached an impasse.

"Put it away!" Elijah shouts, snapping me out of my torturous thoughts. His face is hard, and I follow his callous stare to the back of the room and notice Seth's crimson face as he slides his phone into his pocket. I turn back to Elijah, and his intimidating glare shifts to my left. He charges down the aisle and snatches a girl's phone out of her hand. Then he marches to the back and stands before Seth. "Give it to me."

"I put it away, Slate," he whines.

Elijah says nothing and the room is dead quiet, except for maybe the pounding of my heart. Seth's phone is barely out of his pocket when Elijah rips it out of his hand. He brushes past my desk and throws the phones in his desk drawer, slamming it shut.

"The next person I see with their phone out will be sent to the office. The person after that won't be allowed to take the final."

"Damn," someone mutters behind me.

"He can't do that," someone else whispers.

"Watch me," he says sharply, silencing the room.

I study him throughout the rest of the hour. I've never seen him this way and realize I can't leave it like this. As much as I don't want to make the first move, I need to talk to him. *Was I too quick to break it off?* Maybe I'm being unreasonable about the whole thing, I don't know. But one thing I do know is how naïve I was the night I showed up on his doorstep. Even though he tried to warn me, I never predicted it would be this complicated.

This complex.

This . . . confusing.

When class lets out, I make my way to his desk.

"Hey," I say after the last student leaves the room.

He doesn't respond to me as he shuffles papers, refusing to make eye contact. An empty feeling swells in the pit of my stomach.

"Look, I know we don't have much time, so I'm just going to say it," I say, glancing at the door. "I'm sorry about yesterday. I didn't mean to be so—"

"You were right," he says, his gaze finally latching onto mine. But his eyes are flat. And his voice is bitter. Like a sharp, frigid wind. "It could never work. You're too young for me, Kaley. I'm sorry I ever let anything happen."

His words rip open my poorly-stitched wound, and I try to take shallow breaths to prevent it from bursting open. *He's sorry it ever happened?* And instead of saying *we* could never work, he said *it* could never work . . . like he's already detached from *us*.

"You're sorry? Like you regr—"

"And I trust you'll keep everything that *did* happen to yourself?" He states it like a question. A question wrapped around an unbending, rigid demand.

He can't mean this. He can't mean these words. I search his eyes for the warmth I've grown accustom to, but all I find is ice-cold forbiddance. A brick wall. The twinkle I've loved from the first day we met is nowhere to be found—he looks at me like I am a stranger.

He looks at me like I am a student.

I open my mouth to speak, but my throat is quicksand, trapping my desperate voice, so I give a jerky nod. He rips his gaze from mine, leaving me hollow and cold, and goes back to sorting his papers just as the door swings open. I turn away from him and rush out the door.

"I NEED TO get out of the house," I complain to Emily during lunch.

She listened intently as I caught her up on my parents' new temporary living arrangements. Having her support and attentiveness feels like a soft, warm blanket around my lacerated heart. I miss her so much.

"I don't blame you," she says. "That's pretty disturbing, Kay. At least it's only a week."

"Yeah, we'll be one big happy family." I roll my eyes. "I need to get out of the house, though. Like, permanently. I don't think I can live with my mom."

"I can't believe we're not going to be dorm mates—it feels so wrong. Have you thought any more about transferring to NAU in the spring?" I notice she's barely touched her food.

"I don't really want to be that far away."

"We were planning on moving to Los Angeles for college, Kay. I thought you couldn't wait to get out of here."

"Well, yeah. But at least it's warm there." I ignore her eye roll. "I want to get out of my house, not out of town."

Even though I know it can't work with Elijah, I still can't imagine leaving the area completely. He still holds me down here, whether I like it or not.

"Maybe I'll just get my own place. Like a little studio or something." I lean my elbow on the table and rest my chin in my hand. "I need a job."

"Derek's brother is hiring." She elbows Derek in the back to grab his attention.

I sit up straight and raise my eyebrows. "He is?" A little ray of hope glimmers back into my life. "Oh my gosh, that'd be perfect for me. It's right next to ASU and it's *always* packed. I should be able to save up in no time."

Derek turns in his chair. "You wanna work there?"

"More than you know," I tell him.

"All right," he says. "Come by after school."

A grin stretches across my face. "I'll be there, thanks."

"See?" says Emily. "You'll be out of the house faster than you think."

I clap my hands enthusiastically and squeal. "You have *no* idea how happy I am right now!"

Avery's face lights up as she looks over my shoulder. "Hi, Mr. Slate!"

My heart catapults into my throat, and I whip my head around. *Did he hear me say how happy I was?* His indignant eyes hold mine a brief moment before he returns a stiff hello to Avery.

"Donovan," he says in his strict teacher tone.

Donovan stops mid-chew, lowering his pizza slice.

"Sup, Slate," he says with his mouth full.

"You were supposed to meet me during your lunch to re-take your test. You do hope to graduate, yes?"

Donovan's cheeks flush as he rises from the table. He slogs out of the cafeteria after Slate, and I turn my attention back to the table.

Avery rests her head in her hand and stares off dreamily. "Does anyone else find him extra sexy when he's angry? He was furious in class today—totally turned me on."

I glare at her. "I see domestic violence in your future," I say, without a trace of humor.

Emily's eyes widen. "Kaley," she whispers.

Avery doesn't flinch. "Doubt it. *I* know how to keep my man satisfied."

Derek leans forward. "*Your* man? Or other people's men?" he shoots back at her.

Avery scowls, and several people at the table laugh. I glance at Tommy for a split second—just long enough to notice him squirming in his seat.

My eyes meet Derek's, and I mouth "thanks." His loyalty comforts me.

He gives me a quick nod. "I'll see you after school, Kay."

JACE HIRES ME on the spot. I fill out my paperwork in his office as Derek scarfs down a plate of nachos next to me, watching a game on TV.

"I wish you were twenty-one, Kennedy," says Jace from behind his desk. "I really need a bartender."

"Oh. I'm sorry," I say as I hand him my completed stack of papers.

He glances at Derek, who is zoned out to the game, and lowers his voice a little. "To tell you the truth, I don't actually need a server."

"You don't?" My shoulders drop. "Then why are you hiring me?"

He smiles. "Don't worry. It might be hard to give you as many hours as you'd like at first, but I'll try to hook you up. Besides, someone's bound to quit sometime. This is the restaurant biz after all."

I try to summon a smile. So much for burying myself in a job.

"Let me show you around," he says, rising from his chair.

"She's been here like a zillion times," says Derek. He's finished his nachos, and a commercial break has broken him out of his trance.

"Not in the back, dumbass," says Jace. "Get this junk out of here." He gestures to Derek's greasy plate and pile of wadded up napkins.

"Calm down, dude," gripes Derek, propping his feet on my chair after I stand up.

Jace turns to me and rolls his eyes. "This is why I don't hire family."

He gives me a tour of the kitchen, which is clustered with bustling bodies as they prepare for the happy hour rush. He shows me the computer that I'm to clock in at and introduces me to several servers. I know a few of them from the times I've hung out here. When we arrive back in his office, Derek's feet are still propped up on the empty chair and he's holding a guitar in his lap, fiddling with the strings.

"You're still here?" says Jace, snatching the guitar out of his hands and kicking his feet off the chair.

Derek catches himself before falling over. "Dude! I'm waiting for Kaley."

"You're lucky I don't knock you out right now. *Don't* touch my guitar." He carefully leans the guitar against the wall behind his desk, while Derek flips him off behind his back.

"I should probably go," I say. I don't have the patience to listen to brothers bickering. I'm on edge. "Unless you need me for anything else," I say to Jace.

"No, we're good here," he replies kindly. "Let me walk you out."

"She's not a fragile little bird, Jace," Derek says under his breath.

Before I can look at Derek, Jace places his hand on the small of my back and gently guides me out of his office and outside into the twilight evening. *Is he being protective of me?*

"Okay, so what did Derek tell you?" I ask as we stroll to my car. "That Tommy slept with Avery? Or that my mom had an affair and my dad's leaving town?"

Jace strokes the side of my car, then leans against it, and I'm instantly reminded of . . . *him*. The first time I was alone with him in the school parking lot floods my vision, the memory threatening to break me.

"Both," replies Jace, pulling me back to the present. The deep-orange sun shines on his face, making his green eyes electric. "I'm really sorry to hear about your parents. But as far as Tommy goes, he's a bastard." He glances behind him, seeming to make sure Derek is still inside. "I know he's D's best friend, and like a brother to me, but he's a complete fool. And Avery of all people?" He shakes his head.

"Avery's pretty, come on." I appreciate his support, but I don't need to be lied to. She's far from ugly.

"She's all right . . . but you're beautiful."

My ears grow hot, and I curl my arms around myself.

"Sorry," he says, "but come on. He knows he could never get anyone better than you."

I shake my head and glance at the ground. "That's not true. Look, I don't hate him or anything. It's . . . complicated."

He pushes himself off my car and folds his arms. "Are you thinking of taking him back?"

"No," I say shyly.

I'm not used to Jace being so personal with me. I've known him as long as I've known Derek, but he was out of high school before I even started. We've always had a surface-level relationship. Maybe he's opening up to me now that I'll be working for him.

"I'm just saying," I continue, "it's not all his fault." *And I was seeing his baseball coach behind his back, so yeah. We're kind of even.*

Derek appears next to us, and Jace eases his stance. My heart softens as two pairs of familiar green eyes stare back at me. I've never noticed how striking their eyes are. One pair is filled with brotherly affection . . . the other with mystery.

"Thanks for hooking me up, guys," I say, running my hand through my hair.

"No problem, Kay," says Derek. "I have to pick up Emily, you good?" I nod, and he gives me a tight squeeze around the shoulders and gets into his car.

Jace opens my car door, spiking my nerves, and I hop in. My window is down and he closes the door, resting his hands against the ledge.

"You've got to let me get behind this wheel sometime, Kennedy."

"You got it," I say, smiling.

"This beauty has serious potential. I tried to get Tommy to supe it up a little for you, but he wouldn't go for it," he says with a playful laugh.

I shake my head. "Is there *anyone* who didn't know about him restoring my car?"

"Hmm." He pretends to think really hard, pressing his index finger to his lips. "Nope. Just you, I guess."

I laugh. "Great." I glance behind him. Derek's car is already gone.

"I'm going to be out of town for a couple days," he says, "so I can't start your training right away. How's Friday after school sound?"

"Sounds great," I say.

"Great. I'll see you then." He holds my gaze for a moment, then pats my car and goes back inside.

A sliver of warmth pierces my cold, heavy heart, and I let out a shaky sigh as I glance at my phone before driving home.

No messages.

Jace caught me off guard with the way he looked at me just now, but I am in no shape to think of him in that way.

Maybe I misread him—he's probably just being protective. But for whatever reason, I saw him in a different light tonight, and it gives me a fraction of hope that maybe—*just maybe*—one day I'll be okay and able to move on.

CHAPTER TWENTY-EIGHT

THE REST OF THE WEEK flies by as all the seniors cram for their finals, and I'm surprised at how contagious the excited energy is. I'm looking forward to graduation and working all summer. Even though I'm dying inside, I'm holding it together the best I can manage. I can't let myself think about Elijah's harsh words, or I'll break. Studying for finals helps keep my anguish at bay, and by the time my body hits the mattress every night, I'm too exhausted to think of anything else. It never stops me from checking my phone to see if I have any messages from him, but I'm doing pretty well, all things considered.

We rarely make eye contact when I'm in his classroom, and when we do, it's as if his eyes don't even remember what we shared. I find myself wanting to approach him after class—just one more time. But I never do. What would I say, anyway? He would contact me if he wanted to make it work.

But I haven't heard from him.

The finality of it all has me in a fragile state, but I know the suffering won't last forever. It can't. Pain always fades.

Love fades.

I just need to keep busy and push through.

DEREK, EMILY, AND Tommy come into Velocity to support me during my first night of training. Emily was kind enough to send me a warning text that Tommy was tagging along, but I have no time to worry about him. My nerves are on over-drive—training on a busy Friday night seems like a terrible idea. But Jace insisted I dive right in. After shadowing his top server, Staci, all afternoon, I am given my first solo mission: serving my friends.

"Looking sharp, Kay," says Derek, as I step up to their table.

I nudge his shoulder. "Shut up."

"I'm serious!" He grins. "Looking legit."

I laugh, then take their orders—avoiding Tommy's shameless gaze the entire time.

"We're all hanging out at Derek's tonight if you're interested," offers Emily. I shoot her a look, but pull it back when I see the sadness in her eyes. She misses our group. She misses me. And she's losing Derek. "What time do you get off?"

"I'm not su—"

"Depends," Jace's voice interrupts from behind me. "She's doing awesome; I just might keep her till closing." He leans his elbow on my shoulder with ease.

"I've barely even taken an order yet," I remark.

"You're doing great!" He casually adjusts his arm so it's around my neck.

Tommy's eyes drop to Jace's arm while Emily gives me a guarded look.

"Don't you guys think?" Jace asks the table.

"Hear! Hear!" says Derek, raising his water glass.

Jace drops his arm to his side and narrows his eyes at Derek. "You're drunk."

"I am?" says Derek in mock astonishment. He lifts his glass to Tommy. "Hear! Hear!"

Tommy breaks into laughter.

Jace glares at all three of them. "Are you *all* drunk?"

"I'm not even drunk, bro," says Derek. "Just buzzed. Chill."

Jace crosses his arms. "Who drove?"

"I did," Emily speaks up. "I'm the DD, don't worry."

"Aw, don't worry, babe," says Derek. "I'll fix you a nice drink when we get back."

Part of me wonders if Derek's self-medicating. He's got to be hurting over moving away from Emily.

Jace lowers his face inches from Derek's. "If you act out *one* time, you're out of here. Do you hear me? You're a liability right now. Both of you." He glances at Tommy. "Find somewhere else to get drunk."

As I turn to leave, Emily grabs my elbow. "Are you sure you don't want to come over?"

Tommy looks at me with anticipation. I know I'd get ten minutes with her before she and Derek would sneak off to his bedroom.

"I don't know, Ems."

She slumps down in her chair.

"I'll call you when I get off," I appease.

That perks her up a little, and I rush to the kitchen to place their orders. On my way back, Jace meets me in the dim hallway.

"You don't have to hang out with them if you don't want. I was going to let you off after they're done, but I can tell them I'm keeping you."

Servers and bussers brush past us, and he nods toward his office. I follow him in, and he shuts the door behind me.

"Sorry if I'm being overprotective, but you'll just end up alone with Tommy all night if you go over there. I just wanted to give you an out."

I groan. "I know. But Emily needs me right now. She and Derek are going to different colleges soon, and—"

"I know. But I worry about you being in that situation." He takes a seat behind his desk. "Unless you *want* to be in that situation."

"No!" I blurt out. "No, no. Not at all."

He laughs quietly. "Okay, I didn't think so. Just say you have to stay till closing."

"Okay, thanks." I kind of wish he *would* keep me till closing. I'm not up for Derek's, but I don't feel like going home either. Maybe I can go to the bookstore. I haven't been there in months.

"No problem," he says. "You did really great today; I wasn't playing around."

"Thanks. My feet are killing me, though."

He laughs. "Yeah, welcome to the restaurant biz." He pauses for a moment. "Hey, can I ask you something?"

I clear my throat. "Sure."

Why am I nervous all of a sudden?

"Are you and Tommy really over, or do you think there's a chance you'll get back together?"

I hesitate. "We're . . . done. Why?"

His eyes penetrate mine, and I force myself to hold his gaze.

"Are you seeing anybody?"

I glance at my shoes. "No," I say, my voice weak.

"Am I making you uncomfortable? I mean, I know I'm technically your boss now, but I've known you forever. There's no pressure."

"It's okay, Jace," I say, tucking my hair behind my ear.

He leans back in his chair.

"I'm probably too old for you, anyway," he says with a slight smirk.

He's two years younger than Slate.

"No, actually. Not at all. But aren't you with Rebecca?"

"Nah, we broke up months ago."

"Really?"

Hmm. They were together for at least two years.

"Have dinner with me tonight."

"Jace," I say, shaking my head. I glance behind me

through the small window in the center of the door. I can see part of the table where my friends are sitting, and I watch as they laugh together, seeming so carefree. I feel a twinge of jealousy and turn back around. "I can't. I'm sorry, I'm not ready."

He leans forward in his chair and rests his elbows on the desk. "He's not worth it, Kaley."

I don't think I've ever heard Jace call me by my first name. It catches me for a moment, causing the dormant butterflies to stretch their wings inside me.

"It's not just him," I say, playing with a loose thread on my apron. My heart throbs, reawakening the pain, and I push back the sudden tears. I don't want to think about *him*.

"Hey," he whispers. He springs up from his chair and is beside me in an instant. "Don't get upset, I'm sorry. I shouldn't have been so forward." He places his hands just below my shoulders. "Forgive me?"

I push a smile through my blurred vision. "Of course. I'm sorry I'm such a wreck."

"He really did a number on you, didn't he."

Elijah's face appears in my mind, the merciless pain becoming almost unbearable. I don't want to think about him anymore. He chose his career over me. I don't blame him for that, but it's the harsh truth. It's over.

Done.

"It's not Tommy," I say. "I mean, it's . . . it's a lot of things. I don't want to talk about it."

"Damn, I'm sorry."

"Quit apologizing. I'm not upset with you. Just the situation."

Aren't I too young to be this bitter? If my heart were intact, I just might give Jace a shot.

But *he* ruined me.

They both did.

"I'm here if you ever need to talk, okay? As a *friend*." He puts his hands up in defense.

I manage a weak smile. "Thanks."

"Are you okay to go back out there?"

I nod and turn to the door just as Avery joins the table, standing next to Tommy. *What is she doing here?!* Emily's face looks strained as she glances around the restaurant. Looking for my whereabouts, no doubt. Panic grips me, and I spin back around before Jace can stop his stride, and he knocks me against the door, the back of my head smacking against the glass.

"Oh!" He steps back in a flash. "Are you okay?"

"I'm fine, sorry," I mumble, clutching the back of my head.

"Okay . . ." He waits for me to speak or move, but I can't do either.

Is Tommy already moving on? Elijah clearly is. I think about my mom's affair and her new boyfriend and wonder if my dad will have a girlfriend soon. Everyone just moves on. *Everyone.* And here I am, suffering. Stuck in limbo.

Stuck in despair.

Stuck in the shadows of Elijah's cutting words: *You're too young for me, Kaley. I'm sorry I ever let anything happen.*

"Hey, are you okay?" Jace's voice pulls me back to the surface.

The top button of his shirt is undone and I catch the edge of a tattoo, but can't decipher what it is. When I lift my gaze, his eyes give away that he noticed me noticing, and I feel myself blush. He's undeniably sexy, but there is no way I'm ready. No way I can trust him.

I glance behind me through the little window again. Avery is now sitting at my table. *What the hell?*

When I turn back around, Jace is only inches from my face, his jade-green eyes laced with solicitude. "What's the matter?"

I grab his collar and pull him close, pressing my lips against his. He slides me away from the window, and I hear the door lock as he presses me up against the wall. My heart pounds against my aching chest as his tongue tangles with mine. *Wow.* He's highly skilled, but it isn't the same as—*don't say his name. Just feel something.*

Anything.

I slide my arms around his neck, slipping my fingers into his hair as he wraps his arms around my waist. *Don't think.* He squeezes me tightly against him as his lips maneuver expertly around mine. He almost kisses like it's some kind of art form. If my heart ever heals, I could have fun with these lips.

The door handle jiggles, and I jump. He breaks away, but keeps his eyes on me as he tries to catch his breath. Someone pounds on the door.

"Did they see us?" I say, gasping for air.

"No, it's okay." He reaches for the door, but I stop him. I wipe the smeared lip gloss off his mouth, and he gives me a half-smile that makes my stomach flop.

He cracks open the door, using himself as a barrier between me and whoever is outside.

"I'm in a meeting," he says with authority.

The noise from the kitchen drowns out the person's voice.

"It's fine, just go," he says. He closes the door and turns to me. "Well, my manager is sick, so I'll be covering tonight."

"Okay." I suddenly have trouble keeping eye contact.

"I'd still like to have dinner with you. What about tomorrow night? My place."

Whoa.

"*Your* place?"

"Yeah, I'll cook."

My chest swells. He's a fabulous chef, and his gesture catches me off-guard.

"You want to make me dinner?"

"I'd love to."

"Well, my mom's moving back in tomorrow," I say, "and we're supposed to have dinner together. I could probably cancel, though."

"No, don't do that. Are you going to D's graduation party on Thursday?"

"Of course."

"I'll be there too, if you want to hang out. Then dinner on Friday?"

I hold my breath. "Okay."

A faint smile crosses his lips, and he leans in, raking his fingers through my hair, and kisses me artfully, suggestively . . . finishing with a gentle tug on my bottom lip before leaving the room.

I exhale as I tighten my apron.

What did I just do?

My hands shake as I pull on the door handle, and I pause before heading back out to the floor. I dread returning to my table, but I can't stay in this office a moment longer. If I don't deal with Avery right now, I never will. I boldly step out of the office and stride up to my only assigned table as all eyes fall on me.

"Will you be joining us tonight, Avery?" I say with an arctic smile.

She hesitates, which is rare for her. "Actually, I'm with that group over there." She points to the booth adjacent to the table, and I glance at her Skank Squad.

"Oh. Well, perhaps you guys would like to switch to a larger table, so you can all sit together." I don't know what my face looks like, but if everyone's expressions are any inclination, it's anything but pleasant.

"No, that's okay," says Avery. She actually seems afraid of me.

I rest my hand on my hip and tilt my head at her. "Are you sure? It's no problem at all. I'm here to accommodate *you*, girl."

"Kaley," says Emily, lightly touching my arm.

"I'm serious!" I laugh, brushing her hand away. "It's no big deal. People change tables all the time—this *is* America, right?"

Four pairs of eyes shift to my left in perfect synchronization, and I follow their gaze.

Jace is beside me. "Everything okay here?"

I flash a smile. "Everything's great."

Emily tries to nonchalantly shake her head at Jace, but I catch it.

I narrow my eyes at her. "I'm *fine*."

She squints at me and stands, wiping the side of my mouth. "Your lip gloss is all smeared."

Heat spreads across my face, and I hope the dim ambience hides my embarrassment. But Emily is too close to me. She glances back and forth between me and Jace.

"*Is* everything okay?" she says only loud enough for me to hear.

"Yes, I'm fine."

Her expression is wary as she slowly sits back down.

I clear my throat. "I'm going to go check on your orders."

I pass Jace without making eye contact and stop in the dark hallway just before the entry to the kitchen. I press my hands on my knees and lower my head, taking in a deep breath. I hear someone mumble "new girl can't cut it," but ignore it. Someone lays a hand on my back, and I jump up.

"Kaley," says Jace, concerned.

"I'm sorry, I just got lightheaded. I promise I'll be better. I can handle this job, I—"

"Shh, it's okay. What, you think I'm going to fire you right now?" He chuckles. "Are you going to be okay? Avery went back to her group."

"I'm fine. I'm sorry. I don't want him back, I swear, it's—"

"Hey, I get it. No worries."

A boy younger than me walks by, and Jace stops him. "Can you run the order out to table nineteen?"

The boy nods and rushes back into the kitchen.

I groan. "Oh, great. Everyone's going to think I can't handle this job. I have *one* table and someone has to run my order out?"

He smirks. "He's a runner, Kennedy. That's his job. I always have runners on staff during peak hours."

"Oh."

He laughs. "Come here." He leads me to the soda machine and pours me an ice water. "Stay hydrated, okay?"

I nod and take a sip.

"I have to take care of some things. Just take care of the knuckleheads, and go ahead and clock out afterward, all right?" He lowers his head close to mine and glides his hand along my side, holding my hip. "I'll see you later," he whispers.

And like that, he is gone.

I turn around and catch Avery's stare as she stands paralyzed in front of the door to the ladies room. I shoot her a vicious glare, and she breaks away, slipping inside the bathroom.

"Shit," I whisper.

I toss the Styrofoam cup into the trash and head back to table nineteen.

CHAPTER TWENTY-NINE

"I WANT TO HAVE EVERYBODY over after your graduation ceremony," my mom announces. She's officially moved back into the house, which means my dad has moved into the den. Personally, I think he deserves to sleep in his own bed, but I stay out of it. He's keeping himself busy packing up the rest of his things, while I eat dinner with my mom in the dining room. If it wasn't for my Dad forcing this shared meal, there's no way I'd be doing it.

"Who's everybody?" I ask, taking a final bite of my meal. Even my mom's amazing spinach and feta stuffed chicken can't ignite my appetite.

"You know, Emily and Derek," she says. "And Tommy."

"Mom," I warn. "Tommy and I broke up, remember?"

"I know, but he's been such a part of this family. I want you all here. At least let me take some pictures of the four of you."

"No can do, Mom. Derek's having a big graduation party at his house. Half the graduating class will be there."

"Well, when does the party start?"

"Like seven or eight, I think."

"That's plenty of time for the four of you to stop by."

I groan as I sit back in my chair. "Mom, that is so awkward, you have no idea. They probably won't even want to come. Everyone's going to be busy getting ready for the party."

"Please, Kaley. At least ask them."

"Whatever." I sigh.

"Thanks, sweetie." She kisses me on the cheek and begins to clear the table. It's annoying how happy she is while our family is imploding. It's the love-sick kind of happy, and I know it's because of her home-wrecking boyfriend. It infuriates me.

I meet her at the sink and hand her my plate.

"I still don't see why you had to get a job," she says, rinsing my dish. You should be enjoying yourself this summer. I'd also like to go on some trips with you before you start college."

"I need to work, Mom," I say. "I want my own money."

"Trust me, Kay," she says, loading the dishwasher. "You have your whole life to work. You should enjoy these last few years under your parents' care."

I lean against the counter. "Well ... I kind of want to move out."

"What?" she says, gaping at me.

"Mom, I'm going to be nineteen this summer; I want to be out on my own."

"And you think waitressing part-time will help you accomplish that?"

"Jace says he's going to get me as many hours as possible." I'm surprised at the nervous flutter in my stomach when I say his name.

"Yeah? And what about when you start school? How are you going to keep up with extra hours *and* homework? College is different than high school, Kaley."

Her haughty tone makes me want to remind her she doesn't have the authority to speak on that, but I bite my tongue.

"And Emily's going to be hours away from you."

"What does that matter?" I ask.

"Well, I don't see how you're going to pay for everything on your own. You'd need a roommate."

"Mom, I can do this! Why are you so negative?"

"I'm not negative, Kay, I'm experienced. You won't be able to afford it. Just stay here. I'll be sure to buy you clothes and whatever else you need."

"I don't need clothes; I need to be out on my own," I mumble.

She's quiet for a moment. "You don't want to live with *me*, is that it?"

A pang of guilt twists in my chest, and I step away from the counter. "Don't do that to me, Mom."

"Do what?" she says, pouring the soap into the dispenser and closing the dishwasher.

"Don't guilt-trip me just because I want to grow up."

She turns to me, and it's like looking into my own eyes, except for the small lines etched around her eyelids. Her love-sick glimmer has temporarily been replaced with distress.

"Kaley, life is short. Don't rush into growing up. I'm not making you stay here to hold you back. I want you to live your life. I want you to chase your dreams. I want you to explore classes and figure out what you want to do with your life. I don't want you stressed out about money or tied down to a dead-end job. This is your time. Go experience all that you can. I never had that luxury, and it's my biggest regret."

"And yet another thing to blame me for," I mutter.

"That is not what I'm saying," she says in defense. "I'm just saying that you're still so young, Kaley."

I know she didn't mean anything by it, but that last comment hurts worse than the previous one.

"I'm not *that* young," I say quietly.

She gives me a benevolent smile. "Enjoy your youth, sweetie. It's a good thing. Trust me."

Elijah's vacant eyes flash in my mind: *You're too young for me, Kaley.*

I turn away from her. "I'm not giving up the job, Mom," I say, my voice hoarse. "It's just something I need."

"That's your choice in the end," she says. "But if you decide to move out, I'm not paying for your books."

I jerk my gaze back to her. "Are you serious? Do you know how expensive those are?"

She laughs like I'm ridiculous. "I certainly do."

"So, you're going to punish me if I move out? What if I want to go live in the dorms?"

"You're more than welcome to live in the dorms, Kay."

"You'd still pay for my books?"

"Of course."

"But not if I move out on my own?"

"That's right. I know what's best for you. Trust me; I'm saving you from a huge mistake. And don't think about getting your dad to pay for your books behind my back. He'll agree with me on this."

Her words are suffocating, and I lash out. "Are you planning on bringing your home-wrecker to the house?"

I've never asked her who he is, or where they met. I know nothing about the man. I don't want to know.

Her gaze falters. "No, of course not. You don't have to meet him until you're ready."

"I'll never be ready," I say bitingly. "So, I guess he'll be able to come over in about, what? Four years or so? Assuming I graduate on time."

"Kaley," she warns.

"What? I'm serious. I *never* want to meet this jerk. And since I'm stuck here until I graduate, then I guess we're left with no other choice. Well, that's if this fling even lasts that long, right Mom?"

She doesn't look at me as she wipes down the counter.

"You'll thank me one day," she says quietly.

"Pfft! Sure, Mom," I say, stalking off. I catch the side of her face before exiting the kitchen, and the sorrow in her eyes lassos me with guilt. Her happiness has disturbed me, sure, but seeing her disheartened is much worse. But she is right about one thing: *This is my time.* And I'm still determined to save up and get the hell out of this house. Then *she* can have her man, and *I* can have my freedom. . . . Maybe she'll be thanking *me* one day.

AFTER I SLIP into my pajamas, I check my phone again.

Still nothing.

At only eighteen years old, I've already learned that love just isn't enough. I crawl into my desolate bed and grab hold of my pillow, clutching it to my chest, hoping the pressure against my wound will slow down the bleeding. A stream of tears fall from my face. *I just need to get through this next week.* It isn't even a full week—three days of school, then graduation on Thursday. And then I'll be free.

Free of high school.

Free of Tommy.

Free of him.

CHAPTER THIRTY

EXCITEMENT FILLS THE AIR AS the seniors anticipate graduation. Emily is a ball of emotions—shrieking with laughter
one moment, collapsing in tears the next. I try my best to
console her, though I am in great need of consolation myself.
If only I could share every part of my life with her. . . .

It's difficult to focus on my math final, but I studied hard
for it, and I'll be damned if I embarrass myself with anything
less than an A. It's the last bit of pride I have, and I cling to it
with every ounce of my hollow soul.

The hour is winding down, and I'm one of the last to finish. I drag my gaze to his desk and soak in the last view I'll
ever have of him from where I sit. He stares vacantly at the
back wall, resting the tip of his pen against his lips.

What are you thinking about?

My chair squeaks as I rise. With my stare fixed on him, I
make my way to his desk, but he doesn't move. I feel like a
ghost from his past.

I would say I wish Tommy had never yelled at me the
night of Derek's party, but I can't. I know now that he and I
aren't supposed to end up together. But I do wish I would've
gone to the bookstore that night, instead of the movie theater. Then Elijah never would have taken me home. He never
would have made me feel so beautiful . . . so alive that night.
I never would have sat on the back ledge of his Tahoe after
the baseball game, and he never would have looked at me in
that way that makes every cell in my body dance. I never
would have taken a cab to his house after prom. . . .

I never would have fallen in love.

He would just be that hot math teacher that I had a silly crush on in high school. Emily and I would laugh about the days we used to watch him walk the halls, or that time we drove by his house, or that time she conspired to get him to take us home.

He still would have changed me in some way, though—woken me up to womanhood before I started college. I do believe that. But that would be it. There would be no unbearable pain. There would be no tormenting memories so vivid I'm forced to lock them in a vault deep in my soul. There would just be the joyous memories of my senior year, graduation, and the anticipation of college.

I hold out my final, breaking his trance. He glances at my hand as he takes it from me, but never lifts his eyes to meet my face.

"Here," I say softly, setting the pencil I had to borrow from him back on his desk.

I wait for a moment, but he keeps his head down, looking over the stack of finals. I can't believe our epic romance has come to this. I hastily spin away from him, heading back to my desk. Am I foolish to even think we *had* a relationship?

His harsh words echo in my mind: *I'm sorry I ever let anything happen.*

Had it simply been lust on his end? Infatuation on mine? Whatever it was, it wasn't enough to hold up against the odds.

We were doomed from the very beginning.

I grab my bag and slowly walk out of his classroom for the final time.

I don't look back.

CHAPTER THIRTY-ONE

GRADUATION DAY FINALLY ARRIVES, AND I think back on my life as I finish curling my hair. So much has happened in the last few months—things I had never expected. A quick love affair with my math teacher—if you can even call it that—my parents separating, my mom's affair, my breakup with Tommy, and my best friend moving hours away—not to mention my father. I step back and take in my reflection. My gray pencil skirt, white button-down blouse, and nude heels make me feel sophisticated—like an adult, even. But it isn't just my ensemble that has me looking older—it's my eyes. They've changed over these last few months. They know more, they've experienced more. But hopefully, over time, they won't always look this dispirited. I sigh into the mirror. Why do we even bother dressing up for graduation, when we just cover it up with the most hideous get-up imaginable?

Emily and I are set to walk together during the ceremony, behind Derek and Tommy, and I can't help but think how differently I expected this day to be. The four of us would've partied all night and enjoyed a blockbuster summer together before heading off to college. But instead, we'll be celebrating tonight with awkwardness to the tenth power. They all agreed to hang out at my house for a couple hours before Derek's party—much to my mother's delight—so we decide to ride to the ceremony together.

One happy little dysfunctional foursome.

Derek picks me up in his Beemer, and I climb into the

back seat with my gown swung over my arm. Emily turns around from the front seat, scrunching up her face.

I tilt my head. "What?"

"I have to tell you something before we pick up Tommy." She and Derek exchange a glance.

"Okay . . ." I hold my elbows tightly to my sides, bracing myself for whatever she has to say.

"Tommy's taking Avery to Derek's party."

A sharp laugh bursts out of me. "Of course he is."

Emily bites her bottom lip. "Are you really cool with it? Or are you going mad?"

"Neither, Ems," I say. "I just want this entire day to be over with."

She gives me an empathic smile and turns back around.

Okay, so Tommy's taking skanky little Avery to the party. He's moving on. If that's who he wants to move on with, then so be it. At least he'll be getting laid tonight, so maybe he'll be in a civil mood.

"Wait," I say as we pull into Tommy's driveway. "We're not picking her up before the party, are we?" I may want everyone to move on, but I don't think I can handle being squished in the backseat with the slut bag.

Emily tightens her lips. "Um . . ."

"Seriously you guys?"

"Not if you don't want us to," Emily assures me.

I slump back in my seat. "I'll just drive myself to the party," I mutter. "We'll be at my house beforehand anyway."

"I'll ride with you," Emily says in a firm voice.

"Thanks." I smile at her as Tommy climbs into the backseat behind Derek. I scoot away from him.

"You look nice, Kay," he says.

I give him a phony smile before peering out the window. I can't believe his nerve. At least I can be freed from some of my guilt now that he's dating Avery. We ride the rest of the way in silence.

I HOLD EMILY'S hand throughout the ceremony. We need each other more than ever right now. Her world is crumbling as she counts down her last days with Derek, and I long to fill her in with all the secrets I hold. As we walk down the aisle, I feel my chin quiver, and I'm surprised by my rush of emotion. It's agonizing to remain composed when I see my parents in the crowd sitting next to each other. This is probably the last time I will see them side-by-side, and I burn the image into my memory.

Just before the commencement speaker officially announces our class graduated, I look to my friends—even Tommy. We're finally graduating high school and moving out into the real world. With everything I've gone through this year, I wonder what life will bring as I make my way into adulthood, and I feel a twinge of excited anticipation.

The most surreal moment of the day is saying good-bye to my dad after the ceremony. He's about to drive hours away and create a new life for himself. I can't fathom not seeing him every day. When my mom is done taking pictures of us, he hugs me tight and says in my ear, "Call me if you ever need anything, Kay. Day or night, I will always be there for you." His voice breaks.

"Thanks, Daddy," I whisper.

There is something humbling about seeing my father break down. He's no longer the strong, invincible man I once admired as a little girl. . . . He is a human being, just like me.

And he is broken.

I squeeze him tight before letting go—I refuse to let him see me cry. I don't want him harboring any more guilt than he already does. He deserves to get away and have a fresh start.

We all do.

DEREK, EMILY, TOMMY, and I all pile into the Beemer.

"See you kids at the house!" My mom waves at us as she heads to her car.

"Your mom seems really happy, Kay," Emily observes from the front seat.

I roll my eyes. "Yeah. I think it's the whole 'new boy-friend' thing."

"That is *so* weird," she says.

"You have no idea."

Derek has to stop for gas, so my mom ends up beating us to the house. She has the door open for us when we arrive, and the coffee table is filled with snacks and beverages. It's not quite the grandiose display one would find in the Larson household, but what is? She means well, and I appreciate what she's trying to do for me.

"Do you want to take pictures now or later?" my mom asks.

"Now, please," I say. It's the last thing I want to do, but I want to get this over with.

She whips out her camera and snaps several group photos of us. Then she takes a few of just me and Emily. She then has the gall to snap a few pictures of Tommy and me alone. I grit my teeth as I smile wide for the camera, his arm wrapped tightly around my waist.

When our photo shoot is finally over, and my mom is out of earshot, Tommy turns to me.

"Hey, I hope you're okay with me bringing Avery to the party." His inflection is sincere—well, as sincere as Tommy knows how to be.

My gaze cuts to his hand still on my waist, but he doesn't take the hint.

"No problem," I say.

"Are you sure?" he asks. "I wasn't going to bring her—in

fact, I was going to ask *you* to be my date. But Emily told me there was no way you'd say yes."

My body goes stiff. "Emily was right," I say, stepping out of his hold.

The fact that he even considered asking me solidifies the fact that he always gets his way in life. He doesn't seem angry, though. It's more like he just doesn't know what to do when someone tells him no.

"You can do better than Avery, though," I say over my shoulder as I walk over to the coffee table.

Tommy sits down adjacent to me as I dive into my mom's famous peppermint meringue cookies. She always saves them for the holidays, but she knows they're my favorite, and I'm touched by her sweet gesture. Although I could really use a shot of vodka right now, sugar will have to do until I get to the party.

The evening isn't as uncomfortable as I expected it to be. We find a light banter between the four of us, and Tommy and I even share a few laughs. Maybe this summer won't be a complete travesty. Maybe we really can find common ground and just be happy for each other.

Before I know it, two hours have passed, and I find myself laughing so hard I have to hold my stomach as we reminisce over the last school year. My mother looks triumphant as she dawdles around the house. Emily is in the middle of retelling the story of the disastrous night she and I snuck out of her house to meet the boys, only to realize when we got back that we had locked ourselves out in the rain and had to wake her parents up by banging on their bedroom window. The four of us double over in hysterics as she acts out her father's angry rant in his underwear.

My mom's voice breaks through our laughter. "Do you kids know anyone in a black Tahoe?"

The room instantly falls silent as my body goes into

shock. Emily's widened eyes meet mine across the room. I slowly turn to my mom as she's peering out the front window.

"Why?" I croak.

"Because a black Tahoe just pulled up," she replies.

My pulse sprints through my veins as Emily glances at the boys for answers.

"And a very well-dressed young man is walking up, carrying . . ." her voice trails off.

"Did you invite him over here?" I hear Tommy ask Derek.

Derek shakes his head, then pins his eyes on me. He appears more stunned than angry, and I force a quick glance at Tommy—he's followed Derek's gaze and is also now staring at me. I realize my jaw is still slack, and I clamp my mouth closed.

The doorbell pierces the silence, sending shockwaves through me, and I drop my gaze to my knees, trying to pretend three pairs of eyes aren't boring into me. My mom opens the door, but my body won't move. I don't know if I want to run to the door, or far, far away from it.

Then I hear his silky voice resonate from the doorway.

"Hi. I'm here to see Kaley."

A squeal escapes Emily, and she cups her hands over her mouth, her eyes dancing at me, and my face feels like it's on fire. Derek squints at her, then looks back to me.

"Kay?" my mom calls over her shoulder, her voice wary. "Someone is here to see you?"

I push myself up onto my wobbly legs, ignoring Derek's hardened stare, and face the door. A small laugh of nerves—or hysterics, I'm not sure—bubbles out of me. Elijah stands in the foyer, wearing a black long-sleeved shirt with dark-gray pants, flawlessly tailored. He is a walking Armani ad.

He holds up a large bouquet of long-stemmed lavender roses. Fear and euphoria collide in my chest, threatening to strangle me, and I have to remind myself to breathe. I give my mom a stern look as I make my way to the door. She hesitates before stepping away.

"What are you doing here?" I whisper. Everyone is within earshot, and I imagine them craning their necks behind me.

He speaks clear enough for the room to hear. "I was wondering if you would do me the honor of accompanying me to the movies tonight."

My heart lurches into my throat, rendering me speechless. I hear Emily squeal again, and I squeeze my eyes shut, forcing myself not to look back at her. I open my eyes, but can only nod like a muted monkey, and he gives me a heartbreaking grin and extends the beautiful bouquet.

"Thank you," I say, finding my voice again and accepting the flowers. "But are you serious right now?" I glance behind me, then lean in and whisper, "Are you sure you know what you're doing? You don't have to do this, I—"

His lips cut off my words as he parts my mouth slightly, teasing me with the only lips that can evaporate my surroundings. When he releases me, I falter in my heels for a moment and place a steadying hand on the wall.

He turns to the living room with unwavering confidence. "I hope I'm not intruding on any plans," he says to my wide-eyed group of friends. I pull my attention from Elijah and turn to them. They all remain paralyzed with shock. Emily is actually standing, and I have no doubt she popped up off the couch like a meerkat when he kissed me.

"We're just going to Derek's party, Mr. Slate," Emily says bashfully.

My vision narrows to my mother's enlarged eyes, and I feel faint. I shoot her another warning look.

He clears his throat. "Please, call me Elijah."

"Oh. Okay," Emily replies, blushing as she slowly sits back down.

I can't bring myself to look at Derek, but I do glance at Tommy—his skin is a pale shade of green.

Elijah takes my hand, sending a jolt through my nervous system. "Are you okay missing the party?"

I nod, finding myself speechless once again.

He leans forward and whispers in my ear. "You look insanely beautiful, but would you mind doing me a favor?" His breath tickles my neck, and it's all I have not to drop my bouquet and have my way with him right here in the doorway. "I'd love it if you wore the dress you had on the last time we were at the movies." When he straightens, his eyes peer down at me, glinting with desire.

Hmm, he has a plan.

I grin at him with an irrepressible glee. "You got it." I lead him into the living room, avoiding my friends' gawking eyes, and hand my mom the roses. "Can you put these in something? I need to go change."

She grabs my arm as I turn for the stairs. "Why don't you help me for a minute," she says with a sweet tone, but threatening eyes.

I turn to tell Elijah to have a seat, but he's already making himself at home on the couch, greeting the boys with their signature handshakes. The back of Tommy's neck is red as he embraces his former coach, cloaking me in sweet validation. Emotions I've been suppressing for weeks come flooding back and have me struggling to keep my guard up. I watch Elijah grab a peppermint cookie and sit next to Emily casually. Emily, however, looks like she's about to pass out.

I meet my mom in the kitchen as she's pulling a vase from the cupboard. When she senses my presence, she spins around.

"*Mr.* Slate?" she scolds. "He's your *teacher*?"

"Mom, it's not what you think."

She lifts her brows. "Oh no? He just brought you two dozen long-stemmed roses. He's surely not here to tutor you, Kaley."

"Mom," I say with a nervous laugh. "He's not that much older than me, it's okay."

"This is not funny, Kaley Christine. You are so lucky your father isn't here. He's your *teacher*," she says. "How long has this been going on?"

"*Was* my teacher," I correct. "And Mom, do you really want to talk to me about morals right now?"

She steps back and puts her hands on her hips. "Excuse me, little miss, *I'm* an adult."

"So am I," I yell in a whisper. "And so is he. He's not what you think."

"So what is he then?" she says, her face livid.

"Well . . ." I hesitate. "He just might be the love of my life."

"Oh, Kaley," she says, waving me off.

I'm too stunned and confused to react to her condescension. "Mom, we'll talk later. I have to go."

"I can *not* let you leave with him, Kaley, I'm sorry. I need to know more about this man."

"Mom, please. Go in there and talk to him then. I need to go change. I'm not going to have this discussion with all my friends in the next room."

She stares me down.

"Come on, Mom," I beg. "You know me. Just please trust me on this."

Her eyes soften slightly. "I do trust you, Kay. I'm just . . . a little shocked right now."

"I know."

"How old is he?"

I bite my bottom lip. "Twenty-five."

"Kaley," she chides. "I'm . . . concerned."

"Mom, give him a chance, please. He's amazing."

She sighs before a slight smile betrays her face.

"Well," she says. "I'll admit he certainly *looks* amazing."

My mouth drops, and I laugh. "Mom!"

"Go," she says pointing to the living room. "But we're talking about this when you get back."

"I promise," I say, then rush back into the living room.

Elijah is settled into the couch with one arm slung over the back, coolly chatting away with my friends—who are all clearly on edge. I think back to the barbeque at Coach Miller's, when all of them were clamoring to join the Mr. Slate Fan Club. A laugh escapes me, and everyone's eyes pivot in my direction.

I flush. "Um . . . I'll be right back, guys. I'm going to go change real quick."

"Okay, baby," says Elijah.

Tommy grows pallid and glances at Elijah, then back to me. Elijah winks at me, and I hold back a grin—he's enjoying this way too much.

I turn for the stairs.

"Wait!" Emily calls out. "I'll help you!" She scrambles up the stairs after me and practically tackles me when we enter my bedroom. She stands with her jaw hanging open, gaping at me in silence.

"Are you mad at me?" I say, cringing.

When she finally speaks, her voice is loud. "Are you kidding me? *Slate*?!"

"*Shh!*"

She lowers her voice. "I know I should be totally mad at you for lying to me, but I'm too busy *freaking out*. I *knew* something was up! I mean, I thought I was crazy, so I let it go, but I knew something was off with you guys lately. I just wasn't sure what it was. Are you guys like, just sleeping to-gether, or are you like a real thing?" She sits on the edge of my bed like a dog begging for a treat.

"We haven't slept together," I say as I slip off my shoes. "We came close a couple times though."

She lets out an agonizing sigh and throws herself back on my bed. "Tell me *everything*, Kay. Everything!"

I laugh. "I don't have time to tell you everything right now, but I will. I promise."

"Kaley. You almost had sex with Mr. Slate. Professor Mc-*Freaking*-Hottie! You have to give me *something*."

"Okay," I say with a smirk. "His body is even better than you can imagine. It's *insane*."

She squeals into my pillow, squeezing it to her chest.

"But he's more than that," I say as I pull my black dress out of the closet. "Actually, I kind of broke it off with him a couple weeks ago. It got super complicated really fast. And I was so sick of lying to everybody—especially you—and when he told me he still wanted to keep us a secret for an-other year, I just couldn't deal. We haven't spoken since."

"Are you serious?" She jumps off the bed and helps zip me up. "So, is this like his declaration of love for you?"

My cheeks burn. "I don't know. Maybe. To be honest, I'm too shocked to comprehend anything right now." I slide into my black strappy heels and continue. "I thought it was over. I mean, I cried hard over him, Ems. We were *done*." My hands shake as I transfer my belongings from my purse to my neon-pink clutch.

"Whoa," she says. "So this got deep."

"Yeah," I whisper.

She clasps her hands together. "Swear to me that you will tell me everything. Every. Single. Detail."

"I promise," I say as I check myself in the mirror. I can't believe she finally knows the truth.

"Wait!" she says as I grab the door handle.

"What?"

"When did this happen? Like, when did something actually happen between the two of you?" Her eyes gleam with anticipation.

"Like small things? Or big things?"

"I don't know!" she cries. "When did you become official? Or were you ever official?"

"We were." My stomach clenches. "You might get upset," I warn.

"Just tell me."

I hesitate. "It was prom night."

She falls to her knees. "Get. *Out!*"

I laugh at my lovingly dramatic best friend.

"I am dying!" she shrieks. "After you left the hotel?"

"Yeah. I stayed over at his house that night." I still have the urge to be careful, but it's too hard not to tell her everything. My best friend is back, and I never want to let her go.

"Prom night," she whispers to herself. "Oh my gosh. . . . Oh my *gosh!*" I watch her face as she recalls the details of the evening.

"Are you mad?" I ask again.

She thinks for a moment. "You know what? No," she says firmly.

"I mean, Tommy would've cheated anyway, I guess. He thought you went home. We all did. I never wanted you to be with a cheater, Kay. I was just devastated over the whole thing. I'm sorry you didn't think you could talk to me about it."

"Don't make me cry right now," I say, laughing as the tears start to swell. I pull her off the floor and gather her into a hug. "I'm still worried you're going to be mad at me."

She pulls back. "Why?"

"Because I . . ."

"Hey!" she warns, noting my expression. "Do *not* cry. Did you *see* your gorgeous date down there?" She laughs. "You cannot ruin your makeup!"

I laugh and grab a tissue from my nightstand, carefully blotting underneath my eyes. "Ems, I cheated first. . . . I'm a piece of shit."

"No you're not! Tommy's the piece of shit."

I laugh again. "What?"

"He banged Avery after he thought you went home."

I shake my head. "It doesn't matter. I made out with Slate way before that."

"When?" she asks.

"After his study session."

She presses her eyes closed, and I wait for her tongue-lashing. "Okay, look," she says, opening her eyes. "I get that you feel bad. And I don't think cheating is cool. Ever. But let it go. Tommy can't defend himself here—he cheated on you anyway. No offense, but you guys were kind of a disaster." She clutches my shoulders, startling me. "And holy shit, his study session? You have to tell me about *that* later!"

"I promise we'll talk about everything tomorrow. Come on, I don't want to leave him alone too long with Tommy and my mother."

She giggles. "Kaley, did you see Tommy's face? It was priceless."

"Yeah. The only thing better would've been seeing Avery's face," I say. "That bitch was always throwing herself at him in class." We burst into laughter as we enter the hallway.

"Hey, I'm sorry for bailing on the party," I say. "And I know he just showed up to my house, and it's super crazy, but please don't gossip about it tonight. He could be in some serious trouble now. Tell the guys, too."

She mimes zipping her lips, then takes a step back, arching a single eyebrow. "Um, Kay? Isn't that Tommy's favorite dress?"

I bite my lip. "Elijah asked me to wear it tonight . . . so I guess this dress belongs to him now."

"*Elijah* asked you to wear that?" Her eyes bulge as his first name tumbles awkwardly out of her mouth. "I'm dying to know how he even knows about this dress."

I can't hold in my grin. "I have so much to tell you, Ems."

"You better call me tomorrow," she warns, "or I will never forgive you."

"I will," I promise.

As we descend the stairs, I find my mom sitting on the couch next to Elijah, chatting with the boys. Bizarre doesn't even come close to describing the scene. Tommy's mouth goes slack when he sees me, while Elijah strides over to meet me at the bottom of the stairs.

"Hey, beautiful," Elijah says with a heart-wrenching smile.

Emily slips past him with an expression that I will forever regret not capturing on camera.

"Well, we should probably get going," says Derek, appearing eager to escape the situation. He jerks Tommy to his feet and discreetly shoves him toward the door.

"You guys be safe tonight," Elijah calls to my friends as we follow them outside.

I tilt my head at him in disapproval. It's clear he's getting way too much enjoyment out of torturing Tommy.

Emily gives me a tight hug and whispers in my ear, "Every. Detail."

"I promise," I say. "What about you, though? Are you going to be okay? I hate leaving you like this."

"I'm not thinking about my problems tonight, Kay. I can't." She shrugs. "Derek says he wants to stay together after he leaves for college, but I don't know . . . I just want to enjoy the night, and you should too."

I gather her in another hug. "Okay. Have a blast. I'll call you tomorrow."

She opens the passenger door of Derek's car and yells in mock excitement, "We're going to go pick up Avery!" She gives me an exaggerated thumbs-up, and I can't help laughing. It's such a relief to have my best friend back.

Tommy's eyes meet mine from the back seat just as Elijah's arm slips around my waist, and he quickly turns away. *I don't look too pathetic now, do I buddy?* It's not my intention to torment him, but part of me finds it quite satisfying—even though I know it's wrong.

"Well, it was nice meeting you, Elijah," says my mom, reaching out to shake his hand.

"The pleasure is all mine, Sharon," he replies smoothly.

Even my mom seems a little smitten with him as she watches him open the passenger door of the Tahoe and assist me in. After he climbs into the driver's seat, she goes back into the house. If she was captivated by Tommy's charm, I know she won't be able to resist Elijah's.

"Your mom's really nice," he says, turning the key in the ignition. "I wasn't sure what to expect showing up like this." He grabs my hand, lifting it up to his lips as he drives down the road. He kisses each finger before resting our interlocked hands on the console. "Thank you for coming with me tonight. I didn't know if you'd accept."

"I honestly didn't expect to ever see you again," I reply.

"Me neither, Kay," he says, his voice tight.

"I can't believe you did this," I say. "I don't know what you're thinking. You could be in a lot of trouble now, right?"

He swerves the Tahoe to the side of the road and slams it into park, startling me. He unbuckles his seatbelt and leans over the console, locking me in an urgent kiss. His mouth feverishly searches mine, and I grip his hair, returning his vigor.

Oh, how I've missed this.

He releases me, pulling back just enough to look into my eyes. "Kaley, I just experienced the worst two weeks of my life. I thought for sure this was over, that we were doing the right thing . . . that *I* was doing the right thing." His voice reveals the anguish that he's been shielding from me. "But nothing about it was right. I can't believe I almost let you slip away." The intensity of his eyes sear into me as he brushes my cheek, running his fingers through the side of my hair. "I'm in love with you, Kaley."

A quiver ripples down my spine as his words weave through my chest like thread, slowly stitching up my wound. *He's in love with me?* He wraps his lips around mine, his gentle kiss attempting to heal my bleeding heart. He slowly breaks away to return to his seat, but I tighten my grip on him and lean over the console, our faces nearly touching.

"I'm in love with you, too," I say. "But you *do* know you're crazy, right?"

He grins as if the weight of the world has been lifted off his shoulders, and he rushes to my lips. After paralyzing me with another kiss, he leans back in his seat and refastens his seat belt. "Just crazy for you, Kaley-baby."

"Hey," I say after he pulls back on the road. "I hope you know I'm not trying to make you parade me around and get fired. Honestly. I'm all for a little subtlety."

He chuckles, grabbing my hand again. "I'm not trying to be completely stupid, Kay. But I'll be damned if I'm going to lose the best thing that has ever happened to me."

His words instantly resurrect the butterflies in my stomach into a full flutter.

"I'm taking you to a movie in downtown Phoenix," he says. "I hope that's fair enough."

"That's perfect," I say. "Then maybe we can grab some dinner and go back to your place?"

"Anything you want, baby."

As I relax into my seat, holding onto his warm, strong hand, I gaze out the window.

Anything I want?

I'm going to hold him to that.

CHAPTER THIRTY-TWO

WE PULL INTO THE PARKING lot of the movie theater, and Elijah slides into an empty space and kills the engine.

"Wait here," he says just as I'm about to open my door.

Confused, I watch him walk around the back of the Tahoe, then open my door.

I arch a playful brow at him. "Chivalry isn't dead, I see."

When my feet hit the ground, he envelops me in his arms, exhaling into my hair.

"Damn, this feels good," he whispers.

With his hand cradling the base of my neck, he teases his lips against mine, pulling away slowly each time I lean in.

"Slate," I groan.

He chuckles, then presses his body against mine, backing me against the passenger door, kissing me without restraint. When he breaks away, I struggle to recover my equilibrium.

"Come on, baby," he says, taking my hand and leading me to the box office.

I feel like the luckiest girl in the universe with our fingers entwined for the world to see. After purchasing our tickets, he leads me to the concession stand.

"Watermelon Wedges?" he asks.

I grin. "Absolutely."

He never lets go of my hand as he pays for our candy, and I can't take my eyes off him. Somewhere in the irrational part of my brain, I fear he'll disappear if I do.

Most of the seats are empty when we arrive in the dimly lit theater, and he guides me up the stairs to the very back row, stopping just before the center seats.

"This is more like it," he says, sitting down with a relaxed sigh. I've never seen him so unfettered before. Though we aren't exactly in the clear yet, the air feels lighter around us. It's thrilling to see him so unrestrained, so . . . carefree.

"Okay, I know what I want for my graduation present," I say.

He cocks an eyebrow.

"Not that this isn't enough," I add.

"Please, Kaley. Taking you to the movies and having you wear this dress is a graduation present for *me*."

"Can I take a picture of us?" I cringe, waiting for his rejection.

Much to my relief, he smiles. "Why the hell not."

He pushes the adjoining armrest up and slides his arm around me, pulling me closer. I hold my phone out at arm's length as we press our cheeks together and smile as I snap the picture.

"Okay, one more," I request.

He turns his head, kissing me on the cheek as I beam into the lens and take another one.

"Ooh, that one's wallpaper-worthy, Slate," I say, grinning. "Thank you."

He snatches my phone from my hands and for a second I'm worried he's going to delete the photo. Instead, he enters my contacts list and scrolls down to "Garrett" and taps on the screen. I feel my eyes widen as he deletes the name and replaces it with "Elijah Slate."

He returns my phone, and suddenly it's as if helium has replaced every burden in my body, and I feel like I could float away.

"Thank you," I say, my voice barely above a whisper. "This is seriously the best graduation gift I've gotten."

"No, thank *you*," he says. "For coming with me tonight."

His eyes slide brazenly down my body. "I love you in this dress. You have no idea how badly your legs were killing me that night." He rubs my thigh, leaving a trail of goose bumps behind.

"You didn't bring a jacket for me this time," I tease.

He shrugs. "I figured if we got cold, we could warm each other up."

An excited flutter tickles my lower stomach, and I cross my legs toward him, scooting closer.

"Wanna open these?" He nods to the bag of candy on his lap. "Sorry, I could do it, but I don't feel like freeing my hands right now." He traces his fingers up and down the back of my thigh, igniting a fire in the center of my body.

I open up the bag, taking out a Wedge, and place the candy between my lips and mumble, "Want one?"

His smile slowly vanishes, and he pulls my mouth urgently to his. He grabs the candy with his teeth, and his tongue meets mine as the sweet-and-sour candy dances between us. He slides his hand higher up the back of my thigh, slipping it underneath my dress, and kisses me with a passion that makes me want to skip the movie altogether. Breathless, he breaks away, taking the candy with him.

"Sorry," he whispers.

I notice the theater filling up and blush.

"I wanted to do this the last time you were sitting next to me in a theater," he says, sliding his hand farther up my dress, cupping my backside. His fingers play at the side of my satin thong, and my breath pulls in slightly. A group of guys enter our row, and he swiftly pulls his hand out, tugging my dress back down.

He kisses me softly once more as the previews begin. He keeps one arm around me and his other hand on my leg. Throughout the two hours, he intermittently strokes my thigh, sending fiery chills up and down my body. In turn, I feed him pieces of candy between my lips, and he slowly takes each piece with his mouth, brushing his tongue against mine.

"I could get used to this," he whispers in my ear.

I snuggle into to him, drawing in the once-forbidden scent that enlivens me, yet calms me at the same time. I inhale sharply and close my eyes, wanting to savor this moment. My mind wanders back to the fateful night I accidently sat next to him in that darkened theater and how different this experience is. . . .

I could get used to this, too.

WE STOP FOR Chinese takeout after the movie, before heading back to his place. He's already risked so much for me tonight, I'm not about to push our luck by sitting exposed in a restaurant together. When we're almost to his house, he turns up the music that has been quietly playing in the background.

"This song reminds me of you," he says.

I recognize it right away and my pulse quickens.

"It's a Def Leppard song," I say. Not only is it a song on the album I bought, but it's *the* song . . . the one that reminded me of him.

He lifts his brows. "Yeah, you know them?"

I nod, pursing my lips together. "I do, actually."

"Do you like them?" he asks, trying to decipher my reaction.

"Love them."

He leans forward and taps the screen, starting the song over, and cranks up the volume. The Tahoe's impressive sound system engulfs me, and I am soon lost in the music.

"OKAY, I KNOW what I want for my *real* graduation present," I announce as we walk into his house. "Not that I'm not grateful for the pictures and movie and everything," I'm quick to add.

He belts out a laugh. "The movie was inspired by that dress, Kaley. I had nothing but selfish reasons for wanting to do that. I already told you, that was just as much a gift for me as it was for you."

I bite my bottom lip. "Well . . . maybe this one will be too."

He lifts an eyebrow as he sets the bag of takeout on the kitchen counter. "Oh yeah?"

"Yeah," I whisper.

He leans against the counter, both hands gripping the ledge behind him, his eyes drinking me in as I saunter toward him. I slide my hands up his shirt and across his mountainous chest, gazing up at him.

"Kaley, we can still take it slow. It doesn't have to be tonight."

I rise up on my tip toes and grip his neck, bringing his lips to mine. He cups his hands around my face, embracing me in a slow burning kiss.

"Please don't make me wait any longer," I breathe.

A low, deep chuckle rumbles in his throat. "I'm really trying to be a gentleman here."

"I want you," I whisper. "Right now."

He presses his forehead against mine and lets out an exasperated sigh.

"Please," I beg.

His eyes wander down my dress, and when he lifts his gaze back to mine, my legs sway as I read the hunger in his eyes.

I lift my mouth to his ear and whisper, "Please, Elijah. Make love to me."

He doesn't respond.

In a flash, he scoops me up and I shriek. He carries me

down the hall with my legs wrapped tightly around his waist, kissing me without reserve. When we reach his bedroom, he leans forward, dropping me on his big lavish bed, and climbs on top of me. I tremble at his aggressiveness, fully aware he isn't backing down this time. Flaming heat licks at my inner thighs, travelling up the center of my body as he kisses me with a startling new fanaticism.

"Hang on," he says, breaking away.

He hops off the bed and reaches for the sound dock on his dresser, clicking it on. A song I've never heard before softly plays through the speakers as he turns to face me. With his eyes fixed on mine, he grabs the hem of his shirt and slides it over his head, tossing it to the floor. He pauses, looking at me, and I take the moment to skim my eyes over his massive upper body.

I can't believe he's all mine.

His movements are slow, deliberate, reminding me of a jungle cat as he moves closer, climbing back onto the bed and hovering over me. His lips tease mine, and I reach for his shoulders, gliding my hands over his taut muscles, feeling them move as he pulls the dark bedding out from underneath me. His cool, white sheets feel smooth against my skin as I lie there, watching him rip the comforter completely off the mattress.

His deep-brown eyes lock back onto mine as he slides off his shoes and socks. I try to hold his gaze as he kneels before me, but my vision keeps slipping to his chest, his shoulders, his abs. *Damn, those abs.* I sense a smirk behind his eyes as he watches me. He takes hold of my right ankle, lifting it to his mouth, kissing the inside, nibbling on the bone.

"I love your ankles," he says.

"Really?" I ask, realizing I'm near breathless.

"Yeah," he says gruffly. "Sexy-ass ankles. It was hard for me not to stare at them in class."

The confession sparks a new urgency in me, and I practically squirm, waiting for his next touch. His eyes continue to paralyze me as he patiently unbuckles my stiletto, then tosses it aside.

"I liked watching you erase the whiteboard," I say, almost giggling at my admission.

A broad grin stretches across his face. "Did you. . . . Hmm." His lips are back on my ankle, then travel up the inside of my calf, and I giggle when he reaches the inside of my knee, tickling me. He doesn't falter as he trails his kisses up my inner thigh, his gaze steady on mine, dissolving my laughter into an intense ache below me. I bend my knee as he presses my leg back, hiking up my dress. Every fiber in my body tightens as his mouth reaches the silky barrier between my legs. Instantly, I'm struck with fear and vulnerability, fully aware of my inexperience.

"Relax, baby," he whispers against the satin. He kisses me over the silky fabric, shattering all my insecurities and coherent thoughts as unfamiliar pleasure takes over. He seems to be watching my reaction to every move he makes . . . with enjoyment.

Before I'm ready, his lips retreat, continuing the path of kisses down my left thigh. Taking his time, he moves down to the side of my knee and down my calf, paying special care to my ankle bone before removing my left stiletto.

"There's a pink dress you wore in class," he says, kissing the arch of my foot, then lowering my leg back down. "I'm going to need you to wear that again soon." He remains kneeling before me. "I had some impure thoughts that day."

I bite my bottom lip, sinking into the mattress, my legs almost numb from relaxation. "I used to watch you instead of my boyfriend during baseball games."

A wicked grin stretches across his beautiful face. "I wanted to know what your lips tasted like every time you put on your chap stick." His eyes stalk me like I'm his prey as he unfastens his pants. "Then when I finally tasted them, I was dying to know what the rest of you tasted like." He slides his pants off, and I take in the glorious sight that is Elijah Slate in black boxer briefs.

Oh, help me.

I reach around my back, grabbing the zipper on my dress, but he lurches forward, pulling my hands out from under me, clasping my wrists together.

"Uh-uh," he warns. "That's my job."

He lifts my right hand to his mouth, his seductive, caramel eyes stupefying me, and kisses the inside of my wrist with the same slow burning intensity he ravished my legs with. Continuing up the inside of my arm, he whispers to me in between kisses. "You are the most . . . beautiful . . . woman . . . I've ever . . . laid . . . eyes on . . ." His sensuous mouth moves like butter across my collarbone. "You . . . make me . . . so . . . crazy." I gasp when he nicks the left side with his teeth, sending unexpected electricity down to the depths of my belly.

He makes his way down my left arm, brushing his lips across my wrist, then kissing the palm of my hand. He kisses each fingertip before he slips my ring finger into his mouth, sucking it, titillating my senses, seeming to enjoy watching my reaction.

"I want this finger to belong to me one day," he says.

Wait. What?

He laughs. "Does that scare you?"

It takes me a moment to find my voice. "I think so."

"Good," he says, leaning in to kiss me, "'cause you scare the hell outta me."

He reaches behind me, grasping the top of my zipper, and I arch my back as he slides it down. I sink back into the mattress as he slides my dress down my body, pulling it all the way off.

"Mmm." He takes a moment running his eyes over me and shakes his head. "Unreal," he says under his breath.

He leans over me. "Take off your bra." He says it with an edge of authority that ignites a mixture of fear and excitement within me.

I do as I'm told, tossing my bra to the floor. "Yes, Mr. Slate."

That catches him.

"Kaley," he warns, and I giggle.

"Oh, you think that's funny, do you?" he says, his voice charged with playful menace.

I bite my lower lip to stifle more laughter.

"Let's see if you think this is funny," he says, his eyes glinting with intent.

With his dark eyes fixed on me, he lowers his mouth over my right breast, circling his tongue around my nipple before blowing gently, watching it rise and harden before pulling it into his mouth and sucking. Using his lips as a barrier for his teeth, he clasps my nipple between them, suddenly tugging hard, and I inhale a sharp gasp as an electric current strikes every nerve ending in my body. He moves to my left breast, gathering my nipple in his mouth, gently sucking and a clamorous moan rises out of me. He repeats his actions, teasing, biting, sucking, my breaths now unsteady.

"Not funny?" he asks quietly.

I shake my head, and he springs forward, his lips rushing over mine.

"Relax now, okay, baby?" he whispers against my mouth.

I nod, dizzy from his skillful touch.

He kisses my throat, his hands skimming my breasts, as his lips travel down the center of my chest, slowly making their way down my ribcage, his hands grazing my sides, sending shivers through me. I wrap his hair between my fingers as his mouth travels down my stomach, and I feel my body stiffen as he passes my belly button. An impatient, but nervous whimper escapes me as his lips meet the hem of my satin thong. He hooks his fingers in the sides of my panties and slowly pulls them down, breaking away momentarily to slide them off.

Lowering himself down, Elijah presses my thighs farther apart, and I try to remain calm. He reaches for my hands, lacing his fingers in mine, steadying me as his mouth makes contact below my waist. An intense breath pulls into my lungs as his mouth moves against me, and I grip his hands tighter. I hear a deep moan in his throat as he consumes me, devours me, stimulating every cell in my body, all the way down to the tips of my toes. He pulls his hands out of my clasp and clutches onto my waist, bringing me closer to him as his tongue circles around, darting, teasing, and switching rhythms.

I grasp the pillows beside me, thankful for the music surrounding us, as foreign sounds release from my lungs. The overpowering ache intensifies, building to a place that is almost unbearable, and I cry out to him, unintentionally tightening my thighs around his head. He presses his hands back against my inner thighs, not letting up, and I feel like I might black out. Just when I'm about to become unhinged, he breaks away, and I slowly fall from the high as his mouth makes its way back up my body.

Panting, I grab the sides of his head and pull his face to mine. "I need you," I beg. "Now. Please." I've never needed anything or anyone more than I do right now.

His broad shoulders hover over me. "Take them off," he commands softly.

My arms and legs struggle through their weakened state as I reach down to the hem of his boxers, sliding them down part way, then fall back against the bed.

"I can barely move," I breathe.

I think I hear him chuckle, but I'm not sure, and he slides them the rest of the way off.

With his face directly above mine, his intense brown eyes enrapture me. "I love you, Kaley."

His lips are on mine before I can respond, and he lowers himself between my legs.

No more barriers between us.

My heart races, small beads of sweat forming between us as his body meets mine. He gradually eases forward, and I wince.

His body goes still.

"Are you okay?" he asks alarmed. "Am I hurting you?"

I shake my head. "Keep going."

"Baby—"

"Please."

I bite my bottom lip as he gently pushes forward, and the sharp pain returns. He stops, and I clutch the sides of his torso.

"Keep going," I say.

He pulls back, then presses forward again, moving slowly, carefully, the discomfort eclipsing every sensation for a few moments before pleasure eventually overpowers the pain. I exhale, my body relaxing as he continues to move with caution.

"I'm okay," I breathe, as a new stirring gathers inside me.

I pull his face to mine and kiss him with a desire I've never known before and glide my hands over his muscular back, my need for him burning deeper. When he realizes I'm pain free and pleasure full, he steadily increases his rhythm. He's gentle with me, yet commanding, and faintness starts to spread through my limbs.

Leaning himself on his forearm, he traces his fingers down my stomach, positioning them below my waist. His fingers tease me, circling around as he presses himself deeper inside, and I moan uncontrollably as the new sensation rocks me. He lowers his face next to mine, his heavy breaths sending shivers down my sides. His fingers masterfully swirl against me, and the pressure begins to build with a dizzying intensity. My body tightens, and I clutch onto his powerful back.

"Relax, baby," he whispers in my ear. "I've got you. Let go."

His words put me over the edge, and I let out an eager gasp as pleasure I have never felt before erupts from deep within me. An unhindered moan bursts out of me as my body quakes, and I cry out to him as the euphoric sensation pulsates through me. He holds me close as I come undone, my back arching in submission to the release of pressure.

When I fall back into the mattress, he positions his arms on either side of me, steadying himself on his forearms, slipping his hands around the back of my neck. He presses his chest against mine, and I hold onto his dominant shoulders as he whispers my name, causing a soft gasp to catch in my throat. His rhythm escalates, and I grip his ripped back with all my strength, feeling the slickness of sweat across his muscles.

He slides his right arm underneath the small of my back, lifting up my hips. The feel of him intensifies, almost too much for me, too deep. But I don't want him to stop—I want him to overpower me. I sense his body begin to tremble as he intakes a sharp breath and thrusts into me. I glide my hands down his back and cup his backside, pulling him in deeper, and a deep groan releases from his chest as his body quivers over me. Once he stills, he kisses me intently, my mouth inhaling his ragged breaths. He soon withdraws himself and lies beside me, our heavy breaths overwhelming the music.

After a minute, he turns, caressing my hip. "How do you feel, baby? Are you okay?"

A satisfied grin expands across my face. "Never better."

"You're not hurt?" He brushes a few strands of hair out of my face.

"I'm fine," I assure him. I'm a little sore, but right now my fulfillment trumps any sort of pain.

"Come here," he says, turning me on my side to face him.

He rubs his thumb against my mouth, pulling down my bottom lip and leans in to kiss me. His love for me permeates through his kiss, like a key gradually unlocking the door of my heart.

This is love . . . it has to be.

"We're going to work this out somehow, okay? I can't lose you—at least not because of our situation. If you end up falling for someone in college, or don't want to be with me anymore, that's one thing. But I don't want this to end because of me. Because of my career."

I prop my head on my elbow. "Fall in love in college?"

He lifts a shoulder. "You never know. You deserve to experience college, Kay."

"You really do think I'm too young for you, don't you," I say quietly.

He squeezes his eyes shut for a moment. "Baby, no. I'm sorry I said those things. I didn't mean any of it. . . . I just knew—or thought, rather—that we needed to end it. And I wanted you to stay away from me—I needed you to. I thought it would make things easier . . . for both of us." He sighs. "I almost made the biggest mistake of my life."

"Well, if you don't think I'm too young for you, then why would you say I'm going to leave you for some college frat boy?" I ask. "You really think I'm going to fall in love with someone else? Or are *you* the one feeling insecure for a change?" I flash him a sly smile.

"I'm definitely not hoping you'll fall in love," he says.

"Well it's too late," I say, pressing myself closer to him. "Because I've already fallen."

I run my hand through his moistened hair and kiss him. He traces his fingers along my neck and down my spine.

I sigh. "I'm never going to get enough of you, Elijah Slate."

He kisses the side of my jaw before lying back on the mattress, and I rest my head on his chest. We relax for a while with our sweaty, bare bodies entangled.

I eventually break the silence. "I was wrong about the picture tonight."

"What do you mean?" he asks. "I know you'll be careful with it. You were right—we needed a damn picture of us."

"No," I say. "I mean about it being the best graduation gift I received. *This* is definitely the best."

He laughs. "Well, I hope so, or I didn't do a very good job."

"Are you kidding? I thought the first time was supposed to be horrible. I can't imagine it gets any better."

"Hmm . . . I'll take that as a challenge," he says, kissing the top of my head. "Besides, I promised you I'd make it worth your wait."

"You do know that I'm going to want you even more now, right?"

"Any time, any place."

I lift my head and kiss him just as my stomach growls.

He chuckles. "Hungry for some cold Chinese food, baby?"

"Hell yes."

He sits up. "You know, if you keep making me eat like this, I'm going to lose my eight pack," he says with a wink.

"Oh, God forbid!" I roll my eyes. "If you'd like, I'm more than willing to give you a nightly abs workout."

He belts out a laugh and jumps back on top of me. "I like the sound of that," he says, lowering his lips to mine. I wrap my arms around his neck as my stomach rumbles again, interrupting the moment.

"Come on," he says, pulling me off the bed. He lifts my chin, peering down at me. "You are stunningly beautiful, Kaley. Do you know that?" I blush and try to look away, but he holds onto my chin. "I'm serious."

"So are you," I whisper, and he half-smiles.

He releases me and slips into a new pair of boxers, and I pick up my wadded-up thong, wishing for a change of clothes.

I sigh. "I really don't feel like putting these back on. *Or* getting back into that dress. Do you have anything I can wear?"

He thinks about it for a moment, then opens his bottom dresser drawer, pulling out a blue cotton T-shirt from the back.

"Here," he says, handing it to me. "This is too small for me, but you'll probably swim in it."

I pull the shirt over my head, and it drapes just a few inches past my derriere. I peer down at the shirt and notice our school mascot presented boldly on the front, then look up at him.

"*Very* appropriate," I say dryly.

"Go Wildcats," he says with a smirk. "Do you need some shorts or something? Because honestly, I'd rather you just wear that, if you're comfortable," he says, stepping into a pair of jeans.

"Whatever you say, Mr. Slate."

He gives me a reprimanding look before leading me out to the kitchen. When he notices I'm cold, he grabs the blanket from the couch, wrapping me in it before pulling out a chair for me. We sit at the kitchen island, devouring the cold, yet delicious, takeout. I swear, no food has ever tasted so good. My phone rings, and I glance at the screen, realizing it's pretty late. I press my finger up to my lips to warn Elijah before answering.

"Hi, Mom," I say with my mouth full.

"Hi sweetheart, what are you doing?"

"Just eating a late dinner," I say, keeping my voice casual.

"Okay," she says. "I just wanted to know where you were and when you plan on coming home. Are you still with Elijah?"

"Um, yeah, but he's about to take me to Emily's house. I felt bad for ditching her tonight, and we were supposed to have a sleepover. If that's okay with you."

I peek at Elijah, and he winks at me.

"That sounds great. Do you need me to bring you a bag of clothes or anything?"

"No!" I say, panicked. She's really going above and beyond to repair our relationship lately. "Uh, no, don't worry about it. Emily will have clothes for me."

"Okay honey, have fun tonight. I'm so proud of you. And you'll have to tell me how your date went when you get home tomorrow." A shadow of guilt drapes over me, but as I look over at the sexy man next to me, I realize *some* lies are worth it.

"Thanks, Mom, I will," I say.

"And don't forget we need to discuss *him* more—our conversation isn't finished, Kay. I'm serious about that."

"I know, Mom, we will. I'll see you tomorrow."

I hang up the phone and Elijah's mouth is on mine, tasting of sweet and sour sauce.

"I can make a space for you in my closet if you'd like," he offers. "You know, in case of . . ." He pauses.

"In case of sexual emergencies such as this one?" I say, grinning.

He laughs. "Something like that."

His gesture warms my heart. Part of me is scared about moving too fast, but it would only be for convenience, right? Anything to help me get away with spending the night at a moment's notice is good with me, I decide.

After we finish our meal and put away the leftovers, I stroll over to the couch, but he pulls my arm back. "I don't feel like sitting out here."

"Okay," I say, confused. "Where do you want to be?"

He pulls the blanket off me, tossing it on the couch, and nods toward the bedroom.

Well, I'm not going to argue with that.

He has me lead the way down the hall and back to his room, and I climb on top of his big comfy bed—no doubt flashing him in my revealing attire. I let out a scream as he jumps toward me, tackling me onto the mattress. I giggle as he turns and grabs me, pulling me on top of him. I sit up straight, straddling his hips.

"This just might be the best outfit I've ever seen you in," he says, grinning, sliding his hands up my thighs.

"Seriously?" I say, pressing my hands to my hips. "I go to great lengths to look sexy for you, and *this* is what you like?"

"I like it all, baby, but this is so damn sexy," he says with bated breath.

I catch his tone and slip the shirt over my head, tossing it aside. "What about this?"

His grin fades, and he bites his lip as he reaches out for me, cupping my breasts. He sits up, sweeping his warm, dexterous mouth against my chest, and my blood boils. I lower my lips to his, kissing him hard. He grabs a fistful of my hair, and I push him down onto the bed. He groans in surprise as I claw at his jeans, pulling them down with aggression, along with his boxers. I lean forward, kissing him with urgency, and he gasps as I take hold of him, easing him into me. I clench my teeth through the brief shot of pain, then settle onto him. He clutches onto my hips, guiding me, teaching me, and I soon find a tempo that makes us both quiver.

We continue to explore each other into the early hours of the morning, until our bodies eventually force us to rest. I fall asleep with my head on his chest, listening to the steady beats of his heart, feeling entirely content for the first time in my life.

CHAPTER THIRTY-THREE

I SLIDE MY HAND ACROSS the mattress, only to find an empty space beside me. I stretch my arm farther across the bed, feeling nothing but soft, smooth sheets, and I crack open my eyes.

I'm alone.

I lift my head and notice light shining from the bathroom, and I reach for my phone, squinting at the time.

6:17 a.m.

I've only been asleep for three hours.

Ew.

I toss my phone aside and drop my head against the pillow just as Elijah steps out of the bathroom and into his closet.

"Why on earth are you awake right now, Slate?" I groan.

He pokes his head out of the closet, fastening his tie.

"And if you say you went out for a run, I just might kill you," I grumble.

He chuckles, walking to the side of the bed where I lay and leans down, whispering in my ear, "Go back to sleep, baby."

I clutch onto his neck before he can pull away. "Mmm . . . you smell *so* good."

He kisses my neck. "I have to go to work. Just go back to sleep. I'll be back around three."

I spring into a sitting position, wincing slightly at the soreness of my abs, and hold the sheet against my bare chest.

"Oh, crap! I forgot you had to work today. You're going to be so exhausted."

He rests his hand on my shoulder, easing me back down on the bed.

"It was worth it," he says in a low voice. "Now go back to sleep; I'll be back soon." He nibbles on my ear, and my body melts into the mattress. "Thank you for the best night of my life," he whispers. He breaks away, and I try to grab hold of him, but he slips out of my reach as he heads back to his closet.

"How do you expect me to sleep after you say something like that to me?" I whine. I imagine waiting all day in agony . . . then I remember I don't have any of my stuff here—not even a toothbrush. I need a shower and fresh clothes. I sit back up. "Do you have time to drop me off at my house?"

He hesitates. "Yeah, if you really need me to."

"Are you sure?" I ask. "I don't want to make you late or anything. I could call Emily."

"No, I can take you. But I won't exactly be in your mom's good graces if she sees me dropping you off the morning after our date."

"She doesn't work until noon today; I doubt she'll even be awake."

He sits on the side of the bed, slipping into his stylish leather dress shoes. "Will you meet me here when I'm off?"

I smile. "If you want me to."

"I'd really like that." He kisses me on the forehead. "I'll meet you out there, okay?"

After he leaves the room, I jump off the bed.

"Ow," I groan.

Every muscle in my body aches as I rush to get dressed—muscles I didn't even know I had. They complain as I slip into my strapless bra and reach around to zip up my dress. I step into my heels and shove my underwear into my clutch. I hope I don't see anyone I know this morning—I have "walk of shame" written all over me. When I enter the bathroom, I see that he left a toothbrush out for me. *God bless this man.* I open the package and brush in a hurry, then tie my hair into a disorderly bun and rush out to the garage.

"MAN, THE JUNIORS and sophomores are going to have a rude awakening today, aren't they," I say, laughing, as we drive down the road.

"What do you mean?" he asks.

"You're on like three hours of sleep. They're going to be at the mercy of your wrath."

He smiles at me. "Actually, two hours and twenty-seven minutes."

I roll my eyes at his perfect math.

"And honestly, I'm in the best mood of my life," he says with a wink. "I just might hand out A's like an Oprah give-away."

We break into laughter just as he pulls into my driveway. He gives me a quick kiss good-bye, and as I grab the door handle, I notice an unfamiliar truck parked in the driveway.

He notices my hesitation. "What's wrong?"

"I have no idea whose truck that is."

He glances at it. "You don't?" He pauses, pursing his lips. "You don't have to go home right now, you know. You can stay at my place."

I'm not sure why he's saying this after he just drove me home, but I'm too tired to question him, and I know we have to be quick.

He regards me with caution as I open the passenger door. "Hey, I'll have my phone on me today. Let me know if you need anything, okay? And take this." He slides his garage door opener off his visor. "Come back anytime, okay?"

I nod, trying to read his thoughts. A flicker of apprehension crosses his features as I take the garage door opener from him and slide out of the Tahoe. He waits until I'm safely in the house before driving off.

As I walk toward the stairs, I notice a man's shoes beside the sofa in the living room and come to a halt. *Did my dad leave his shoes here?* I drag my fatigued body up the stairs, too sleep-deprived to put the pieces together. The hardwood floor creaks as I tiptoe into my bedroom and peel off my dress. I'm in desperate need of a shower, but all I care about is sleep. I slip into a clean pair of underwear, then throw on a pair of thin sweatpants and a tank top. As I draw back the covers in anticipation of rest, it hits me.

A strange truck.

A man's shoes.

Elijah's concerned face.

I'm a moron.

Anger rips me out of my exhaustion, and I turn from my bed and stride down the hallway toward my mother's bedroom. I wrap my hand around the doorknob, turning it slowly. I hesitate, trepidation filling me as I try to prepare myself for an image that has the potential to burn itself into my brain for the rest of my life.

I push open the door.

Thankfully, they're both under the covers, but there's my mom: sleeping in the bed that she and my father shared for over eighteen years . . . with a strange man.

I slam the door shut and storm into my bedroom. Outraged, I slip into my flip-flops and grab my phone charger, along with Elijah's garage door opener. I charge down the stairs just as my mom scurries out of the bedroom in her robe.

"Kaley," she says, panicked, chasing after me.

"I'm not staying in this house, Mom," I say, my voice

shaking. "You *promised* me you wouldn't bring him here!"

"Wait!" she cries as I open the front door.

"What?" I snap, turning to face her.

"Kaley, I'm sorry. I thought you'd still be at Emily's. I'm *so* sorry."

"Look, I get it, Mom. You moved on before the rest of us even had a chance to. In fact, you moved on before you were even separated—not to mention you're still technically married to my father. I thought I made it abundantly clear that I cannot handle this. It's only our first day living together, and I've already caught you in bed with *him*."

"You weren't home. I was going to have him out of the house before you got back."

"I didn't realize that was part of the deal," I say cuttingly.

"I'm truly sorry, Kay. Please, forgive me." Her tortured face tugs at my compassion. I don't want to stand in the way of her being happy, but it's too much . . . too soon.

"I forgive you," I say impatiently. "But I can't deal with this." I turn and walk out the door.

"Where are you going to be?" she calls from the front steps.

I'm about to tell her I'm going back to Emily's house, but then I realize it doesn't matter anymore.

"Elijah's," I holler as I hop in my car.

As I tear out of the driveway, my vision begins to cloud. Maybe I'm overreacting, but my father's side of the bed isn't even cold yet, and she already has someone in it. She knew about her affair seven months ago—on top of the months of flirting that I'm sure went on prior to that. I, on the other hand, just got blindsided. I've only had a few weeks to get used to this twisted situation, and it's all happening way too fast. All of a sudden, my dad is living three hours away, there's a strange man in my house, and I barely even recognize my mom's personality.

My world has been upended at a time when I'm supposed to be exploring my way into adulthood, not being forced into it. With all the unknowns that lay ahead of me, I feel like I've been sent into battle without any armor, stripped bare of everything I used to cling to. Surprisingly, Elijah is the most stable thing in my life right now. Well, he and Emily. But she's leaving for college soon, starting a new life, with new people and new surroundings.... We'll no longer be minutes away whenever we need each other.

I turn onto Ironwood Drive and pull up to Elijah's house, parking on his side of the garage. As soon as I step into the kitchen, I flip on the coffee maker—I couldn't sleep right now if I tried. I skim my fingers over the glossy island countertop and look around. I've never been alone in his house before; it feels . . . oddly wonderful. As the coffee brews, filling the house with its potent aroma, I scrounge around his cupboards in search of food and find two large shelves that look like they belong in a nutritional supplements store.

"The man definitely likes his protein powder and vitamins," I mumble.

I open the refrigerator, and sparkling clean shelves filled with meat, eggs, fruits, and vegetables stare back at me.

Ugh.

Just as I'm about to close the door, I notice the carton of leftover Chinese food on the bottom shelf and snatch an eggroll from the container. I pour myself a cup of coffee, taking a bite of the cold roll, and plop myself onto the couch.

Breakfast of champions.

I glance at the clock—Elijah's already in second period. I send him a text letting him know I'm at his house.

He replies right away:

Are you okay?

I smile, realizing he knew it was only a matter of time before I figured it out.

Yes, I reply. Just a little slow, apparently. I found them in bed & got into it with my mom.

Sorry, baby.

A strange curiosity comes over me. What are you guys working on right now?

Finishing up quadratic functions.

Ooh, that's so hot.

A student just asked me why I'm grinning. I love you. See you soon.

I laugh as I imagine the clueless student's face. Love you, too. I'll be waiting. :)

Curling up on the couch, I finish my nourishing breakfast and soon become sleepy—the coffee clearly unable to penetrate my oncoming fatigue. I flip the channels on the TV and eventually zone out to a marathon of my favorite show on Bravo. I doze off a few times before plodding down the hall and crawling into his luxurious bed, the dark-gray walls surrounding me in peaceful tranquility. My body dissolves into the mattress as my mind wanders in and out of consciousness. I don't want to punish my mother—I really am choosing to forgive her and want everybody to move on. But not only would I feel disloyal to my father by being around her boyfriend, I really don't think I can handle it. And if this man truly makes her happy, then she should be able to see him.

It's probably best for everyone if I don't live there.

I wrap my arms around his pillow, embedded with his incredible scent, and plan out how I'm going to get my own place as I drift off to sleep.

MY PHONE WAKES me two hours later. I squint at the screen, then answer it.

"Where are you?" Emily demands.

Her voice is way too intense for my groggy state, so I decide to have a little fun with her.

"In Mr. Slate's bed."

She pauses before yelling at me. "I am *driving* right now! You could've caused me to swerve into oncoming traffic!"

I laugh. "You're fine," I say. "What's up? How was the party?"

"When are you going to be home?" she says, ignoring my question. "Don't make me wait any longer!"

The fact that she's so alert before noon after a night of partying makes me take her eagerness seriously.

"I was home for a minute. Slate dropped me off, but I found my mom in bed with her boyfriend."

She gasps. "Shut. *Up.*"

"I'm serious. Do you think I can stay with you until I get my own place?" I ask. "I'm going to take extra shifts all summer so I can save up as quickly as possible, but I've gotta get out of there."

"Totally," she says. "You know my parents won't mind."

"Thank you," I say, relieved. Maybe this summer won't be so bad. "Anyway, I got like *no* sleep last night; can we catch up in a few hours?"

The other end of the line goes silent.

"Let me get this straight," she says. "First, you stayed the night at Slate's house. Then, you tell me you got *no* sleep. And now you want to talk *later*? I hope you're joking."

I laugh. "Okay, you're right. So, how are you and Derek?"

"Kaley!" she whines. "It all sucks, okay? He has a ton of football crap to do, and I just found out he's leaving town almost a month before I am. This whole summer is going to suck, and I don't want to talk about it. So quit dodging my questions and tell me everything!"

My heart aches for her. "It's not going to suck," I assure her. "We won't let it suck. Did you at least enjoy the party?"

"Yeah, but I missed you. . . . A *lot* of people missed you, actually."

Something in her voice catches me. "Really? Oh, wait. Are you talking about Tommy?"

"Oh, he and Avery were *all* over each other—it was so gross. So, yeah, I think that was his way of missing you," she says, breaking us both into laughter.

"Okay, now I'm really glad I didn't go," I say. Over him or not, I don't need to see that. "Well, thanks for letting me ditch. Sorry I wasn't there."

"I wasn't talking about Tommy, though."

"You weren't? Who were you talking about?"

"Jace seemed really disappointed you weren't there last night."

Jace! I completely forgot about our date.

I smack my forehead, but keep my voice steady. "He did?" I try my best to sound surprised.

"Yeah. I think he likes you."

My memory flashes to the kiss we shared in his office. "Please. He's Derek's older brother. And my boss now."

"Says the girl who's lying in her math teacher's bed right now."

We burst into laughter again. I want to ask her if any of them told Jace about Slate, but I don't want her to suspect anything, so I leave it alone.

After Emily swears a blood oath to secrecy, I tell her the story from the beginning. From the tension that quickly built between Elijah and me, to the time Derek caught us in his Tahoe. She freaked out over that one, and I'm pretty sure Derek's going to get an earful for keeping it from her. I continue on with the fateful study session where he kissed me for the first time and explain how we almost got caught by the custodian. I've never talked to anyone about him before, and it's liberating. She's the best audience a girl could ask for—she squeals at all the right places and refuses to let me skim over any details. But most importantly, she isn't judging me.

My heart warms. I have my best friend back.

After we hang up, I glance at the time. We talked for almost two hours, but it felt more like ten minutes. I decide to hop in the shower and get ready. I linger in the hot water, letting the stream relax my strained muscles. As I go through the motions, my mind sweeps over everything I just told Emily about Elijah, and it all becomes clear to me. I remember thinking he was just an escape for me—an escape from my monotonous life. A life I wanted to shake up. But now I realize he was *never* an escape . . . he was everything I wanted all along. He's everything I'd been searching for, but never knew existed. I loved Tommy, I did. But as a child. This is different . . . I love Elijah as a woman.

As I'm making the bed, I hear the doorbell ring and freeze into place. I sneak over to the window and peek through the shutters.

It's Elijah.

I run to the door, opening it wide. "You scared me!"

He gives me a heartbreaking half-grin and steps inside. "Sorry, baby." He cups my face, granting me a light kiss. "I didn't realize I was without my key when I gave you the garage door opener this morning."

"I'm sorry," I say, my face still cradled in his hands.

He steps forward, backing me against the wall and leans down to kiss me. I grab his tie, pulling him closer. His lips are soft, but soon turn eager as he squats down to my level.

"I love coming home to you," he breathes, swiftly lifting me up.

I squeal in surprise, and he carries me down the hall and into the bedroom. He sits me on the edge of the bed, loosening his tie as his lips wrestle with mine. I slip his tie over his head and begin unbuttoning his shirt. He leans into me, and

I collapse back onto the mattress, sliding my hands into his designer shirt, using the access to explore his bare chest. Kissing the side of my jaw, he gently travels down my neckline. Conspicuous chills manifest on my skin as he pushes up my shirt, kissing my stomach. He makes his way past my belly button, and I tremble as he pulls back the waistband on my sweats, his lips teasing the hem of my underwear.

Then he stops.

His eyes burn into mine as he gazes up at me. Flashing a salacious grin, he pulls me into a sitting position.

"Stay with me tonight," he says, kissing my lips.

It takes me a moment to find my voice.

"Okay," I manage. "I have to work tomorrow. But not until three."

He tilts his head. "Work?"

It dawns on me that I never told him. "Oh. Yeah. I got a job at Derek's brother's sports bar. It's right next to ASU. Kind of perfect."

"So you officially decided on ASU?"

"I did," I say, smiling. "Why do I feel like we didn't talk much yesterday?"

"Because we didn't." His eyes twinkle with amusement. "But it sounds like we'll have plenty of time to catch up now that I know you're sticking around."

"What, did you think I was going to move to Flagstaff near my dad?"

He shrugs, sitting next to me. "I wasn't sure after this morning with your mom."

"Oh, I'm moving out for sure. I'm going to be staying at Emily's for the summer and work as many shifts as I can. Hopefully I can save enough to get my own place by August." His expression is unreadable, and I hesitate. "Is that cool with you? She's not going to say anything about us."

"It's fine. I just want you to be happy. I'd still like to give you a space in my closet . . . if you want."

"I *do* want," I say. I check the time and hop off the bed. "In fact, I want to get over to my house and grab some clothes right now, while my mom's still at work."

He stands up. "Do you need me to come with you?"

"No, I'm fine."

He takes my hand. "*Are* you fine?"

"I'm fine. I promise. I just need to get out of there."

He follows me out to the garage and kisses me good-bye.

"Hurry back, so I can finish what I started," he murmurs in my ear.

A shiver tickles down my side, and I breathe him in. "You better."

THE HOUSE IS silent when I enter the foyer. There's no evidence that a strange man was ever in my house, and I'm left wondering if last night wasn't his first visit. A lump forms in my throat, and I swallow it down. I need to do this fast. I sprint up the stairs and pack two large duffle bags, making sure I have plenty of clothes for Emily's and all the essentials for Elijah's.

After packing up the rest of my toiletries, I haul my bags out to my car, cramming them into the back seat. Just as I'm climbing into the Chevelle, I remember my lavender roses that Elijah gave me. I rush back inside and swipe the large vase off the kitchen counter. I know this isn't the last time I'll be in this house, but as I take one last glance around, it feels bittersweet.

Heavy on the bitter, though.

It's a challenge securing my roses into the passenger seat, but I somehow manage to buckle them in without crushing the petals too badly. When I climb into the driver's side, I notice something white, deep in the center of the bouquet. I reach in and pull out the tiny square envelope and open it.

Inside, is Elijah's perfect handwriting:

MISS KALEY KENNEDY,

YOU ARE THE VARIABLE I NEED
TO SOLVE MY LIFE'S EQUATION.
I CAN'T LET YOU GO.

YOURS,
ELIJAH SLATE

I press the card to my chest and close my eyes. All at once, it hits me: Elijah is making a space for me in his closet—making a space for me in his life. After surviving emotional perdition these last two weeks, my first instinct is to protect myself . . . to protect my heart. And though it may take a while to completely trust him—or anyone, for that matter—I pray that one day I can give my heart to him without fear.

I ignore my disquiet and read the card again, unable to suppress a grin. *I swear, he's the only person I know who can make math sexy.*

WHEN I ARRIVE back at Elijah's, the garage door is already open, and I pull my car in. He's at my side before I cut the engine, opening my door for me. I notice he's wearing my favorite athletic pants, and they instantly bring back memories of the embarrassing parking lot debacle involving Derek in the back of his Tahoe, and I suppress a smile. I grab my roses, and he helps me out of my car.

"I didn't want to leave these there," I say, suddenly feeling bashful.

He smiles at me, then reaches into my backseat, pulling

out my bags.

"*Two* bags, Kennedy? Hope I have enough room," he teases.

"It's mostly for Emily's house," I say, blushing. "I'll only keep a few things here, I swear."

He peers down at me, his biceps bulging as he holds a bag in each hand. "Bring as much as you want," he says quietly, turning toward the door.

I follow him inside and set my roses on the kitchen island before trailing him into the bedroom. He sets my bags on the bed, then faces me.

"Make yourself at home." He rubs the back of his neck, dropping his gaze. "I'll take whatever you don't want to keep here back out to your car when you're finished . . . okay?" He glances at me before stepping aside.

"Okay," I reply, moving toward my bags.

He leans on his dresser beside me and chews on his thumb nail.

Is it my imagination, or is he fidgeting? My nerves spring into action, insecurity prickling my insides. Suddenly, I feel like I'm intruding on his territory. *Is he regretting offering me his closet?*

"You don't have to offer me this space," I say, turning to him. "It's cool. I'll be living at Emily's. She's not exactly going to tell on me if I sleep over here." Now I'm the one fidgeting.

He brings his eyes back to mine and stares at me for a moment. "I want to share my closet with you," he says, but his voice sounds off to me.

"Are you sure?" I ask.

He nods, and I hesitate before unzipping a bag. I take out a small stack of random shirts and timidly step into his closet as he watches me. An entire wall has been cleared out, and my heart melts. He's giving me two full rods and three shelves.

"Oh, I forgot to bring hangers," I realize out loud.

"I have extras," he calls from the bedroom.

I set my shirts on an empty shelf and just as I'm about to exit, a glimmer above me catches my eye. I look up and see a silver key dangling from a red ribbon on the empty rod above my head. I take in a sharp breath as my brain attempts to comprehend the situation.

Elijah appears in the doorway of the closet with a stack of hangers.

"Here," he says softly.

I drag my gaze from the key, locking my eyes onto his.

He glances at the key, then back to me. "Are you freaking out?"

A moment passes before I can respond. "W-what is this?"

"It's a key to my house . . . if you want it."

I try to speak, but the words don't come.

"Kay," he says, setting down the hangers. "You don't have to take it if you don't want it. I just wanted to offer. You can come over here whenever you like." He clears his throat and continues. "Or . . . you're welcome to stay here until you get your own place. Instead of Emily's." He pauses. "Or you can just . . . move in."

"Move . . . in?" My mouth suddenly feels like it was just stuffed with cotton. "Are you asking me to move in with you? Like, permanently?" Clearly, I've misunderstood, and he's going to explain himself.

He rubs his jaw and chuckles nervously. "Yeah, I am. If you want."

I can't breathe.

"Slate," I say, moving around the tiny room. "Are you insane? We've barely—I mean, it's only been—that would be *crazy* . . . right?"

He laughs, clearly amused.

"What?" I say, a little too on edge.

"You're literally pacing, Kaley," he says. "Come here." He grabs my hands and pulls me close to him. "It's okay if you don't want to."

I hesitate. "Well . . . it's not that I don't want to; I just don't think it would be smart."

"Why?"

"*Why?*" I didn't think it required an explanation. "Because it's too fast. And because you're friends with Mr. *Bentley*. What's your family going to think? What's *my* family going think? And what about your career? There are a million reasons," I say, panicked. "This isn't exactly being cautious, Slate. What if you lose your job?"

"I won't," he says, his tone unconvincing.

"What if you do?" I demand.

He shrugs. "Well, then I guess I'll go work at Daddy's law firm," he says, his mouth almost twitching into a smile.

"Be serious."

His caramel eyes pierce into mine. "I *am* serious."

I pull away from him, wrapping my arms around myself. "You would seriously go to law school after just completing your master's degree in education."

"I'd get ten degrees if it meant that one day I could call you my wife."

The air sucks out of the room and my vision pinholes. I shuffle back a few steps and grip the edge of a shelf.

"Kaley," he says, carefully stepping forward. "I didn't mean to say that . . . I know that's heavy, I'm sorry." He rests his hands around my shoulders. "But it's the truth."

My limbs go cold and I try to step back, the narrow space closing in on me. "I can't marry you."

He smirks. "I'm not asking you, my darling."

"I'm serious, Elijah. My parents got married at my age—I can't." My mind races as I pull my hands through my hair.

"I don't know if I'll ever want to get married. I don't want us going through what they did. It's not worth it. I love you; I don't want to end up hating you."

"Kay." He steps forward, causing me to back into a row of his neatly pressed suits. "Your parents got married because of a baby. There are no obligations holding me to you—just an insane amount of love that I never knew existed."

I meet his eyes and take a deep, steadying breath. "So, you're telling me you want to marry me . . . but you're not asking."

A smile plays at his lips. "Exactly."

Silence fills the small space as I stare back at him, dumbstruck.

"I don't understand."

"Kay, I knew I wanted to marry you after these past two weeks of hell—I've *never* experienced agony like that. It changed my life forever. *You* changed my life forever. I drove to your house yesterday because I knew I was making the biggest mistake of my life. I had to take a chance. You are the only thing in my life I have no doubts about. When I told you that I've never felt this way before, I meant it. . . . I've never wanted to marry anyone before."

I raise my eyebrows. "Never?"

"No. And if that scares you, and you want to run away screaming, I'll understand—it'll kill me, but I'll understand," he says, chuckling softly. "I know I'm saying this prematurely in our relationship, but I almost lost you, and I need you to know where I stand. I know this is fast, baby, but this entire thing between us has been fast, and it's been out of my control from day one. I mean, I thought I'd experienced love before, and I guess I did on some level . . . but nothing like this. It's like the force of gravity, Kaley. You can't fight it, no matter how hard you try—it's scientific *fact*. It can be challenged, sure, but it can't be stopped. And the heavier some-thing is, the stronger the pull. And I've *never* experienced a pull like this. I'm done fighting it."

He lifts my hands to his chest, and I feel his heart pound-ing. "You've made me impulsive, Kaley. . . . You make me feel alive. You inspire me; you make me want to strive to be the best man I can be. I want to be the one you call on, the one to protect you. . . . I want to start a life with you." He takes a breath. "But I'll wait until you're ready." He releases my hands and kisses me on the top of my head. "And listen, I don't want you feeling trapped or anything. If after you start college you decide you're not ready for all of this, I get it. Just be honest with me—that's all I ask."

"Are you nervous about me starting college? You keep mentioning it."

His eyes soften. "I want you to go to college, Kay. I want you to experience a full life. But I'm well aware that we're in very different places in our lives right now. I've been where you're at before. I know what it's like. I don't ever want to hold you back."

I shake my head. "I don't see it that way. I don't care about parties, or boys, or the college life—I never really have. I've always wanted something more, but I never knew what it was." I pause. "That is, until I met you. I just want to get my education and live my life . . . with you."

He smiles, relaxing his shoulders.

I glance up at the key. "Can I ask you something?"

"Of course."

"Was that *her* key?"

He belts out a laugh. "No, baby. I had the locks changed the very next day. Even had to pay double for a rush ap-pointment. Actually, I just had this made for you while you were at your house grabbing your clothes.

"Really?"

401

"Really," he says.

I clear my throat, fidgeting with the drawstring on my sweats. "So, you're *not* asking me to marry you."

He smirks. "No, Kaley." His face grows serious, and he cups my chin. "You'll know when I'm asking you."

Holy hell.

I swallow, glancing up at him. "Okay . . . but you *are* asking me to move in with you."

He reaches over my head and unties the key.

"Yes," he says, dropping it in the palm of my hand.

I stare at it, twirling it around, as memories of our journey together flash through my mind. He's right. . . . Everything spun out of control the morning I walked into his classroom. And no matter how scared I am, life will never go back to the way it once was . . . nor would I want it to. His love has pulled me in so deep—I never want to come up for air.

I clutch the key in my palm and gaze up at the man who has dramatically changed my life, releasing a long exhale. "And you *do* know that this is completely insane, unwise, and utterly crazy, right?"

"Yes," he says, his eyes laced with anticipation.

I slide my arms around his neck as a slow grin stretches across my face. "Then I'm in."

EPILOGUE

Slate

THERE ARE THREE TYPES OF probabilities in the world. There's the theoretical method, my personal favorite, which is solved by dividing the number of ways an event can occur by the total number of possible outcomes. It's basic. Straightforward. Black and white.

I like black and white.

Then there are empirical probabilities, which are based on observations and experiments. I'm good with this, too. I like evidence. I like dealing with facts.

But then there are subjective probabilities—the gray area of statistics. An estimate based on experience, or intuition—not hard facts. Kaley and I have already beaten the odds of our improbable relationship. And the outcome?

Pure bliss.

Another improbable statistic is sitting in my classroom right now. According to Kaley, his parents are making him take this class so he won't be behind when he starts his first semester here in the fall. He tries to act natural around me, but I can sense his discomfort. As long as he keeps his mouth shut, I'll do my best to treat him with respect.

I get up from my chair and make another round. Some kids are still on the first page of the test, and it pains me. Math doesn't have to be so bad, it's just not meant to be crammed into five short weeks. And the three-hour class blocks are information overload for the average human brain, especially for a college-level math course. Frankly, I'm against it. But I need the money and hope to teach at a university one day. Until then, I'm making some extra cash by teaching intermediate algebra at the local community college in the sweltering July heat. Sure, there's air conditioning, but the insulation in this building is a joke.

When I return to my desk, I see a text from Kaley:

I'm off to work. :(Love you.

I can almost hear her irritated voice through the screen, and I stifle a laugh. She has no idea how cute she is. She's upset about having to work on her birthday. She tried to get it off, but her boss wouldn't allow it. Kind of harsh, but at least we're both off the next two days and can start our celebration. I reserved a suite at the Royal Palms Resort and Spa in Phoenix for two glorious nights. I can't wait to surprise her.

Love you, I reply. I'll see you when you get home.

If you really love me, you'll tell me what you have planned.

Not a chance, baby.

I glance at the time and give a ten minute warning to the class, and most of the students straighten up as they frantically race the clock. Bradford hands me his finished test, and I give him a nod. It's the best I can do, given the fact that I can't stand the punk.

WHEN I GET home, I change into my workout gear and down a protein shake. I'm barely holding onto a six pack these days. She doesn't seem to mind, but she's young, and I'm trying to at least keep up with her energy. I walk back to the spare bedroom that I converted into a home gym and slide my iPod into the dock. I turn up my favorite eighties rock playlist and rack the weights.

It's chest day, and I start with the flat bench. The weights clang against each other while I think back to my life without Kaley. Memories come flooding back like a movie reel, all the hours I spent in here trying to work her out of my mind. It all seems so long ago. Now, we not only share the same bed, but we share our lives together. We've made love just about everywhere . . . in the spa, on the side of the spa, in the pool, in the shower, on the couch, the kitchen island, even the hallway one time when we lost ourselves in the moment. She even interrupted one of my workouts and had her way with me on this very bench, while I watched her through the mirrors.

After about an hour of hard lifting, my muscles finally reach fatigue, and I take a quick shower. I grab a protein bar from the kitchen, then turn on ESPN and lean back on the couch. Eventually, I pull the stack of tests out of my bag, and I'm still grading by the time she walks through the door.

"Hey, baby," I say. "Happy birth—" I stop when I look up at her. "What's wrong?" I toss the papers on the coffee table and turn to her.

"Nothing," she says. "Why do you think something's wrong?" She smiles but it doesn't meet her eyes.

"It's obvious something's wrong."

"Ugh," she groans. "You can always read me; it's so annoying."

I fight the urge to laugh and tell her that anyone can read her. Instead, I stand up and walk over to her.

"I'm fine, Slate," she says. "I just want to take a shower."

"Bad day?" I ask.

"You could say that."

"I'm sorry." I grab her slender arm and pull her in for a hug. "Happy birthday."

"Thanks," she says, muffled into my chest.

I let her go, and she walks down the hall and into our

bedroom. I sit back down to continue grading, but my gut gnaws at me, and I decide to go check on her. The shower's on when I find her in the bathroom, but she's still clothed, standing by the sink. I catch her wiping a stream of tears off her cheeks, and my adrenaline instantly begins to fire.

"Kaley, what's wrong?" She jumps, and I soften my voice. "Sorry, I didn't mean to startle you."

"I'm fine," she says, turning to me. "Just a bad day. I'll be okay."

"Is it your boss? Is he making you work tomorrow?" For some reason there's been some tension between them, and I'm not sure why. My only guess is it's because he's the brother of one of her closest friends and maybe doesn't approve of our relationship.

She shakes her head. "No, it's not him. He wasn't even there today.

"Then who?" I ask, causing her tears to spring up again.

"No one, it's stupid," she cries, hiding her face.

I pull her into my arms and stroke her hair. "Just tell me, baby," I say, resting my chin on her head. I'm careful to appear at ease, but I'm dying to know who made her cry.

"Tommy came in today," she says.

The hairs on the back of my neck start to rise. "What'd he do?"

"Nothing," she says, pulling away. "He was just being a dick. It was bad enough I had to cover his table, but then he made some snide comments about you. He usually only comes in if Derek's there, so I wasn't expecting it. And he brought Avery—not that I care—but she laughed along like the little slut bag she is when he was talking about you."

I couldn't care less what Bradford has to say about me—I know I have nothing to worry about. But nothing enrages me more than how he treats Kaley. It infuriates me and takes a massive amount of self-control not to beat his ass.

"Are you mad?" she asks.

I let out a sharp laugh. "I want to beat the hell out of the little bastard."

"That's why I didn't want to say anything. He's not worth it, trust me."

"Oh, I'm well aware of that," I say. "But I can't let him treat you that way—just know that."

"Slate," she groans.

I rub my face and let out a deep breath. "Get in the shower. I'm taking you out."

"What are you talking about? I thought we were celebrating tomorrow."

"We are. But I'm not going to let you have a bad birthday. Besides, I want to try that new Italian place."

She blinks at me. "I don't know what's more shocking. The fact that you want to take me somewhere in town, or the fact that you want to go to a restaurant that serves pasta and bread."

I erupt into laughter. She's the only one who can diffuse my anger in a moment like this, and my love for her deepens. "I want to take you out. You deserve it."

"Okay, but let's go somewhere out of town, like usual," she says.

"I'm tired of that," I say, touching her cheek and watching it blush. "I want to have a normal life with you. I love you, baby. Let me do this."

"All right," she says with a sigh.

I draw her in for a kiss, and she slides her arms around my waist. The soft touch of her lips runs through me, and I can't believe she's all mine. She doesn't deserve some jackass disrespecting her—she deserves the best. I wish I wasn't the little weasel's teacher. Then I could just sock him in the mouth and be done with it. I'm definitely going to have a talk with him after class on Monday.

It's tempting to slide into the shower with her, but I leave her alone to get ready.

SHE ENTERS THE living room wearing one of my favorite dresses just as I finish grading the last test. She hasn't worn it since she was my student, and the yellow looks incredible against her tanned skin.

"Hey, beautiful," I say, rising from the couch. "I feel like it's *my* birthday."

She blushes, and it takes all I have not to wrangle her into the bedroom right now.

"You don't look so bad yourself," she says, admiring my attire.

I lean down and kiss her flavored lips as I reach behind her head, fastening a silver chain around her neck. When I step back, she touches the necklace, peering down at it.

"Is this . . . a *real* diamond?"

"Of course," I say. I'm not going to spoil the moment by telling her how I went to my sister's jewelry guy and used her discount. It's quality jewelry, no doubt, but I got a great deal.

"Elijah," she whispers.

I press my finger to her lips. "If you tell me I shouldn't have, I will seriously get upset. I was going to give it to you tomorrow, but I wanted to take this moment to remind you that you have a worthy boyfriend now. Who's madly in love with you. Who wants to take you out in the actual town we live in. And who wants to come back here and make passionate love to you all night long. Is that okay with you?"

She smirks. "In the Tahoe?"

"What?"

"We haven't had sex in the Tahoe yet."

I shake my head, and she laughs.

"It's my birthday," she pleads.

"Whatever you want, my love."

She reaches up to kiss me, throwing her arms around my neck. "I can't believe you did this." She pulls back, admiring her necklace. "It's unreal."

"Let's go celebrate your life, baby."

I'M IN THE middle of my entrée when I see him. Our eyes meet across the room, and I'm relieved that Kaley's back is facing him—but I need to think fast. I should get up and go over there to avoid him coming to my table. I nod his way, and I'm about to tell Kaley I'll be right back when he narrows his eyes at me, causing a heaviness to hit my stomach that's in no relation to the plate of pasta I ordered. He glances at the back of her head, then glares into me again.

Is he really not going to nod back? He can't even be polite? We golf together every Sunday. He's opened up to me about every detail of his life. We're pretty close . . . he has to know his behavior is rude. He breaks his stare, and I bring my focus back to Kaley, but it's impossible to pay attention to what she's saying, so I just nod along.

I glance back at him a few times, but he's no longer looking my way. I don't think I know the man he's with, but I can't be positive because it's difficult to see his face from this angle. I don't understand how he can recognize Kaley so quickly from the back of her head. *Did he see me come in with her?* I really didn't pay attention to my surroundings when we first sat down, which isn't like me at all.

"You full already?" asks Kaley.

I realize I don't even have my fork in my hand. "Yeah. Not used to eating pasta, I guess."

"So, I take it you don't want dessert?"

"Huh? Uh, no. No thanks."

She tilts her head, noting my odd behavior.

"I'm sorry, do *you* want dessert? If you do, maybe we can

go get some gelato somewhere."

"They serve gelato here," she says.

"Right," I say. "Well, we can do that. Whatever you want."

"No thanks," she says. "You'd probably make them sing happy birthday to me, and I'd have to leave you."

I laugh along with her, but it's forced. I raise my hand to the server, and she makes her way to our table.

"Any dessert for you guys?" she asks.

"No, just the check please." I glance at Kaley. "Oh, are you even done?"

She sets down her fork and gives me a slight nod.

Our server looks back and forth between us, then slides the check on the table. "Whenever you're ready."

"We're ready now," I say, scrambling for my wallet. I pull out my card and hand it to her.

"Is everything okay?" asks Kaley as soon our waitress leaves.

"Yeah, why? What's up?"

"You're acting a little nervous. I was perfectly fine having dinner out of town like normal."

Yeah, and I should've listened to you.

"No, it's fine," I say.

I was so at ease when I came in here with her earlier. Didn't feel stressed at all. I let my damn guard down. How could I do that? I never do that when I'm in any type of public setting with her. The one time I do, my boss sees us. I glance back at Stan, catching his hard stare again.

Mother of God, this is bad.

When our server comes back, I snatch the check out of her hand and sign my name, leaving a thirty percent tip. I rise from the table, refusing to look Stan's way. Kaley follows me, and my body goes rigid as she slips her arm around mine. Any chance of lying my way out of this is now gone. She pops a mint in her mouth from the host desk and grabs one for me. I cringe as she turns, revealing her profile to Stan, and presses the mint to my lips. I part my lips just enough for her to slide it into my mouth. Bad decision on my part, but I don't want to alarm her, and it's obvious he already knows what's up anyway.

Anxiety shrouds my thoughts as we drive home. I do a pretty good job at maintaining normalcy, even asking her if she wants to grab dessert. She doesn't, and I'm relieved. As we pull into the garage, she's quiet. I hop out and meet her on the passenger side, opening her door as she slides out. I take her hand and start to lead her inside.

"Wait," she says, pulling her hand away. I turn around and she opens the door to the backseat. She gives me a shy smile and runs her hand through her dark hair. "You promised."

"Now?"

She ignores my hesitation and grabs my hand, pulling me into the back. She's practically on top of me before I can even shut the door. I still can't understand her fascination with the Tahoe. As soon as I can afford it, I'm trading it in for an Escalade.

The taste of her lips slowly withers away my stress. She unbuttons my shirt, and I slide my hands up her silky, smooth thighs.

Damn, she's incredible.

"You feel tense, Slate," she murmurs as her lips run down my neck.

"I'm good, baby."

Stan is the last thing I want to discuss right now. And I don't need her worrying about it. She's had enough stress to deal with this year. This is *my* problem.

My big, huge, gigantic, worst-case-scenario problem.

Her lips return to mine as she unfastens my belt, and

Stan's hard stare dissolves in the back of my mind. This girl is worth it. And I'm not just saying that because she's unbuttoning my pants right now. She's the most intoxicating woman I've ever met without a trace of pretentiousness. She's funny and charming and down to earth—and much more innocent than she realizes. And these lips—*good God, these lips*. I never want to let her go. I won't. I can't lose her again—no matter what happens. I scoot down on the seat and lean my head back. The tension from tonight's disturbing dinner quickly fades into the background as I let the most beautiful woman in the world take control.

ACKNOWLEDGMENTS

First and foremost, thank you, God, for your endless amount of love and forgiveness—and for calling my bluff. Your blessings continue to amaze me.

And thank you to:

Darin, for always challenging me to be the best version of myself, for never letting me settle in life, and for never letting me give up. *LFL* You are my rock. And I am in awe of you.

Brandi, for giving me a safe place to write, the courage to dream, and for talking me off countless ledges. Thank you for encouraging me to write this story. OMS!

Regina Wamba, for swooping in mid-series with nothing but confidence and assurance. Not only did you bring my visions to life, but your patience and professionalism match your incredible talent. The revamp of this cover is absolutely stunning, and I cannot wait for the world to see what you did with the rest of this series. Thank you for saving me and for taking care of my baby!

Brent Kobayashi, for my original cover design—I will always hold it near and dear to my heart! Thank you, always.

My wonderful behind-the-scenes team, Darin Stevenson, Brandi Kobayashi, Camay Rooney, Cheri Rooney, and MacKenzie Allyn. Thank you all for loving this story as much as I do.

Mary Jo Risse, the only teacher who never punished me for daydreaming. . . . Thank you for seeing in me what so many others couldn't.

My big sister, Camay, for reading to me constantly when I was a child, for teaching me that imagination is limitless, and how even when all your toys have been shipped off to Seattle, an empty room is full of possibilities. I fell in love with stories because of you.

All my friends and family who have supported me throughout this crazy ride. The success of this book has been nothing short of a dream. To all of you who reached out to me, supported me, and enthusiastically spread the word—from the bottom of my heart, thank you.

And last, but far from least, a very special thank you to Arizona summers and mathematical unicorns. . . .

ABOUT THE AUTHOR

Kelly Stevenson is the national bestselling author of *Force of Gravity*. She resides in Phoenix, Arizona, where she is currently working on the next installment in the *Gravity* series. When Kelly is not writing, she enjoys dining with her husband, horseback riding, and anything that surrounds her in wilderness.

Force of Gravity is Kelly's debut novel.

To learn more about the author please visit:
KellyStevensonAuthor.com